Born in Guildford in 1971 J.P. Cansdale is a horticulturist who has been constructing and working on large private gardens and estates around the UK for the last twenty years. He also writes schemes of work for Youth Drama and has a real passion for creativity. He lives in Cheshire with his wife and two children. *The Dark Echoes* is his first novel and is the beginning of a trilogy.

The Dark Echoes

J.P. Cansdale

The Dark Echoes

Vanguard Press

VANGUARD PAPERBACK

© Copyright 2014
J.P. Cansdale

A CIP catalogue record for this title is
available from the British Library.
ISBN 9781 84386 756 2

Vanguard Press is an imprint of
Pegasus Elliot MacKenzie Publishers Ltd.

www.pegasuspublishers.com

First Published in 2014

Vanguard Press
Sheraton House Castle Park
Cambridge England

Printed & Bound in Great Britain

Contents

PART ONE

ONE

Joshua

Whether or not he had always been true to his wife, his family or himself was a question that had preoccupied Joshua as he entered his sixties, and whether or not his blindness was the punishment his son had said it was, he'd had plenty of time to consider.

Today even before he started his first yawn to consciousness, the cracked and cold London pavement had hurt his frail body. Joshua sighed, the layers of cardboard beneath him were providing little more sanctuary than the once thick blanket Al had given him for his birthday. He yawned again and opened his eyes, blinking regardless of his lack of vision. Surely it was too early to get up. Forty yards beneath him however, the third underground train of the day deposited those who disagreed in the Central Line station close by. Yet it was the sweet smell of collected tobacco, burning through a coveted cigarette paper, that finally stirred him properly.

'Well Joshua, since you've stopped snoring, I'm guessing you're awake. So I think I'll take a piss before our public arrive,' Al said from the end of Joshua's make shift bed. His accent thick and true to his roots of Birmingham city, and the council houses he had been proud to build.

'Charming,' Joshua replied from beneath his blanket. 'Don't worry I'll keep your place.'

'"Posh bastard" that's what they'll put on your headstone, and under it they'll write "A snob till the end".' With that Al rose, leaving the sound of his footsteps and the smell of crushed embers to mark his departure. Joshua was left with the displaced sounds of early traffic, and a breeze that snatched the first drying leaves of autumn from the railings behind him, and sent them scuttling across the pavement and up a drainpipe close by.

Sitting up and pulling his blanket hood down, Joshua revealed his greyed long hair and thick beard. He wiped his mouth with his sleeve, and listened to the first spatters of the commuting masses begin to step past him, heading to and from the depths of the underground.

'They'll be playing fucking "Jingle Bells" next,' Joshua said loudly to nobody in particular. His scholarship to Winchester fifty six years ago had quickly rounded his vowels and taught him some words his mother was not proud of. Though his accent was tempered now with travel and pain it was still unmistakably that of the English gent. Joshua disliked the onset of autumn, it only lead on to winter. Pulling the blanket tighter round his shoulders Joshua reasoned that three days without Al's mixed tobacco was long enough. He'd give up properly in the New Year. So, if the cold brought out the best in the public's spare change today, he'd give Al the money for some real filter tips wrapped in foil, unspoilt by concrete or dustbin lid. Joshua shuffled in discomfort, their home may only be fifteen paces from the underground entrance, twenty if his hip seized up, but his own bladder would have to wait, they couldn't risk more than one empty hat.

'I give it a week,' replied a voice that stopped any further thought or complaint. It wasn't Al, but someone unfamiliar and different to the thousands he heard each day. Joshua was sure no footsteps preceded it, yet it had been so deep and clear, it was almost inside his own head.

'My apologies, what do you mean?' Joshua asked.

'I mean nothing, I agree… il tempo passa così velocemente.' The Italian accent heavy now, confirmed by the use of his own language.

'I'm sorry, I'm not sure.. Could you…?' but Joshua was interrupted.

'Time passes so quickly,' the voice translated.

'It does, it does. Forgive me I thought it was only Al who ever listened to me.' He waited, but this time there was no continuation, or reply, and no footsteps attempted to remove its owner. Joshua tutted, rubbing a dirty hand over his blind face, conceding that his perception of footsteps were fading with age. Then came the crash of a coin on the ground, only inches from his feet, except Joshua let it lay, anxious and now unnerved.

'It won't pick itself up,' Al said, his voice welcome. His touch more so as he opened Joshua's hands and placed the coin into one of them.

'A shilling, I think,' said Joshua from its weight and size.

'Well done. Blimey I hope you're not losing your marbles as well as your sight,' Al said.

'So do I. What time is it?'

'Time to sit up straight and smile, I think I can smell our lady friend from here.'

Joshua placed the coin into his pocket, and started to stand as he picked up the scent of the six-fifteen lady, often the

17

highlight of their daily conversation. The sound of her stilettos played upon his vertebrae like piano keys to a deft touch, lighting his senses to ignite her scent until a shiver reached the base of his spine and spread quickly throughout his old body to his toes.

'Morning,' Al said to the woman. There was no reply other than her unhindered steps and Al's attempts at small talk. Al sighed and helped Joshua to his feet. 'Too slow old boy. She smiled at me again this morning, that's the second time this month.' Al's guttural cough followed, the antidote to any erotic shiver the stilettos may have provided.

'But you know Joshua, I'm glad you're blind because she pouted her lips and blew me a kiss. What a woman!'

'You know, I'm glad I'm blind Al. That way she will always be Aphrodite. That way Al, I won't be able to tell if she's extremely fat with clothes which are far too tight, but has a step so light the Moulin Rouge would dare not turn her down.'

'Alright alright, I'll have to add "grumpy" to your epitaph.'

'Or Al, to that matter, if she wears knickers bigger than this fucking blanket you gave me!'

'Alright, alright, what's bitten your arse this morning?'

'Blindness Al,' Joshua picked up his latest guide stick. 'Now it's my turn as you say, to take a piss.'

'Careful Joshua,' Al called after him, showing a small sign of his affection.

'Yes, Yes' Joshua replied already making his way to the underground entrance. He could hear the newspaper boy setting up his stand, and smell the tightly wrapped bundles of paper being set free and placed out.

'All I need now is the smell of coffee and I'll be back in my breakfast room,' Joshua said.

'You what old man,' the boy shouted at him. 'Here, don't spose you want one of these papers, all the latest from Monday 18th September 1967,' he laughed. 'More revelations about April's Air France robbery.'

Though the temptation was there to strike out with his stick, Joshua managed to restrain himself. 'No thank you. You must be new?'

'Yeah, just started today fella, how did you know eh? Thought we'd all look the same to you,' he laughed again.

'Yes yes you do, you're right, but you're older than the other boy – 16 or 17? Not from Hackney like that boy Tom, but more local? And you're late? Tom would have been here before six fifteen.'

'Eh, what you on about?'

'I'm blind, not deaf. But if you do have any papers left over, please give them to me. Helps against the cold, "fella!". Now if you don't mind I really must be getting along.'

'Oh right, sure.'

The air turned stale at the underground entrance, the updraft inside bringing with it the sounds from the tunnels below, not least the smell of greased escalators and expectant aftershave. Joshua reached out, the hand rail was still there to guide his body down the fifteen steps, then two paces then seven steps down to the ticket booths and more paper stalls. Thirty five paces straight ahead to the opposite wall, then left by what ever was required to find the entrance to the gents. Once inside, the cubicles could be identified by their smell, the urinals were best avoided. After an unsatisfactory start to the day Joshua ran cold water onto his dirty hands, and over his lank hair, and beard. Then with his ablutions complete, Joshua retraced his unsteady but calculated steps back to resume his place beside Al. The pair he often thought were just flotsam, in the rising of the commuter tide. Al had for once agreed with the analogy, but preferred shorter descriptions to their current situation; 'dishonoured' was his favourite, 'destitute' was his friend's.

'Of course, you've got the fucking master card,' Al would say if his hat was empty. 'I fought in the war, you're just an old blind bastard! Give me that money and I'll get us some tea.'

The day passed and Joshua stood, sat or crouched depending on how well his hips behaved, sometimes he sang, mustering enough breath to give clear voice to the tune that played inside his head. Daylight passed and night closed in until the reluctant companions made their minds up whether to stay put, or head for some sort of shelter. It was during the night that they talked about the comrades they had lost, and Al's stolen medals, ripped off him by thieves who had ignored the fear on his face, oblivious of the depression that had taken hold on his return from the war, so acute that it had soon driven his dear wife away. Sleep would come to Al, as he sipped gin to stifle his nightmares and then Joshua would give into exhaustion. If they were lucky, they escaped the malice of alcohol and the screams of fighting cats.

The following morning Joshua lay buried beneath his blanket again, dreaming of his last lover, of her dark curls and the way her stockings fell at his gentle instruction, when he was woken by two voices near by. Even though his head was covered, the voices were very clear, just like the day before.

'Listen, I don't care what we said last night. I want you to buy up all the derelict land next to the river. We'll stop that man in his tracks. I don't want his influence getting out of hand.' It was that same Italian voice.

'Of course I'll buy the land, but why the change of direction. He could be a powerful friend?' the second voice questioned, lighter than the first, his accent Spanish, no it was Portuguese Joshua reasoned.

'A powerful friend maybe, but we can't afford any risk of him becoming a negative influence in the Chambers, can we.'

His voice drifted as his head turned, they must be moving away, but then just as the day before no footsteps could be heard.

'Yes,' said the second voice, Joshua thought the Italian to be sturdy but not fat, the second a thinner man, eleven maybe twelve stone.

'I need a new dinner jacket for Daniel Weaver's visit. I want to take him somewhere special as it's his first time over from New York. Call a taxi, I don't want to use the underground now, let's get up to the flat in Burlington Gardens. Oh, did you remind Daniel to bring over the Pipp ball?'

'Yes of course.'

'Make sure he brings it. I think that we may need it a little sooner than expected. Maglanis you know, I think we'll forget about this meeting'

'With respect we are not far away.' stated the second man, now sounding more and more like an assistant to the first. 'We've made it this far and you did insist that the meeting could be a useful opportunity.'

'Very well, but lets make it brief.'

Joshua pulled the blanket from his head determined to hear some other distinguishing sound. There was a slight sigh of frustration from the second man followed by a silence.

'There's nothing quite like the ritual of dress,' Joshua volunteered from the pavement. Maybe they would hear him, maybe not, but the continued quiet urged him on. 'I think the Italians cut a suit too slim, a man of heavier build is better suited in Savile Row.'

'You are right old man,' came a reply with a gentle rumble of laughter. Then the voice came closer, the Italian must be crouching down. 'I just love the steady hand of that street, and you know, it is a long way to Milan.'

'Milan is such a vibrant city,' Joshua said, finding a little confidence, 'but I think it has little beauty, not like a sunset across Lake Como.'

'Ah,' the Italian breathed in the image. 'You are so right; tell me when did you last see Lake Como?'

'I travelled a little, between the wars,' Joshua raised himself up and pulled the blanket round his shoulders.

'You were a lucky man, I know the lakes well.'

'I danced aboard the Coco on Lake Garda.' Joshua felt his warm breath rise out into the chill morning air as he remembered. 'A thirty foot launch, with lanterns warming her wooden deck,' he smiled to himself. 'We laughed into the night, the women were so liberated so... they wore a more gorgeous short skirt then, and bobbed hair and... you could drink in their perfume, and I.., I can hear their laughter. We all tried to dance the Charleston and the ah... well that was nearly forty years ago and I forget the names of those other dances.'

'What a mystery you are!' The Italian spoke quietly now, his voice close, 'tell me when did you last have a hot meal?'

'With respect Sir, your meeting at nine?' reminded his assistant.

Joshua felt a cool hand on his. It gently pulled him to his feet. 'You will have to excuse me as I have a meeting but I think, I think I'd like to hear more of your memories. I myself remember that Italy, before the war took hold.'

'It would be a pleasure sir,' Joshua answered, running his free hand over his beard.

'Joshua I think I should offer you a better place to rest your head, at least for tonight. You could clean up and we could talk tomorrow?'

'Thank you but forgive me, I don't know you,' Joshua laughed.

'Come now I'm sure we have much more than sunsets in common. I may even have sailed on the same launch,' the man gently squeezed Joshua's hand. 'You look like you could do with a hot meal, that's all.'

'Thank you, if we could just wait for Al. He is my eyes so to speak, but deserts me at least six times a day. Or you could give me your address, and tell me when you would like to receive us.'

'I fear old man, I only have room for one lost soul and I'm only in London until tomorrow afternoon. Let Mr Maglanis here take care of you. I have a house not far from here in Notting Hill.'

'Another time then,' Joshua said. 'Perhaps when you return to London.'

'Then Joshua our chance meeting today would be lost into the "what ifs" and "maybes". Remember opportunities don't always repeat themselves.'

'Si deve andare,' Maglanis said

'Very well, the choice is yours Joshua.'

The implication of lost opportunities, and the retelling of a past Al had no connection with stirred inside. Something else too that his waking mind could not place, an attraction he dare

23

not allow to blossom into free thought. Instinct then would have to drive his choice.

'Yes, very well, if Mr Maglanis helps me write a note I'll come with you. You'll forgive me for not staying the night. Al will think I've been abducted. But it's been a long time since I had a good wash, and my clean return will make him laugh.'

'So be it,' said Mr Maglanis clearly agitated. 'I'll take care of our new friend, but you really must be going now.'

'Thank you, and make sure Al is given a little something to ease his suffering,' the Italian said his voice fading.

'I'll return to collect you as soon as I've dropped Mr Peterson off,' Maglanis concluded.

The taxi ride passed in silence between Joshua and the assistant. Maglanis gave off an air of efficiency, and a desire to have Joshua out of his company. Fortunately, it wasn't long before Maglanis was asking the driver to stop and wait. He guided Joshua out of the cab, then up five steps. Less than a minute after the loud tap of the brass knocker, Joshua heard the door open.

'Stevens, please meet Joshua Peterson. Mr Rodiani has requested that Joshua is cleaned up and given something to eat. You know I think… find him some new clothes, something suitable for dinner. I'll be back around eight for supper.'

'Will Mr Rodiani be joining you Sir?' Stevens asked.

'No, he'll come later, he should arrive around eleven.'

'And will you both be staying the night sir?'

'No it will just be me. Joshua, Stevens here will take good care of you.' With that Maglanis turned leaving the two men at the door.

Upstairs in the hot water of a bath, Joshua felt his body lighten and his hips ease, the scent of the bath salts wafted up clearing his head. The bathroom was large enough for sounds to echo off its tiled walls and before Joshua had finally removed his soiled clothing he had paced the seven yards from the door to the bath that was placed alongside the far wall. There was a toilet and sink to his right, and a large radiator on the other wall that fought off the cold of the outside walls, now wet with condensation. Leaving what was left of Joshua's shoes in the hallway, Stevens had guided him here, from the top of a long flight of stairs they had passed through two other rooms identified by their door frames and carpet. Their conversation had consisted only of hazard evasion. The butler's confident tone and guiding hand, betrayed his discomfort at the prospect of undressing a tramp.

'I can manage thank you,' Joshua said, when he heard the taps turned closed. Even with the door clicked into place, Joshua had waited until he heard the third door to the landing shut before he disrobed. Nakedness was more uncomfortable than Joshua remembered, but the water's blanket was welcome, more so when he finally let it slip over his head.

He found the soap and a scrubbing brush and he did what he could before giving into his muscles that screamed for a cessation to the proceedings, they needed soaking not working. Then just when he had finally given in to relaxation there was a knock at the door. This act to protect his privacy, so alien to him that he did not answer until a muffled voice called out. 'It's Stevens sir, I've brought you some new clothes.'

Joshua chuckled to himself then replied. The door opened and he heard the footsteps of the man approach then stop beside him. Stevens coughed as if he needed to make his position in the room known.

'I doubt it's often you have to polish an old turd like me,' Joshua asked before Stevens could speak. 'Don't worry, I think I've got the worst off.'

'I do whatever I'm asked to do. Any hesitance you sense Sir is based purely on your protection not my own,' Stevens replied. Joshua could hear him collecting up his ragged clothes from where he had dumped them at the side of the bath. 'Now would sir like some assistance to wash his hair and shave?'

'I'm sorry please forgive my manners. I should get out.' Without waiting Joshua unsteadily got to his feet and stepped onto the floor reaching out for a towel.'

'No please, I prefer to save my towels from unwashed marks. You stay there and I'll refill the bath and we'll clean you up properly.'

Joshua did not complain, only covered his crotch with his hands as he waited. 'Al told me shaving was not for old blind bastards like me, and please call me Joshua, it's been too long since I was last called sir to deserve the title now,' Joshua sighed. 'In case I forget later, thank you.'

With Stevens' gentle assistance, years of grime were removed from his hair, and the beard that Al helped with from time to time was cut back until it could be shaved. Stevens trimmed the back and sides of Joshua's greyed hair leaving the top long enough to be pulled back revealing a less furrowed brow than of late. Joshua felt far removed from the street, and the café where the tea was served luke warm and was strained from reused bags. The new shirt on his shoulders felt like the re-enactment of a dream. The tailored jacket fitted his buckled malnourished frame well enough to revive a smile, and to reveal a handsome man long since concealed.

He thought of his lover Marcella, of kissing her hand before leading her aboard the Coco and could almost smell her black hair when a familiar voice reminded him of the reality of his transformation. Joshua accepted a sandwich offered with a glass of water in the drawing room then sitting back in the luxury of a leather chair listening to the crackle of a fire, he nodded off.

He was woken at half past six by a gentle shake.

'Champagne Sir?' asked Stevens.

'No, Mr Stevens,' Joshua replied standing up and brushing himself down. 'If you don't mind I'd like a cup of tea with a dash of milk, and one sugar. Then, I think I'll leave, get back to Al.'

'You are a new man Joshua, no longer the vagabond,' Maglanis exclaimed. He must have been sitting in the room watching him sleep. His voice unnerved Joshua who managed to react with his head.

'I wish Al could see me now,' Joshua said with a calm pride, running a hand down a lapel. 'The man I really am, or rather, used to be.'

'You should see yourself,' Maglanis gestured, 'Maybe; just maybe, you have left the street behind my friend. After all it's never a good idea to go back! Sit down for a while and we can talk before we eat.' The warm room chilled a little at Maglanis' instruction.

'The loan of a new suit hardly constitutes a new life,' Joshua said defensively.

'I have prepared a hot pot sir,' said Stevens breaking the tension a little. Joshua was hungry; he would eat before returning to Al. Maybe he could ask for some to take back. 'Would you like me to guide Joshua to the dining room sir?'

Stevens's voice grew nearer as he spoke, and Joshua reached out to receive his arm, grateful to escape.

The question of whether or not to drink wine with the meal was answered when Stevens placed a glass into his hands followed by a reassuring pat on his arm. The smell of red wine intensified with the touch of glass to his lips, and though his tortured taste buds did not pick out the refined flavours that his host enthused about, the warmth grew in the pit of Joshua's stomach and slowed his racing heart. Much as Joshua enjoyed the food, his hands quickly started to cramp up as he held the cutlery, and his napkin wetted with frustrated hunger. Pushing his plate away Joshua became suddenly tired of Maglanis' increasingly slurred account of great wines lost during the war. His host was adamant that the Germans shouldn't really be blamed for hoarding them for their own consumption.

Halfway down his fourth glass Joshua asked the question that he had dared not to ask before.

'Mr Maglanis, how do you know my name? Who are you?'

Tristao Maglanis stopped talking and sighed, his answer delayed by the sounds of Stevens clearing their plates away.

'Will that be all sir?' Stevens asked.

'Just a bottle of the fifty four, wait no the err, the forty eight please Stevens.'

'Very well sir.'

'Joshua, I must apologise for my over-indulgence in German history.' He went quiet again, easing himself forward to remove his jacket. 'Alessandro is a man of many talents and much laboured skill. I fear it would be unfaithful of me to try and explain his motives, nevertheless I can say he has a lot to offer you, especially a man with your talents.'

'Then I am grateful indeed to you and for your master's hospitality, but I saw what the Germans did. You will have to excuse me or I'm afraid I might outstay my welcome.'

'How so?'

'Because I can't understand how in this fine house you defend their butchery Maglanis? Because your words crash hard against the memory of the women I saw raped, and the children who starved in their camps.'

'You worked for them didn't you Joshua?'

Guilt spiked against Joshua's skin, and a cold grip of anxiety took hold of his stomach. The air ached in its silence, desperate to be filled with an explanation. Stevens placed a new bottle onto the table and the embrace of the door by its frame marked his departure.

'I had a wife once, tall and beautiful, and a son handsome and strong,' Joshua started, but his own anger silenced his reply.

'Was it your son who blinded you Joshua?'

'When your fingers are bloodied, bitten and chewed as they fight back against your suffocating hand, and those who watch…' Joshua stopped himself and drank his wine, gripping the glass with whitening knuckles. He should have stuck with the tea.

'Alessandro was right then. We have seen your work.'

'What do you know young man?' Joshua asked. 'What do you know Maglanis, of those who beg for mercy? Or of their last gasp before they confess. '

'I know how duty can turn to pleasure Joshua. I know how the light in the eyes of those who scream least, are the last to fade,' Maglanis provoked.

'It is as you say, a life I have left behind,' Joshua reached forward to pick up the bottle from where he'd heard Stevens place it. Already uncorked he filled his glass, dripping wine over his hand and onto the table.

'Please allow me. At least, let it breathe, it's a…' but Maglanis stopped himself.

'I think you had better take me back to the pavement,' Joshua said quietly.

'There is a place for you still Joshua; men of your talents are very few and far between. Work for us and be our link to our past. I think Mr Rodiani would allow me to say that together the opportunities are limitless.'

'I was never true to my wife,' Joshua said standing up and pushing his chair back. His clean clothes now felt heavy and tiredness ragged at him. 'But she was the only one whom I loved. She was so wrapped up in the stale bubble of her father's wealth. During the thirties, Mr Maglanis, we travelled the world in luxury avoiding the great depression as it wrecked lives and… I saw the tears in her eyes as they left her to bleed and I felt the hatred in my son's voice, as he sought me out on the streets.' Un-wiped a tear fell clear of Joshua's cheek, a second followed but the third did not leave his eye. He breathed in deep and sighed heavily letting his shoulders drop. 'Nothing can hurt me now, you have nothing to bribe me with. So if this is dressed up revenge for a contract long fulfilled, then Mr Maglanis, I would prefer it if you just pulled the trigger. Or I will ask you again, please take me back to where you found me.'

'There is no need for a confession Joshua, please sit down.' The sound of another bottle being opened was followed by the clink of it's neck to the glass. Joshua did not sit down, he was growing angry, if this was not his demise, why then was he here? If they worked for the police why not just arrest him, but these were no policemen, they had their own courts.

'Yes I worked for the Germans and I worked for the fucking Yanks, whoever paid the most,' Joshua said, growing impatient.

'We know, please sit down. We are not here to punish you for your past.'

'Oh I have been punished for my past,' Joshua said. 'By those who have tracked me down before you. There are others Mr Maglanis who know of my past.'

'There can't be many Joshua. Where did they find you?'

'In 1952 I took up residence in a boarding house five stops from the underground station where we met,' Joshua hesitated, regained his seat and reached out for his glass, taking a sip before he continued. 'I had only lived there for six months… when I returned one night to be knocked unconscious. When I came round I had been tied to a chair, a cloth pushed deep into my mouth. In the middle of the room, under the bare light sat what looked like the Devil himself. He looked at me Mr Maglanis, and I gazed into his dark eyes. He told me how I should be admired but how did he put it? It was time for a little "dark reflection." Then you know, he smiled at me. A simple smile. It was the last one I saw so I've had a long time to ponder its values, the tilt of his head and the soft punctuation of the lines that crossed his face as he stood up.'

'What happened Joshua, What did he do to you?' Maglanis asked.

'He crushed the light bulb in his hand and I heard him move toward me in the blackness, and then… he whispered into my ear "You may be good. But in the dark Joshua, it's just you and I". Nobody could hear my muffled screams as he scratched at my eye's, burning them with the dirt beneath his broken finger nails that he clicked together next to my ear. He kicked me down the stairs and out into the street. "I know you're not dead, not yet!" he said as the rain pissed down on me, then he was gone.'

'So there you laid in the gutter Joshua, until years later Alessandro spotted you and here you are. Where there will always be a place for you. A place where you can rebuild your life and revive those skills that you honed to such perfection. Joshua, you once walked amongst your victims, their sweat dripping from your knife edge, their heartbeat in your hand. You could track a man across continents tracing his scent until you ate from his table, and slept with his wife. There's no need for you to suffer anymore.'

'Mr Maglanis I can barely find the fucking toilets let alone one of your enemies. Please let me leave.'

'At least sleep in a bed for one night my friend. Clear your head and leave with a full belly in the morning.'

After a long silence, Joshua replied, 'Very well'

'Stevens,' Maglanis called out. The butler could not have been far away because the door quickly opened. 'Guide Joshua to his room please. I'll wait for Alessandro in the drawing room.'

Too tired to try and find a way back to Al, he took Stevens' arm. Too drunk to sleep he lay awake fully clothed on top of the bed, stuck in his darkened world waiting for the morning to come. Without the tick of a watch or Al's dreams to stir him he finally drifted off into a dream. He was eating chips at the seaside with Anna on the day they had first met. The daughter of a wealthy textiles merchant she wanted to travel the world, live the dream, work was for others. Joshua had loved her from the first time they had met, and she loved the attention. Proud and forthright, Joshua's father had hated her, his son should become a teacher and a scholar, not the plaything of new money. Everything in Joshua's dream was in black and white, a negative image to the reality it had been. Joshua held white railings that marked the promenade's edge where he had remembered the fresh smell of black paint. The only colour was the defiant ruby red lipstick that Anna was applying. A little way along the promenade, a middle aged man was watching the young couple. He ran a hand over the top of his thinning hair and smiled at them. Despite the sound of the children playing on the beach, and the waves against the pebbles, the man's cough sounded as if he were much closer. He walked up to Joshua until he filled the whole dream, and spoke. His Italian accent strong, his voice deep. 'No more darkness for you Joshua!'

Joshua jumped back up onto his pillows but the man was still there, his image floating, projected out of the dream state into the room. Joshua reached up to his face then his eyes, checking the fingers on his own hand. He could see. At first he smiled and then he did not, the heat that the wine had generated in his body, was suddenly replaced by the cold sweat of fear. In his dimly lit bedroom where the darkness showed up in a negative white out and a lamp on the bedside table gave off a black glow. The man moved forward and sat upon the bed beside him, hair white where black hair grew. His face was like a frosted steel sculpture, the cold finding its way in to highlight lines across his forehead, and a short scar on his left cheek. A grey hue darkened under each piercing eye, fixed upon Joshua.

'Please Joshua relax. I may not have got your sight just right,' he smiled, revealing black teeth, obviously pleased with his achievements, then continued. 'It's a bit like the tailors we spoke of Joshua; the first pattern of cloth does not always fit. However my friend at least we can now meet face to face.' He extended a hand that Joshua nervously accepted trying to separate himself from his nightmare.. 'My name is Alessandro Porta Rodiani, why not join us in our quest?'

'Because I'm sixty seven, you fucking idiot.' Nausea rose from Joshua's stomach, a hangover from the unfinished night. Why had he ever spoken up on the street. He should have just kept to his pitiful self. 'What the fuck are you doing to my head?'

'I'm letting in the light Joshua.'

'Why? I live on the streets, what possible use could my battered body be to you?'

'Now now don't even think of age as a barrier. I can help you overcome any insecurities that the streets have caused to your body, you'll soon limber up. After all, you are, you might say Joshua, my link to the past,' Rodiani said leaning forward and reaching out for Joshua's shoulder.

'You are just chasing memories then, like so many others before you,' Joshua said recoiling.

'I will forgive that comment only once,' Rodiani said, his voice gaining depth and irritation.

'Please Mr Rodiani, I'd rather you didn't threaten me, whatever you've done to my eyes. I do not fear you. If you want to dispatch me, do it now.'

'Believe me Joshua, there are worse creatures for you to fear than myself. Huayna has far more inventive ways to end your life than I would have patience for.'

'Then what do you want from me, if you already have a killer?'

Rodiani gave a rumbling laugh and leaned forward placing a firm hand on top of Joshua's own. 'Let's just say even if he was in my employ you have a subtlety he lacks. Besides you have been waylaid in penitence for long enough to concern yourself with a rival. Now I have a man I need you to find, an old acquaintance that may tax even your abilities.'

TWO

The Faces Amongst Us

Up until his sixth birthday Cieba had slept each night as any active boy should, with a proud father to kiss him good night and a mother to embrace. He would snuggle down into woven blankets of alpaca wool, and dream of the adventures of his forefathers. In the last thick clusters of trees that clung to the lowest peaks of the Andes, his father watched him sleep until the embers spluttered out on the fire that warmed them. For two years this had been a temporary home, while they searched for their lost company. Two years of safety that ended in the deathly grey cold of this spring pre-dawn, when a small scout party of the Pelecaras broke through the tree line.

They were the remnants of Incas and those that had dissected them, fuelled with jealous hatred for a religion that had desecrated their sun god and obliterated their people with sanctimonious greed. The solidifying Pelecaras spirits swept through the village cracking the skulls of those who woke unprepared, their blows accompanied by their own cathartic cackle. It took ten minutes for the sun's vital rays to start breaking through the trees, outlining those of Cieba's Etéreo tribe who bravely fought back, and the sixteen bodies which bloodied the floor.

'Get the children out!' screamed Cieba's mother as she shielded her son. 'Split the light and get them out!'

Shielded within their parents' arms, the children were guided away from behind trees and out of their huts; the muffled screeches of the Pelecaras broke between the prayers of their mothers. Like his friends around him, Cieba recognised the grass beneath his feet as the centre of their village and the urgent cry of Nasua his grandfather. But unlike the rest of the children Cieba felt the warm flow of his mother's blood cross his face, taking with it her hand that had shielded his eyes from what pursued them.

It took a heart beat for the others to register what had happened, and see the monster that stood but a pace from a motherless son. Elongated and shredded by despair, the tattered Pelecaras Huayna cackled, his fragmented form giving off a radiant click as he gained strength from the boy's fear. Like all the Pelecaras, Huayna was hairless, scraped clean by each other in an effort to both relieve and concentrate their hatred.

Frozen by fear, Cieba had to watch his mother's blood run across Huayna's desiccated hands then drip from his shredded nails. Withered black lips broke across his skeletal mouth, forming a cynical smile below dirty yellow eyes which held the only colour in the predator's body, and bore down on the shrinking child. Catching a frightened lung full of putrefied breath Cieba knew no more than the pressure of hands which covered his own eyes and pulled him away.

When he woke Cieba heard the whisper of his grandfather's reassurance and he felt the warmth of others as they huddled together in pitch darkness. He rubbed his eyes to revive his sight, but no leaf or branch came in to view. There was no smouldering fire or chink of moon to catch their unseen breath escaping into the cool blackout that surrounded them.

'How many?' came a voice clearer than all others, that Cieba recognised as his father.

'Too many Eubucco,' replied another in the darkness. 'There were too many for us to fight.'

'We lost too many!' said another, the desperate anger in his voice mixed with spittle.

'Including Evallea…' Eubucco said his voice breaking down as he acknowledged the murder of his wife, Cieba's mother.

No more words broke in the darkness, only the slight shuffle as the Etéreo sought each other's embrace and the tears of loss could be heard. As the hours began to pass Cieba felt his grandfather's gentle embrace start to stiffen, as revenge stirred in his old bones.

'Grandfather…?' Cieba eventually dared to speak, but his question was quickly interrupted. 'Hush Cieba,' Nasua said. 'Sleep if you can, when you wake the danger will be passed.'

The exhausted tribe waited in the darkness without sun or stars to mark time, and Cieba drifted in and out of sleep, each time waking with a shudder, to the resonant image of Huayna, and the death of his mother. Eventually though, the fatigue of grief overwhelmed him, and he slept without subconscious interruption. It wasn't until he felt the warmth of the sun on his face, as he was lifted up, did he wake to a clear and unbiased light that broke over the Etéreo. The sunshine flooded across them through a vertical line in the darkness that stretched from the ground high up into the clouded sky outside.

Eubucco stood in the doorway looking back at his people his face darkened, his body a silhouette. 'Look at the faces of your friends. Help them,' he said, then with a deep sigh turned and stepped back into the village which they had fled the day before.

Following their captain from the cold hard floors of darkness, and out into the late afternoon sunshine, the Etéreo worked quietly to retrieve the bodies that littered their home. Dismantling their huts they built fires and as the day began to reach its end, Cieba stood silently while Eubucco lit the wood of his mother's pyre. Fifteen other funeral fires burnt into the sunset, lifting an orange hue on the snow covered slopes behind. The smoke rose high toward stars which had already started to shine.

Two days after the massacre the Etéreo tribe started the long trek back to the cloud forests of their ancestors, the place his grandfather protested they should never have left. The journey was long and difficult as the leaf litter beneath their feet turned to shale, then into rock then ice and snow. Finally after five weeks of transient camps and distorted dreams the frozen winds of the mountains slowed amongst trees and humidity took control again. From the night that they had set off Cieba's sleep had become short, snatching an hour maybe two every night, until his slender frame could cope no more and exhaustion took over. Eubucco would wait up, hoping that his presence would help his son, but Cieba learned to fake sleep and take solace in the half light of smouldering fires and the sleeping noises of others. Sometimes but not often, Cieba would rise and step between those who protected him, he would stand at the edge of the fire's glow listening to the mutters and wind of his people.

He felt at his closest to them now.

On the eve of his seventh birthday, as Cieba waited for sleep, he heard them. Just whispers to start with but it was definitely them. Sitting up Cieba watched the moonlight reflecting off the half built structures of their new home and the sleeping bodies resting to the smell of cut timber and shredded leaves which lingered from their daily toil.

'Can you hear them Cieba?' Nasua's whisper made the boy shiver.

'Yes.'

'Good,' was the simple reply as Nasua slowly and unsteadily got to his feet. He had weakened considerably since the long walk back to the cloud forests. It was stupid, he had said all along, to cross the snow passes of the Andes and leave their home behind. "Why go from where the sun rises to where it sets. Why are our warriors more likely to reappear on the western slopes?' There had been no answer, only the repetition of his son's determination that they must do and try everything they could, rather than just wait. After the death of Evallea the old man realised his son Eubucco needed to be left to make his own decisions.

'I was beginning to think I was the last. Follow me,' Nasua said. He led Cieba through the sleeping bodies of their kin and into the trees of the dense Peruvian cloud forests where their ancestors had always lived.

'Where are we going grandfather?' Cieba asked reaching out for a guiding hand. 'I don't want to see Huayna again. Where are you taking me?'

'To start your journey son,' Nasua said smiling back at the boy. 'Shh, now and step where I step.'

After half an hour of watching his grandfather's footsteps they arrived at the edge of a clearing lit by the moon. Standing back from the perimeter they didn't have to wait long for the voices to return. There was no malice in the chattering, that quickly rose into a disorganised clatter of humour, which they could hear from behind the silvered branches opposite them. Cieba felt his hand being gently squeezed and he looked up to see Nasua's face set with a wide expectant smile, an expression the boy had not seen from him before. The voices were now accompanied by the sounds of branches being pushed aside, and just at the point Cieba wanted to run back to his father most, the excited spectres spilled out through the trees.

'They are Xapiripe spirits. Can you see them Cieba?' Nasua barely whispered into his ear. The boy nodded his reply, his father forgotten. Never dull like humans, but always magnificent, the spirits were half dancing, half walking. Cieba saw their red and black painted bodies, heads covered with vulture plumes, armbands of beads and parrot feathers, and about their waists toucan feathers. Cieba counted fifteen or sixteen in the clearing but many more could be heard in the darkness beyond. Iridescent and magnificent the Xapiripe noticed the intruders and their march halted, their chatter silenced.

Indicating that his grandson should copy his actions, Nasua stepped forward until they stood in the middle of the clearing, only a pace away from the spirits' sharpened spears. The Xapiripe clustered together to confer. With whispers of judgement they surrounded the pair and Cieba's heart sank into the memory of his mother's death. He felt mocked and ashamed by the Xapiripe, their confidence crushing his own, just like his father had said, there were too many. Without warning Nasua let go of his hand and stepped back leaving the boy alone in the eyes of this jury. Fighting back tears Cieba

41

took a deep breath and stood up strong, clenching his fists. He might only be seven but he wasn't going to die without a fight.

'Put your fists away, Huayna can't be beaten with your anger,' Nasua said, stepping forward and placing a hand on the child's shoulder. Cieba's hands opened and he bowed his head, his fate was set. His journey at its end, not as Nasua had said, at its beginning.

The action met with approval from the spirits, their buoyant chatter returning with a clattering of spears against their shields. Nodding their approval to the young boy, the Xapiripe dispersed to continue their journey, those closest laying their hands on Cieba's head to ruffle his hair. He felt their touch and breath as they bustled past, and with their talk mischievous once more, they left the clearing.

As the last branch sprang back into place, there was a moment of still and quiet relief, followed by a wave of subtle satisfaction that the exchange between the living and the dead had passed without bloodshed.

'Come,' said Nasua suddenly serious, the delight which had covered his face lost to a look of vulnerability, 'We must leave.'

'But grandfather?'

'Not now young warrior. We must get back before they find us here alone.'

'Is Huayna close?' Cieba asked, stepping back between the trees. Nasua looked down at his grandson and nodded with a deep sigh. 'He will never now be far away,' he said taking the boy's hand again. The comfort of his grandfather's palm which had lead him here, was now replaced by a firm callused grip that led Cieba in fear.

'Now get back to your father's side,' Nasua said, gesturing across the sleeping tribe.

Exhausted, Cieba took his place and slept from the moment his head rested against his woollen pillow. He awoke to the sound of construction and raised voices. Rubbing clear his vision, he could see Eubucco and Nasua arguing.

'He is not old enough,' Eubucco said firmly. 'And he is too vulnerable!'

'And I am getting too old to teach him!' Nasua said, his hands slowly clenching and unclenching as he spoke. 'If your mind had not been so closed I could have taught you. Maybe then we would not be in this mess,' Cieba sat up but neither man noticed him.

'You cannot blame that attack on me father. That is unfair!' Eubucco snapped back.

'If you had let me and my brother train you. We could ......All of the Etéreo could have left.'

'But where and for how long. How you can justify splitting the light as an ends to all means. Not when…' Eubucco suddenly noticed Cieba watching them and lowered his voice. 'Not when the Pelecaras have been stalking us for so long.' Then he whispered. 'Not after what happened to his mother.'

'That was your choice, and they are just stalking your fear Eubucco. That boy is a gift and you are wasting time.' Nasua shook his head and left.

Meeting the Xapiripe and the exchange between his elders did not readily leave Cieba's thoughts. As the days that followed turned into months, he was left alone to play with his own generation, of which there were only nine in an Etéreo village of one hundred and eighty five. When the new village was complete, construction gave way to hunting, feeding and honouring the cloud forests of their birth.

43

In line with their tribal traditions, at twelve Nasua and his elder brother Naiba had been withdrawn from the forest and placed into the spectral darkness so that when they returned they would truly appreciate all that surrounded them.

The boys had grown strong and, as a man, Naiba took charge of his tribe. He declared that no longer would they fear the fierce cannibals or the spirits of the land. He trained his men hard and the women made arrows which were poisoned and swift. Within a year they were no longer hunted, and only the Pelecaras stood between them and peace.

Whether it was fear or not that kept the spirits at bay Naiba did not know, but the attacks stopped, and his people hailed him. Time passed and the warriors who had fought so bravely bore children who idealised their leader. However, Naiba sadly never found love easy, mainly because women did not understand his ways. Instead he rejoiced in his brother's children and watched them grow strong. In his fifty second year Naiba announced that before he died he would track down and destroy the Pelecaras, so that after his own death the Etéreo would live forever in peace. His warriors rallied to his call and they left in strength, they would split the light one more time and surprise the spirits when least they expected. At dawn they had disappeared leaving the village in Nasua's hands.

A year passed without attack or their warriors return and the Etéreo dared to think that their warriors had been successful. Un-checked rumours spread of a mighty battle in which their heroes had tracked down and surprised the Pelecaras, defeating them with both great bravery and loss. Nasua quickly latched onto the idea that his brother would soon return and all they had to do was be patient. A month later the Pelecaras returned, only in small quantity and without Huayna but no less venomous. Nasua had fought them back into the forests. Furious that his brother's gamble had not worked, he took on two of the spirits, receiving a near fatal wound that rendered him unconscious and bed bound for three months. When he awoke Eubucco had taken charge, with a clear message that without their warriors the Pelecaras would quickly slaughter what was left of them. They should leave the cloud forests as quickly as they could and travel west.

Now back in their home, Eubucco needed time to think. His decision to travel west had been costly, not least because he had lost contact with his motherless son. A woman he had loved since his fourteenth birthday when she had brought him flowers after Nasua had scolded him. With each day he saw Cieba grow weaker and he feared he would die, why the child could not sleep he did not know. Nasua seemed to understand, but then his father was more interested in training Cieba in the old ways, something that only filled Eubucco with fear.

With so many demands on his time Eubucco agreed that if Nasua did not discuss the Xapiripe or Huayna, he could mentor Cieba, teach him what Evallea had started; the guidance she found from her belief in Pachamama, mother earth, and Aratum who guided the visions of the Shaman.

Nasua's lessons were interspersed with stories of his own childhood and the warrior his brother had been. Sometimes they would walk quietly down to the stream or up to a ridge where they could see down through the valley. Once Cieba remembered they sat up high letting the rain fall on them in complete silence, until it passed over and in the warmth of the returning sun, a rainbow formed with beautiful ambition.

'It's a shame that it should be corrupted,' Nasua said under his breath.

'Do you mean by Huayna, Grandfather?'

'No Cieba, that creature must never be let inside. That's what he wants, more than anything.'

'Is that why they chase us?'

'Yes. It is, but your father has asked me not to talk about it.'

'Why? I saw him close.'

'Eubucco feels the best way to protect the Etéreo is to be ignorant of our past. Now come, before I say too much and get both of us into trouble.'

Throughout his long life in the foothills of the Andes, Nasua had only known the daily rains to come in the afternoon, when the rising high humidity of the forests met the cold of the mountains above. He could count on one hand the times he had woken up in the dark to rainfall, and each time the Etéreo had lost more than he dared remember to the attacks of the Pelecaras. So when he woke to the sound of water running from his roof he rose quickly. Shouting out the alarm and reaching for his bow Nasua got to his doorway just in time to see Cieba standing at the edge of the tree line. Illuminated by their defences scrambling torchlight, it was obvious the boy intended to leave.

'Cieba!' shouted Eubucco following the gaze of Nasua, but it was too late, the boy had stepped from sight. Nasua felt the wrath of Eubucco, but he did not have time to look. Nasua realised that Cieba was heading back to the clearing where they had met the Xapiripe, and picked up his pace.

'This is your fault!' Eubucco shouted as he followed. Despite being half Nasua's age he was no match for the older man's agility through the thick forest, and the rain only aggravated his fear. He had tripped twice and was desperately fighting back anger as he burst out into the clearing to find both generations safe. Nasua was crouching in front of Cieba and Eubucco could only look on as his father wiped the boys' tears aside.

'Cieba this is no time to run off crying! This place is not safe!' Eubucco shouted, jealousy rising above his fear.

'This place is no more safe than the village. Let the boy cry, he is frightened,' Nasua said. He pulled the boy into his arms as he had done so many times before, the rain gathering in the creases of their embrace, the ground rapidly softening to mud beneath their feet.

'He is *my* son,' Eubucco shouted. 'Not yours'

Nasua spoke as calmly as he could. 'He is your son, but when have you ever shown him the love that he needed?'

'It's me he comes to when he needs to sleep!'

'Only because his mother told him to,' Nasua said stepping behind Cieba, a hand now on each shoulder 'You cannot replace the years Eubucco when you should have nurtured him, when you should have trained him.'

Out of the darkness behind, serrated screams crashed through the trees from their home. The desperate voices cut deep into the party, and all three generations recognised the sounds of death.

Eubucco stepped forward. 'Cieba we must return to the village, please, our people need us.'

'No,' the boy replied wiping the rain from his eyes and taking a step away from Nasua.

'If your brother had not been so stupid...' Eubucco growled.

'Then learn from his mistakes,' Nasua answered. 'They will not stop Eubucco...we must get away from here, and head for the rising sun.'

47

'Take the boy,' Eubucco whispered back, 'I will do what I can until the dawn.'

'No, we should stay together,' Cieba said defiantly.

'I don't want my son to die,' Eubucco said stepping back between the trees.

'Then we must leave the rest of the tribe,' Nasua said his voice barely audible.

Eubucco stepped back into the clearing and took hold of his son's hand. 'Cieba, we'll head for the rivers and follow their course away from here. The water might shield our scent.'

Between tree and through water the boy was carried, his elders taking it in turns to cradle or carry him across their backs. They did not eat for three days, only taking sips of cold water from the river when they dared. On the morning of the fifth day they reached the Apurimac river and rested until dark in the shadows of a rocky outcrop. That night they did not stop at all, the few words they might have uttered were put aside until dawn broke once more.

'The boy needs food, and I cannot go on at this pace' Nasua said coming to a halt with the sun rising behind them.

'Then the time has come,' Eubucco said crouching down beside his son. 'I cannot protect you any longer Cieba.'

THREE

Notting Hill

After fifteen blind years on the streets of London, Joshua William Peterson woke with a start. His dreams had blanked out the night before. Instead of Rodiani they concentrated on his son David, the way that he used to giggle, and the first time he had tottered unsteadily across the grass in their own London garden. In the subconscious re-enactment of outstretched hands to catch his boy, Joshua had cracked his knuckles on the corner of the wardrobe and jolted himself awake.

With the daylight being held back by thick curtains, the negative image of his room was much the same as it had been before fatigue had finally overtaken him just after four in the morning. The wooden floor beneath Joshua was made all the more uncomfortable by his new suit, which cut off the circulation to his left arm, causing pins and needles to mix unpleasantly with sore knuckles. After Alessandro had left, Joshua had withdrawn into this corner of the room; he needed the constant of the hard floor more than the comfort of a bed.

Joshua wiped his eyes, sore from his new vision and the tears that had overwhelmed him. Getting unsteadily to his feet, Joshua straightened his clothing (the belt that held up his trousers had not prevented them twisting around his waist) and found a clock. It was ten thirty five, and he needed tea. A knock at the door decided his next move.

'Who is it?' Joshua asked groggily.

'It's Stevens Sir... I thought you may appreciate some breakfast.'

Joshua opened the door to meet the relieved face of the butler. Stevens was carrying a breakfast tray which he placed on the table beside the window on the other side of the room.

'Forgive me for asking Sir... It's just you look... did you not sleep in the bed?'

'No, I'm not sure that I did' Joshua replied, rubbing his head watching Stevens as he tucked barely ruffled sheets back in, and brushed flat the blankets. The butler was a little shorter than himself, and he was wearing a suit. Joshua wiped his eyes again with his handkerchief allowing him to focus a little better. Stevens' hair was parted to the left, his concerned face betraying his usual detached efficient manner.

'Thank you for letting me sleep,' Joshua said.

'You are welcome.' Stevens wasn't going to admit he'd been knocking gently on the door every hour since seven. This was to be his last try for a response, then he was going to have to open the door and face whatever was in here . 'I had just finished a few errands for Mr Rodiani and I wanted to make sure that well...' He hesitated whilst he finished putting the pillows in his correcting order. 'I was a little concerned that after so long without a proper bed to sleep on that...' He stopped talking when he realised that Joshua was looking at him properly and not vaguely in the direction of his voice like he had the day before. 'Did Mr Rodiani help you with your eyes... Forgive me it's just...'

'Yes,' Joshua replied, before Stevens could stumble over his words any more. Instead the butler stared at his guest for fully half a minute before turning to open the curtains.

'No,' Joshua shouted covering his face. 'Please. Leave them shut.'

'I'm so sorry sir. I wasn't thinking. Can I get you anything else?'

'Some of that tea would be much appreciated, but I can pour it,' Joshua started to remove his jacket, which Stevens took from him and hung inside the wardrobe door, then he insisted on pouring the tea.

'Would you join me?' Joshua asked. 'I feel a little uncomfortable drinking by myself.'

'Just as I would feel if I stayed Sir. Now if you'll excuse me, Mr Rodiani has requested that you are to have lunch together. At one o'clock.'

Joshua didn't reply. He felt his chin to find stubble starting to re-grow then removed the tie that hung loosely around his neck and pulled his shirt out from his trousers.

'I'm scared Mr Stevens,' Joshua said flatly, after a sigh.

Stevens moved closer and placed a friendly hand on Joshua's arm. 'You have no place on the street. You are a gent Mr Peterson and if you did not have something to offer Mr Rodiani, I can assure you, you would not be here.'

'You realise of course that you sound exactly the same as your employers.'

'There are new clothes arriving for you shortly,' Stevens ignored Joshua. 'In the meantime I'll get some fresh tea and toast.'

When he returned twenty minutes later Stevens found Joshua had showered and was preparing some soap with which to shave. Reluctantly he conceded to allow Stevens to take over but not until they had both had some hot sweet tea. Joshua's new clothes arrived at eleven thirty. He insisted that he be left alone to dress himself. At twelve forty five Joshua left his room and made his way carefully down through the house where he found Rodiani waiting for him at the bottom of the stair.

'I knew I was right about you Joshua,' Rodiani said looking appreciatively up. 'You are a fighter, someone meant for better things than the gutter.'

Joshua kept descending, he'd heard enough of his own promotion, but his fight against it gave him a strange new confidence that grew with every step. At the bottom stair Joshua waited for Rodiani to acknowledge this change and move out of the way.

'Let's have some lunch and get down to business,' Rodiani said regaining his stature. He stood five feet ten possibly five-eleven in polished shoes. He wore a white tieless shirt tucked neatly into slacks and as he waited for Joshua to pass, he pulled a hand back over the top of his receding hair, his cufflinks catching the light from the front door window. They moved through to the dining room without speaking.

'Thank you Stevens,' Alessandro said as he took a few neatly cut sandwiches from the assortment on the table. 'Tell me Stevens, how many bottles of the "Forty Eight" has Maglanis left me?'

'I think there are around seven bottles left Sir.'

'Around seven, Mr Stevens?' Alessandro asked a notable change in his tone.

'Six to be precise sir, and eight of the "Fifty Four" Sir.'

'Don't let him drink anymore of either, not unless I'm here to enjoy it as well,' Alessandro said. 'Now, more tea Joshua or would you prefer something a little stronger?'

'Tea is fine thank you,' Joshua replied, pushing away the half eaten sandwich that lay on his plate.

'I'm thinking it must be nice, not to be in the dark?' Alessandro asked finishing his fourth. He sat back and pointed his folded napkin at his guest. 'Don't be angry with me Joshua. I know your eyesight is not perfect but it will allow you to see things that Maglanis or I cannot.'

'Mr Maglanis suggested that you dealt with the Nazis. Is that where you gained your doctrine…? And may I ask did your studies touch on the occult?'

'No Joshua, the Nazis as you call them had their own ways.' Rodiani cleared his throat. 'I cannot deny that I did business with them. Then again, neither can you.' He cleared his throat again and smiled. 'But ultimately my "doctrine" preceded theirs.'

Joshua closed his eyes, placing two fingers on his temple as a new point of reference. A headache was fighting against clear thought, and the momentary darkness eased it. He could hear Rodiani's steady breathing, unchecked by Joshua's withdrawal, and calm in the face of his creation. There was no pressure to rejoin his new life other than the chink of china as Stevens poured his tea and placed the cup and saucer in his hand.

'Who do you want me to find?' Joshua asked focusing once more.

'Ah good, back to business,' Alessandro wiped his mouth again and threw the napkin onto the table. He smiled and opened his hands.

'I'll need to know a few things.'

'Of course, ask away.'

'What was or is his name Mr Rodiani, what nationality is he, where he was born, is he or was he married, if not, does he have any children or significant relative? Where was he last seen?' Joshua cupped his hands together under the saucer and sat forward so that he looked his host in the eye. 'Lastly may I ask what does he have that you do not?'

'Very impressive Joshua,' said Alessandro, sitting back in his chair and laughing gently. 'The man you are looking for is a South American Indian. His name? The last I heard, he was going by the name of Nathaniel. I have no second name but I doubt that will slow you down. Many years ago he was called Cieba, back then unfortunately he had just lost his young wife, but listen to me.' Alessandro shifted forward in his seat, so that his elbows rested on his knees. 'This is not the sort of man you can tackle in your present state. He has abilities that shall we say, are rarer than even yours. You need to grow strong again. Maglanis will look after you; get you back on your feet.'

'Then just one last question.'

'Of course,' Alessandro rumbled. Picking up his glass and draining it. 'But then my friend I must go.'

'Did you have his wife killed?'

Rodiani rose from the table, calmly manoeuvring his chair away and pushing it back. 'You of all people should know Joshua, that in business sometimes we have to make choices that are shall we say… less palatable.' Rodiani offered his hand. A clean hand Joshua noted, with manicured nails and soft skin more suited to shaking hands and folding money than loading a gun. Joshua stood up and shook it, his employers grasp was firm and unexpectedly aggressive.

'So do we have an understanding, an agreement?' Rodiani asked

'Yes I believe we do.'

'Good.'

FOUR

Into the light

In 1763 the man whom Joshua had been charged to find was only twelve. It had been five years since he had been left frightened and alone beside the first fast flow of the Apurimac river, here the water was coldest and the terrain bleakest. Five years of waiting, five years of learning, too many years of recounting the words that his father had left him with.

'Forgive me my son,' Eubucco had said, 'I pray that the Pelecaras leave you to grow old.'

Shaking his head to try and clear his mind, Cieba knelt on one knee and took a deep breath. In front of him the endless rainforest had been interrupted by a fallen tree, its branches had crushed everything in their shadow, opening up a glade of forty or more paces in each direction. The boy closed his eyes to feel the warmth of the rising sun, its red glow translucent through his eyelids, its warmth only interrupted by the gentle sway of the living leaves behind him; before him, the sun gave a golden hue to the moss which still clung onto the once mighty tree. Cieba waited until the clear bright morning blurred with the high humidity of the afternoon, and the rainforest mists lifted to meet the cold of the mountains, so that rainbows formed above him. One formed now above the clearing, not because of natural intention, but because he had asked it to.

'Arutum,' Cieba said aloud, 'I call upon your spiritual force to drive my vision.'

A chill spread, and the drips of humidity faltered upon each leaf. The dead were close.

Drawn to the boy like Nasua said they would, their imminent presence pushed aside the endless call of the forest creatures who shrank back or fled. In the quiet that followed the saturating damp evaporated into the air to form a cloud which quickly rumbled above with a darkening menace, threatening his creation.

'You are strong,' his father had said as he'd left. 'Remember what your mother taught you. Let Pachamama guide you, trust in Arutum, trust in yourself.' Cieba had had no choice. He shivered now, but there were no more tears, he had shed enough. He was stronger and older, he should not doubt himself anymore.

The thunder above gave way to a profound silence in which not even a drip dare fall.

After his elders had left, Cieba had followed the river downstream into the broken forests where he had been rescued from the cold by Iquitos, an elderly Quechan man, who had come down to the water to wash. Iquitos had slowly, and tentatively, approached the abandoned child, whose eyes had been fixed out over the water. Unresponsive to the old man's call, Iquitos had circled the boy, wading out into the river to convince himself that Cieba was not part of a trap. Content with his life without this interruption, Iquitos had had to pluck up courage to move closer, his heart pounding louder than the river's flow, his hands shaking back the compassion that had started to grow. Then just when Iquitos was within a stride, Cieba had collapsed, and he'd had to move swiftly to catch him.

Iquitos carried Cieba back to his home which sat comfortably a little way down river, on a patch of open grassy ground, well above the water line. There he lived with his wife Suomi. It was only one room but they'd built its walls together from the largest stones they could carry from the river bed. They'd finished their home with a strong roof of stripped timber and flattened leaves. On the night of its completion the couple had cooked fish from the river and relaxed in their new home. They'd chosen the spot well, and soon Iquitos placed out stones in order to slow the river's flow and make a pool that corralled the fish. Now they could trade his catch for alpaca wool and monkey meat.

When Iquitos had returned with Cieba, Suomi had looked over the starved child he'd laid on their floor. Disgusted that such destitution should find one so young, she had turned without speaking to stoke up the fire and prepare some hot food.

In the shadows of the trees the Xapiripe watched relieved. Cieba, they hoped, would be safe with the couple for as long as he needed to be. Suomi would provide not only the comfort of a full belly, but the gentle hand of care Cieba had not had since his mother had died. Most of all Cieba slept like he had not done for years, and he talked, learning and overcoming the differences in their languages quickly. He laughed too, happy to be free of the nightmare life he had been living for so long. Iquitos though, took time to accept the boy for more than just a refugee. Surely someone would come for Cieba, yet they did not, and as one month became six he began to relax, they would feed up the boy, keep him safe.

All was well until one night, when the cold crept up from the river and snuck beneath their blankets. It was then the couple first heard Cieba talk in his sleep. He spoke indecipherable words, often barely audible, then erratically shouted out. Either way he could not be stirred, leaving Iquitos and Suomi to wait up unnerved in the darkness for him to settle down, so they could sleep again. When they questioned him in the following days, Cieba swore he had no recollection, regardless of how aggressive or agitated he had become in his dreams.

After eight weeks of this same exhausting routine, Cieba had become withdrawn, with little appetite. As he grew weaker Suomi feared Sharm's evil spirits had infected his mind. Death, she thought, could not be far away. They were destined, it seemed, never to have a child.

Then as sudden as the disturbances had begun they stopped. Suomi's relief was palpable and she encouraged Iquitos to embrace Cieba as the son they had always wanted rather than a just a pitied refugee. The boy's appetite returned and he caught fish and repaired the dam.

Suomi taught Cieba how to skin and smoke the fish. Above all else, laughter radiated the days as months turned into a year, then two.

Cieba never spoke of the Pelecaras; instead he said that treacherous cannibals, avenging their leader's murder, had massacred his people. He had been the only escapee.

Unsure of how best to celebrate the passing of the time, they used the day that Iquitos had found Cieba as his new birth date. It was the one time in the calendar when Iquitos would take his son to meet other traders and come back with a celebratory spear, or blade.

It was a full cycle of the moon after Cieba's fifth year with them, that Iquitos woke to a heartbreaking whisper. The boy was talking in his sleep again. Daring not to wake Suomi, Iquitos watched the comatose Cieba get out of his blankets, stand up and leave their home.

Bravely, Iquitos searched in the dark, until he found Cieba at the tree line, eerily whispering conversations to an unseen other. The old man was so unnerved, he dared not disturb his son and stayed back to finally follow him home. The next night Iquitos dared not sleep, hoping against all hope that the whispers would not return. But they did. Night after night the same pattern repeated, and Cieba started to withdraw again, away from food and affection.

Without knowing what else to do, Iquitos continued to follow the boy, watching from afar, until finally his patience broke, he could not see Suomi suffer anymore. He would do all he could to stop Cieba's decline. Boldly lighting a torch he convinced himself he had nothing to fear, as he strode forward. The child must be exhausted, what harm could he be?

'Cieba,' Iquitos called, with all the confidence he could muster. 'How many times must I follow you out here? Really child come back to the hut.' Preoccupied by ensuring his footing was sound in the flickering light, Iquitos did not look up until he stood behind the boy at the tree line. Determined that he would not falter nor listen to the whispers, Iquitos reached out. His touch was met with a chill that passed through him almost stopping his heart.

When he woke the following morning Iquitos had to clutch at his chest to ease himself upright. It was then that Suomi pulled open the door with tears in her eyes. 'Thank the stars. Thank Pachamama. You were so pale I thought you were going to die.'

'Where is the boy?' Iquitos said by way of reply, his voice blighted by his pain.

'By the river. Why?'

'No reason,' Iquitos lied, rubbing the bruises he had found on each arm. He had no memory of how he dropped his torch nor how he had arrived beneath his blankets, and he quickly decided he did not want to recall. He would pass off his injuries as a slip down the bank in the dark. Somehow Cieba must have brought him back. Iquitos winced, whatever had happened, he would not follow the child again. It would be better to wait until the time was right, send him downriver with the monkey traders, it would break Suomi's heart but the boy was dangerous. There was only one certainty, that Cieba's strength could not last with so little food and sleep. For the next few weeks the old man moved more slowly about his work. He would just be patient. Until then Suomi could deal with the weakening boy.

Three weeks later, Suomi found Cieba as the sun rose across the river's edge, what on earth they were going to do with him she did not know. His eyes were totally focused on a group of rocks not far from the shore line, he was unresponsive, even to her waving hand.

'Cieba, come home, please get some rest,' Suomi reached out just as her husband had done. This time Cieba's reaction was slower, allowing it into her memory without blackout. Grabbing her hand Cieba held her motionless, and stared hard at her, with a rage she had never seen. The broken child whom they had nurtured, now crazed and fearless. It was obvious now how Iquitos had been harmed. Why had he not told her?

From within, the woman who had fought against her own parents for this peaceful retreat by the river, came a scream of injustice. With every syllable her cry carried the sadness of her miscarried children and with a strength that she seldom unleashed, Suomi pulled free from Cieba, breaking his gaze and waking him from his chimerical state.

'I'm so sorry,' Cieba said. He shrank back. His power lost in a gentle voice.

'What is happening to you child, why are you behaving like this?'

'My father left me, he just stepped between the light and disappeared,' Cieba said quietly.

'I don't understand Cieba. That is no reason to hurt Iquitos, he means you no harm,' Suomi said rubbing her wrist. She took several steps backward, then turned to take a few more, 'I think that you should leave.'

'He would not take me with him Suomi, he said that someone might protect me, keep me safe... If not, he said it was safer to be left to starve than if they found me,' his voice now innocent.

'Who is trying to find you child?' Suomi looked back to see Cieba skimming stones across a flat calm that had appeared on the water. He was lost in his pursuit fully transformed into the child again. She could not fight the mother's bond which compelled forgiveness, it forced a retracing of her steps toward him. More gently this time Suomi repeated the question.

'Who is trying to find you Cieba. Tell me?'

'Grandfather said that the gaps in the darkness are like skipping stones,' Cieba said weighing up a pebble in his hand.

'Cieba. Please stop talking in these riddles.'

'He said that they would come for me no matter where I went.'

'Cieba...' Suomi hesitated, she needed her husband. 'Cieba. Let me talk to Iquitos.' She turned and headed up the bank toward Iquitos who had appeared out of the hut. It was the chill from the river, she told herself, not fear, that ran a shiver down her spine.

'Train him as a warrior,' Suomi said as Iquitos took her hand. 'Either that, husband, or kill him.'

So, each day Iquitos took the boy further into the forest, challenging him to climb higher into the trees and deeper into the ravines. Iquitos taught Cieba how to use a bow, and how to fashion a new one from the best timber, which they steamed, then cooled, a technique unique to Iquitos' family. When the old man needed to rest, Cieba would work on his aim or be sent out into the water no matter how cold. Fate would decide whether the child would perish.

As moonlight followed the setting sun, a hardened youth formed from the shell of a child.

'Look how he sleeps now,' Suomi whispered into her husband's ear. 'You have done well Iquitos.'

'At least he sleeps,' Iquitos said grumpily. 'I wish I could. I always feel like I'm being watched.'

'Nonsense,' Suomi said kissing him on the cheek. 'You should be proud.'

'I'd trade my pride for half... No a quarter of the energy that boy has now. I'm going further still in the morning; I'll take him out toward the falls.'

'Just be careful old man, remember that Cieba is only twelve,' Suomi teased. 'Think wisely on the route you need to take.'

It took three days of hard trekking through the thick forest to reach the falls; the journey took its toll on the old man's body. This would be the hardest test of his long life, Iquitos thought as he slashed away with his new machete he had traded all his last catch for. Its blade was nicked in a couple of places but it would make his life easier. With his heart pounding and the sight of the falls appearing through the trees, he could hold his tongue no longer.

'Cieba I must rest. I am getting too old for these long treks.'

'You look tired Iquitos. Yet the water is just there,' Cieba replied, catching up to his adopted father. 'Rest, I will come back with a drink to refresh you.'

'I don't want to be left alone Cieba. My heart pounds and my body sweats like the rainwater from our roof.'

'You will be fine. Rest here and I will return soon.' The boy waited, placed his hands on his hips and looking down at his frail father said confidently, 'Then I think we should return home.'

'Since when did you make the decisions? It's bad enough that I should have to...' Iquitos started, defiantly standing back up on shaky legs. But he had to sit again, clutching his chest. 'Very well,' he conceded, waving Cieba away. 'Be quick, my mouth is dry and I want to talk to you. It's about time that we... .that I...' but Iquitos winced in pain. 'Go Cieba, be quick.'

Iquitos closed his eyes and thought of Suomi, he touched his cheek where she had kissed him farewell and felt the warmth of her embrace as she whispered her affections in his ear. The old man gave a half smile remembering the children they had wished for. His heart began to thud slowly and when he opened his eyes the vibrancy of the rainforest had dulled, his memories forced aside by whispers. They were crass, menacing words that preyed on his weakness and, through his fading vision, he saw them.

Like moon lit strands of spider web, the Pelecaras surrounded the dying Iquitos, baring their teeth, hungry for flesh and soul. Nonetheless Iquitos' defiant cheeks stayed dry, his father had told him once that it took a proud man to recognise his own fate with dignity. He was trapped in a body incapable of returning their malice. His machete now useless, he could do little more than retain his self respect to his last breath.

He counted five deathly creatures, his life would end quickly. He knew his life had been good, though he had longed for a son of his own and would have wished to die at Suomi's side with their hands intertwined. He felt her love now. Iquitos withdrew within himself, in the depth of his fear he found a calm that numbed the cuts to his flesh, and fingers at his face. With his last heart beat he forgot the glare of their eyes and thought one last time of Suomi.

Without sound to hear him nor sight to destroy the last image of her husband, Suomi felt his violent passing. She put out the fire that crackled beneath its welcoming stove, and pulled over the shawl he'd made for her so many years ago, a gift she remembered which crossed all boundaries of gender. The same gift which had persuaded her to follow him here. It would keep her warm on her journey ahead.

Daring not to go back to Suomi, Cieba followed his instincts to return to the last home of the Etéreo. With the memory of Iquitos pushing him on, he retraced his steps west following the Apurimac toward the higher cloud forests and the Andes beyond. This time there was nobody to carry him, or a shoulder to lean on, only the overriding fear that they would follow.

For two weeks he had run, slept and walked, his bow across his back crisscrossed with the now empty leather satchel of food Suomi had given to him. Eventually he found the last remains of the camp where his friends had died and a few hours later he walked into a stand of trees, whose trunks were less thick. Here, where the daylight could still be seen through its canopy, he spotted a fallen tree. Once a giant that had touched the moon it now lay still and silent, it marked the centre of the clearing where Nasua had first introduced him to the dead.

Walking amongst the narrow stems Cieba ran his hands over smooth bark and under the leaves. The sun was rapidly setting, its warmth replaced by shadows stretching up from the ground and across his torso. From where he stood Cieba took ten strides to the fallen tree and then turned right along its length for another ten until the rougher thick trunk of a mature tree met his touch. By the time he'd found the complete circumference of the whole clearing it was completely dark and, just before the clear cut stars could be blotted by the gathering clouds, Cieba returned to the centre and sat down.

Through the night he heard the Xapiripe start to arrive behind him and one by one they began to sit down at the edge of the old forest. Their movements signified by sound alone, they brought with them the sounds of his memories. The voices of his father and Nasua, the voices of the day they had left him.

'He is not too young,' Nasua had said that day.

'He is far, far too young,' Eubucco replied angrily.

'So you risk his life leaving him alone, when in there, where there are pathways and choices he could make... You know that if Huayna finds him here he will tap his skull and gut him.'

'I do, and then he will die at their hands just as the rest of the Etéreo have. Look at me. I know the risk I place my son in.'

'So you risk all?' Nasua shouted. 'Against everything that you have learnt and seen. You risk the history of our people.'

'Yes, because father, the Pelecaras are at our backs and if they follow us into the spectrum they will slay and slaughter years off his life, then he will not have time to learn…'

'At least he would be alive,' Nasua interrupted.

'Then I will have to risk his soul. You are strong Cieba,' Eubucco had said calmly, crouching down to his son, 'Let Pachamama guide you, trust in Arutum, trust in yourself. You will know when you are ready to call the pathways to you.'

What stirred Cieba from his dreaming state was neither word nor memory, but silence and the warmth of the returning sun. Rays unhindered, crossed his face and when he opened his eyes he found himself in a clearing, the saplings gone, only the fallen tree remained.

'Pachamama, Arutum, let the light that binds us come forth as it did for my father's people,' Cieba shouted, the rest of his words lost as the earth rumbled. Above him clouds gathered, darkening with brooding intention bringing with them a fine mist that crossed the sunlight to form a rainbow above him. Cieba crouched. The dead had taught him what Nasua could not, filling in the gaps of his grandfather's theory with their observations and enthusiastic promise. Now it was up to him to do the rest. 'You will know when,' he heard his father's voice again.

'Arutum, do not let your fears stop this,' Cieba spoke clearly to the forest floor, his lips brushing against the earth as he did so. The rich scent of damp leaf litter lifted from the ground and he tried hard to stifle his nerves as the Xapiripe clattered and whooped for joy, delighted that Nasua's prodigy had been heard.

Above him the rainbow began to split into irregular blocks of light which loosely undulated in a blanket of colour banishing the clouds, rain and sun alike. Measured by metre and nanometres, blues, greens, reds, yellow, primary, secondary and tertiary colours were splitting out of the light spectrum, and covering the sky. Then, at Cieba's command, they were forced individually, straight down to the forest floor in clear shafts of distinct colour.

Firstly to his left at the side of the clearing, a vertical column of yellow light descended, a man's whole stride wide, incinerating the leaves which caught against it. This first column was quickly joined by another of orange. To his right the pillars were of warm chrome, scarlet then vermillion, and through thinning trees now drained of colour, Cieba brought down magenta and violet. To his left, the spectral yellows were backed by shafts of greens then blues and finally purple. All sumptuous to the eye and inviting, but he remembered the concentrated light was deadly to the touch. 'Beauty and pain,' Nasua had whispered into his ear at his mother's cremation.

His mother's memory closed his eyes. Her murderer, Huayna was close, his whispers of decay now spreading through grass and bark, he had picked up Cieba's scent.

Cieba did not need to look to know that the columns of colour were converging, creating a wall of light. He spoke again to the converging spirits', now methodically to prevent nerves cracking through. Time was running out, the Pelecaras are close. There are six, maybe seven, he guessed, too many to fight.

Just as they had done when his father had left him, the brilliant rays of light vibrated with energy. They resonated again

67

now with unanswered clarity, until without thought, a cancerous blot formed in the spectrum that rapidly ate its way out to join another below it, creating a line between yellows of Immaculate Conception. The black line grew vertically apace until it stood boldly reaching into the sky. Equal in width to the other columns, its darkness invited shelter and terror alike.

'You are a fool,' his grandfather had said to Eubucco. Then just as he stepped inside, he had turned to Cieba. 'The fate of the Etéreo lies with you. Be strong and learn quickly.'

'Cieba, forgive me my son. I call to Pachamama to guide you, and pray that the Pelecaras leave you to grow old,' Eubucco said and disappeared.

At his back Cieba felt the cold prod of Huayna's lifeless finger, its malice almost stopping his heart as it had done to Iquitos. The boy dared not turn; he needed all his courage to move forward.

'Forgive me Iquitos for not saving your life,' Cieba's words were met with cold whispers of indignation, and a grasping hand on his shoulder.

'Father,' Cieba whispered, 'I do not know what else to do.'

Without looking back, the boy shrugged off the deathly hands which taunted him, took a deep breath and followed his father into the dark, vanishing from site.

Never before had the Pelecaras been given such an invitation. There, in front of them, as the boy's creation faltered, was an opportunity they could not resist. Pushing each other with nervous delight, they followed. Five of them made it through before the doorway shut, and with unannounced delight they sought out their prey.

FIVE

Joshua begins to dream again

For Joshua the negative whiteout of the long dark winter nights in London made it impossible for him to leave the house for more than a few hours at a time. To start with Stevens accompanied him through the same city streets that had for so long been the subjects of touch and scent to him. That's not to say he hadn't heard the sounds of the sixties psychedelic culture drift out from vehicle and building alike, but Joshua had had to remain concentrated on avoidance rather than pleasure. Nor had Joshua been deprived the scents that accompanied the designers flourishing in Carnaby Street, as free love mingled with the judicial mod footsteps that made their way past his outstretched hands. The worst of his senses Joshua mused, was now taste, his wrecked by nicotine and the inflamed gums of malnutrition.

Stevens however was blessed with patience and an unbiased fascination with the world that surrounded them. He was as happy discussing the merits of Merc and Mary Quant, as he was the tragic statistics emerging out of Vietnam. The butler also liked to listen to the off-shore radio, its volume often barely audible, which was Stevens' own way of controlling its pirate chaos in his ordered world.

He helped Joshua whenever he was allowed, reacquainting him with the use of kitchen and washing facilities. After a week or so Joshua started to make his way out alone and quickly recognised that in the seeing world the confidence he had built up during his blindness needed re-establishing. The late sixties may have been a time of liberty and expression but his new eyeballs were only black spheres and for someone his age they drew unwelcome attention, not least because of the way they irregularly wept blood, an incidence that usually followed acute flashes of colour that brought to life, for an instant, the world much described.

It took patience to get used to his mostly negative world and though he liked the cut of the cloth that met his softening hands, he disliked the image that met him in the mirror. His white eyes especially irritated him, closer examination only revealed black veins that stretched and broke like lightening across each round mass, this he found particularly distasteful.

The black comedy of Al's friendship was now replaced by the moments when Joshua found Stevens dancing alone in his kitchen. Never aware that he was being watched, the butler would unleash his own quiet tributes to The Stones and Hendrix alike, doing his best to fashion a guitar from his selection of frying pans and playing air drums with two spoons. Sure that Stevens would be mortified if discovered, Joshua would slip back upstairs or out the front door, choosing a place far away to gently laugh.

Joshua heard very little from Alessandro Rodiani, and it took fully three weeks before he met with Maglanis again. When the Portuguese man did return he was well suited and stood with a straight back. From his voice Joshua had estimated the man's height and weight correctly; slim build, around six foot one and in his early forties. Joshua had also guessed correctly that from his accent Maglanis would have olive skin and black hair. So he was pleased to see his predictions were mostly right, though Maglanis' hair was shorter and more wiry than he'd expected and his face slightly thinner. Joshua's intuitive practice of weighing up his victims' actions, and reactions to make their dispatch more organized, had in the past proved both efficient and irritating, especially when dealing with the opposite sex. With Maglanis however, there were several things that did not add up; mainly why he never looked at anyone directly, but spoke with an undiminished arrogance. The other was his habit of subconsciously, almost nervously touching his shirt sleeve cuffs. The one thing that Maglanis was not, was insecure.

Joshua tutted, he was too old to care about the idiosyncrasies of others. He should concentrate on getting fit and well, for which he needed to give into his body and sleep. Strangely it was at this point as he settled into his bed, that Joshua realised that this new life was real, that he wasn't about to be given back to the streets and the dependence of loose change. The full stop of one life saturated with eclectic sound and Al's dulcet humour had been replaced by the pinking of radiators flushing with hot water, and the unopinionated polite conversation of a perfectly dressed professional butler. However tangible this new path was any exchange with Maglanis often dried up, leaving him detached and cushioned, the very factors that had caused Joshua's own restlessness as a young man, and had driven his career.

Nethertheless, as he recovered from his exhaustion, he often thought of his old friend. Was it better to leave Al in the past? Joshua could not and would not want to patronise him with a visit that culminated in the uncomfortable folding of money into his friend's hands. Al would not allow that attack on his own pride. Instead Stevens had agreed to visit the tube station, returning with news that all the homeless had been moved on, leaving Joshua anxious enough to go there himself. Unfortunately the paperboy was unwilling at first to accept Joshua's transformation.

'Bloody hell, look at you. All tarted up like a flamin' Christmas tree,' the boy said at the same volume he sold his papers. 'Did you all get the Royal treatment then? Cos you all disappeared at the same time. One day you're all there, with yer coughs and yer 'ats out.' The boy stopped to smirk at his own observation. 'And the next, all gone off to get suited up. "What happened?" I should ask that of you fella, on account that you can see after all!'

Eventually he agreed, after an exchange of three shillings, to give Al a message if he returned.

'It's a shame that you have been unable to contact your friend Mr Peterson,' Stevens said when Joshua returned.

'If Al does ever show up here, I would be grateful if you would give him this money,' Joshua reached inside his jacket, took out his new wallet and handed over three five pound notes. 'That will at least provide him with food for a while, or a roof over his head for a night or two. I can't describe him in absolute detail I'm afraid, as I never saw him.' Joshua laughed at his own words 'He was from Birmingham. A little taller than I, and was more than a little coarse I'm afraid,' Joshua sighed then smiled. 'I have to say though he is extremely good company.'

The visits of Tristao Maglanis to the Notting Hill house were always accompanied by the smell of strong coffee and cigar smoke. Stevens knew Tristao had a key, but surmised this as his only gesture of decency not to let himself in. Without a set pattern he would arrive early morning, between six and seven thirty, hand over his coat and make his way into the drawing room, where he liked to read through Stevens' collection of Life magazines. He would thumb through them happily until his coffee ran out, at which point he would stand up, throw what he was reading onto the table, say something in Portuguese and leave the room. After many years of this routine Stevens would wait out of sight until he smelt the relit cigar from the entrance hall and hear his name being called for instruction.

'Óculos de sol, qué o que ele precisa!' Tristao said, one October morning as he stepped out from the drawing room. The sun was spilling in through the glass of the front door casting half of the hallway into shade. There followed a long silence which left Stevens on unfamiliar ground, the quiet lasted so long that he was compelled to peek around the doorway from the dining room. Maglanis was stood facing the mirror, with one hand holding out a pocket watch, and the other holding his cigar, from which he was taking short puffs.

'Mr Maglanis?' Stevens inquired.

'Sunglasses!' Maglanis translated, he turned and left the house flooding the hallway with light.

Stevens could do no more than shrug his shoulders and close the door after him, the draught sending the abandoned cigar smoke spiralling up the staircase. It wasn't until he went to clear away the coffee tray, that he found a magazine left open on a page reviewing the film, "Two For The Road". On the right leaf was a photo of Audrey Hepburn wearing her white sunglasses. Within the hour Maglanis was knocking at the door again.

'Give these to Joshua,' Tristao said pushing a small case into Stevens' hand, then he distractedly pulled out his watch again. 'I'll return tomorrow.' Wishing to provide some anonymity for his employers new killer, Maglanis had brought a pair of dark glasses to cover Joshua's eyes. Without wanting to reject them instantly, Joshua decided to try them on outside. As he stepped out, he found the ground still wet from the previous night's rain and a wind so cold he pulled his collar up around his cheeks. In spite of the chill. the sun was unhindered and provided some warmth especially when he stepped inside a shop doorway to put on the glasses. It only took a few paces however to realise that the new style of "Sunnies" caused people and objects to float into view at the last moment, too late for Joshua to swerve or avoid contact.

'Thank you for the gesture Maglanis, but I think I would be better making my own choice of spectacles,' Joshua said the following day. Tristao was beginning to grind, some of his habits were more than a little infuriating. Especially his lack of interest in Joshua's previous life on the street. In particular, the whereabouts of Al and his regular lectures about the need to use the underground as much as they could, "to blend in with the crowd".

Joshua lay awake that night, his dislike for Maglanis plateauing at half past four, he was stuck with the man and would have to be patient until he was strong enough to properly challenge him. Until then he would have to laugh off the man's banter as misplaced affection.

Joshua continued his solitary walks, and afterwards, if Maglanis was not there, he would spend an hour or two with the butler. Stevens told Joshua that he had looked after the house since his father had passed the job on to him. He also said that apart from the wiry Maglanis, the house was mostly empty (which did not stop him airing and cleaning the rooms each day). Routine, he said was much preferred, as Mr Rodiani would drop in when you least expected it. It hadn't taken long for Joshua to tire of being third party to Stevens' workload and as his eyesight settled he helped clean, insisting that it would build up his strength.

On Thursday the second of November Tristao knocked at the door at five thirty am precisely. With no apology or conversation he drank his coffee and read his paper. Stevens readied himself to hear that Rodiani would be arriving imminently and waited on edge for his instruction. So when Maglanis appeared to have become totally engrossed in a magazine, reporting on the anti- war march on the Lincoln Memorial, Stevens finally decided to disturb him.

'Early start this morning Mr Maglanis?' Stevens asked, opening up the curtains and lifting up the tray of cold coffee crockery.

'Yes,' Maglanis said lazily, then yawned without even lowering the article.

'I see,' Stevens said with unreserved indignation, he turned and left closing the door with less than his usual precise calm. He found Joshua in the hallway pulling on his coat.

'My friend. I really don't know how you do it, but I'm afraid that I'm going to have to escape,' Joshua said. 'I cannot abide that man at the best of times and especially not today. You see somewhere out in the world my son has just turned thirty one and well…' Joshua sighed heavily. Not wanting to continue or look at the butler he took out his wallet and thumbed through the notes he had inside. He looked up to find his eyes met, and for a fleeting moment in the hallway, the butler and the killer understood each other completely.

'Then Mr Peterson, I'm sure I can pass on any messages upon your return. It might perhaps be prudent to return for some lunch. It's just gone seven forty. If you are agreeable I could have soup and a roll ready for one?'

'One o'clock would be very acceptable,' Joshua said. He managed a smile as he stepped out into a squally morning. No sooner had he left than Maglanis walked out into the hallway looking for him. Disgusted that Joshua had gone. He left a message that he would return at two that afternoon to take Joshua away.

'Make sure he is ready,' Maglanis said.

Nervously but efficiently Stevens pressed then packed Joshua clothes, and put them into an old suitcase which he found in the attic. He had to wipe it clean and air it first, it was well travelled and a bit frayed and so he thought quietly, it would be well placed in Joshua's life. In the middle, between two pairs of trousers and some vests, Stevens carefully placed his transistor radio, packing each side of its wooden casing with socks and making sure the aerial was secure. Maybe he would buy another one, but not in the near future, he was unlikely to see Joshua again and he'd rather leave the house quiet for a while. He took the case downstairs and busied himself in the kitchen. When Joshua returned a fresh pot of tea was waiting. The butler relayed with a sigh that Joshua was to be moved to a small flat in Ealing at the end of the central line.

Joshua had wondered what the next move of his employer was to be, so he did not put up a fight when Maglanis arrived half an hour early clearly agitated. He tutted as Joshua took the time to shake the hand of Stevens thanking him again for his kindness.

The journey via the tube to the flat was a quiet one. Neither man spoke until Joshua purposely used the jerk of the train as it moved out of Notting Hill Gate Station to lean against Maglanis.

'Is it possible that you can spare Stevens' life?' he asked. 'I think, unlike my friend Al, he can be trusted to keep quiet about me.'

'If you are sure?' Maglanis replied.

'Yes I am sure.'

'So be it,' Maglanis said bringing the short exchange to an end. Ironically he was pleased that Al would have met a clean death under Maglanis, it was better that way. The rest of the journey to Ealing passed without conversation, until they stepped inside the front door of a two storey block of flats on Grange road.

'I'm beginning to wonder if this is another bad joke Maglanis. I thought after the sunglasses you were done tormenting me?' Joshua said. Tristao ignored him, disappearing into the flat at the top of the stairs, leaving Joshua to curse him and follow on up. He knew he was on a different street but it was just like his last home, even the smell of curry from the ground floor flat was the same.

'This really is not funny...' Joshua faltered, 'Maglanis this surely is a copy of my old flat.'

'You mean the place where you saw the Devil?' asked Tristao with a wry smile. He closed the door behind Joshua, 'the man who took your sight?' Joshua took his time not to reply, instead he used his energy to familiarise himself with the identical layout.

'You still don't get it, do you Joshua?' Maglanis said finally, his voice once more agitated.

'What, that I should be grateful for your generosity?' Joshua asked entering the same room as Maglanis. 'I think I'd like to meet up with Mr Rodiani again, express my thanks.'

'All in good time Joshua, all in good time.' He threw Joshua the keys and left.

From that day onward, and for the next three weeks Tristao would visit just as erratically as before, but Joshua only drank tea, not coffee, and avoided the papers, so his guardian usually arrived early evening. More often than not Maglanis was on his way out for the night which made their meetings brief, insisting only that Joshua gave him a rundown of his day.

Joshua hung up his new suit, bought some jeans and more comfortable clothes and opted for a wide brimmed hat to cover his eyes. He placed the radio in the kitchen just as Stevens had, but rather than music, he mostly listened to panel shows or the news.

Joshua learned to walk in the first light of day when the white out turned grey and winter birds sang. He began to walk further and further, often into the late morning. It used up his new found energy he'd gained from the move. With some of his new allowance he bought tickets to travel along the underground or bus routes, and found comfort in a sporadic group of shops spread from the Edgware Road to Feltham. Through these he could stagger his food purchasing, it drew less attention to himself. As a blind beggar living off the detritus of others, food had often become impregnated in his beard and clothes. This was now a bad memory that rapidly developed into an obsession of cleanliness, he especially hated crumbs. As a result Joshua hardly ever ate in the flat, and the weight he had put on under Stevens' care turned lean to muscle. All the time his determination grew that this last chapter of his life would not be wasted, he just needed to be patient.

In his wanderings, Joshua found his old launderette down the Uxbridge Road which he'd used in the fifties, but having sat in it for a while listening to the machines spin he decided that he would not walk the extra ten minutes back to his old lodgings. Instead when his clothes were done he returned to his new flat, and to the biggest luxury he would allow himself, almost greater than the roof over his head, his kettle. Much to Maglanis' humour he bought it on the first day there. No longer did he have to rely on guidance from a kind hand, or Stevens' ornate china. He now took great satisfaction in being able to brew a small pot of tea for himself, which he would drink hot from a clean mug, with a dash of milk and one sugar.

The flat was stark; consisting of a bedroom that contained a lumpy bed and a wardrobe, a kitchen diner that had a bay window in which was placed a small rectangular drop leaf table with a chair either side of it and lastly a bathroom in which the pipes rattled when the taps were turned. Maglanis bought Joshua an electric heater, but he left it off, after all there was no wind to chill his bones and there was a bed to sleep on.

On the streets, Joshua's dreams had at first been full of the regrets that his career had brought him, and the fear that he had squandered the time he should have spent as a father. As time passed his dreams began to mingle with the lovers he had flaunted in Paris and Milan and the jazz clubs he had loved but his wife had hated.

Apart from the occasional sip of Al's Gin, Joshua had never sought to blank out his mind with alcohol or drugs, he had always thought he deserved his punishment, and hardened by time, his sleeping mind reflected mostly on his comfort zones. It was the thought of removing Marcella's clothes, or the sight of her laughing with her friends that brought a smile to his heart, and more latterly the smell and taste of tea and toast took him right back to the kitchen at his father's house in Hampshire. All reflection had stopped however, when he regained his sight, and for the first month he could not recall dreaming at all. However, on his second night alone on lumpy springs, with the sound of the late buses on the Ealing street below, his imagination started to spark as his eyes closed. If nothing else, the puzzle of his dreaming state gave him pause for thought until daylight returned.

On the evening of Friday the 1st Dec 1967, Maglanis dropped off a package, about the same size and weight as a bag of flour. He needed it storing for a couple of days, but spent most of the time boasting about a beauty he had bedded the night before, and the one he was taking away for the weekend. Joshua was well and truly pleased to see him leave, because today, he had decided when all this was over he would do the one thing he most feared, to contact his son. That afternoon he'd even spoken his name aloud, "David" named after Joshua's father. Maglanis had distracted his new determination, and he needed a walk to settle his thoughts. The Indian couple downstairs were arguing when he returned, so he turned the radio on and went to bed recounting Maglanis' bragging. That night he dreamt again of Marcella and how she had always wanted to make love in a waterfall, a feat they had managed only once. His mind's eye could see her naked, luring him into a deep pool. The waterfall crashed into it so loudly, he could not hear her words.

Invigorated for the first time in many years, Joshua's libido followed the woman, no longer Marcella, into the water where she now swam. Then from above, the water began to fall as snow. The heavy flakes were picked up by a breeze, and blown against the trees around them, they hardened and turned into the rigid shapes of brick and glass, forming houses. The pool Joshua had swam in had turned into cold tarmac, slimy with a fluid that stank like gasoline. There were no sounds of wind or the street, only a radiant click which Joshua later considered sounded like fingernails being scraped over each other. Shaking his unconscious head Joshua saw the woman disappearing towards a road junction just in time to be hit simultaneously by two cars colliding. The ensuing blast finally woke Joshua with a start. He rose with a shiver and headed straight to the kitchen to fill the kettle.

SIX

The Cruel Sea of Green

On and on the tributaries of the Amazon River drop away from the Andes, gouging through rock and cutting through trees. Leaving unforgiven foes on their shores and collecting new treasures in their flow, bowing to no man until, with great respect, they must yield together to form one, that spills out into the Atlantic with undiminished historical force.

In the upper reaches of the Tuichi tributary, hundreds of miles south from the Apurimac, but no less potent, the first rains of 1774 had started. Caught in the downpour Cattleya reached the top of the first waterfall which marked the last few miles of her journey home. Despite her weariness she moved silently through the dense shade of the Amazon rainforest leaving no trace of her passing. She'd left her people before sunrise eight days ago and would be lucky to arrive home before nightfall. After an easy descent, she continued to follow the river's course inside the shelter of the tree line. Always in sight was the edge of the canopy, it was dangerous to wander too far from the curtain of rain, it was dangerous to wander too far from the river. The rain's intensity created a blanket of noise that tilted the odds in favour of the predators of the forest, their prey left to retreat in fear, eyes peeled, waiting for the downpour to pass.

High above amongst the bowing branches, the blurred eyes of two spider monkeys peered down through the battered foliage to watch Cattleya's careful steps beneath them. Other than avoiding them, the spider monkeys knew little of humans. As for Cattleya and her people, they knew nothing of the western world. They had been left untouched by the Jesuits, the Portuguese and the Spanish who played with the spoils and the borders of her country. The monkeys shook off the rain so that their ears might hear better the hunter who stepped over the roots of giant kapok trees, her arrows still thankfully held. It was better to be still and to wait, their instincts decided, than to run and be shot at.

On the forest floor Cattleya's journey had faltered to avoid a colony of army ants that were making their own lethal rivulet across her path, and she watched the birds picking off the insects as they fled the ants' destructive course.

Naked, but for a short skirt of cloth around her waist, a bow across her back and five arrows in her left hand, Cattleya detoured around the ants and covered the following mile to the top of the next waterfall. It was a much harder descent this time, but she easily made her way down the steep sixty feet drop through trees that clung to the thin soil defying gravity and reason. At the bottom she rested by its pool and watched the rain bounce off the surface as if it were rock. Moving closer to the waterfall she reached out a hand to cup the cold water. It was chilled from the seasonal snow melts of the Andes which had started to swell the river's flow, and soon, many miles to the east, would flood the Amazon basin once more.

The cold water revived her tired body and she thought of her father awaiting her return. She missed him and his understanding that her visit would be brief, and that she would love him more each time she returned from her restless adventures. She was nineteen but her father still looked at her with the same hopeful eyes he had done since she was seven. The thought of her family's warm embrace brought a rare smile to her face; the hard life of the jungle was made harder still by the solitude she had chosen.

Stirred by her memories, momentum beckoned, and she focused across the pool to where the water flowed back into a river and the rainforest became impassable. From here her journey home had to be taken up through the shallows, stirring up the clear cold water as she waded along the river's edge.

The rain still hadn't stopped when she saw the vapour rising from the horizon marking the last waterfall of her journey. At over a hundred feet tall, the impressive cascade created a determined crescendo that began to suppress all other sound. Feeling suddenly vulnerable, Cattleya removed the bow from her back.

Thirty paces from the sheer drop Cattleya reached the tree with the three forked branch and thankfully headed back into the forest. Here a very narrow track took her through the thick undergrowth and around the edge of the waterfall until the ground began to fall away sharply. After a journey which had incurred no injury, she did not want her parents' smiles stolen by broken bones or bruises. So she stopped short of the edge, re-slung the bow across her back, and planned a route.

This steep slope didn't allow the undergrowth to survive, and so Cattleya had a panoramic view through the thinning trees. Breathtaking glimpses opened across the top of the canopy as it followed the steep valley away into the sea of green that filled the horizon. The picture was framed on her right by the waterfall that fell into a wide dark pool, and on her left by an outcrop of rock. Cattleya wiped her brow as the rain finally stopped and over the vastness before her, wisps of mist started to form in the high humidity.

Suddenly noticing something in the pool beneath her, Cattleya instantly dropped behind the tree in front. Waiting moments only she rose to risk a second look, one hand gripping the bark of the tree the other tightening upon her arrows. She was right, it was a big monkey, or a man in the pool, but it was too far away to be sure. Father had told her how cannibal tribes trapped their victims like this, and she swallowed in the fear that her throat was about to be slit. Cattleya crouched back down behind the tree and tried to listen above the fear in her heart. Nothing could be heard apart from the waterfall, and the call of the monkeys swinging out from their hiding places to declare the end of the rain to all that would listen.

Brave but not stupid Cattleya rose slowly then looked again. The body was face down. Cattleya held her breath and watched, if it did not come up for air before she needed to breathe, she would go closer.

After too short a time Cattleya gasped in some air. Calming and convincing herself this was a corpse, she started to creep forward descending the long steep slope to the pool, eyes always fixed on the body which still floated motionless. She stopped abruptly and grabbed hold of a branch, suddenly remembering how the children sometimes used tubes made from the Liana climber to breath underwater. Scrutinising the figure she could see no such device.

Finally, she reached the pool's edge to find that it was the body of young man. Without being able to see a face she could be sure of only one thing, he was not from her village. His bow was made in a different way, and its wood was a lighter colour. He also had a bag that floated beside him, its strap wrapped round his left arm, her people did not use bags, only slings. He was not marked by tattoos, but by a scar on his shoulder. Dead though this stranger must be Cattleya's racing pulse had not calmed. She stepped into the water and a shiver of goose bumps spread up through her body as she poked the corpse with her bow. It did not react in any way. So she stepped back to the shallows placing all but one arrow on the shore.

Resolved to retrieve the bow and the bag for her father, Cattleya waded into the deepening water, adrenalin wiping away the fatigue in her legs. The closer to the corpse she stepped, the more the cool water did its best to take her breath as it wrapped round her body, and as her arms lifted, it rose under her armpits chilling her spine. With barely two paces left Cattleya held up her arrow like a dagger and reached out with her other hand.

Panic crashed through her, no cold flesh was there to meet her outstretched fingers. The body was warm. Terror drew every last drop of blood from her still heart as a hand, lifeless for so long, reached up and grabbed her shoulder. Cattleya let out a scream that would chill the heart as the body in front of her drew breath.

Her hunter's legs gave way, her feet slipping in the circulating flow of the waterfall and her head, which had stayed strong over many days of wandering alone, slipped beneath the surface. As the last decibel of fear left her mouth the water poured in.

Cattleya's keen eyes which had seen far into tree tops were now blurred, witness only to the flickering light of the rapidly disappearing surface. She was pulled ever deeper and deeper, her hands aloft. There would be no embrace she thought, no homecoming this day.

Lastly as she reached the bottom, Cattleya's body was spun by the flow, her head struck the rock and she dropped her last arrow. Her fingers outstretched with her final ounce of determination to find it, met instead the touch of another, her hard hands which had taken so much life now received the grasp of a saviour.

SEVEN

Joshua finds closure to a
life less ordinary

True to his word, on Monday the 4th of December 1967, Tristao returned to collect his parcel from Joshua's flat. He weighed it in one hand, scrunching its brown paper cover with his grip. Tristao shook his head muttering half in English, half in his own tongue, so that the smouldering cigar in his mouth seesawed up and down. 'It's good quality for the price I tell him. But you know Joshua, still "levá-la de volta" he says "tem sido cortada, diz ele".' Joshua could only guess that drugs were inside the parcel. Tristao became increasingly agitated, gesticulating as he headed back for the door. 'It's too cheap not to be cut I told him, but oh no Joshua, I have to go through with the deal. Now there is no fucking deal. Cut he says, É claro que a sua foi cortada porra!' At which point Tristao left, leaving the door wide open for Joshua, and the rest of the house to hear him stomp down the stairs slamming the front door behind him.

Three days went by before Maglanis returned, this time a little calmer as he knocked on the door. Joshua had just sat down at his table, he was trying to stem a trickle of blood from his eyes before it reached his collar. His afternoon had been consumed by choosing a bottle of gin, which he hoped would cure the hideous insomnia he'd been suffering since Tristao's last visit. Without Al to talk to, the recent nights had been lonely, and his desperately short naps were full of tortuous dreams that always woke him with a start. In the last twenty four hours his eyes had not closed at all. To make matters worse, the couple downstairs had argued from five thirty this morning, right up until the ten o'clock news. Once the shouts died down they had made love. Their pants gaining momentum until she had climaxed with a cry Joshua likened to a dying wolf. By the time they had completed the process for the third time; Joshua had mentally strangled them both and efficiently dispatched their bodies around the London wastelands.

He could not go down the prescriptive route, so he would have to try and rely on alcohol. It had been two years since he had drunk gin, so it would be kill or cure. Either way, he would sleep and the couple downstairs would live for at least another day. Joshua hesitated as he passed their door, after he had slept, maybe then he would kill them. Fatigued to the point of dizziness he slowly made his way to a shop about ten minutes walk away.

The journey out was uneventful, however crossing the road on his way back with the bottle in hand had been a different matter. The flickering light inside the corner shop had agitated his vision and he became so preoccupied with his bleeding eyes, it was all his numbed senses could do to jump out of the way of a bicycle. The cyclist had approached at such speed that Joshua did not hear the wisp of his tyres, but he had heard the man shout at the last second. The shock of the near miss induced such clear colours to his sight, that before he could get his bearings, a taxi blared its horn. The driver fixated on the gin and the assumption that Joshua was drunk.

'You look absolutely terrible,' Maglanis said without compassion when the door was opened to him. He stepped past Joshua and went through to the kitchen picking up the bottle of gin to inspect the label. 'You'll have to pull yourself together old man. I need your help,' he said.

'Well those are a few words I didn't expect to hear from you!'

'You should consider it a little test.'

'I have a feeling this has something to do with your drugs'

'Not my drugs Joshua. I don't think our employer would allow me to use you to my benefit. This, my friend, is your chance to put your old skills into practice. It's a situation which needs rectifying quickly Joshua.' Tristao hesitated, touching his shirt cuffs, then looked straight at Joshua. 'You know I would take care of it myself but Mr Rodiani thinks I need to distance myself. They won't be expecting you.'

Within the hour Joshua was standing on the underground's District Line heading east. His body running on adrenalin his mind focused. An hour after that, blood, which had long since been washed from Joshua's hands, warmed his skin once more, as he took care of three men in a dimly lit car factory in Dagenham. They were setting out their plans for a drugs cartel of their own in the East End. Joshua had felt a little rusty but, as Alessandro had pointed out, his skills were unmistakably still there. He left the men dead, with a small note from his employer tucked inside each surprised mouth. It read "Il diavolo non è mai lontano", "The devil is never far away".

That night Joshua slept fully sixteen hours without anger, gin, fear or regret. The following day Tristao woke him just before the grey drizzle of the morning could pass into an afternoon full of rain. He followed Joshua into the kitchen and watched him fill the kettle.

'Drugs can be quite a useful ally, Joshua,' Tristao remarked, moving through to sit at the table in the bay window, 'You know I think I might just be able to teach you something yet.'

'Am I to take that as a thank you?' Joshua said, sitting opposite while the kettle gathered momentum.

'You are quite a piece of work Joshua,' Maglanis said reaching inside his blazer pockets to take out two thick bundles of ten pound notes and place them on the table between them. 'There is five hundred English pounds in each. That is to say thank you.'

Joshua had taken his first life at the age of 27, when a night in Milan had taken an unexpected direction. His wife, Anna, had chosen to spend the weekend with her parents, and his lover, Marcella, had preferred to stay in Como with her friends. So Joshua had made plans to have a bit of fun. He was dropped in the city by the family's chauffer and had made his way to the low lit city jazz bars, where he sipped cocktails and enjoyed the attention of many women. Around two in the morning he struck up a conversation with a Spanish business man, going by the name of Ruiz. The two men were soon laughing and joking like old friends, each trying to identify the most beautiful women in the room or postulate over the quality of the music. Swept along in this new friendship Joshua found himself explaining how, despite his lifestyle, despite his lovers and his wife's money, there was something missing in his life. The two men had laughed at his words, downed their drinks, shouting for the barman for more. It was five o'clock when they stumbled out onto the streets in the company of two equally inebriated French women on holiday from Provence.

'I wonder Joshua,' Ruiz said, stepping out in front he turned and faced the group. 'As beautiful as these fine ladies are, would you help me with an errand I have just remembered?' Full of alcohol Joshua had laughed and agreed. Kissing the women farewell, the men had walked quietly for half an hour through the dark streets, marked out by the waking coughs and late night laughs which spilled out from the open windows above. Eventually they stood outside the shadowed outline of a door, Ruiz produced a knife, its keen edge glinting in the lights from above.

'The man inside has stolen a lot of money from my employer. A third of it will be mine which I will share with you, if you help me.' Fuelled by an exhilaration he would never be able to explain, Joshua had nodded. The man inside the flat did not give up his money without losing his life, yet the speed and detached way in which Ruiz handled himself from the moment the door was open, to the moment they stepped back into the street, was incredible. The power over someone's life questioned everything that his education at Winchester and his family had taught him. Joshua accepted his payment and the men parted. Two days later, as he was getting ready to leave Milan, Ruiz turned up at his door with a job offer, which was a world away from his marriage and the control of his father.

'Tell me about this man you want me to find' Joshua asked Tristao. 'I think I'm ready.'

'It would also appear old man, that Mr Rodiani feels the same way.'

'I get the impression 'young' Mr Tristao that the man you are looking for is not in the business of ammunitions, or drugs, perhaps not in business at all… Would I be right in thinking that this is somewhat of a personal matter?'

'Yes. You have passed the test,' Maglanis gave a half smile. 'Nathaniel holds a journal which our employer would like returned.'

'And I take it that journal ties Mr Rodiani to something or someone…' Joshua stopped momentarily trying to choose his words carefully, but was interrupted before he could continue.

'Again you are correct. But alas… it would be wrong I think to discuss… the journal.' Tristao's words were deliberate between his own pauses. He seemed suddenly to struggle with his English, so gave into his own. 'Se há uma verdade a ser dita, é Rodiani que deve dizer isso!'

'I'm sorry it must be an age thing, what did you say?'

'Mr Rodiani… will tell you the truth… if there is one to tell.'

'Indeed,' Joshua sighed, Tristao was obviously on sticky ground here. 'Let's stick to the basics then. Where was he last seen?' The shift from Rodiani's involvement relaxed the air and brought bravado back into play.

'I saw him last amongst the crowds of Wall street, on October 24th 1929,' Maglanis replied sitting back at the table, and stared out of the window at the rain. He drew a fine leather shoe up onto his opposite knee and rested an arm on the back of his chair. They sat for a moment watching a bus come to a stop in the street below. People got off, turned up their collars and pushed up umbrellas against the rain, as they made their way home.

Joshua knew the date of the stock market crash well, he had been twenty nine, with six hits under his belt. The burst of the economic bubble had brought him his first target in New York. Pulling a handkerchief out of his trouser pocket Joshua eyed up Tristao, who was still staring out of the window. 1929 was nearly forty years ago, yet Maglanis had the looks and nature of a man in his late thirties and he had thought Alessandro Rodiani to be fifty six, fifty seven at the most. The same feeling that he had had so many years before in Milan was starting to creep through him again. This was something different.

Joshua needed a moment to think. He got up and collected the money from the table and placed the bundles in his jacket pocket. He disappeared into the kitchen to re-boil the kettle.

'Quite a day Tristao,' he said as he returned, with a cup in hand.

'Yes,' Maglanis said proudly. 'I was there protecting Alessandro's interests. So, you see, I did not have time to chase Nathaniel. I saw him there though, standing behind a camera; you know the ones they have on legs, with the big bulb. It was definitely him.'

'I was in New York on business the following spring,' Joshua said, but Maglanis was paying little attention, he was far more intent on his own story.

'Let's just say a couple of Alessandro's brokers were reluctant to repay his generous interest in their companies,' Tristao said.

'I take it you were more successful than many others that day?'

'Always successful, or I'd be working for nothing. If I learnt nothing else from Rodriguez it is to protect your investments.'

'Who is Rodriguez?' Joshua asked.

'Your predecessor on this particular case, but I always thought he had too many distractions. However, you, Joshua, are much more focused, if you pardon the expression.'

'Yes, very droll,' Joshua sighed. He wetted the corner of his handkerchief in his mouth then wiped beneath each eye. Relieved they were only wet from his saliva, but disappointed that the colour had gone, he continued. 'It was thirty eight years ago when you last saw him. Did the war stop Rodriguez looking?' This question was answered first by laughter, and then a lengthy silence during which Maglanis stared out of the window blankly.

'I'm afraid Rodriguez lost his life to a woman before the last war broke out. Alessandro has tried other ways to locate Nathaniel, but none have been successful. I think my friend, he has been waiting for the opportunity to employ a man like yourself.'

'Oh, I see. Obviously the world has changed, nations have been scattered, ravaged and reduced somewhat. Are you sure that this Indian is still alive?'

'Alessandro is sure. As for his whereabouts, Rodriguez used to say that only six people separate one man from another, even on the opposite side of the world.'

'Yes well, I am, of course, aware of that little gem of information. But it doesn't appear to have done him any good.' Joshua stood up again, this time through frustration. His movement making Maglanis laugh once more.

'You are right, and it is better not to mention Rodriguez to Alessandro. Instead concentrate your mind on Nathaniel. I can tell you he is not to be underestimated.' At this, Maglanis stood up as well, pushing his chair backward as he did so and buttoned up his coat as he spoke. 'I must go, I will pick you up at six tomorrow night. Alessandro has requested we join him. So get yourself cleaned up and put that suit on I gave you.' Joshua watched him pull the cuffs of his shirt through so that they were accessible just inside his coat sleeves. 'Now I must leave. I'm going out tonight!'

'You do surprise me. Is it any particular occasion dare I ask?'

'I have a few plans Joshua. Yesterday it was my birthday, but as you know, there was not the time shall we say, to enjoy myself. So tonight my friend I think I will have a few drinks with a beautiful woman, sleep in a five star bed and reflect on a long life.' He laughed this time to himself, pulled out a fresh cigar and lit the end. 'Sleep well Joshua,' he said through the smoke and left.

By five thirty the following afternoon Joshua had done as he was bid, clean shaven and suited, by six fifteen the two men were in a taxi driving across town to Alessandro's house in Notting Hill. Neither spoke, until they pulled up outside. Tristao paid and as the diesel engine departed, they found themselves shoulder to shoulder staring at the door.

'Forgive me Tristao, where are my manners. How were your delayed birthday celebrations?'

'Como mil sonhos!, like a thousand dreams!' Tristao actually placed a hand on Joshua's shoulder. 'Enough of me Joshua. Alessandro is a great host my friend, and he's been looking forward to tonight.'

They walked up the steps to the opening door, except where Stevens should have been a young woman stood in the light of the hall. With a seductive smile and flirtatious eye, she introduced herself as Candice and led them through to the drawing room. Opposite them in front of bookshelves, previously unnoticed by Joshua, stood Alessandro Rodiani. He was pouring red wine from a crystal decanter, which he returned to its silver tray. He cleared his throat and turned with an appreciatory smile, approaching them both with the offer of a full glass.

'Benvenuto! Welcome back to my house,' he laughed like an old friend. 'Please take a glass of wine to ward off the winter cold.' Somehow refusal was not an option.

'Thank you,' replied Joshua receiving the glass and taking a large swig. The blackcurrant tannin's masking the alcohol immediately washing through his blood stream, the effect awkward on his hands as he fumbled for a handkerchief. Blood was wetting the corner of his left eye; colour was flickering in his right.

'1948 Gattinara Fratelli Berteletti Riserva Piemonte,' Rodiani announced lifting his glass and tilting it to the light. 'The last of the few eh Tristao! I'm sure you'll enjoy a glass my old friend, especially tonight.'

'Grazie Cardinale,' Maglanis took the glass bowing his head slightly as he did.

'How about you Candice?'

'Yes thank you,' she replied, doing her best to drift across from the door without an inebriated slip. Unfortunately, however, she couldn't help but stumble, spilling wine from her half full glass as she staggered slightly back. It was an awkward action that the other three observed, her cheeks turning red as she realised.

'I've given Stevens the night off. So I'm afraid I haven't prepared much in the way of food my friends, but the girl is yours Joshua,' Alessandro said, waving a hand coldly in Candice's direction. Her smiles at Joshua were full of promise.

97

He followed her long blond hair as it parted and fell loosely across her patterned blouse, deliberately open enough to reveal her cleavage. She ran a seductive finger around the rim of her already empty glass then touched the tip of it to her tongue. She giggled at the emotionless man and blew him a kiss, assuming that he wouldn't last long anyway, so it was worth the promised cash.

With no other sound to fill the room, the ticking of the clock above the fireplace filled the void until Tristao coughed, his direction clear enough for Joshua to speak. 'Thank you, but Candice, as beautiful as you are, I'm afraid you're a little young for my old body. I think I'd prefer to get down to business.'

'I wish I had had the benefit of your wisdom when I was younger,' Alessandro said, refilling Joshua's glass as Tristao instantly relieved the girl of hers and led her out of the room. Joshua heard the front door close behind her, and watched Alessandro gently run a hand over his receding hair, then smile at him.

'Very well, let's get down to business. We made a deal. I've taken you off the streets, fed, clothed and housed you. In return you have taken care of a small oversight by my dear Tristao.' He drained his glass and placed it on the table. 'Indeed I would say Joshua you have proved yourself. All we need now is a direction for you to move in. If you're lucky we might just get a glimpse of him. How are your eyes, they look sore?' Tristao re-entered the room. 'Has the colour taken over yet, or are we still in time?'

'Mostly my vision is negative. However the colour, as you call it, is coming more often… And lasting longer.'

'And now as we stand here. What can you see now?'

'It's best described as changeable but... unpleasantly negative at the moment.'

'Then we have no time to lose, Please follow me,' he passed Joshua and led him through the hallway and down into the cellar, the one place Joshua had never visited during his stay here.

The three glasses of wine he had drunk in quick succession did not prevent the damp cold of the poorly lit basement creep around Joshua as he followed Alessandro down the wooden stairs. Nor did Tristao's much coveted vintage ward off the chill of fear, as they passed wine racks and into a larger room than those above. It was illuminated by globes of naked bulbs strung loosely from the ceiling, beneath which a complex pattern of silvery white lines stretched out on the floor in every direction. Joshua stood looking down over it, hardly noticing Tristao pass him and start to light candles on the pattern. Each ignited with dark combustion, until the entire room was alive with black flame licking the air, sending dark rays out into the room. The design grew stronger almost elevating and vibrating with intensity.

'It's quite beautiful isn't it?' Alessandro's steady deep voice resonated. 'It's taken me a long time to recreate it, but Joshua, unfortunately it's not quite finished.' He walked out into the pattern. 'There are many more like this in my journal' Alessandro walked on 'Nathaniel has that journal and I want it back. You'll need to bring him back too, he is the author after all, and the key holder to, well... You see Joshua each pattern contains a doorway that not everyone can see'

'I don't understand?' Joshua said trying to keep his voice strong, he'd only seen a pattern like this once before, in Florence, beneath the body of his Anna. Her blood flowing

99

through his hands as he'd tried to stem the bleeding, the tears of her torture settling on his shirt while he had screamed out his revenge.

'Nothing good ever came from interfering with the occult' Joshua said beneath his breath.

'I'm sure you won't be surprised to hear that the Nazis helped me to get it this far' Alessandro's voice boomed as he strode right to the end of the cellar where he picked up a large book from the floor and headed back 'The journal you must find looks just like this one, Joshua. There are only two. This one belonged to Samuel Richardson, but don't try and trace him. It only contains a couple of designs, how do you say it Tristao? la punta di un iceberg'

'The tip of the iceberg' Joshua heard Tristao translate, his own head spinning.

Alessandro growled, clearly now agitated as he spoke 'Now enough, let's get on with it'

Joshua looked up into the darkness and tried to control his breathing. He knew it had not been Rodiani who had murdered Anna, because he had avenged her, but the memory of her death bludgeoned his mind. Caught with the same knife, which had killed Anna, in his hands, Joshua had been labelled with the crime. Somehow, however, the press were silenced by the Firenze Polizia, so his photo never reached the papers, nor did his case come to trial. Instead he was knocked out in his cell, and transported to the back streets of Milan. He awoke untied, in a small flat, with a pistol on the floor beside him and a few lira in his pocket. It took him four days to assassinate all those he had thought responsible.

'How is this supposed to help me find Nathaniel?' Joshua asked trying to focus his mind.

'That my friend, is where you come in,' Tristao said appearing next to him. 'You perceive things differently, you have more finite abilities. So look at the pattern Joshua, what do you see?'

'Nothing but memory.'

'Tristao, perhaps...' Rodiani said not finishing his sentence.

Tristao moved between his master and Joshua and placed a baseball in Joshua's hand. It was hard and greyed, its stitching intact, though a darker red than it had once been, it was no different Joshua decided later, than many he had seen during his travels in the States.

'Listen Joshua, and smell, use all your senses, close your eyes again if you need to.'

'Forgive me Mr Rodiani, what is the ball for?'

'Throw it onto the pattern and look not to where it lands, but to where you hear its echo.'

Rubbing his head in frustration, Joshua caught a scent, a perfume that proliferated then mixed with the smell of paint and sea air. He threw the ball as directed and heard the sound of its bounce echo to his right. Opening his eyes he had to reach out to steady himself, like his dream of awakening upstairs, he now stood on a promenade his hands finding security on the railings.

In front of him Anna was blowing him a kiss from her ruby red lips and giggling as she promised security away from his fathers plan with the prosperity from hers. He felt the touch of her hand as she stepped closer revealing the desire in her eyes, then the soft pampered skin of her cheek to his ruddy face as she whispered her dreams.

A little way along the promenade, a deep shadow loomed and despite the sound of the children playing on the beach, and the waves against the pebbles, the radiant click which emanated from the darkness filled his ears.

'No more darkness for you Joshua!' he heard Rodiani say from somewhere outside of this bubble.

The seed of doubt was planted so the question had to be asked, 'Was it you who killed my Anna?'

'Joshua? "Your Anna?" Please.'

'I still loved her, whatever you think you know,' Anna was still standing before him, teasing him, luring him with a finger.

'We can all regret our past Joshua. Can you honestly say that bystanders were never caught up in your deals,' Rodiani said.

'I'm afraid you have the wrong man. I'm too old now...' Anna's face had changed, her lips had turned pale, her hands now clutching her stomach. From the pebbles on the beach, the children ran to jostle their elbows and heads to see over the rounded concrete walls of the esplanade, screaming as Anna started to bleed.

'Il diavolo non è mai lontano da tutti noi Joshua. We're all getting older. So there is no turning back.' Anna slowly slumped to the ground, blood seeping through her blouse, one hand around a knife's handle.

'Then weight my old bones down and throw me in the Thames,' Joshua said faintly.

'Then the devil has won Joshua, and you will never have revenge.'

Joshua couldn't stop his momentum re-enact history as he grabbed hold of the knife to pull it free, only to find the woman beneath him was no longer Anna. She was not white nor clothed but younger and Brazilian he thought. As Joshua pulled her toward him he realised she was pregnant. She was dying from the same wound that had killed Anna and she desperately tried to speak. Joshua's eyes began flickering between the negative and the colour of the dim lights as he lifted her head in his hands, the blood bubbling in her mouth as she spoke. 'He is here.'

Along the promenade, through the screams and the scraping click, a creature stood – more corpse than man, his face fixed at a point past Joshua and the girl, his white body transient on the edge of the darkness behind him. Joshua followed his hollowed eyes to Rodiani.

From somewhere close, Tristao asked, 'Where are you Joshua?'

'Trapped in a nightmare Tristao,' Joshua whispered not caring if he was heard.

'Can you see a door Joshua?' Tristao asked.

Wiping his face clear of his bleeding eyes Joshua realised the creature stood in exactly that, a doorway. In the same place the echo had come from.

'Yes,' he replied.

'What can you see through it Joshua?' Tristao's words were fainter now, the breath behind them shallow and failing.

'Death.'

'Beyond him… Joshua.'

Joshua looked down as he felt the weight shift in his arms, the dead girl's eyes fixed on him, the blood now congealing at the edges of her mouth and on his shirt. To his left the children stood, cold and destitute, silent as the spray from the rising sea whipped at their backs. In front of him the darkness had widened into an opening at least as wide as the promenade. The creature gone, its click with it, leaving only the roar of the ocean as it swelled and chilled Joshua to the bone. Death had won, crass hideous and unrelenting it swept the children into the sea. Its last prize now cold in Joshua's arms.

'Why leave me, you bastard of the devil,' Joshua screamed letting the girl slip and headed to the door. At its threshold he found the answer to Tristao's question. A wooden farmhouse stood alone, its peeling white paint luminous to the pitch black that surrounded it. Iconic and unmistakeable in the American landscape Joshua had seen many like it before in the farming heartlands. His next step forward was halted by Rodiani's voice.

'He left you Joshua, because you have work to do. Step back Joshua, your time will come.'

Turning around, Joshua found the promenade had gone, with it the sea, leaving only a body on the floor. It was clothed now, suited in fact.

'Anna. The girl. It was Tristao all along,' Joshua said, dropping slowly to his haunches next to the dead Maglanis.

'He was a good man. A brutal one, but loyal Joshua, don't fail him.'

'Why should I stay?' Joshua said looking back to where the vision of the door had been.

'Because he gave his life so that you can fulfil yours! Besides, the doorway has closed,' Rodiani said. Lit by the naked bulbs, he collected the baseball from the far end of the room, then he returned, crossing the pattern on the floor to retrieved the dagger Joshua had pulled from Tristao. He stood quietly for a moment wiping it clean with his handkerchief.

'What did you see in the darkness?' Rodiani eventually asked.

'A farmhouse, I've seen them before in Nebraska.'

'There, you've got your direction Joshua. That's where he is. Bring him and the journal to me. I've waited long enough, so

104

don't disappoint me. Contact Daniel Weaver in New York, he'll sort out anything you need. You'll find him via the 'Il Circolo.' It's my club. '

'Yes of course I…'

'Oh and give this to Daniel, he'll know what to do with it,' Rodiani threw Joshua the baseball.

'Mr Rodiani, this ball…'

'No more questions Joshua, no more questions.'

EIGHT

The boy in the blue coat

Back in the Ealing flat, Joshua lifted a second cup of steaming tea to his lips and looked out of the bay window onto the street as it came to life this Saturday morning. The grey dawn had gone, and in the dark patches of his daylight he could make out a little boy, giggling as he ran along the pavement towards his waiting mother.

'Come on little man, before all the sweets have been sold,' his mother called. They were heading for the corner shop four doors down. Just as they passed beneath Joshua's window the light changed, flickering until the image was flooded with glorious colour, but as Joshua blinked, the image sadly reverted to the negative. Joshua sighed, closing his eyes tight to hold onto the memory of a happy boy, in a blue coat, running after his mother on a cold winter's day.

This time Joshua let his eyes bleed freely onto his collar and drip into his cup.

'You always were a fool old man. Who is going to pity you now?' Joshua repeated out loud the last words David had said to him. Shrunk by his own voice, tears pushed aside the blood and he wept freely. 'At least father, your blindness will prevent you from hurting anyone else.'

The next words had been Al's angry defence, to which David did not respond, other than to turn on his heel to mark his departure, with the toss of his small change onto the ground.

As the boy outside disappeared into the shop, Joshua rose from his table feeling all of his sixty seven years again. He cleaned his face and collected up the unspent cash that Maglanis had been leaving him for housekeeping. He placed it into the old suitcase along with the money that had been given to him as a reward. Joshua also packed the radio and a small cardboard box of narcotics Tristao had left him to use at his discretion.

From his blazer pocket, he pulled out Rodiani's baseball, but instead of placing it straight inside the case, he found himself passing it between his hands. The leather still soft to his touch as he gripped it, then rotated it in his fingers. It was a strange moment, during which he thought of nothing else other than the curve of the stitching and the fading marks of the signatures once written upon it. He wondered briefly how many others had held it this way.

Joshua tutted to himself and placed the ball amongst his socks in his case, snapping the locks shut when he'd done so.

Straightening himself up, Joshua picked off a hair from his lapel. He was still wearing his fine suit, despite the slight smell of smoke which had attached itself during the night before. Lastly, Joshua pulled on an overcoat and pocketed his passport, also courtesy of Maglanis. Checking himself in the mirror, he wiped a dirty mark from his shoulder with a clean handkerchief and stepped out of the flat. He closed the door behind him and headed for the train station.

PART TWO

NINE

The Rejuvenated Man, Part One

Six and a half weeks on foot downstream from the treacherous pools that had halted Cattleya's journey home, stood the last outpost of the Portuguese. Despite its remoteness it was a growing community of traders using the river for transport. The Jesuits had settled here first, but had moved on, travelling ever deeper towards Bolivia, away from the river and the attention it brought. A further day's walk south into the forest, at the end of a track stood what was left of some stable outbuildings, a small chapel, and a two storey house. All were surrounded by a high wall to keep the forest at bay. The dwelling had been built by the wealthy Fernandez Peixa, using the church's money for his lover Consuela to live in (it had also housed his horses and his money). She waited there while he invested in the main structure of the trading post and allowed her to name it after his home town in Portugal, Praia da Viera, where he had been a fisherman. He had lavished Consuela with silk and lace and furnished the house with whatever she wanted. But when the formidable Fernandez had fallen ill and died, Consuela had no choice than to offer firstly her clothes, then her beauty to the highest price. Having arrived in luxury from the port of Lisbon she had died as a prostitute on the streets of Santarem. The large house of Fernandez had been pillaged and lain empty for years, until that is, the Vatican had looked upon it as a suitable solution to a small problem they were having.

Inside the echoing halls of St Peters, the voices of the church had carried with unquestioned gravity.

'We think Cardinal Rodiani, that it's best that you take this opportunity, to shall we say, put these indiscretions behind you,' stated one.

'The Amazonia's are exactly the place that the church needs a man of your, your obvious talents,' said another.

'Above all Cardinal it will give you time to reflect and grow' were the last words he heard on the subject. Within a month Rodiani was heading via the slave routes to Brazil.

In the same year that Cattleya had overcome her fears and stepped into the cold water up river, the disaffected Cardinal tried to ease his nerves with some very specific bathing arrangements of his own in the Fernandez house. Steam rose off the surface of the bath and drifted up onto the ceiling, water droplets formed against the walls and the shutters that blocked out the night. Around the bath, tall candles lit the new resident as he attempted once more to relax and remind himself of the comforts he had once enjoyed at his home in Florence.

Unfortunately the horrors of the journey to this new life had plagued the portly Cardinal with impotence, and the pleasures of the flesh he had for so long delighted in, now filled him with a frustrated rage that had left the blood of several "unsuitable" natives spread across the floor of his less than opulent quarters.

The tide of hot water quickly rose around Rodiani's pale body, momentarily finding the top of the deep bath before it spilled unevenly over the sides. He settled himself in, pleased that his instruction to fill the tub completely had been carried out, especially now that his knees and torso were submerged. Rodiani rested his head back onto a towel and let one arm follow the water's course, where without looking, his hand found a glass of wine. Its precise placement identified by Agustin who at seventy seven had learned from his mistakes.

Beneath him, the spilt water gathered momentum seeking out its escape over once polished mahogany floorboards that now tolerated blood stains and wax. Slipping over the dark surface the water disappeared between the gaps, splashing onto the kitchen's tiled floor below. Now as the scent of bath salts started to lift into the room, the Cardinal shouted for his entertainment.

'*Agustin*!!'

On the other side of the door, Agustin had been watching, his knuckles whitening around the latch, desperately trying to keep the door open by the very narrowest of gaps, that allowed him an eye on his master, and kept his own face in the shadow. In the passageway beside him two carefully selected women from the town waited nervously. The first, Maria, felt Agustin's hand start to push her forward as soon as he had seen the wine glass lifted. When the call came, Agustin quickly let her through, only to resume his previous position immediately.

With practiced sultriness, dressed in a loose cotton shirt, Maria accurately moved toward the bath, taking care not to make eye contact with the bathing dignitary. Standing behind him she picked up a jug of warm water from beside the tub and poured it carefully over Alessandro's receding hair. As long as she did not look at him, all would be well; she just had to stay calm. When the jug was empty, only the sound of water dripping onto the floor beneath them could be heard. It was an uncomfortable cold sound that fought against the heat of the room. Maria felt compelled to sing a lullaby in her native tongue to fill the void. Her subtle song only just masked Agustin's concerned intake of breath.

Seemingly undisturbed by the change, Cardinal Rodiani stared unblinkingly toward the candles at the end of his bath, and Maria began to pull back through his wetted scalp with a whale bone comb. The silver strands marking his hair that, before the journey, had remained throughout his fifties the deepest black.

Firmly and without hesitation she pulled the comb from the front of his receding hair to the nape of his neck, sending electrifying sensations shivering through his body. If her hand was steady all would be well. Yet Maria could not help but notice how the Cardinal had sweat beads rolling down over his short stubble and secondary chin alike. Gabrielle, her friend, had heard that the Cardinal sweated pure wine and if you looked closely enough you could see it was red.

Agustin now gave Gabrielle a gentle shove into the room, a welcome sight for Maria, that gave strength to her song. Stepping as swiftly as possible, Gabrielle took the same path as her friend, her eyes on her and not the Cardinal. Dressed the same but more heavily built, she approached the bath.

'Ahh,' the Cardinal sighed, his body starting to relax enough for his loins to awaken and swell with his intoxicated blood. He tried his best to focus on the flickering candle light, and not on either woman, the excitement was in their presence, not in their discloser. His heart began to pick up pace and the briefest sensation of sexual desire began to obscure his desperate situation in this country.

Gabrielle gently scooped a little water over his shoulders, taking great care not to splash. The Cardinal sighed again, she did not want to look down for fear she may lose her calm or worse giggle. Instead she found herself staring at the smile that had started to cross his face. She cupped the water again, and wondered whether he was as bad as the rumours made out. She looked up to the comb and the slender hands that pulled it, then up to the concentrated face of Maria who had stopped singing. Returning to her task she cupped the water once more, only to find the Cardinal's unblinking eyes upon her, his smile gone. Chilled and suddenly frightened by his stare, her nervous hands spilt water over his face.

Cardinal Rodiani closed his eyes to avoid the unwanted spray and the brief moment of enticement was lost. The splash of water brought with it the horrors of an ocean that he sought so desperately to forget. All too quickly the demons that haunted his fragile mind swept across the water that encased his frustrated body. To Rodiani the spirits of his memory swirled with the steam of the bath, and chilled the water to the temperature of the ocean. On the voyage over from Africa, their ship had been lifted and dropped by the raging Atlantic in swells so deep it was a miracle that any had survived. Lifting his arms to shield himself from his vision the Cardinal slipped in the enclosing bath, and the water that Agustin had boiled clean of impurities felt filthy as it washed over his face.

Trapped by his tortured vision of the past he tasted not bath water, but the foul salt water that had poured down through the deck hatches of their ship *Meridian,* the slave ship that had brought him to Brazil. Rodiani slipped deeper down, submerging his head. He reached out to grasp a remembered ladder, which had been the only thing to stop his fall lower into the hold.

He had held onto that ladder with all the strength he could, and if this was a further torment from the devil he would not give in now. Not after he had stared into the eyes of the slaves trapped in front of him, chained horizontally between low beams, trapped in their own faeces and the vomit of fear. No matter how desperately they cried for release he had held on. He could not save them from the rushing water, so he closed his eyes, and did not open them until the ship was still and the deck hands tried to pull him free, but his arms were locked despite being badly bruised. It was Agustin's words that finally released his grip.

'They are all dead Alessandro. You must leave them in peace,' Agustin said.

The memory flooded back filling the petrified Rodiani's mind until he could stifle his own scream no longer.

Gabrielle grabbed hold of his arm in an effort to aid his pitiful state, but her attempts to calm the Cardinal were met with deranged blows as his mind fought to get up and break free of this horror. His actions causing Maria's comb to stab into his scalp.

'Agustin!!' Rodiani screamed now, as he had done so many times before, scrambling at the edge of the bath to escape. His flailing arms suddenly found enough support to pull his bright pink body shakily out of the bath. He shuffled forward only to slip backwards on the wet floor and fall heavily, knocking himself out with the impact. Agustin watched his master fall unable to stop the two women rush past him as he did so.

Agustin knew that the demons that swam in the recesses of the Cardinal's conscious mind did not recede immediately when he passed out, he'd seen this all before. He watched his master's eyes roll white as he twitched on the floor, until his spasms slowed and a sleep of recovery took over. Agustin went to fetch help and some towels thankful that his master had made it out of the bath this time.

'*Mateus, Francesco!*' the old man called from the doorway down into the courtyard .

Having already heard the Cardinal's screams from above, the men had intercepted both women before they'd disappeared out of the gate and into the night. Maria and Gabrielle were reminded that the second half of their payment would only be made once their silence was ensured.

'It's a good job the Cardinal has so few bathing companions,' said Francesco, placing his hand upon Agustin's shoulder as they looked upon the Cardinal's flushed body .

'My friends, we must move his Eminence to his bedroom. It would appear once more that he has drunk a little too much,' Agustin said.

'Is he not a little too hot?' asked Mateus.

'Maybe we should let him cool down while you get some help Agustin,' said Francesco straight faced, he stood with his hands on his hips, stretching his back.

'His Eminence I'm sure would be extremely grateful if we could move him now, before any more "help" turns up,' Agustin replied. He was used to their jibes, but at twice their age knew without them Alessandro would stay where he lay.

'I'm not taking the legs,' said Mateus, dismissively gesturing his hand flatly down. 'I saw enough of the Cardinal last time.'

'Agustin will make sure that the towel is more secure if you help me roll him,' said Francesco with a smile. 'Unless you would wish to dry him first Mateus?'

'No I don't want to be that close to his Eminence and anyway, you should take a turn at the leg end Agustin.'

'I would my friend, but I no longer have the strength in my arms or legs that you have.'

'And I have not the strength in my stomach,' laughed Francesco.

'You would if your stomach were a little smaller,' fired back Mateus, 'very well "Ad majorem Dei gloriam",' Mateus sighed quoting the Jesuit motto. 'I will take the legs Agustin.'

'Ha!' laughed Francesco. 'Very good and how gracious you are "to the greater glory of God",' he translated.

'Though it'll be the last time if the towel comes off,' said Mateus.

'Just keep your eyes on me Mateus,' said Francesco, 'and we'll try to protect this dignitary's dignity today!'

'I fear it may be a little late for that my friend,' winced Mateus as they rolled the Cardinal for Agustin to wrap a towel around his waist.

In the bathroom the three men got into their respective positions. Mateus between the Cardinal's legs with a sweating knee over the crook of each arm, and Francesco taking the greater weight at the shoulders, with Agustin assuming the supervisory role.

Eighteen months ago Mateus and Francesco had been accompanying the Jesuit Father Matthew on his way from his mission in Paraguay to the port of Salvador de Bahia. Sadly only three weeks into their journey Father Matthew had contracted malaria and by the time they carried him into Praia da Viera he was barely breathing and died within two days. Agustin had been sent in response to a letter Alessandro had received from the town authorities.

'Be mindful Agustin,' Alessandro had said, 'Jesuits stir up trouble. Bury the monk and bring back any papers he was carrying. Get rid of anything else.'

The ceremony had been short and as the last prayers at Father Matthew's graveside faded and their bibles closed, Mateus and Francesco had been shackled together. At the end of the rope that held them, the tall and wizened figure of a mercenary stood high booted, his black hair dusty and his hard stare indicative of his unforgiving life.

'Where are you taking those men?' questioned Agustin, with Matthew's papers under his arm.

'These men are Guwarii natives in brown cloth,' the mercenary said coldly. 'They are out of your hands and into mine. I think you will find that Rodriguez Taveres' name will carry greater weight in this town than your own, Agustin!'

'What about the Cardinal Rodiani's name?' replied Agustin. 'I think, Maglanis, that he would prefer these men to stay out of the sugar plantations.'

'The Cardinal knows better than to get mixed up with the Affairs of the Portuguese Crown. Or to that fact the Jesuit order. So you'll need to provide some evidence of your Cardinal's concerns.'

It was not often that Agustin forged his master's writing, but having cared for him for the last thirty five years, he was very proficient when the need arose. With every word he wrote to ensure the men's release, he remembered the white churches in the port of Loanda, where the slaves were christened before being packed into the *Meridian*. He would not stand by powerless again.

Agustin had been a week away from his seventy-sixth birthday when the town's authorities reluctantly ignored

Sebastao de Maglanis and released the two men to his master, and the dwindling power of the Catholic Church. 'You can be sure that Rodriguez will be told about this,' Sebastao had said as he removed the shackles and lit a cigar.

'I'm sure you will give him your unbiased account.'

'Be sure too old man, that Rodriguez will get them back one way or another.'

Based on the conversations conducted on the way back to Alessandro's house, Agustin was able to persuade his master that Mateus was a skilled carpenter, and that Francesco was a capable painter. As both skills were desperately needed in his home, Alessandro had agreed in return for food and safety, that their trades could be plied in order to overhaul the property. However, the agreement would only last until the work was done.

After nine months, Alessandro had given up asking why tools and materials took so long to arrive and why Agustin managed to misorder badly enough that only oils and canvas turned up instead of brushes and white wash. Francesco painted nonetheless, with some of his creations decorating their new home. Mateus' epic restoration of the heavy main gates ended with them opening effortlessly. It was just unfortunate that Alessandro managed to burn a part of the roof, (which he blamed on Agustin's choice of candles) and smash a couple of windows. With the unforeseen delays and misunderstandings of the country, alongside Agustin's habit of breaking things, it became thankfully clear to Cardinal Rodiani that as Agustin got older, the two newcomers were becoming invaluable.

'Every time,' whispered Agustin under his breath as they moved Alessandro out of the bathroom, down the corridor and into his bedroom. Each year as his hair grew whiter, he occasionally dared to remind himself that he had once been stronger, and at least four inches taller. Still for humility's sake, his two companions would eke out the move a little more, taunting him gently, playing on his fear that they should be discovered.

'At least this time he was out of the bath,' Mateus said, with laboured breath keeping his eyes on Francesco's grimacing face, who was barely contending with the weight.

'At least this time he had not made it down the stairs,' wheezed Francesco laughing at his companion as the towel slipped off, he ignored Alessandro's bloodied hair that wetted the front of his shirt.

Agustin finished their thoughts as they laid the Cardinal into his bed, 'At least this time Alessandro, you did not make it out into the courtyard, and increase the burden on these two fine men.'

Francesco and Mateus took their cue and left. It was only during these vulnerable hours that Agustin could see the man whom he had known so many years ago, a man once innocent to the vulgarities of human nature. His unconscious face relaxed, Alessandro's soul, his aide surmised, was open once more, if only briefly, to the Holy Spirit.

TEN

Yesterday's Tomorrow

For Cattleya the watery darkness of the waterfall pool was replaced by the hard sensation of rock against her face, and the taste of blood in her mouth. Momentarily disoriented, the crash of the waterfall quickly brought clarity to her memory. Relief turned to fear, she had been tricked, the floating body had been a decoy, or somehow alive. How could she have been so stupid? Cattleya cursed herself. With no strength to pull away, her left arm felt trapped beneath her, her right outstretched, its fingers claustrophobically touched by another. She could not give in, she must not give in and with concentrated effort her will power managed to override exhaustion, enough to flicker first one then both eyes open.

Almost everything was blurred apart from the rock, her outstretched arm and the hand that met her own. Her heart pounded again, it had to be the man from the pool she could see, the man who had tricked her. He was stirring, but she could not move. Cattleya closed her eyes and tried to concentrate her breathing.

'Good to see your eyes open,' the man said, barely audible above the waterfall.

Cattleya reacted instinctively to his voice, snatching her hand away, then rolling onto her other side to get up and flee.

Except she could go no further than onto her knee before the pain around her ribs pulled her up fast, she had to stay seated, hunched up, looking away.

'The undertow of the waterfall is deceptive,' he continued. His voice strained as he sat up, 'and you are heavier than you look. You must have hit the bottom before I got a proper hold and pulled you out...! Please I mean you no harm.'

Cattleya kept her silence, but decided to turn and face the man. She thought him lean, hungry and like herself, in a great deal of pain. Wincing he reached over for his bow and hauled himself up, leaning to take the weight off his right leg. The stranger was taller than her father. His torso, like his back unmarked by paint or tattoo, nor did he have any piercing or opened ear lobe; he was part of no tribe she had ever seen or heard of.

'Did you fall?' she asked, finding courage in his friendliness.

'Yes,' he said laughing gently. 'I fell.' He leaned forward a little, offering his hand to help her off the rock. 'My name is Cieba.'

'What were you doing in the water?' Cattleya asked, warming to his smile and reaching up to regain his touch. 'I thought you were dead.'

'No not dead...' Cieba's words were abruptly silenced. His explanation interrupted by a blow Cattleya did not see. The man's face she had just met was momentarily puzzled by a lack of focus. Then he fell, crumpling in front of her, forcing her to step back, until his face smacked hard against the rock they had laid upon. Behind him stood her uncle Mikania. The waterfall's sound must have concealed his approach, and now he stood with his eyes burning furiously, his club poised ready to end Cieba's life.

'No,' cried Cattleya. 'No uncle, don't kill him. He saved my life.' Mikania, took a long questioning look at his niece. He put a foot onto Cieba's back and rocked him. When he was satisfied that the stranger was not going to get up he lowered his club.

'Still searching for your brother Cattleya?' Mikania asked mockingly.

Cattleya ignored him, moving as quickly as she could to crouch beside Cieba and push aside the bloodied hair from his face. He was still breathing, slowly and quietly, the opposite to herself. Cattleya pushed at her uncle's leg. 'Luckily for you Mikania, I don't think he's about to get up and fight back. So take your weight off him before you crush him anymore.'

'Always the rebel Cattleya. I would have thought by now you would have calmed down, found a husband or been killed by the jaguar you hunt.'

'No uncle, I'm nineteen summers old and you are still the most dangerous creature I have met.'

Mikania shook his head, he could be rid of her now, dump them both back in the pool. He stood back, watching her tend to the stranger. He took a deep breath and realised his momentum was gone, she would fight back now.

'Maybe you should ask your father if he still wants you to search for your brother, or is this his replacement?' Mikania taunted instead, moving forward to rock Cieba with his foot again.

'Maybe I should slit your throat, and tell my father we were all attacked,' Cattleya replied, looking up. 'That way it might look like a fair fight.'

'It's a good job your father's heart still beats strong,' Mikania replied, bitterness rife in his voice as he gripped the handle of his notched club, his knuckles whitening with the pressure of his frustration.

'Yes it is,' came the steady voice of another stepping out of the darkening forest and into the clearing of the pool.

'Father,' Cattleya said relieved.

'Cattleya, I was sure I'd heard your voice,' said her father Pentas. He steadied himself and caught his breath, looking at his daughter with the same pride and relief that he always did. Pentas had counted every sunrise his daughter was away, and asked Pachamama every night to protect her from the jaguar that had taken his son. 'Eight days,' he said under his breath.

'What are you both doing here?' Cattleya asked standing up reluctant to leave Cieba.

'We're following one of your uncle's visions,' Pentas said. 'You're not exactly what he saw, I think. Unless of course I misunderstood you Mikania?' He frowned looking down at Cieba. 'Yet whatever your uncle saw, I am very pleased to find you.'

'The paths of the future Arutum shows me are sometimes unclear, but brother, she has brought us to save your daughter from this man,' Mikania's tone was contemptuous; he pushed the body hard with his foot and stood back.

Pentas moved forward and picked up the stranger's bow to inspect it, he gave a respectful nod at its construction then crouched beside his daughter.

'Hunger has aged this stranger. I doubt he is much older than you Cattleya. He doesn't look like a cannibal, and you are both wet and injured. Why did you hit him brother?'

'It was only a matter of time before she was followed back. He was about to kill her, you could see it in his face' Mikania replied angrily.

'Do you know this man Cattleya?' Pentas asked quietly leaning closer to his daughter.

'Only that he saved me and that his name…' Cattleya tried to explain.

'Look at him Pentas; he could be from anywhere'Mikania interrupted.

'Maybe he's from the mountains Cattleya?' Pentas proffered, gently placing a hand on her arm and getting to his feet.

'Maybe he was on his way to murder us in our sleep!' Mikania ranted, this time moving away to temper his anger. He went and washed his club off in the pool, the rest of his scorn inaudible.

There was no mistaking the brothers' tribe, both with hair flattened across the brow and bands of red paint around their heads. A thick black band of paint covered their eyes and each wore a stud of wood in their lower lip. Mikania the shaman wore a necklace of intricately carved bones, the work of their grandfather's third wife.

'Your heart still beats as proudly as ever Cattleya,' Pentas said placing his hand on her shoulder.

'Yes father,' Cattleya replied.

'Your daughter wishes us to befriend this stranger?' Mikania asked returning from the water's edge and poked his club at Cieba's leg.

'Is this so Cattleya?' Pentas asked.

'His name is Cieba, he saved my life……… from the water,' she replied, pointing toward the pool. 'I slipped in the rain,' she lied.

'Then I think we will not leave him here to die. Brother, Mikania our shaman, maybe Arutum did guide us here. So don't hit him again,' Pentas said calmly. 'I think we shall take

Cieba to our home. There we will see if there is anything left of his brain!'

'Very well,' Mikania sighed. The decision of Pentas, the tribe's leader was final; the shaman must do as he was told. 'As you wish Pentas, but I doubt he will survive.' Mikania picked Cieba's fragile frame up and over his shoulder.

'You lead the way Cattleya,' Pentas said. 'I'll follow you and our guest Mikania.'

'Are you afraid that I will drop him brother?' Mikania asked slyly.

'Our people will be waiting for us to return Mikania, and I will be pleased to tell them that your visions have led us to Cattleya and this Cieba from the mountains.'

'Thank you,' said Cattleya embracing her father properly for the first time.

'Cattleya you are hurt,' Pentas said as she tensed in his arms. 'We must get you home to your mother. She'll know how to heal you both, I think you will mend faster than your new friend.'

'At least my bruises happened in the water father, and not under Mikania's club,' she said.

'That's enough Cattleya.' Her father's words were firm and the four did not speak again as they made their way back through the shadows of the forest.

After three hours of silent walking later they stepped between the familiar huts of their village. Many of their people had retreated to their beds, but those who were awake quickly gathered around to greet their leader. They acknowledged Cattleya with silent nods, preferring instead to ask Pentas about the stranger. Whispers spread as whispers will, that they had brought back an attacker who would be executed at day break, but then another rumour started that Cattleya may finally have found her brother.

On the second day after arriving in the village, Cieba woke from a dreamless sleep. He had been placed in a hammock, and from the corner of his eye he saw a woman sitting beside him. In her lap the beginnings of a woven basket, her hands were plying the leaves around its base, and she had not noticed him stir. From somewhere behind, the sun broke into the hut gathering dust in its rays, lifting its flecks into a static galaxy at the other end of the room.

The throb in the back of his head and the pain that shot up his leg convinced him this place was real and not dreamt. It was then that he noticed the girl he had dragged from the pool, she was leaning against the door frame opposite him. The golden stars of dust surrounded her as the sun caught her dark hair, glossing it, and lifting a smile on her face. She must have been watching him from the shadows.

'My uncle the shaman says you should be dead,' the girl said.

'Oh,' Cieba replied. Her face was softer than before, its periphery newly painted with short waves of charcoal, accentuating her beauty. Her eyes were the same, still intoxicating.

'My father, he says you should be dead too!'

'Your uncle says a lot of things Cattleya,' said the woman beside him. 'But has he fixed your bruised ribs?'

'Mother!' said Cattleya annoyed, retreating into the shadows and out of the room.

'My daughter Cattleya likes you,' the woman Laelia said when they were alone.

'Cattleya,' Cieba repeated.

'It's a long time since I have seen her interested in anything or anyone,' Laelia said, remaining seated her hands still at work.

'Oh,' Cieba answered, not sure of what else to say.

'Who are your people Cieba?' Laelia asked.

'They were murdered in the cloud forests,' her patient said, the throb in his head evident in his voice. He looked across at the woman, her persona reserved, her eyes on her work.

'It is sad that you are alone,' Laelia said gently, she was quiet for a moment holding her basket up to the light. 'You should rest. Pentas will want to talk to you as soon as he hears you are awake. So sleep while you can. You are safe here with me Cieba,' Laelia started to rock his hammock gently and began to sing softly.

'Please,' Cieba said holding a hand up. 'I need to be still'

'You are lucky to be alive,' Laelia said taking her hand off the hammock. 'Your body was broken before you saved my daughter, before Mikania struck you. You are lucky too that Pentas loves his daughter more than he trusts his brother. If you can sleep it would be best. You will need your energy to walk again.'

Laelia started tentatively to sing again and Cieba sighed. Her song like her care was genuine, he felt safeguarded. He should relax his shoulders and not fight her lullaby.

'Thank you,' he said, watching her work.

'My son was taken by a jaguar, that the men caught by mistake…' Laelia said trailing off to place the basket on the floor. 'It was trapped all night before the men found it. They came and got Pentas, for his strength and his brain. He didn't spot our son run after him, a spear in his hand to protect his father. Together with my husband, the men tried to set the Jaguar free, but it was too late, the animal was infected with

Sharm's anger, and it jumped... It leapt from the pit without their help, and dragged my son off into the forest in vengeance for its capture.'

'When did this happen?' asked Cieba.

'Many, many years ago when Cattleya was only seven,' Laelia replied finally looking at her patient. 'Get some sleep Cieba. Please rest while you can.' Laelia went back to her work, singing softly again.

Cieba did not want to sleep, not again, but the woman's song was a comfort longed for, reminding him of his mother so cruelly put to death. This time he could not fight her gentle melody, and exhaustion overrode any defence that lingered. He dreamt of his mother's love, and his own abandonment by the river.

Six years had passed since he had stepped inside the spectrum and started his journey to the waterfall pool. Then, at twelve he had been so intent on getting into the dark that he had not even thought of how to get out. It was a mistake which he'd regretted almost instantly, because as the doorway closed behind him there had been nothing, no sound, no structure and no light, nothing to mark his path or his passing.

'Father,' he had called out into the cold. 'I am here!'

The response from the void was as blank and hard as the floor he stood upon. Cieba could hold back his tears no longer, all of this was for nothing. His father, like his mother, was dead and he was truly alone. Without shadow or sun to mark the passing of time he could not know how long he stayed curled into a scared and empty ball, nor how long he kept his eyes closed, yet when he opened them he decided to move. Getting up onto his feet and striding out, hands outstretched in the direction he thought he had come from.

Then he heard them, first the scrape, then the click. He could smell their breath, tarred with a menace that lingered in the growing cold.

With the scent of the Pelecaras at his back Cieba stopped walking and stood still. He should not be frightened; Iquitos's training had sculpted his body into a hardened youth. He had hunted peccary with the ease of a man twice his age. His adopted father had given him confidence, aggression and above all determination.

'Show yourself,' he shouted, raising his fists and spinning around to meet his predator. There was only blackness that, despite his resolution, filled him with a fear that he was going to die.

It was a fear he could not face, what choice did he have but to run. Faster and faster his feet pounded beneath him. Always the ground unchanging, the darkness unforgiving and the smell of pierced, bloated innards caustically savaging the air as the dead chased him.

Then they had spoken, the five in turn, their words tripping him, sending him sprawling onto the floor where he felt his knees graze and his palms tear. The boy cried out in pain, no longer a warrior but the child again. Before he could pull his knees to his body or resume his flight, a cold and fleshless foot pressed hard between his terrified shoulder blades.

'Like father like son,' a crude and emotionless voice of Azuay whispered. 'Always running… no direction.'

'And you cry like your mother did,' Yupanqui added.

The words were designed to hurt and they did. Their emotional pain backed by the physical when their voices were joined by jagged fingers which they ran through his hair, scratching his scalp and drawing blood. The pressure preventing any attempt to escape.

'Where are you running to boy? Tell us, we'd love to know,' was the guttural taunt of Atoc.

Somehow as Atoc pushed his broken nails across the top of the boy's ear and into his left eye, a thought grew in Cieba's mind.

'You are as trapped in here as I am,' he said quietly.

The reply was unquestionably violent. A harsh hand pulled Cieba up and off the ground by his hair, his feet not touching the ground his legs flailing and striking out at the spectres defiantly.

'Who are you, if you have nothing to feed on,' Cieba shouted.

'Then we shall feed on you,' screeched Hernan, his spiny fingernails scratched down Cieba's back, the pain it caused drawing the boy's legs down.

'Then who? I'm the last who can open the door.'

In the lengthy silence that followed Cieba was released onto the ground. He quickly pulled his bloodied knees up and for some small comfort closed his eyes. His scalp felt like it had been torn from his skull, but he dared not touch it for fear of what he might find.

'Why don't you run?' Huayna asked, his voice rasping.

'Where would I go that I could be free of you' Cieba shouted out now, waking in his hammock six years later, shaking his head fighting the image and the pain until Laelia's gentle hand settled on his shoulder, her song reminding him of where he was.

'Calm yourself,' Laelia said. 'Sleep, you are safe here,' she was willing him back to sleep, and it worked, her presence now enough to stay his memories and he slept without dreams.

'Maybe Pachamama, you have brought me a new son, just maybe,' Laelia said when she was sure he was asleep.

When Cieba finally woke it was the afternoon of the following day and he found food and water waiting for him. 'Eat it,' said Cattleya, looking at him from the same position at the door. 'You're so skinny that the ant birds could carry you away.' His belly craved and grumbled. It had been a long time since he had been offered food in such plenty, and the thought of eating under Cattleya's gaze made him anxious. He'd rather talk to her than eat.

'Your family are very kind,' he started to say looking up, but she was gone.

Cieba overcame the ache in his body and managed to swing his legs round so he could get out of the hammock. After a few tentative mouthfuls he finished everything that had been left. With a full belly, he peered out of the hut to hear women folk chattering just out of sight. From his right a young boy ran into view, he stopped in his tracks to stare Cieba up and down, then ran off giggling. Cieba stepped out of the doorway to watch the boy run. Following his course he could see that Laelia's hut was the end house of maybe thirty other small dwellings, all set out in a wide oval, that must he thought, be fully sixty paces across. In the centre was a much larger hut into which the boy disappeared momentarily, only to be followed out by Mikania. The shaman glared at Cieba and went back inside.

Looking between his hut and the next, Cieba could see that there was nothing between him and the trees. His leg was sore but it just took the weight of his body so he walked out a little way and relieved his bladder. Feeling lighter Cieba reached up to rub the back of his head to find a small swelling where Mikania had struck. He smiled to himself, he was alive and out in the sunshine, that was worth the sacrifice of a small lump.

Cieba turned sensing somebody behind him, and saw Laelia with her hands interlocked.

'Did the jaguar take you from your people Cieba?' she asked.

'No,' he replied, 'but I have watched him sleep and looked into his eyes as he waited in the rain.'

Laelia shrugged in recognition that this could not be her son. She had known it all along. She would have to listen to her heart that knew he was still alive, and not her head and the shaman who told her he was dead.

'Come with me Cieba, the elders are waiting for you,' she said quietly.

Laelia let him lean on her to take the weight off his leg. She led him back between the huts and across to the open ground where the children played. At its centre stood the communal meeting house, twenty paces long and ten wide. When the pair arrived at its entrance, the voices of the elders carried hard out into the humid air. It was clear that they were deciding Cieba's fate and Laelia held him back to listen.

'Pentas, the boy should be dead I tell you,' said Mikania.

'It's a good job I didn't hit him,' said Aechemea, the most feared hunter of the tribe.

'Yes it is,' clearly the voice of Pentas, 'and I am glad that it was not. He risked his life to save my daughter from drowning!'

'But Pentas, it's not just the cracked skull that Mikania gave him, but broken ribs and a broken leg. But now, but now shaman, it is fixed! It's only three days since you brought him here from the waterfall,' said Custus, the butcher of the group. He was a fat heartless man only happy when he had blood on his hands, which were swift and accurate with a blade.

'I say we should listen to his explanation, we owe him that at least' said a voice Laelia could not recognise. A murmur of approval passed through the men and Laelia smiled at Cieba.

'Thank you for saving my daughter,' she whispered.

'I think the Pelecaras are swelling in his brain. I have heard him speak in his sleep!' shouted Mikania. The last thing he needed was a union between this boy and Cattleya. She would never settle down and Pentas was getting old. They needed a strong leader, a spiritual one.

'And so have I!' added Phaius, stout and proud in Mikania's company, he had always marvelled at the spirit world and collected what plants he could to help produce his shamans dreams. The other men did not question his devotion, it was bad luck to question the spirit world, besides Phaius was a terrible hunter.

'I say we throw him back into the river, weighted down, see how long he can hold his breath this time,' said Drosera the eldest of the group. He did not like having this stranger in the village. He couldn't sleep at the best of times, and since Cieba had arrived he had only managed an hour or two each morning just before the sun rose.

'I think this would be a good time to show your face, don't you?' Laelia said nudging Cieba forward into the dark interior. The voices from the other end died down, the elders bodies dark, the fire behind them sending shadows across the ceiling.

'Look at him, he walks now!' exclaimed Custus exposing the big gap between his front teeth.

'He is young and strong Custus,' said Pentas.

'Yes and it was you who brought him to us,' growled Drosera, 'what if the rest of his tribe have followed him here and are waiting to attack?

'I should seek guidance from Arutum,' said Mikania.

'Let me question him,' said Custus. 'I'll cut of his balls, that will calm him down.' The others murmured their approval.

'Why don't you let him speak, why are you so frightened of him,' Cattleya passionately called out from another entrance.

'Pentas please,' shouted Custus. 'Have you no control over your daughter?'

'Custus if you do not show some respect, it is I who will cut off your balls!' Pentas shouted, his fury quieting the group.

The silence was filled by Cieba, the elders turned back to him as he spoke. 'Maybe they are right to be frightened of me Cattleya, for the same reason they are frightened of you, I think.' Cattleya laughed at his words, which only upset her uncle more.

'Why can't you get it out of your head Cattleya?' Mikania raged, waving his hands at her. 'Always the first to challenge everything, even our security.' His voice echoed in the grumbles of the others.

'Maybe she's right. Did you ever consider that, brother?' Pentas said clearly and loudly which sent another wave through the room.

'Was she right when she ran off to find your lost son?' Mikania said, then hesitated hoping for support, that this time did not come. 'Is she right when she breaks your heart each time she walks out into the trees? Disappearing for days and weeks.' His words were lonely.

'Maybe not brother, but she was right when she walked back into my arms at the age of seven dragging her big

136

brother's spear behind her.' His voice was resolute 'Do none of you remember that! She showed her courage to me then, as she does now!'

'Then maybe it is she who should be left to deal with this stranger, this man who should have died?' Mikania said, shaking his head and leaving the hut, muttering under his breath.

'If you give me permission, I will father,' Cattleya said.

'Very well,' said Pentas. 'So it shall be. That concludes this discussion. My decision has been made.'

Pentas was the last to leave the shadows of the hut, he wanted a moment to clear his head. Except the voices of the others barely faded when he heard Custus laughing. Pentas found him outside pointing to Cieba whom appeared to have fainted and was slipping out of Laelia's grasp and onto the ground.

'Maybe he is not so strong after all!' Custus said.

Cattleya rushed to his aid, but her hands were too late, it was just like it had been at the waterfall.

The debate of the elders had soured in Cieba's mind. Their words scratching at him, just like the Pelecaras had done. Cieba could not fight off past and present at the same time. All their voices swelling in his brain rapidly blossoming into a migraine which he managed to control until they had stepped into the blazing sun. The migraine blurred his vision and turned his stomach, to the point that his already weak legs could stand no more, and he slipped into the echoes of the past.

'Get up you fool,' the spirit Hernan poked, his words full of spittle.

'Get up,' Atoc repeated.

Cieba had not replied, because the taunt in their voices had softened. For too many days he had walked in the spectral darkness, their whips across his back, the blood scabbing and rubbing free from his skin. He had become too scarred to feel and too numbed to notice the cackle of their voices change. There was no point to the chase, enough was enough, and he stopped, firstly sitting then laying down on the endless smooth surface of nothing, he dreamt of death. They could do as they wished, his resistance was gone. It was an action that was met with a cessation of cruelty.

'Get up. The air is changing,' Huayna rasped.

Cieba felt it too and looked up, it was growing colder, and from above in the endless dark a snowflake fell, so radiant as it drifted down that it highlighted the spirits that surrounded him. How long had it been since these creatures had marvelled at anything except their own judgement, Cieba could not guess. Their expressions of delight were unmistakable.

He felt the change too on the ground he laid upon. It was no longer smooth but pitted and rough beneath his fingers. A second snowflake was followed by another, until a flurry illuminated the darkness laying onto the floor and creating a pathway as wide as a river. There were definite edges to this route, on which snow now drifted collecting up against structures that rose on each side, reaching into the sky. The blizzard marked out windows that were illuminated from within, defiant to the cold, they cast more light onto the unfolding vision.

Was this his choice, Cieba thought as he stood up. Was this his choice to walk forward into this, let his feet chill in the snow, let his body freeze in the blizzard that was wrapping itself around him.

'You have no choice,' the Pelecaras said.

On his left a leafless tree took shape, on its branches it bore words and letters that Cieba could not read, spelling out, "7th Avenue" and 142nd Street". Somebody pushed past him, he wanted to reach out but they were gone, walking into the snow until they disappeared. The whole mirage was suddenly clarified by the winter sun as it rose up from his left forcing its way between the buildings and bringing with it all the sounds of a city. More people overtook him, and cars that the world had not yet seen hurtled past through the slush.

The chaos, that had grown from a snowflake busied itself without rhythm or repetition until it violently ended. Cieba heard the screams before he saw what had happened. The cries of disbelief around him quickly countered by cackles of delight from the Pelecaras when they found the collision of two cars. As quickly as they had arrived the people left, their footprints in the snow mingling with the broken glass that covered the ground. Their departure momentarily blocking Cieba's view of the body that had been thrown out onto the road.

In the vehicle closest, a couple were trapped, their faces bloodied and still. For some unknown reason Cieba knew their names and realised that he must save the woman. His instinct then overrode his confusion and without hesitation he ran to them climbing up onto the bonnet. With the stench of gasoline filling their lungs the couples' eyes flickered open to meet Cieba's approach. They could just about make out his translucent form taking shape in the miasma. The woman smiled through her pain, the sight of his face taking the fear from her eyes.

'It was all true,' she said quietly. 'You came back to me.'

Cieba reached down to brush his hand across her cheek and looked over at the driver.

'Help me free her, Joshua,' Cieba said. 'She doesn't have to die.'

The blue lights of the emergency services halted back from the junction, their cries of order and safety filling the air. With Joshua's help, Cieba just managed to guide Mary's outstretched arm for the paramedics to pull her free from the wreckage.

'Nobody else goes in!' shouted Fire Chief Bill Maguire stepping in to prevent the ambulance crew from further rescue. Standing back onto the sidewalk Cieba could clearly see the gasoline outlining the body on the ground, the liquid touching the butt end of a cast off cigarette, the flames leaping back up to their source, igniting both cars, and sending billowing flame high up into the cold January air.

'You see,' came the familiar wheeze of Huayna. 'We can work together.'

ELEVEN

The Rejuvenated Man, Part Two

Seven days after his unfortunate fall in the bathroom, Cardinal Rodiani finally acknowledged Agustin. It wasn't the first time that a deep silence had grown between them, but this last week it had been even harder than usual to attend to the Cardinal's daily needs. Agustin assumed that in addition to the weight of the Cardinal's sexual guilt, the two letters he had received recently had only added to his troubles. The first had borne the seal of the Portuguese Crown, the second followed within a week from Spain, the latter not Royal but official nonetheless. Unusually Agustin had been unable to read them, and their concealment worried him, not least because they had compounded his master's bleak mood.

However, as Agustin did not particularly wish to converse with the Cardinal, intuition would suffice, and with practised ease he'd let the days pass until a more favourable air moved through the house. Today however, Agustin needed to break the silence, if only long enough to relay some pressing domestic issues.

'The household needs supplies and I must post your report to Rome,' proffered Agustin, while he cleared away the morning tea. Alessandro looked up in response, his eyes questioning every syllable of the suggestion.

'And we are running low on wine Your Eminence. I will need to take both Francesco and Mateus. There is a lot to do but, God willing, we shall return before nightfall.' If they left early enough he might even get time to walk down to the river, he knew a place away from the main trading jetties where he could soak his feet and think of home. Fernandez had chosen the town's location well, because here the Beni river was just wide enough to slow down for a mile or two, and when the rains came, the town did not flood. For Agustin the opportunity to paddle in the shallows even just for a few minutes was blissful.

'Very well,' Alessandro answered gruffly, casting his eyes to the sky and then back to the papers he was studying. He waved Agustin away, as he always did, despising the thought of having to fend for himself even for one day. Agustin retreated slowly down the corridor waiting for his master's voice.

'Oh Agustin!' Alessandro called.

'Yes Cardinal?'

'Don't buy any of that shitty Spanish wine again… only Italian… and… don't forget the candles.'

'Very well Your Eminence, I will see you tomorrow night.'

In the grey dawn of the following day the trio set off, sitting alongside each other on the rickety old cart that Alessandro refused to spend money on. It was not on his list of priorities, after all it did the job required, and at seventeen the pony, Luca, had strong legs. Agustin had once bartered for a few cushions to protect his piles from the hard seat, but lately even they were getting thread bare. Strangely however once they were aboard and on their way, the sway, caused by the uneven track, and the patched together chassis, distracted Agustin so much, he would drift off to sleep. He would dream of his childhood, when he sat beside his beloved father on his fishing boat gently rocking on the waves.

Eventually, thanks to the steady pull of Luca, the trees began to thin and they entered the outskirts of Praia da Viera. Francesco and Mateus learned at their first stop, that in the three weeks since their last visit, the Bandeirantes had travelled through the town on their way back to St Paulo to report the results of their expeditions. Their presence had been replaced, by the fear of the slave trader Rodriguez Tavares. Having exhausted his routes up the main tributaries to the north of the Amazon, Rodriguez was now following where the Bandeirantes had been, closer to the Jesuit settlements bordering Bolivia and Paraguay. His rationale that the natives were being drawn out of the jungle by the Jesuits, into more concentrated groups, making it easier for him to capture, was bearing fruit.

'Look Agustin,' said Francesco nudging the old man awake as they entered the main thoroughfare.

'What,' Agustin replied sleepily, lifting his head off Mateus' shoulder. 'Are we half way yet? Don't forget to stop and pick up the shaving strap before we get too far into the town.'

'Wake up Agustin. We are in the town's centre,' said Mateus wiping saliva off his shoulder. 'And yes we've picked up the leather.'

'Ah, I must have drifted off,' Agustin protested.

'Old man, you sleep more each time we take this journey,' Francesco laughed.

'It's this fine pony you have trained so well,' said Agustin straightening his bent back and coughing to clear his throat in the hot and still air, 'and the smooth ride on this cart that you have fixed so well Mateus.' His words made the other two laugh.

'You old fool. Look Agustin,' said Francesco more seriously, as he pointed up the street. Agustin followed his hand to a small herd of cows being steered towards them between market stalls, bellowing as they smelt the water nearby.

'It must be true what they said about Tavares,' said Mateos watching as the cattle moved away to reveal two columns of slaves behind. Each line fastened to the other by shackles that were rubbing at their wrists, and each man attached to the one in front by chains that rattled between their shackled feet.

Dust rose from the surface of the street as the column moved closer and like a myriad of tiny swarming flies, fine particles of soil, once held together by the roots of trees clawed up at the captives, sticking to their skin and filling their throats. Bound at the wrist there was no chance to swat aside the dust's menacing onslaught, except only an attempt to stagger blindly with a hope not to trip.

The first two men were pulled left by the rope at their wrists. At the helm Maglanis yelled in Portuguese then yanked the rope again. He was following the herd down a side street of white washed buildings, away from the bustle and shouts of the market pulling the columns behind him.

Counter to the teachings of Father Matthew, Mateus and Francesco's first instinct was to protect themselves. Even Agustin shrank into the safety of the cart and his robes, all three subdued by the memory of Maglanis as the slaves moved past. Not just men, but women and children made up the lines, their faces set, their tears dried on makeshift shirts or crystallised in the corners of their bloodshot eyes.

Mateus was counting, 'Fifty three men, twenty one women... eight boys,' he broke off while he finished his addition, '...and ten girls, that's ninety two.'

'Look at them,' Francesco said and sighed quietly. 'There are too many, even for you to save Agustin.'

'Hmm,' Agustin replied signing the cross.

'It is unlikely we would escape twice. I doubt that cruel bastard will even let them drink from the well.'

'We should move,' Mateus said, taking up the reins to usher Luca on.

'I doubt also that the fine ladies of England will ever hear of the blood that drips from the wrists of that child, as they add a second spoon of sugar to their tea,' said Agustin quietly to himself. Then more audibly he continued, taking hold of Mateus' hands as he did. 'Whoa Luca. God may have forsaken them, but I shall not.'

'Agustin, I really don't think you can help,' Mateus said, as the pony brought the cart to a stop. 'Maglanis is not alone this time; he is hardly likely to listen.'

Agustin stood up, and Francesco let him squeeze by, so he could tentatively climb down.

'Would you two young gentlemen be kind enough to attend to the groceries that we require,' asked Agustin. 'My old legs need to be stretched a little, before I can carry anything.'

'Be careful,' Francesco said reaching down to shake his friend's hand before he left. He knew there was no point trying to change Agustin's mind.

'Just don't forget the candles,' Agustin said, his face resolute.

TWELVE

The love of your life

'Wake up Cieba,' Cattleya's gentle voice cut through the hangover of his collapse. The inebriated murk that the Pelecaras had battered into his subconscious was replaced by a dappled shade, and an affectionate touch. 'Wake up. Come back to me.'

Her voice became firmer as he stirred, commanding his waking, its urgency underlined by the squeeze of her hand against his arm. Cieba remembered her face before he opened his eyes, and tried to reach out, but just missed her retracting touch.

'It's good to see you,' he said, watching her stand up and move back.

'And you,' she replied. 'You spend more time asleep than you do awake.' She stretched and ran her hands through her hair, finally looking back at him. 'You've been unconscious for two days. I thought you were going to die and prove old Custus right.'

'No, I've survived this long, I'm not ready to die yet,' Cieba said. He took a deep breath and exhaled slowly. 'Do you ever get stuck in the past Cattleya?'

'Sometimes,' she replied, suddenly becoming embarrassed by this admission and looked away.

'I'm glad it's not just me,' Cieba said. He got to his feet unsteadily and reached out to Cattleya, only to be denied again when she took another step back.

'I must get you some food, and tell my father you are awake.'

'You can tell Custus that I am returned from the dead,' Cieba laughed and followed Cattleya shakily back to her mother's hut.

Over the following days Cieba rapidly healed and began to spend more and more time with the woman who had found him floating in the waterfall pool. She did not ask how he had got there, and took care to let her mother feed him properly, though she herself would often eat alone. In return Cieba did not press her about her brother or why she found so much comfort in her solitude. He also chose not to tell Cattleya of the whispers that he heard from those villagers who had watched her grow up and would see him cast out. Fortunately the whispers never grew into words, subdued by respect for Pentas; time, the gossipers concluded, would play out the couple's fate.

Cieba thanked the sun each day for rising and as one week rolled into another, he dared to wonder if he had found a new home, and a life that may have freed him of his past. As he grew stronger his flashbacks came less often but when they did, they were acutely debilitating, pushing aside the actual, and dragging him back through the past six years of wandering with the Pelecaras. The pitch dark, and their mutterings, were only punctuated by physical transitory experiences of years yet to pass.

For Pentas, the sight of his daughter smiling each day outweighed his concerns about Cieba and the pressure from Mikania. However with Cattleya so close to home, he could not help his protective instinct, and he posted a watch on the pair. Whether Cattleya worked out his plan he did not know, but she started to take Cieba further out into the forest which quickly made any surveillance far too obvious. Pentas would just have to trust his daughter and worry in silence.

Cattleya had never found any serious attraction in the boys of the village, preferring adventure to love. Her closest friend was her father. In fact, since her brother had disappeared twelve years ago, Cattleya had had little in the way of prolonged communication with anyone, and it had left its toll on her toughened shoulders, leaving her shy to her growing feelings toward Cieba.

In the end it took the adrenaline of a Peccary hunt to loosen her tongue. Cattleya showed him how to drive the wild pig from its foraging, through the forest and into a pit. This time, however, as the creature fell into their trap it completely missed the stakes prepared to impale it. Instead of an easy kill, the hunters had to watch the pig run wildly against the sides, splintering the wood and squealing furiously as it started to break down the soft walls. Determined that its fate was not set, the animal left its pursuers without a clear shot, their spears growing heavy in their arms, as one hour followed another.

Out of the corner of Cieba's eye he saw Cattleya looking away, her spear hesitating, its point slowly tilting toward the ground as the peccary's snout cleared the pit's edge. Without saying a word Cieba lowered his own spear and retreated into the shadows. Would that he could have told her, history was unlikely to repeat itself and they would be safe. He felt Huayna's ridicule, that Cattleya deserved what she got, and he felt Iquitos yelling at him to kill the animal, except Nasua's memory was stronger still; this was not Cieba's fight.

The couple never spoke of the incident again, so their questions went unanswered; suffice it to say that the animal went free without retaliation. Sitting on the edge of their empty trap, Cattleya accepted the drink he proffered and told him of all the beauty she had seen in the forest and of all the sadness that still weighed heavily on her mother. She talked of her father Pentas, of how his warm heart measured his words before he spoke. Pentas was a proud man to whom she was indebted, for he had welcomed Cieba into his household.

The two new friends began to joke and tease each other as they walked between the trees, and as the days turned into weeks Cattleya began to let their eyes meet, and the touch of their hands was inevitable.

It was a touch that neither wanted to release, because when their fingers disengaged doubt surpassed desire. Independence was at stake, and whilst Cattleya's mind drifted to the mountains, Cieba fought back the bravado the Pelecaras had beaten into him, and the boldness to challenge all that surrounded him.

By the time Cieba was fifteen, his eyes had become used to their fluctuating incandescence and their subdued bullying. The five now saved their malice for the meandering visions they vied to control, and the respite between allowed Cieba to gain strength and listen, eavesdropping on the dead. As he lay close by on the flat surface of nothing, he heard them talk less of their vengeance and more of the past lives when they breathed freedom and tasted food without taint. It was when they spoke like this that the rasping click they radiated, slowed and almost petered out, leaving their ragged flesh to glow calmly. There was no doubt however from their words that all five were murderers or that any of them could blame their crimes wholly on circumstance. Neither was there any doubt that none showed any remorse except in the occasional subtle hesitation of a word, or the delayed stare in their guilty yellowed eyes.

Somewhere in the blackout that year, Cieba had woken uncomfortably to find himself laying on pebbles. Though he couldn't see the stones, they shifted and slid beneath him as he sat up. He gathered one and threw it, not expecting any sound; anything he'd ever thrown before had simply disappeared. But this time Cieba heard the pebble land, then slide like a shard of ice, until its momentum was stopped by a solid object, leaving a dark echo to fill the void.

Instinctively Cieba strained his eyes in the direction of the echo but could see nothing. His ears were more successful, closing in on the sounds of a river coming closer to him with every heart beat. Getting to his feet the pebbles beneath him flushed with water covering his toes and rapidly rising around his ankles and up to his knees. Calmly Cieba reached down to cup the flow and bring it to his face, it smelt clean and inviting. Suddenly the need to taste it was overpowering, there was something so familiar to its chill.

He was distracted by a cold moon that appeared above, not only highlighting the river's flow but the banks beyond. Cieba smiled to himself realising he was standing just up stream from Iquitos's fishing pool. He laughed gently, he was safe here, and should not fear the water. So with his mind persuaded, he drank deeply.

Full and comforted, Cieba fell back into the river, with arms outstretched he felt free. He stood up to rub the water into his hair and gratefully wash beneath his arms. The reflecting moon lifted his eyes up the bank to find Suomi's home on the horizon. Even from where he stood Cieba could see the building was derelict. Its disrepair accentuated by the silhouetted skeletal figure, that stood clothed in tattered black cloth holding out a blunted sword. Cieba recognised it straight away as Yupanqui, the smallest of the five Pelecaras; he was stunted by a shattered right leg, that no longer fully extended.

'Ah look. She's dead, your poor stepmother is dead,' Yupanqui's cracked.

'Leave her be,' Cieba shouted in anger. Around him the water was now rising up his waist forcing him to wade, increasing his frustration as he tried to get to the bank and the creatures on it.

'And you thought she had left your family's nest,' Atoc irritated further.

'Let her be!' Cieba shouted finally free from the river's clutches. All five Pelecaras stood outside his old home, peeking through the collapsed roof and pulling at the old dried leaves.

Azuay blocked Cieba's stride to the doorway, his face solidifying into muscles that stretched and retraced as he snapped his teeth and prodded Cieba away with a sharp finger. Behind Azuay, Huayna had started to pull open the tattered leather that had once made up the door.

'At last,' Huayna rasped, 'we can lap up what's left in her skull, give us a little food for thought.' All five screeched with delight.

'Just like we did with her husband,' Azuay whispered, through lips that had gained colour and definition. He laughed and pushed Cieba to the floor with such force that it winded the teenager. Holding his ribs Cieba got to his feet. Something snapped inside and he yelled out for justice. With all the force he could muster Cieba grabbed Azuay, pulling him away from the door, and shoving him to the edge of the bank. It left Cieba's hands covered in a gritty black slime and the smell of decomposing intestines. Retching, the boy targeted Atoc next who fought back with greater strength than the last. He held Cieba by the throat starving him of oxygen and a fighting stance.

Pulled to the tips of his toes Cieba had to watch as the spirits pulled apart what was left of his home, scattering it's construction and snuffing out any semblance of habitation.

'Only bones' Hernan coughed, pulling Alpaca wool from his mouth.

'To think you were their only son' Yupanqui screeched. Atoc dropped Cieba to the ground, then kicked him before he could gain his balance or ease his throat. Then Yupanqui kicked Cieba so hard on the thigh that he dropped to his knees, clutching at his leg. A second kick, this time to Cieba's shoulder, forced him off balance and over the edge so he tumbled sideways down the steep bank. He finally came to rest at the river's edge, his cheek hitting the wet pebbles of the shoreline, his head and his stomach churning.

Cieba stayed where he lay, persuading himself that somehow Suomi was safe. Above, the clouds cleared completely from the moon and he caught sight of his reflection in the water. No longer the boy but a young man. He needed to stay calm, do what Nasua had told him and mould his anger into determination. Looking up from the water to the opposite bank and then downstream to where the river cut deeper into the landscape he noticed something odd. Cieba blinked and refocused, there downstream from the direction he had first walked over this riverbed, was a horizontal line of ripples in the water like the water was hitting a ridge of glass. It was so subtle that he had to stare. Yes he was right, there were imperfections and faint differences on either side of the ripple. The more he stared the more obvious they were.

It was then he realised two things; firstly that he was looking at the spectrum, no longer reliant on the morning sun, but subdued and accepting of the available light and secondly that the pebbles' echo had led him out of the dark.

'You've done it,' Huayna said behind him, his rasp less potent. 'You've done what Nasua could not.'

'Not yet,' Cieba replied without turning. He let his shoulders drop, and breathed slowly. He realised now why his father had always been at the entrance, he must have stayed in touch somehow with the doorway, else they would have been lost like his uncle.

'Can't you feel that breeze or the grass beneath your feet?' Cieba asked, still not turning. Huayna only wheezed painfully. 'Or can you only smell death Huayna?'

'We've all got to eat,' the spirit laughed, 'and I don't seek an education in the filth that lies beneath my feet.'

'Then what. Why chase down this?' He pointed to the spectrum and the dark line that had started to form vertically at its centre. 'What is it that you want? Other than to relive a life that you threw away decades ago?'

Huayna growled, marking his reply by placing his hand on the back of Cieba's neck and running a cold broken nail into his flesh slicing it across his shoulder.

'Time passes so quickly child,' Huayna whispered into Cieba's ear. 'One year in there and you come back into the real world three years older, but boy, it will be the only time you will age.'

'Then I will stay here,' Cieba said resolute despite his pain, 'and not age at your command!'

'We cannot stay here, not after all that you have shown us, think of the fun we could have with your whispers of the future. How do you think the people of this forest, or this country would react, if we told them what was going to happen. Even you could not be that cruel.'

'Then I have no choice.'

'Cieba. You have slept enough, wake up.' It was Cattleya's voice. 'Enough of your dreams.' She was shaking him awake again. 'Unless of course you are just being lazy.'

'No not lazy,' he replied opening his eyes to meet hers. A look that lingered, encouraging the kiss that followed. Cieba gently touched her shoulder, then ran the slightest touch down her back.

'The day is passing,' he said, 'we should return home.'

'Let us stay here, just a little longer,' Cattleya said kissing him. Her passion growing with her hands upon him. Without the apprehension that had stopped them before, they made love where they lay. Afterward they held each other until the sun began to set and Cattleya found herself touching the scar on his shoulder.

'We must return, or your uncle will be pleased, and your father heartbroken.'

'How can you be so content among them?'

'Because without you Cattleya, your family are alone. At least for a little while, make them happy.'

THIRTEEN

'53 Men, 21 Women... eight boys and 10 girls'

'In the name of the Father, and of the Son, and of the Holy Spirit,' Agustin whispered before he took another step. He pulled out his rosary beads from the waist pocket of his faded black habit, bleached by the sun, his white tunic beneath flecked with dust and humidity.

'Come on Luca old boy. On we go,' Mateus called behind for the pony to move on.

Agustin continued his prayer when his companions were out of sight. Moving the beads steadily around the leather, he caught sight of the column of slaves in front. Focusing on little else but their plight, he continued to follow, quietly breathing the words of his recitation.

'I believe in God, the Father Almighty, Creator of heaven and earth and in Jesus Christ, His only Son, our Lord. Who was conceived by the Holy Spirit, and born of the Virgin Mary. He suffered under Pontius Pilate, was crucified, died, and was buried. He descended into hell...'

Agustin stopped, up in front about thirty paces away, he could count five mercenaries, who had halted the slave march. These men were drinking from the well, which was shaded by a few trees, that dissected the red dusty road with green.

Agustin felt very old, and very tired, he looked up into the cloudless blue sky and sighed. Had he not seen enough of this torture for one lifetime. He sighed, and worked out it had been four years since the *Meridian* had docked in Loanda, and they had watched the war lords of Angola offer up their own people to the slave trade in exchange for weapons.

Agustin had retched then at their desire for power which had infected the African countryside with fear and savagery. Even his Cardinal had been silent to the scale of misery that touched each new face. Even his misguided master had stood back when they asked him to bless the slaves before transportation. If nothing else Agustin would always respect him for that one act of defiance.

'Now death waits patiently, only shrunk to the midday sun,' Agustin said still looking upward.

'They're ours Priest! …your robes will not protect nor save them this time.' The voice was unmistakably Maglanis.

'Won't you let an old man take a little shade and a cool drink?' Agustin asked. He sighed again and moved closer looking over the slaves, he couldn't put it off any longer.

'Be careful old man,' Maglanis said throwing a half cup of water onto the dusty ground.

'Of course, I'm far too old to trouble you.'

The other four mercenaries laughed, and taunted Maglanis for his stupidity. One even refilling his cup from the freshly pulled pail and gesturing it to Agustin.

Agustin smiled and as he walked closer to receive it, his eye was drawn to a boy in the middle of the column. He was desperate to lift the shackles from his ankles, but his action was tugging the chain through from the man in front, and pulling him off balance.

'St… stop it… st... st... stop it Icka,' said the man, struggling to speak through spluttered coughs.

'Shut up, shut up Tumi!' the boy responded pushing the man hard. With no free hands to steady himself and weak with malnutrition Tumi started to collapse. It was a movement that captivated Agustin, as it stretched in a slow unravelling motion, the shadow beneath Tumi growing with each faltering second, and death's spectre darkened, ready to relieve his pain.

Then, like poetry rising from the pit of despair, a tender unnoticed hand reached out to stop the collapse. Whoever was standing behind Tumi had reached out just in time. Quite how the other man had managed to achieve the intervention without pulling the other slaves after him, Agustin could not fathom. And how he managed the rescue without being noticed by the guarding mercenaries, made the act that much more miraculous.

'Death has stalked these ninety two men, women and children long enough don't you think Sebastao? Why not give them some water? It's hot and Fernandez didn't dig that well just for you!' Agustin said emboldened by what he had just seen.

'You maybe a fearless old fool, but you are outnumbered with only your cross to protect you,' Maglanis said, pulling himself up straight and re-lighting a cigar. He puffed it into life and stood tall, his right hand finding the hilt of his sword the other his hip, he added, 'The will of the church is waning priest. I doubt this time even a letter from your Cardinal would stand up in the courts of Portugal… you should think hard before you say anymore.'

'Ah fearless you say!' Agustin laughed. 'I have often wondered, if this body of mine had been stronger, if, if I should

157

have taken up the sword. Then I could have waved cold steel in the air and not my useless words.'

'Then we could have fought like men and not...' Maglanis was cut short by an approaching horseman.

'Take your hand from your sword Maglanis,' said the newcomer in a low gravely voice. He was stockier than the other mercenaries and better fed, the luxury of a saddle he thought suited his status in mid life and it saved his energy for the many women he often boasted to frequent. The stranger rolled his braided beard between his fingers and eyed the situation. Agustin could see his other hand atop a loaded musket, which was balanced across his saddle. The chestnut coated horse beneath him was tall, well groomed with an Andalusian majesty that was a rare sight in this town.

'Give the slaves some water; they look more fucking dead than when I saw them two days ago.' The horseman fixed Maglanis with an unforgiving stare, then cleared his throat to spit onto the floor. He continued in a cruel tone, perfected only by those who have found peace with their own violence. 'I told you then to look after them, and why are their fucking legs still shackled?' He spat again, wiping his beard free of phlegm with the back of his hand. 'You're supposed to be in charge! If we lose any more it's coming out of your share.'

'I see your financial intentions are as intact as they were when we last met Mr Taveres,' said Agustin, relieved that his own stand off with Maglanis had been a benefit to the slaves.

Rodriguez Taveres had arrived in the town the night before to satisfy his loins before the long boat trip to the plantations. He hated the water and to distract him had started the day with a large breakfast washed down with a little wine. After gathering his things, he'd collected a bottle of rum before mounting his horse to catch up with his men. This early intake of alcohol was obvious in his voice. His men, he thought were too relaxed especially when a priest was stood before them. Possession of the land here was sensitive enough, without upsetting the Catholic Church. At least for a little while longer their blindness to his trade was necessary. Looking down at Agustin he nodded slightly and gave a wide smile.

'I trust Cardinal Rodiani is well?' he asked.

'Yes the Cardinal is in good health...'

'The slaves were watered yesterday Rodriguez,' Maglanis interrupted defiantly. 'After all we've been through I don't see why we should pander to the wishes of the church.'

Without thought or hesitation, Rodriguez leant back in his saddle, hoisted the musket to his shoulder, aimed and pulled the trigger. The ensuing blast resonated around the street with profound effect. The sound captured by the depth of the well, its echo escaping, seeking out any silence in the surrounding streets.

Every man, woman and child felt the chains that bound them together pull tight as the led shot passed through Tumi, and into the miracle man behind him. Through the screams that acknowledged death's patient reward, Agustin, Maglanis and the other mercenaries heard Rodriguez Tavares declare, 'I warned you Sebastao, those two are coming out of your share. Now give them some fucking water.'

Agustin slowly knelt on one knee and closed his eyes, blanking out the shouts and the cries of injustice with a prayer.

Hail Mary, full of grace,
The Lord is with Thee;
Blessed art thou among women,

And blessed is the fruit of thy womb, Jesus.
Holy Mary, Mother of God,
Pray for us sinners,
Now and at the hour of our death. Amen.
Glory be to the Father,
And to the Son,
And to the Holy Spirit.
As it was in the beginning, is now,
And ever shall be,
World without end. Amen.

FOURTEEN

The Fear of Love

'Look at the sunlight bouncing off the river,' Cieba said, watching how its rays shone in his lover's eyelashes. Cattleya sat beside him looking down toward the water. Her black hair that she had grown, now reached her shoulders and glistened, its darkness lost in wisps of electrified strands, lifted by a gentle breeze. She felt Cieba's gaze and her smile grew a little wider as she turned toward him.

'Are you dry from your swim yet?' she asked.

'Nearly,' he said. 'You should have joined me.'

'I never thought you would go back in the water,' Cattleya said ignoring his invitation, 'let alone swim like the fish that live in it!'

'You should try swimming with them instead of eating them,' he laughed and reclined back on his elbows, closing his eyes to the afternoon sun.

'You were nearly fish food when I found you,' Cattleya said playfully poking Cieba on the arm.

'Ha ha. Maybe so,' he recoiled, laughing again. 'But this is a good spot to swim, you should try it.' He sat up his body shading Cattleya from the sun. 'A little further down stream and the Caiman will get us both.' Quickly he grabbed her legs, playfully pulling them left and right to mimic the reptile's attack. Cattleya giggled, kicking her legs and pushing him off, then she leant back and pretended to look the other way.

He moved to her side, and Cattleya sat up to rest a hand gently on his shoulder. She looked into his eyes and then up and down his lean body.

'I just think you're not the swimming kind,' he said.

'You're right, I'm more the... hunting type,' she said, pulling an imaginary blade and pouncing on him. 'Got you!' She laughed pinning Cieba down. 'I just think, you're not the hunting kind.'

'Ha, I should throw you in, just so I can rescue you again,' he said, pushing her over so that the two of them rolled toward the edge of the flat rock they were on. It was wide and projected out over the river not far from the village, a favourite place for sweethearts to meet.

'Oh no, no. It was me who rescued you,' she shouted, pushing him off rolling them over again, this time right to the edge.

'If your uncle hadn't hit me over the head... you would have seen who rescued who.'

'He's got to be the worst Shaman ever, if my father didn't protect him the others would kick him out. I'm sure of it.' She laughed. 'You know he's only been right twice. The first time was when it rained for twenty days without stopping, and the second time is when he "saw" something that led to finding us by the waterfall.'

'Truly a great man,' Cieba said faking seriousness.

'Well I'm not sure the second was such a good vision,' she giggled.

'You shouldn't make fun of him,' Cieba said perfecting the serious look now. 'No really Cattleya. Because... My love...

he's behind you... with his club.' His voice panicked as he pointed past her. 'Oh no, Mikania don't hit her,' Cattleya turned round swiftly enough for Cieba to dislodge her from on top of him, rolling back up the rock and pinning her down.

'Oh that was too easy, now I've got you,' he laughed.

'You shouldn't ...' she said but stopped herself.

Cieba jumped up and offered his hand to pull her up after him, but she refused, making her own way back over to the rock's edge. 'I'm restless Cieba,' Cattleya said looking out to the horizon, her tone suddenly defensive. It wasn't the first time that her mood had changed rapidly in the last few days.

Cieba sighed to the river and the trees and to this woman who filled his heart with such love and fear. 'Always the flow of the water, or the bird that flies north Cattleya, always the need for you to leave!'

'If I did not have that desire, you'd be dead in that pool,' she said.

'We should stay for a little while longer,' he said flatly. He did not want to get into a fight, not at the end of this day, a day when they had been so happy and Cattleya had been so at ease.

'My mother is not always right Cieba,' Cattleya said, not turning her gaze away from the horizon. Cieba restrained his words, allowing the sound of the river to calm his reply.

'She's right often enough for us to wait,' he said. 'Maybe we will be thankful if your uncle continues to be wrong. But if your mother is right will that not make you happy?'

'I should just take off for a few days like I used to,' Cattleya said ignoring his question.

'Cattleya! She's right often enough for us to wait, ten days, a few more at the most.' With the impatience that drove his words he got up and walked away. 'There is a change in you.'

'That change is you,' she replied. 'Not some mysterious claim that I'm pregnant. I wish all of you would for once live in the real world. Stop relying on your stupid visions to guide your every step. It's not difficult you know. Feel this rock beneath your feet or the touch of your lips to mine, those moments are not dreamt, nor is my love for you. It is actual and beautiful and not to be forsaken.'

'Then if it is not to be cast aside I do not understand why you must leave me here. I do not want to leave! I have travelled enough! Like you I want a life that I can reach out and grasp. Not a life of recollection. You complain about your people, but you have no idea about the life I have left behind.'

'No? Then you must think that I ignore the constant chatter in your sleep? You look to fit, and fight your dreams, and when you dream like that, it takes you an age to wake. It's like you are living two lives. Tell me Cieba, if I must explain to you about my life. Tell me where you go to in your dreams?' She crossed the rock to Cieba, who stood with his arms crossed looking away.

'Or Cieba answer me this, which one you would choose if… which life truly would you choose if I made you decide between them? Like you are asking me to choose!' She did not let him reply but instead held up her hand. 'I need to feel like I used to, just for a day or so. Surely you must understand the need to stay in contact with that old life?'

'I understand,' he said quietly.

'Then let me go, as you go.'

'I understand,' he repeated. 'But Cattleya, I fear we should heed your uncle's fears.'

'Which one, that you are a greater shaman than he will ever be, but are too frightened to tell us, just in case he slits your throat? Or that he has begun to see white men, men filled with Sharm's anger that would bind our hands and bleed us? Or worse still that I may be carrying your child?'

Cieba spoke slowly and tried to choose his words carefully. 'Then I will tell a little of my life, maybe then you will understand. Sit with me and listen. Up in the cloud forests where the high humidity readily forms rainbows, my forefathers devoted their lives to the beauty of light. The way it divided into bold curves or was split in the fine mist amongst the trees. They learned to capture these mists in clearings they had made. Then one day countless generations before I was born, one of them discovered an imperfection in the spectrum in front of him. It was a dark line, an empty space where no colour could penetrate. He asked the Xapiripe spirits for guidance but they only laughed, warning him not to meddle in what he could never understand. One day, as the mist re-appeared in the highest clearing, the eldest shaman ignored the advice of the Xapiripe and called upon Pachamama for safety, and Aratum to drive his vision. Together they solidified the rainbow so it formed solid lines including the black one in front of him. The Xapiripe retreated annoyed that they had been rejected, their colourful dress dulled by the spectrum.' Cieba stopped, unfolding his arms and clenching fists. He couldn't decide whether he should continue. Cattleya was looking straight at him trying to work out if this story was simply that, an attempt to distract her with a tale.

'This is better than Mikania's stories,' she said reaching out to unclasp his fists. 'What happened?'

'My forefather was convinced that it was a pathway which would lead him to a new life. He would not listen to reason and stepped inside, disappearing completely only to return five years later full of wonder and fear of the things that he had seen.'

'So what did he…' Cattleya started. Then she asked. 'Did he pass down this gift to walk into rainbows?'

'Yes.'

'Then take me there.'

'Cattleya. Its not a place that you should wish to go.'

'But I thought you said he was filled with wonder…'

'And fear,' Cieba interrupted

'So it is just a story?'

'It's… Cattleya…' he paused, wishing that he had not started. 'The light around us is our perception of our surroundings. Like you see the way the river flows differently to me, or not at all.'

'Are you trying to tell me that the river is not there?' Cattleya asked pointing down to the water.

'No.'

'And the pathways?' she asked.

'Places beyond your nightmares, where even the Pelecaras step carefully.'

'You are sounding like Mikania again. Prove it; show me how to pull a rainbow out of the sky.' Cattleya laughed, but stifled her giggles when she saw her lover frown. She had hurt his feelings enough by wanting to leave. Was it only her father who saw things as they were in this world?

'I should not have started this,' Cieba said. 'It is impossible to describe.'

'Teach me, show me.'

'No, if you are carrying our child we should wait.'

'Then I will wait Cieba. Except I still believe you should be the village shaman.'

'Mikania is the shaman and must remain so.'

'Why?' Cattleya said exasperated and bored with the conversation. It was all leading back to her need to be alone.

'Because few people can see beyond what is in front of them, and your uncle could do great harm. He is not without power and I feel his premonitions of white people could be true. I have seen them many times but not surrounded by trees and not yet.'

'Not yet. Does that mean you see into the future as well? If this is right, my people must leave. Maybe your pathways could lead us somewhere safe.'

'Don't patronise me...'

'You'll be telling me next only men can travel into the darkness. I've had enough of your visions and predictions!' Cattleya's annoyance was bubbling over. 'If I had slipped in the rain, or stayed away just one more day we would never have met, and you know if I really try and remember what happened in the waterfall pool, I would swear that you had tried to pull me under, but I was too strong for you!'

'Cattleya, mind your words, they mock us both.'

'It's all just aspirations and monkey shit Cieba.'

'Cattleya?'

'You see I don't need you to teach me how to swim,' she shouted.

'Then tell Custus to cut off my balls,' Cieba said smirking. There was a moment of silence, broken by his laughter, that Cattleya could not resist. Their happiness pushing aside the argument to allow an embrace.

'Can we agree on one thing?' Cattleya said quietly. 'That our love is real?' Cieba nodded and tenderly squeezed her.

'I think my mother might be right. So you'd better be a good father,' Cattleya said.

'Oh, well I think I would like to try.'

'Or Custus…'

'Don't tell me…' They both laughed again.

'Whatever happens…' Cattleya whispered into his ear. 'Keep us safe Cieba.'

FIFTEEN

Muse

At the same time as Agustin and his men were entering the streets of Praia da Viera, the Cardinal still lay in his bed, dreaming of his childhood in Italy. The dull light that stole into his room, was just bright enough to illumiate the gentle rise and fall of his stomach as he slowly snored with deafening ease. He was dreaming of the church and those who had tried to mould his young life.

'Why do you cry Alessandro?' Father Marcus had asked one morning when he had approached Alessandro as a boy, so many years ago. He could hear the soft resonance of the Father's sandalled feet cross the stone floors of St Sebastian, and even now was haunted by the chill quiet between the Father's words.

'I think I saw the Devil again,' sobbed the boy. He'd wiped the tears across his face with a chubby hand and looked up at his tutor.

'Ah Alessandro. Be mindful that the devil is never far away,' Father Marcus replied placing a hand on the boy's head, and running his fingers slowly over his hair to the nape of his neck. It was an action that was the only sign of affection Alessandro had ever had, either from the church or his mother, her embrace saved for her eldest. Father Marcus drew his hand along the boy's jaw line to lift up his face. Then the steady patient tone changed, agitated by Alessandro's appearance. 'Look at you boy, your face is a mess.'

'But Father. I think I saw him in the colours of the window.' Alessandro wiped his face with the inside of his sleeve, trying to clear away the mucus that had followed his tears. 'He was smiling at me Father.'

'Then, Alessandro you must learn to live with him child.' The distaste toward this conversation grew in Father Marcus's voice. 'Alessandro I have told you before. You must learn to manage your temptations so that the devil does not control your soul.'

'Father?' But the young Alessandro's doleful eyes had made no impression.

'Hold out your hand Alessandro and we shall see if a little pain can't concentrate your thoughts'

Just as the hard wooden sole of Father Marcus's sandal hit his knuckle, the Cardinal woke, thankful to be in the still quiet of his South American home. He sighed heavily, and rubbed his knuckles, it had just been a dream, and though it was not the worst of his recurring nightmares, it had left him shaken. Blinking he looked around in the stifled light and was quickly reminded of his surroundings. He sighed again in recognition that his plan to get up and finish the document laying on the writing table, in order for it to be sent to Rome, had been foiled when he had opened a third bottle of wine just after midnight.

Without Agustin to wake him, Alessandro could see from the clock that the hours had passed into mid morning, and he could feel the heat of the day starting to creep into his house. Without Agustin the opportunity for fresh cool morning air to relieve the mustiness of the room had been lost. Although the rising temperatures alone didn't stir Alessandro's saturated body, his annoyance that he'd missed Agustin and the smell of his own bowels did, so he got out of bed.

As he crossed the room to inspect last night's work he passed wind repeatedly, filling the air with a noxious odour unrivalled by even their ageing pony. Grimacing at the smell, his eyes re-focused on the spilt ink on the floor and the quill, now dry upon the table. The document that he had toiled over into the early hours, explained once more to his superiors, the difficulties he was experiencing in this new world. He pushed at the letter with his finger tips, it was an indecipherable mess. Sentences that had started with cohesive intention had quickly descended into a chaotic scribble full of his own comprehensive use of blasphemy. He smiled, doubting it would have reached the Popes eyes anyway.

'Fuck it!' the Cardinal concluded and screwed up the letter, throwing it back on the table. He hated every block of stone that the Vatican was made of, 'mandarmi a questo Laire diavoli di un paese'(sending me to this devil's lair of a country), he said to the empty house.

Despite the short notice that Agustin always gave him, his visits to town apparently always coincided with an empty page in Alessandro's diary. "With no appointments or polite conversation, it will perhaps allow you time for a little quiet reflection, your Eminence," Agustin had an irritating habit of saying.

His Eminence placed a hand upon each hip and stretched his back, his limbs felt like lead. Agustin was so very good at filling his days that today, with nothing planned exhaustion took over.

Alessandro crossed the room and collapsed into a chair that looked back across his sleeping quarters.

On the day of his adornment when the pomp and circumstance was over and he was at last alone Alessandro had collapsed into a chair much the same as this one. The room he had looked back upon then had been more sumptuous than this, and his heart had been a little lighter. Alessandro sighed heavily and closed his eyes, tonight he thought he would drink a little less wine.

In order to try and lighten his mood he tried to picture the opulence of his rooms in Florence, and how he would open up his wide windows and look out across the river. Yet quickly the thought of windows turned sour, as he remembered St Sebastian again, and how the patterned glass there had held back the grey dawn, much the same as these shutters held back the day. Nonetheless after the Italian sunrise gave way to the morning, the sun's rays had been refracted through the stained glass with such majesty that the most troubled soul would be lifted. Rodiani tutted to himself, four and half years he had spent under the direction of Father Marcus, thanking the Holy Spirit for the opportunity to kneel at the mercy of such power and promising God that he would never forget His beauty.

After an hour of watching the clock, Alessandro decided it was no good. His stout fifty seven year old body was feeling a pang of hunger, and the need to relieve itself, so he got to his feet. Crossing his room, leaving it unaltered, he caught sight of his little black Bible, he picked it up and made his way down through the house. After his ablutions, he went downstairs to the kitchen to find his aid had laid out all the food he could need for the day, but alas, the heart burn he was suffering through his hangover was so acute that he ignored the stove and simply poured a glass of water. Tearing off a chunk of bread, he left the kitchen and headed back into the main reception room. It was good to feel hunger and not bloated. A little abstention perhaps he thought would be of benefit once in a while.

As the day moved from hour to hour Alessandro got dressed, and unhindered by duty, he put aside any ecclesiastical ambition for the day and decided to re-explore his surroundings. To his approval he found that all was in order, and everything was kept neat and tidy. Without fear of judgemental eyes, he pulled a chair from the house into the courtyard and sat in the sun. It wasn't until he was seated that he realised he'd subconsciously kept the black Bible inside his tunic. He pulled it out and placed it on his lap. The large yard surrounding him was enclosed on two sides by the main house and chapel, and the third side by the end stable wall, on the fourth side was an outbuilding split into two by an archway and the large wooden doors that provided the only entrance or exit.

In his solitude, he thought of his childhood home, on an Italian hill farm above the Casentino valley. As a young boy he had helped his father and his elder brothers between schooling at the church, and wherever his large frame could be of aid to his mother, but he had never felt needed. Not until the cathartic teachings of Father Marcus, and his mother's encouragement, did he start to look at the church as a source of wisdom, where under the guidance of the Holy Spirit he could better himself.

'Your father and brothers are farmers Alessandro,' his mother had said, when she placed the small black Bible in his hands. 'You can be so much more'

Alessandro's day dream was broken by some locals looking for Agustin. They had called out his name and crept around the unbolted gates, which in testament to Mateus' care opened effortlessly, hardly making a sound. At the sight of the Cardinal's dishevelled dress and seated position, the couple urgently retreated signing the cross gracefully and stepped backward apologetically. Their visit stirred the Cardinal from his reflection, and he decided to follow them through the archway, taking a notion to walk the outer perimeter of the wall. It became obvious to him that the areas where he visited least were far from the immaculate standard he required, and in need of some serious attention.

'Agustin!' he exclaimed when he arrived back in the courtyard. He shook his head and moved inside to the wine cellar. This again was a place he had not properly studied for months and he was disgusted at the disarray he found. Of the fifty or so bottles stored, there were at least thirty that he no longer drank. What was Agustin thinking? Did he not have enough to think about without the inadequacies of his staff?

'Curse you Agustin, I told you. No more Spanish wine. No wonder there's not enough fucking room for anything decent!!!!' he shouted.

With the cellar inspection complete, Alessandro made his way up the stairs and out into the fading light of the day. With nothing but water and bread in his stomach he decided his abstinence had been a good reminder of human frailty and headed for the kitchen. Placing his Bible on the work surface, he tore another lump of bread away and braved the carving knife. He cut some cured ham, which was good, but lacked Agustin's presentation. The man should be here with him, not supervising the other two like they were children. Chewing the meat, he looked around, and to his delight he spied in front of him two bottles of his favourite Italian wine. Without thought of his earlier resolution, he removed the cork from the first bottle and poured a glass.

SIXTEEN

Nameless Men

Cattleya had begun to understand Cieba as another human, real and living and for her to know even a small part of his past, was enough for him to rationalise it as exactly that, his past. Surely now his present and his future life were bound to Cattleya and their child and not to the Pelecaras. Within days of their discussion by the river Cieba's blackouts stopped completely and he slept free from the nightmares that had haunted him for so long.

Another two weeks passed by before Laelia suggested Pentas should be told he was to be a grandfather. Overwhelmed by the news, he announced the young couple would have a new hut built for them. Until then Custus would give up his home and sleep in the meeting house. Custus could do little but agree, saving his scorn for the ear of Mikania and the animals he dismembered. For someone so lean it did not take long for Cattleya's belly to swell and as she blossomed into her second trimester Cieba became more and more determined that he would be the best father he could. The whole village it would seem now rejoiced in their love, and Pentas told his daughter she was not to go off wondering, he wanted nothing to go wrong.

So, unseen they came, swift as the lead shot and brutal as the wind, their voices carried through the still humid air.

Whispers of fortune and the bitter western feel of an empty pocket. Crass were the words that offended Cieba's dreams of bliss. Too little and too late did they jar his memories as he slept on until dawn, unable to foresee how determined a bounty hunter can be.

This was not the Pelecaras but the disparate living, their voices were now more real than his dreams, and as reality bit, he heard the first screams from outside their hut. Furiously he followed his lover, arrow and bow in her hand and anger in her soul. Yet before retribution could be wrought, Cattleya's warrior cry faded, her blood falling along with all who dared to fight.

With all his friends who'd been too slow to arms or too weak to fight, Cieba was bound and together they were forced to watch the remaining survivors pulled into line, their hands and feet quickly restrained. For all those who lay still, their Shaman, their leader, and the love of his life, were left dead where they fell, under a rising sun that turned their bloodied shadows red.

Unable to break free Cieba shouted out to the Pelecaras. But his words were no match for the speed of the foot and the butt of a musket that knocked him unconscious.

SEVENTEEN

The Rejuvenated Man Part Three

Above the sobs and the cries of despair, Agustin could hear the turn of rusted pins and the release of chains. He'd knelt on one knee before Maglanis' men even thought to restrain him, and pulled the rosary beads back into his palm before his eyes closed in prayer. The voices of the guards muffled into a stream of commands and the reinstatement of order. Their commander had spoken, his deputy put in place, there would be no further dispute save one last reminder of their destination.

'Maglanis,' Rodriguez shouted.

'Yes,' Tristao replied, he lit a defiant cigar, his eyes narrowing in its rising smoke. 'Yes, Rodriguez?' he repeated.

'You should remember that Mr Richardson likes to receive his new arrivals in good condition. Or he will drive down the price even more.'

'Yes Rodriguez.'

'You remember also what we have gone through over the last three and a half months to get this far.' He hesitated ensuring all five of his employees were listening. 'Do you really want to get back onto one of those stinking ships and go home with nothing. Or is it the rat infested docks you want to visit again. I tell you Maglanis I would rather be out here, than pulling half dead Negros covered in their own piss out of a boat. Well what do you say?'

'They have all been given some water, and my men will get some food from the market.'

'Good. Now get those fucking chains off their legs and get them down to the docks.'

Daring not to open his eyes Agustin thumbed one bead after another along the same leather thong he had owned for nearly forty years. In fear that he may jeopardise more lives he kept his council as the footsteps passed him and moved away. The smell of stale sweat was replaced by the freshly washed steed that neighed beneath Rodriguez.

'You will have to judge me as you see fit priest,' Rodriguez said above him.

'It is not my place to judge.' Agustin opened his eyes but did not stand up.

'A strange admission for one so close to God,'

'I fear Sir that God has forsaken this place, and I would not call upon my faith to understand your actions.'

'So be it friend. I will leave you to pray to whom you see most fit.'

'Thank you Sir, but I doubt we shall ever be friends.'

Rodriguez leant forward and patted the horse's neck. 'Be sure to pass on my regards to Cardinal Rodiani. It is unfortunate that he finds himself so far from his home.' Rodriguez sat himself up and ran his fingers over his beard. 'Your name is Agustin is it not?'

'Yes.'

'Agustin I wonder if you would pass on a message for me?' Agustin gave a slight nod to reply. 'If I can ever assist the Cardinal in any way, he merely has to send word to St Paolo.'

'I will be sure to choose my words carefully, but first if you will forgive me, I wish attend to the fallen.'

Rodriguez pulled his reins tight to steer his grand horse after his men, leaving Agustin to get to his feet. Tumi had been thrown over his one time saviour, so his thighs crossed the other man's face. Why, Agustin wondered, did he care so much in this land of extremes? He should have stayed seated on the cart and never followed the slaves down this road. If it was God's will that he should survive the Atlantic, why taunt him with these deaths? Maybe he thought, he should look to St Jude patron saint of lost causes and despair.

Taking a deep breath Agustin put his beads away and started to pray, crossing the small distance to the bodies as he did so, and as carefully as his strength would allow tried to separate them from each other.

'Oh glorious apostle St. Jude, faithful servant and friend of Jesus, the name of the traitor who delivered thy beloved Master into the hands of His enemies has caused thee to be forgotten by many, but the…' Agustin had to draw breath, he'd unveiled the face of the man beneath Tumi, it was contorted and yet strangely relieved at the same time. Taking hold of Tumi's legs again, Agustin tried his best to pull his body away, but he could only move him half a pace before his back weakened and left him unable to move. So returned to his prayer. 'Church honours and invokes thee universally as the patron of hopeless cases of things despaired of. Pray for me who am so miserable; make use, I implore thee, of that particular privilege accorded thee of bringing visible and speedy help where help is almost despaired of. Come to my assistance in this great need, that I may receive the consolations and succour of heaven in all my necessities, tribulations and sufferings, particularly…'

'Agustin, are you alright?' shouted Francesco anxiously hurrying down the side street alone.

'I promise thee, O blessed St. Jude, to be ever mindful of this great favour, and I will never cease to honour thee as my special and powerful patron, and to do all in my power to encourage devotion to thee.'

'Agustin what happened?' Francesco asked when he reached Agustin.

'Amen,' Agustin completed. 'Francesco, would you please help by taking this poor soul off me. We need to get both these men into the shade.'

'I heard the shot, but it took an age to get back through the crowd,' Francesco said taking the legs and moving both the bodies as requested, leaving Agustin to slowly straighten up. 'Mateus is following with the cart. Are you hurt Agustin? are you alright my friend?'

'Yes I'm fine,' replied Agustin sighing heavily. 'It wasn't me that they shot.'

'Is he alright?' called Mateus as he rounded the corner, horse and cart in tow.

'Yes,' replied Francesco, raising a hand and walking back to Mateus to slow his arrival. 'Would you like a moment or two to gather your thoughts Agustin, can I get you some water from the well?' Agustin did not respond.

'Francesco what's happened?' Mateus asked impatiently.

'Rodriguez Taveres and the slave trade, that's what happened. Now let's get these bodies away. The least I can do is give them a decent burial.'

Without further question Mateus pulled the horse closer and they picked up the two bodies. Agustin walked slowly away down the street toward the river muttering to himself. 'I used to be a proud man,' he said.

'It's odd how different these two look in death Francesco,' said Mateus as he tucked an arm in. 'You see how this one's eyes are closed and his body is cold yet this one … this one, his eyes… look at his eyes Francesco'

'Agustin!' yelled Francesco.

'You really are a miracle man,' Agustin said, returning to feel the slight rise and fall of the man's chest. 'Mateus,' he said calmly, 'it's about time we bought some new cloth for the Cardinal. Please go back into the market and get enough for two robes, and Mateus be generous with the quantity! I think that Saint Jude at least has not forsaken this man.'

Whilst Mateus disappeared back to the market, Francesco collected some water from the well and with Agustin holding the slave's head gently up, they managed to get a couple of sips inside him.

'Pass me those cushions,' said Agustin fussing over his patient.

'Are you sure that's wise?' asked Francesco, trying to lighten the mood.

'Yes it'll support his head.'

'But what about your piles?'

'I'll be fine.'

'And what about this man ?' asked Francesco lifting the cushions from the cart's seat. 'After all, they are moulded to your…'

'Francesco.' Agustin held a finger to his lips. 'Always joking! Maybe we should show this man a little respect.'

'Oh now Agustin, that's exactly what I'm doing,' he lifted the cushion trying hard to suppress his smile.

'Enough Francesco! Did you get the correct wine?'

'Yes, yes and the candles.'

'Good. Now, I think you should lend me your habit.'

'What for? Mateus is getting some cloth as a cover.'

'Surely you don't expect me to sit on that cart all the way back home without a little comfort!'

It was Francesco's turn to shake his head but he took off his habit nonetheless.

'Ah look here's Mateus,' said Agustin. Together they lifted Tumi's dead body and the live slave into the cart and placed the new cloth over the bodies before assuming their places, ready for Mateus to direct Luca toward their return journey. Agustin told them all that had happened and they prayed quietly for the man to survive the rest of the day. If they could get the slave home he might have a chance. So with Agustin sitting on Francesco's habit fingering his rosary beads, he reminded his companions to stop as regularly as they dare to check on their patient.

There was light spilling out from the Cardinal's room when they finally pulled into the darkness of the courtyard of their home.

'Put them both in the far stable next to Luca,' said Agustin 'That way if he dies we'll have them in the same place.' He looked up to the lit window and placed a firm hand on Francesco's knee. 'I'd better go up,' he said. 'Close his shutters and empty his pan.' He huffed at the thought. 'Do what you can with the supplies, but leave me some water in the stable and I'll sit with him awhile when I get back. You two should get some rest.'

After an hour of listening to his master's voice bemoaning the state of the cellar and the weeds outside of the perimeter wall, an exhausted Agustin made his way back to the stable. He crossed the courtyard holding a lantern at arm's length to find both Francesco and Mateus on stools nodding off beside their patient. The candle in their own lantern was flickering on the wick's last quarter inch.

'His breathing is much better,' Francesco relayed sleepily. 'If he survives the night we should give him something warm to drink.'

'He needs food, if he wakes up!' said Mateus. 'There's nothing of him, if he survives the night he'll need to eat. He is starving.'

'Let's just hope then, that he does not die, so we can give him a decent meal,' said Agustin ushering the men to get up. 'I'll watch him now until dawn. Now both of you go get some rest. I've had more sleep than you.'

'We will, but just for a few hours, then I'll be back to take over. The Cardinal is hard enough for you to deal with after a good night's rest, let alone one without sleep. Mateus and I can look after this man,' said Francesco getting up and rubbing his back. Agustin smiled wearily and nodded, it was guilt that forced his first watch, not practicality. Mateus blew out the remnants of his lantern leaving Agustin in the flickering light of his own. Before they left, both embraced the old man. 'God be with you in your vigil Agustin,' they said.

Alone at last Agustin patted Luca on his flank. 'I think that you and I are very much alike my friend. Except that you are blessed for your strength and your loyalty, and I, well perhaps we should ask Saint Jude again,' he laughed gently and reached down for some fresh hay. Luca snorted and bowed his head to receive his gift. 'I think though we can only ask so much of one saint at a time. What do you think?'

Agustin tightened his habit and wrapped a blanket round his shoulders that had been left over the stable door. The material was not for the cold, but for the drying of the pony when he got caught in the rain. It smelt of Luca and the hay that was transported up stream three times a year. Its weight soothed Agustin and he sat down on one of the vacant stools. He was a silly old fool, what was he thinking, the stranger was unlikely to survive the night, which meant in the morning his companions would have two bodies to bury. Then again what if he survived, Alessandro would not take kindly to another mouth to feed, and if he ever found out that Taveres had been involved, this slave would likely be sent to the Richardson plantation anyway.

'Well Luca whoever this man is I do not want him to die. So watch, O Lord, with those who wake, or watch, or weep tonight, and give your angels charge over those who sleep. You know Luca it's times like these, that even I need a little comfort.' He pulled his beads from his pocket.

'These were a gift Luca, from my father, on the last time we met.'

Agustin looked over the beads in the flickering light for a while then quietly began the rosary prayers that he had clung to for so many years.

The repetition of the prayer eased Agustin's mind as it always did. He was relieved that between the different beads he could hear his patient breathing. A comfort that allowed his eyes to close and sleep to creep in. A voice drifted into his dream, it did not challenge, nor fight or even seek solace. It whispered in defence, not for its owner, but its owner's love.

'She didn't cry when she died,' the said in his own language, from the stable floor. Agustin had to look into the darkness. He must have been asleep for hours because his lantern had burnt out.

'What my friend?' whispered Agustin willing one of the other men to come quickly so they could translate.

'She would have fought like a mighty jaguar,' Cieba continued.

'I'm sorry I wish I could understand,' Agustin fumbled for the water and tentatively offered it to the darkness. 'Please take some water,' he said trying desperately to see where the voice was coming from, but there was nothing. Concerned that he might tread on the man he decided to go and get one of the others, surely Francesco wouldn't be far away now. Agustin turned, whispered his brief departure into the dark and headed for where the door had been, except five paces had turned into ten, then twenty. Reaching out Agustin felt sure that tiredness must be playing tricks on his mind, but an icy finger on his shoulder told him differently. His fear was compounded by the grating click that came close behind the touch, the pressure from the finger driving into his shoulder and pushing him down. Agustin was petrified; the devil had come for him, to collect the debt of his survival across the ocean.

'Leave him,' the patient's voice whispered.

Agustin could not stop the tears as the finger was withdrawn. He thought not of his Cardinal, or of his friends but of his family, and the throw of a fishing net onto the azure seas of his childhood. He shook his head and reached out to steady himself, and found the stable wall where it should have been all along. On the dimly lit floor opposite him, his patient had sat up and was taking sips from the cup of water. It was all Agustin could do to make it to a stool and sit down, he would have to let his heart settle before he could speak.

'Thank you,' said the man in Portuguese so that Agustin could understand.

'What is your name, and what just happened?' asked Agustin, rubbing his head with a shaking hand, trying to focus his mind, and stop his headache.

'My name is Cieba, and I am sorry if I frightened you.'

'That I should have lived through so much death and still be alive' Agustin said quietly.

'Who are your people Cieba?' asked Francesco from the doorway, unseen by the other two until he spoke in his native language, one much closer to Cieba's own.

'They have all been murdered. I am at your mercy,' Cieba replied.

EIGHTEEN

Old Bones, New Life

In the grounds of the house that Fernandez Peixa had built for his lover Consuela, Agustin nurtured the life of the slave they had saved. The three men took it in turns to watch over Cieba, and for most of the first forty-eight hours he slept, only waking for long enough to take sips of water and a few bites from Agustin's bread. The men dressed and changed Cieba's wounds. The bullet hole below his left shoulder in particular wept and they took great care to keep it clean. The lead shot had not travelled far into his flesh and was easily removed with a heated blade. Agustin gave way to his companions' understanding of the forest's natural remedies, Francesco especially searched hard on the first day to find the plants he thought would best heal their patient. In his pursuit he found a clearing about an hour's walk from the main track, a place he thought suitable to bury Tumi.

'May God have mercy on your soul,' Francesco said to the body as he and Mateus stood together by the open grave side. 'I thought here your spirit can rise freely to the heavens.'

They covered the body with earth and stood for a moment to reflect and catch their breath.

'You know Francesco,' said Mateus wiping his sweaty brow. 'As we bury this poor man, I am even more grateful that Agustin saved us from Maglanis. We could quite easily be dead.'

'Worse, we could be with Rodriguez,' Francesco replied.

'Francesco, I fear him above all things. He is worse than malaria.'

'You are right, at least malaria brought us to Agustin,' Francesco laughed. 'Come on Mateus let's get him covered up.' After they had knocked in the cross that Mateus had made the day before (Mateus had made two crosses, he'd been sure Cieba would not survive) they left quietly, cleaning off their spades as they headed back to the cart.

'You know. Agustin is a great man,' said Mateus. 'A man of God'

'Ha yes, despite his bad cooking,' Francesco laughed.

'Yes yes and his dozing,' Mateus continued. 'And his piles.'

'Bring me another cushion my friend,' Francesco said bending his back and contorting his face to impersonate the old man's discomfort.

'You know Francesco, I would do anything to keep us out of the plantations,' Mateus said patting his cousin on the shoulder.

'Please Mateus, I don't want to talk of such things. I think that we've had enough death for one day. Let's enjoy the sunshine and when we get back we'll give Luca a good wash and a rub down.'

The day after Tumi's burial Cieba managed to eat more. He spoke a little, mainly of his injuries and then of Maglanis. He talked in his own language mixed with snippets of Portuguese and Spanish, his explanations and actions were understandably slow at first and exhausted. Encouraged by his carers who nurtured his words, he managed to stand and within days was taking tentative steps around the stables.

After his lecture Agustin curtailed the Cardinal's anger by persuading him that the changes he required in the wine cellar were best done first hand. Rodiani nodded his agreement, he could see sense, he said, in his personal intervention. 'After all,' he declared. 'How are you supposed to know what tastes like bottled passion, and what tastes like piss?' Together they spent nearly four hours working their way through bottle after bottle by candle light. Each bottle lifted, described, wiped, placed out on the table, then after tedious contemplation, put back on the rack. After a monotonous lesson in taste, which started with swearing and ended with concise appraisal, none of the wine was poured away. To conclude, Agustin blew out what remained of the wick, thanked his worshipfulness for his time and lead him to the chapel for his prayers.

Just how to approach the Cardinal about Cieba quickly became a pre-occupation for the household. Agustin needed to buy some time, so proposed repairs to the stable, as part of the improved standards that Alessandro expected. Righteously Rodiani agreed to replace broken tiles and the rotten doors inside. It would keep Rodiani away for at least a month, as he would despise the mess, and having Luca in the courtyard would give Cieba more space to move around.

To help them further, Agustin suggested that the Cardinal take a daily walk up the track toward the town, that way he could take fully into consideration the encircling forest and give direction on how they might improve their surroundings. Provoking the Cardinal like this was a calculated risk, if Agustin pushed him too far a storm would rage, and their guest could be discovered before he had gained strength enough to run.

At first this plan worked well, though each time Rodiani's footsteps passed the stable he criticised and complained. Four walks together out along the track was enough, Agustin was waved away. He should know now what he wanted from the property. 'Good God man is it really that difficult?' Rodiani shouted.

The following day Agustin found his master slouched in his chair beside his writing table, his breakfast untouched, his tea cold in its cup. The blinds had been pulled half closed again, reducing the light in the room to a menacing haze that disguised the half written letter he held in his hand. Agustin would have to choose his movements carefully.

'Would your Eminence prefer something else to drink?' he asked. There was no reply. Agustin waited for the silent count of a hundred, and coughed. With no reply and with the Cardinal unmoved, Agustin cleared the breakfast things onto a tray and headed for the door.

'Agustin,' Alessandro's words stopped his aide dead in his tracks. 'You seem a little distracted lately.'

'How so your Eminence?' Agustin replied as calmly as he could.

'Don't lie to me Agustin, I despise secrets, you should know that by now.' His tone grew colder. 'What is going on?'

'Forgive me,' Agustin turned from the door and swallowed hard, he had been as careful as he could possibly be to keep Cieba out of sight. 'Forgive me your Eminence but I do not know what you mean. I thought that your organisation of the cellar was exceptional and the exterior wall will be tended to as soon as the urgent work on the stables is complete.'

'Urgent Agustin, or just a smoke screen?'

'Forgive me, but to what Eminence? Your directive was very clear.'

'Don't play games with me. Have you received any news from Rome? News that you are withholding from me I wonder?' Alessandro growled, his eyes still set upon the page in his hand.

'No your Eminence,' Agustin replied trying to keep his relief disguised. 'We have not received anything from any of the three Jesuit settlements, or Rome. In fact nothing since that last letter from Spain.'

Alessandro sighed heavily and lifted his gaze. 'Nothing from the town, no news from the banderaintes?'

'No, although,' he paused. 'Although I did hear a rumour that Rodriguez Taveres was travelling through this way. But you know what tittle-tattle can circulate in a small town.'

Alessandro sat up and shook his head fixing his eyes on Agustin. The bags beneath them darker than of late, and he ran a hand over his receding hair.

'Why the fuck would Rodriguez Taveres be out here Agustin?' he said.

'I think perhaps for the same reasons as he was in Salvador de…'

'Obviously Agustin,' Rodiani interrupted angrily, 'obviously!'

'Perhaps your…'

'What Agustin! Perhaps what!' He was yelling now his voice reverberating around the house, his face puce. 'Perhaps he is plying his trade inland, picking up what scraps of life the Jesuits are leaving behind. Well Agustin, one thing's for sure, there's fuck all I can do about it. Are my hands not tied by those bastards in Spain and are my eyes not blinkered by the fucking Portuguese? Well Agustin, you tell me?'

'Perhaps your Eminence, you will forgive me while I go and prepare you some fresh tea?'

'You had better not be lying,' Rodiani said waving Agustin away. As soon as the door closed behind him the storm broke. Words followed by ornaments that Mateus would have to re-fix.

'Shit hole of a country… mandarmi a tana di questo diavoli di un paese… Fuck it. Fuck it! Fuck It!'

The whole house shrank as he bellowed his disgust, and Agustin went straight to the stables, the fresh tea could wait. Stooped and visibly shrunk, he sat down on a stool opposite Cieba, looking desperately tired. Agustin sighed heavily and leant forward to put his head in his hands and close his eyes.

'Agustin?' Cieba said in broken Italian. 'I will not stay and cause this upset, I will leave.'

Agustin raised a hand to quiet the gesture. 'You would think Cieba that after all the years I have spent clearing up after that arrogant fat bastard that I would be used to his… to his…' Agustin stopped himself and rubbed his eyes. 'Forgive me for my blasphemy. If I do not rise above Alessandro's tortured soul then I fear the devil will have conquered.'

Cieba gave a half smile. 'I should leave.'

Agustin laughed and rubbed a tear away from his eye. 'No,' he said. 'Tell me about yourself Cieba. If you can… please would you tell me about the woman you spoke of when we first met. Was she beautiful, was she your wife?'

Cieba nodded, understanding just enough of Agustin's words. 'Francesco?' he asked pointing a finger back and forth between himself and the old man. Agustin left and returned with Francesco who gladly translated as best as he could.

'I had been beaten badly when I first met Cattleya,' Cieba started.

'By who?' asked Agustin through Francesco.

'Men from a different place... They beat me with their hard sticks breaking my leg over steps, my arm in a car door... they threw me into an alley... They threw me into an alley and left me to die.'

'Francesco?' Agustin said raising his hands, not understanding what was being translated.

'The frost cut deep into my hands so that I could not even feed myself. The Pelecaras gnawed at me to give in. They pulled me back before I could understand, before I could get to her...' Cieba's words trailed off and he waited for the translation.

'Pelecaras, that at least is a word I understand,' said Agustin. 'So after you were beaten, you were trying to get to...or get back to Cattleya is that right?'

'No,' Cieba was shaking his head before Francesco had finished talking. 'I was trying to find the car crash where I saved Mary. I had it written down on a newspaper. I could only read the date, but I knew the roads. I just had to wait to get back to her again.'

'Agustin, I just don't understand,' said Francesco. 'What is a car? And an alley? Or a newspaper?'

'My friend,' said the old man patiently. 'What was the date on the newspaper that you talk about?'

'1968,' Cieba replied.

Francesco laughed. But Cieba continued, eager now to finish his story.

'The Pelecaras pulled me away, their patience undone, they wanted me, even though my body was broken, I was too weak to resist or to fight. They taunted me with my bow, throwing my arrows onto the floor…' Cieba broke off.

'What happened?' Francesco asked.

'It was raining, in the darkness, it flooded the floor and in their frustration they dragged me back to the gate. They threw me into the waterfall pool to teach me a lesson.'

'The pool?' Agustin asked.

'This real world at last,' Cieba said.

Francesco frowned and stood up. '1968! That is two hundred years away. I think Maglanis has poisoned your brain. Agustin I fear this man is unwell.'

'God forgive me Cieba,' Agustin said, his voice weak. He stood up slowly, his head bowed as he leant against the wall, his rosary beads clutched in his hands. Looking at them for a moment while he thought then asked, 'Is this darkness where you took me?'

'Yes.'

'Who was it that stood behind me?'

'One of the Pelecaras.'

'I am too old for this Cieba. Up in that room I have a man so troubled by what is left of his faith and power, that his shredded nerves keep his mind on a knife edge. Now in front of me you stand with stories of visions, and these creatures that you have lived with for so long. I wonder maybe if they could placate the Cardinal's anger with one of your visions… without killing him.'

'For you… Agustin… Francesco… Mateus… I would do anything.'

'In which case my new friend, it is we who will be at your mercy as now we have something to offer the Cardinal.'

Agustin left Cieba to think and plan, promising that they would do anything to help. A few days later steam rose off the surface of the bath that Cieba had poured for his new master. Vapour drifted up onto the ceiling, and water droplets formed against the walls and the shutters that blocked out the night. In the centre of the room the bath had been raised onto a small short platform so that its occupant could not be leant over.

Cardinal Rodiani entered the room in a long linen shirt and breathed in the sensuous salts that had been added to the bath, the water brimming at its edge, just as he liked it. The candles that illuminated his portly figure had been reconfigured and placed at intervals upon painted lines that Francesco and Mateus had spent most of the day working on.

Alessandro smiled, Agustin obviously had a plan. This new man, if Agustin was to be believed was capable of amazing things. If all went well maybe he should persuade the native to join his household. The lines he thought were a little odd and a bit pagan, but then again, if this man could bring some order to the local women so be it. He just needed some satisfaction. He liked too, the bath's new raised position and was relieved to see his wine glass full where it should be.

'It's good to have a constant in changing times,' he said, raising the glass to take a sip. 'Ah, good choice.' Then Alessandro picked up a different aroma in the room.

'That scent,' he thought out loud. 'Reminds me so…' Alessandro removed his shirt and stepped into the bath, the familiar tide of water washed over the sides as he settled himself in, and he took another sip. Rodiani hesitated where he would have called for Agustin, and for song. The room was so sumptuous that his anticipation washed over the silence just like it used to do in his house in Florence.

'That scent,' he said again. Placing it amongst his memories, he closed his eyes and inhaled deeply.

For the briefest of seconds he felt a cold chill that made him shiver, but laughter quickly stirred him and opening his eyes, he felt the candle lit walls had become a little brighter. Sitting up he was sure he could see the outline of a door to the left, and yes there too, one on the right. This time where previously blind panic would have set in, only lines of curiosity crossed Alessandro's face.

'Who's there?' Alessandro called out self consciously.

Laughter was the reply, from a man and a woman. Lovers maybe, with their soft giggles directed at each other. Their laughter he thought was even more relaxing than the girl's song had been. Alessandro smiled appreciatively and looked around desperate to catch a glimpse of the couple.

'Relax Alessandro,' said the man entering the room, his arms outstretched to pacify the bathing dignitary. For a fraction of a second, the man looked to Alessandro like one of the natives, but no, there stood the handsome frame of Giorgio carrying his bottle of wine. Alessandro sighed and there was a call from the doorway to his right. 'Hello Alessandro.' It was Lisa, Giorgio's lover. Both had been long time occupants of Alessandro's Florentine apartment looking over the Fiume Arno.

'What great vision is this?' Alessandro said, laughing to himself.

'It's what your heart most desires Alessandro,' answered Giorgio.

'Let us bathe you Alessandro,' said Lisa. Her soft voice stirred him, more now than it had ever done before.

'You look so weary from your travels. Fill up his glass Giorgio, and I shall sing softly to him.'

Outside the bathroom Agustin waited for a call that did not come. Cieba had requested that they be cut off from view, so all the old man could hear were muffled voices. No matter how wrong this was to his faith, so far it was working, and if the Pelecaras took Alessandro away like Mateus suggested they would, well maybe there would be even more peace than if his libido was satisfied. God forgive him but if Mateus was right at least his many years of duty would be over. He would take the money from the safe and go home.

'Agustin,' Francesco said, rounding the corner from the stair and sitting down next to him. 'I hope Cieba will cope with the sight of the holy pink body.'

'What could prepare a man for such a sight?' Agustin replied trying not to smile. 'Where is Mateus?'

'I just left him downstairs, he said he would stay there, though I doubt he will. He is more likely to be with Luca, as he is so uncomfortable with this.' Francesco gestured at the bathroom door. 'At least he and I won't have to run after any women today.'

'Ssh, let us wait patiently,' Agustin said. But they did not have to wait long before Cieba let himself out into the corridor. 'He is asking for you Agustin,' he said, heading for the stairs.

On the other side of the door Alessandro stood out of the bath drying himself off with his shirt.

'Ah Agustin, do we have any fresh towels?'

'Of course, if you would just give me a moment.'

Seventy years of disciplined routine saw Agustin out of bed at five each morning and the day after the Cardinal's new therapy was no different. After drinking his tea he would sort out the clothes from the day before and wash as required. This morning as the stove warmed the kettle, he looked out of the one window into the courtyard. Cieba was wandering across the dusty ground toward the archway. Concerned, Agustin pushed the kettle off the stove and headed out after him. On the other side of the great wooden gates, the sun's first rays were breaking against the outside walls, and Cieba stood lit up in its rising glory, his eyes closed in meditation.

'Are you alright my friend?' Agustin asked. 'I hope that I have not dishonoured you?'

'I owe you my life Agustin, you could not dishonour me.'

'I have a little time before I must take the Cardinal his morning tea... Will you sit with me a while?'

Cieba agreed and followed Agustin's gesture toward one of the small alcoves that dented the wall a few paces either side of the archway.

'I have lived through such horrors,' Agustin started as he followed Cieba. He was quiet for a moment as he absorbed the sun's rays, gathering his thoughts and forgetting Cieba's limited understanding of Italian.

'It was the end of the third week of our voyage from Lisbon before Alessandro stopped throwing up. By the time we arrived in Loanda, three weeks after that, he must have lost half his weight.' Unsure of why he had started to tell this story he hesitated.

'It must have been horrible... to watch... him suffer so?' asked Cieba his Italian growing.

'He... he suffered horribly, we used to watch him stagger, and crawl to the side to wretch up his bile. Nonetheless he would not be helped... So stubborn even then, he would rather

199

be left to collapse or just slump against the ropes. If he was conscious he would focus his anger on anything and everything that crossed his path, from the cracks in the decks to the stitching on his shirts.'

'Who else... came with you?' Cieba asked, but Agustin ignored his question to carry on his tale.

'I can clearly remember when the winds subsided enough; it gave us chance to re-hydrate him. I recall him walking along the deck declaring to all who would listen, "Thank fuck, at last I can stand", and Marco,' Agustin laughed now, 'and Marco who was stood right in front of him says "The Holy Spirit has seen you through, Your Excellence" to which the Cardinal replied, "You're fucking right Marco, you're fucking right. Bring me some more wine will you! It'll strengthen my legs."

'Marco?' Cieba asked but again Agustin ignored him.

'When the winds picked up again, and his sickness returned, he got sores on his knees from crawling on the deck, pitiful creature. You know that crucifix which hangs around his neck, that crucifix was the last indication of his faith, his fine robes of office gone, discarded until we weighed anchor outside that hell hole Loanda. Then and only then as the African slaves were led shackled down into the ship's hold did it finally hit home to the Cardinal, the depth of his predicament.'

'Why did he leave his... Italy?' asked Cieba.

'Yes it was Italy. You see Cieba, unknown to Cardinal Rodiani; his sexual tastes were widely known and quickly despised by our new Pope. He was intent on cleaning up the Church's image, and if it wasn't for Alessandro's friends deep inside the Vatican, he would have been excommunicated and cast out onto the streets with no money. Instead those friends decided to send him here, to begin a new life in a new world.'

'Where is Marco?'

'He died Cieba.' Agustin took a deep breath and sighed closing his eyes to the new day. 'Yes he died along with my brother Piero. Buried and drowned along with three hundred festering negros. I swear the angels of death swam up from hell itself to crash upon our ship in that venomous storm. Only fifty five out of four hundred and eighty on board landed in Salvador de Bahia.' Agustin sucked the air in between his teeth and stood up to walk away. 'I must go Cieba , thank you once more. I fear if you are to stay with us, the Cardinal may call upon your abilities again.'

'Agustin,' Cieba wanted to ask more, but Agustin raised his hand to silence him.

'Perhaps we will talk another day Cieba, but I must go to him now.'

NINETEEN

Lessons Between Master Craftsmen

'Agustin!' Cardinal Rodiani called after Cieba had settled his nerves. 'Make sure our new companion is comfortable.'

'Yes your Eminence.'

Cieba repeated his new role twice over the next few weeks and Alessandro's mood lightened, allowing Agustin time to think. To help himself do so he would retreat to the small chapel, which was the only place on the grounds that remained cool and airy, no matter how hot it got outside. Inside there were eight wooden pews, each only wide enough to hold half a dozen people at the most. The pews were divided by an aisle made from flat stones brought up river at great expense by Fernandez. On the courtyard side, facing north, were two stained glass windows, each the height of a man, they provided all the natural light in the chapel as the south side was just solid wall.

'Forgive me Lord,' Agustin said as he knelt before the alter. 'I fear that I may have abused one poor soul to placate another's tortured mind.' He kissed the crucifix at the end of his rosary beads and signed the cross. 'I pray that you will forgive me and give guidance.'

Agustin closed his eyes and felt his old bones lighten and as his breathing steadied, he felt a wave of serenity pass from his white hair down through his kneeling body. It made his faith grow. In his heart he had made the right decision, this way he could help both men. More at ease with himself he unexpectedly felt the presence of another.

'Did you have a place of worship Cieba?' Agustin asked not looking around to confirm his suspicions.

'Between the light that you see, places to negotiate within, threads of another life that I may never understand. Nowhere like this,' Cieba replied from the back of the chapel.

'The Jesuits believe that their versions of my faith and the faith of the rainforest people, are much the same. They say that given time we could find a way together,' Agustin said, slowly standing up, his bones gaining all the weight that they had just lost. He bowed his head, signed the cross again and turned round to face Cieba.

'I fear our paths are very different,' Cieba said, his Italian now very good. 'Agustin before you ask...' But his words were stopped by the older man who held a finger to his mouth, the other hand outstretched. 'Ssh, ssh,' he said, 'I am too old to...' he closed the distance between himself and Cieba before he continued. 'I think what I am trying to say is that I want to try and help you. You are a man of miracles, but you are troubled. Let me help that I might somehow try to repay my debt.'

'Agustin...' Cieba started, but again the old man silenced him.

'I simply want to help you understand yourself, maybe then you might be free.'

'How can you do this?'

Agustin sat down on the back of the pew closest to him. 'Let me think. Other than broken bones and those scars, do you have anything physical from the other time you speak of, your other life, where you say these cars exist. Like a crucifix maybe?'

'No,' Cieba replied. 'Other than my memories, no.'

Agustin looked up through the stained glass opposite him, made glorious by the sun moving directly above. He savoured its glory for no longer than a few seconds, then covering the remaining ground to Cieba, he placed a hand on his shoulder and said quietly, 'I do not wish you any harm, but I think, I think if you could show me something...'

'Something, that you could hold... touch? From a different time?' Cieba said.

'Yes that is what I mean. If you could bring me something, it might help rationalise things. Forgive me I must go Cieba. God be with you.'

Back in the house Alessandro had woken. He stood by the door, placed his hands on his hips and looked back over his large room. His writing table was a mess, and the only things legible on it were not his. He passed wind and smiled, that last glimpse of Florence, the taste of Lisa, had triggered a longing for his old home, too long had he sat and wallowed in this house. The room was over run with important information which he should have attended to, it was high time that he undertook his responsibilities again. Steer clear of the slave traders and their games, rise above the pressures of Spain and Portugal; the Vatican was the only place that could reinstate his old life. To do so, he would need to impress on them that his work here was fully collated and complete. Instantly he resolved to abstain from his new pleasures and sort out the decaying paperwork. Tomorrow he would start, today he would walk, break free of the walls and smell the air.

Even before Agustin arrived with his morning tea the next day, Alessandro was hard at work. Amongst the disorder were detailed records of Jesuit activity in the borders of Paraguay that had lain untouched for years. When Agustin did open the door, he was sent away. From now on Alessandro asked to be served downstairs in the main reception room, which contained a large polished mahogany table that was hardly ever used. After all, Alessandro reminded him, the room was supposed to be used for dining. Agustin retreated dutifully to the kitchen and waited until he heard Alessandro leave his room before he re-boiled the kettle. Once seated at the table the Cardinal complained about the delay and went on to blame Agustin for the overcomplicated way in which the information upstairs had been piled up in the past.

Sipping his tea he focused on the saucer and declared that until further notice his room was out of bounds. He would take his meals here where they always should have been served.

'Forgive me Your Eminence, but surely I should enter your room at least to clean.'

'Surely Agustin, there will be nothing to clean if I am to eat down here, and don't worry I'll leave my chamber pot outside the door when I have used it.'

'Thank you, Your Eminence.'

'Now I must get back to the task. Give me until eleven and then I should like some coffee.'

'In this room?'

'Yes Agustin.'

Agustin cleared away the tea and took it through to the kitchen. He washed, dried then put the crockery back onto the dresser, the same cups and saucers that his brother Piero had carefully packed back in Florence. Piero had insisted on using straw and that all the fine china was double crated. Given the necessary haste to their departure, Agustin had chastised him for his actions, but the china was all that remained of the opulent Florentine kitchen. Other than two heavy chests containing the Cardinal's clothes, the only other possessions to have made it were three paintings; one was of the Holy Mother cradling her child which hung in the dining room, a representation of the crucifixion which hung in the Chapel, and lastly a battered painting of the Fiume Arno which divided Florence, this took pride of place in the Cardinal's private quarters. The latter had been restored by Francesco and his work had been much admired.

'How long will this last I wonder?' Agustin said to himself. With an hour or so before coffee was required, he looked out of the window into the courtyard and wondered how he should remove the Cardinal's bed linen, or whether he should just purchase a new set, though it would have to be ordered. Either way the ones that were on his bed would need burning soon. He shook his head and focused on the courtyard outside, Mateus looked to be questioning Cieba by the gates and obviously trying to get at a piece of paper Cieba was holding behind his back. Agustin tapped on the glass and beckoned for Cieba to come inside, much to the disgust of Mateus.

'Come into the kitchen and sit while I work out how much tea we have left. I think our friend out there may have forgotten to buy some last time we were in town.'

'I have this...' Cieba was holding out the scrap of paper.

'What is it young man, what do you have?'

'As you asked... I went back for this... the paper... newspaper, please read it to me, I know... it leads to the crash... I only held it once before... I cannot read it.'

'It is written in English, I shall try to read it out loud for both of us.' Agustin took the proffered scrap, it was on thin paper unlike anything that he had seen, it had writing on both sides but it was the story on the side up that Cieba wanted him to read.

New Year's Day Car Crash Tragedy

What could bring Mary Swartz from the farming community of Wood River, Nebraska to the intersection of 7th Avenue and 142nd Street? I'm sure our readers will remember what a beautiful morning that was, so I felt compelled to find out more about the couple.

The facts still remain the same. Pregnant Mary Swartz, twenty seven, and the unidentified driver of their car collided with Matthew Modiene, twenty nine, a young musician returning home from playing in the New Year. Both Modiene and Swartz were killed instantly in the first light of New Year's Day, the unidentified man is still unconscious. Doctors at the Presbyterian Hospital say the man is still in critical condition and are unwilling to comment on whether he will recover from his injuries.

Miss Swartz must have been desperate to leave her home town after the suspicious death of her parents.

The page was torn here and Agustin had to lift it up closer to the light from the window to read it.

Grand Island Police have been unwilling to discuss the murder case nor have the NYPD been willing to comment on
but have concluded that Mathe
I will keep readers up to da
New Yorkers should be

'And here Cieba, there is a date at the bottom of the other side – 14th January 1968.'

'Agustin,' Cieba tried to speak but he couldn't continue.

'You are cold Cieba, how did you get so cold?' Agustin took a step back. 'You are filthy, your clothes are ripped… and… you do not look to have eaten in days. I only saw you last night. Where have you been, where did you get this from?'

Cieba could not reply as exhaustion took over. The last thing he heard was Mateus' disgruntled remark. 'I think maybe this shaman might be better off under somebody else's care.'

As Cieba collapsed, Mateus narrowly managed to stop him banging his head and laid him down safely on the kitchen floor away from the stove. Unaware that he was being moved Cieba's mind wandered back over his journey during the last twelve hours.

During this time he could see straight away the Pelecaras had in their own crude way started to work things out, by scratching their fingernails into the smooth floor, and filling the indents they left with silver. These marks were concentrated enough to create a chilling pattern of lines and circles that stretched out fifty or more paces. Across these, more intricate glyphs had been attempted; some ten or fifteen paces across, some only a stride's width in circumference. The more Cieba looked the more pearlescent and incandescent the silver became, its beauty in the darkness hypnotising.

'Do you like what we have done?' Huayna asked, his cold voice grating in the darkness.

'Pretty aren't they!' said Hernan.

'Pathways?' Cieba asked.

'More like… signposts,' Atoc said, considering his answer.

'They mark the way, the ways that we started to find together, before you left us,' Hernan said.

'Is it a map?' Cieba asked.

'Oh so very nearly' Huayna rasped.

'Where do you want to go Cieba? The alley?'

'Yes the alley.'

The five strode towards him, circling and brushing against him with tattered clothes and sharp bones. Their rotation quickly drawing forth the smell of air vents and car fumes, closely followed by the light of a winter's dawn, illuminating a collection of litter beneath their feet. It was then he noticed that the spirits, having been for so long bare footed, now wore shoes, just like the other people he could barely see scurrying past.

A car horn sounded, followed by another, heralding the spoken word of pedestrians making their way to work. Still circling him, the Pelecaras began to pick up a momentum that sickened Cieba to the point where he could not stand, so they let him fall. When he woke he was cold and alone, clothed in a tattered suit, with the alley rubbish as a pillow. Lifting himself up to huddle against the brick wall behind him, he found, in one hand, the last remnants of the newspaper, and in the other an empty bottle. He was so numb he could barely hold onto the clipping, but hold onto it he did. Two blocks away a siren sounded, gathering volume in the quiet cold until its lights raced by, throwing blue and red light onto his plight.

The sound of a homeless drunk pissing against the dumpster close by woke Cieba from his daze. A nameless classic tune lifted into the air alongside the tramp's stench as he tried to stay upright and stumble back out onto the street taking his song with him.

'Enough,' Cieba said.

'So you need us now?' said Atoc, pleased with his work.

'I see he brought you the paper again,' Hernan said poking at the page tearing it part way down so that nearly half of the article was lost.

'He brought it this morning,' Cieba replied, pulling what was left of it to his chest.

'But why bother? She's already dead.' Azuay said flatly.

'Then why do I save her?' Cieba asked.

Huayna pulled Cieba to his feet. They were joined by the others who, wrapping their arms around Cieba, started to rotate again. The alley rapidly deteriorated leaving him standing in the darkness once more. Relieved to still feel the paper between his fingers he took a deep breath, slipped their grasp and ran, following as best he could the pattern they had laid out on the floor.

'Don't ignore our map, brother,' Hernan shouted after him.

In the Fernandez house, Cieba woke to voices.

'Are you going to wake him or am I going to fetch some water?' Mateus said grumpily.

'Why did I save her, and not Cattleya?' Cieba asked in barely a whisper.

'Cieba you are awake at last. You have been asleep for hours,' Agustin said relieved, his voice bringing a full stop to the memory.

'Agustin...?' Cieba asked faintly.

'Yes I have the paper. Heavens preserve us you are as thin as when we first met. Sit up now and I will fetch some food. Mateus please go and tell Francesco, he has been worried sick'

Unaware of Cieba's poor health, Alessandro kept to his new work regime, determined that this fresh act of devotion would work. The harder he toiled, the more convinced he became that when the Vatican read his report and heard of the ridiculous pressures he was under from Spain and Portugal, they would see his position was untenable, and he would be sent for.

For ten days Alessandro read and collated, until on the Thursday morning of the second week he saw the end was in sight, another seven days at most and he would be done. Then he could relax and enjoy the last of his time in this country. That morning he ignored Agustin's attempt at conversation and sipped his morning tea, calculating whether or not they should take the trip down river to St Paolo in anticipation of a reply, or whether it would be better to sail further down to Salvador de Bahia. Then again, he thought with a smirk, that he should request an emissary to retrieve him from Praia da Viera. They could witness first hand how he had stood strong in this wilderness. Either way, once his work was done he should not let the talents of the Indian go to waste.

Pushing away his finished breakfast, Alessandro requested from now on to have his morning coffee in the small reception room just inside the main door. The room only had one small round white ornate table with two chairs, an odd choice given

Alessandro's stature, but Agustin was not going to question him, he had enough to contend with trying to get Cieba back up to strength.

'I think I shall take a little air, inspect your work on the stables,' Alessandro announced standing up and heading out into a cloudy day where the air was getting heavier, rain could not be far away. Agustin watched from the kitchen window as Alessandro looked at the stable roof, turned and walked back to the house, his heavy footsteps rising up the stairs and into his room.

Why on earth the Cardinal wanted to have coffee in such a cramped room was beyond Agustin, but he'd better get it cleaned. He gathered a bucket of water, cloth and mop and set to the task. There was only one small window in the room which faced the stables. Never mind, he said to himself as he mopped the floor and wiped down the furniture, when Alessandro was in here, he was contained.

'Would it be possible Your Eminence, to clean your room while you take your coffee in here?' Agustin asked when the Cardinal was in place.

'Just change my bed and don't touch my papers Agustin,' was the curt reply.

Dreading what he would find, Agustin turned the handle of Alessandro's door. To his surprise he found all the paperwork well organised. He opened the blinds to let in some light which sent dust clouds up into the room making him cough and splutter. He had no choice but to open the window slightly and let in some fresh air. Below he could see Luca eating some oats from Francesco's hand, the two having a conversation without words. Agustin thought to call out but changed his mind and turned back to the task at hand. 'Ah,' he sighed heavily, the

212

room was disgusting, spilt wine stains on the bed clothes and urine splatters on the floor. He would start with the wine bottles and build up his courage to tackle the rest.

Alessandro finished his coffee, rounded his newly clean table and stepped outside feeling confident, especially when above him the threat of rain was being pushed aside by a blue sky.

Admiring the sun as it broke through he noticed, on the other side of the yard, Francesco, Mateus and Cieba had just sat down on the cart. They were laughing and joking in their own language, which, even today, he decided he didn't mind, especially as all three stood up and bowed their heads when he approached.

'Good morning Your Eminence' Francesco said.

'Good morning to you all,' the Cardinal replied.

'A beautiful day Cardinal?' Mateus suggested.

'Yes it is,' the Cardinal replied. 'Yes it is.'

'Are you well on this fine day?' Mateus chanced, and Alessandro nodded, his hands holding his black Bible to his stomach.

'Forgive us Your Eminence, we were just taking a short break,' Francesco said sensing the conversation was at its end. 'We will leave you to your prayers and finish our white washing before it gets too hot.'

'Very well,' Alessandro nodded again. 'However I wonder Cieba if you would walk with me.'

'If you so wish,' Cieba said following Alessandro's lead. They walked across the courtyard and out of the gates without speaking. On the other side Alessandro stood still and pondered his words.

'Is there something different you wish of me, if so...' Cieba said.

'No please. I think maybe if you could follow me back to the house,' Alessandro was uncharacteristically nervous, passing his Bible from hand to hand then waving it in the direction of his home. 'It's perhaps better if we speak privately inside, we could have some coffee. It's very good, the finest I think I have ever tasted, it just needs a scoop of sugar, well... please after you.'

Upstairs Agustin had stripped the bed and decided the linen would survive if he boiled it in his biggest pan. He straightened his back and huffed, he would need more time if he was going to wash the floor too. Suddenly dizzy he closed his eyes and steadied himself. 'Silly old fool,' he said. 'Get some help or this will stay as it is.' With his mind clearer Agustin moved to the window hoping to get the attention of Francesco, instead he saw Alessandro follow Cieba in through the door beneath him.

'Now he's going to want the blessed bath filling,' Agustin said huffing again. Making his way back to the door he passed the writing table on which sat the two royal letters, held down by an unopened bottle of wine. 'Well Your Eminence, it is unlike you to leave stones out to be turned.'

'Agustin,' Alessandro called from downstairs.

What did the letters say? Did they call for the Cardinal's return, is that why he wanted to sort out his records? Or had they told him to do what he was being paid for. Agustin signed the cross, or, he wondered had something happened in the Vatican. Without opening the letters he would never find out and suddenly more than ever, he wanted to see his home near Alassio again.

'Agustin! Are you up there?'

Nervously he moved the bottle to one side and opened the first letter re-breaking the Portuguese seal. The letter was two pages long, and shook in his hands as he skimmed over the elegant writing. There was no doubt in its words that there was a deeper suspicion around the Jesuits, and an accusation of a desire for power that was outstripping and outweighing any good they had initially come to do in the name of God. Worse still it accused the Jesuits of hampering the progress of Portuguese stability in this country. There was no mention of their return and he found at the bottom of the last page the mark of the first Marquis of Pombal. Agustin had heard of his rise to power, this man, otherwise known as Sebastião José de Carvalho e Melo. He was not a man to ignore or conspire with.

'What are you up to Alessandro?' Agustin whispered.

'Agustin!' The Cardinal's voice had grown, and he should go, his hands were on the second letter. Its mark from the Court of Charles the third of Spain. Alessandro's footsteps were on the landing. He should face him, be strong and face him man to man. The door swung open just as Agustin grabbed hold of the wine bottle.

'Agustin what are you doing?' The Cardinal's face was puce.

'Have we not been through enough?' Agustin asked clearly. His stomach churning.

'Agustin, I have not got the patience to talk to you about wine anymore. Put that bottle back and bring us some coffee will you!' his words were deliberate. His temper reined in.

'Eminence.' The moment was lost, Agustin's position had been re-established.

'Two cups!'

'Of course.'

Alessandro walked heavily back along the corridor and down the stairs to his newly commissioned coffee room. He composed himself and placed his Bible on the table.

'I think my friend that I could be of assistance to you' Alessandro hesitated ensuring he was understood. 'Like myself you are a man of great power… And we have both suffered great hardship and well,' he rephrased, 'I think we could be of assistance to each other.'

'Can… you… turn back… time?' Cieba asked, stretching out his Italian, he didn't want Alessandro thinking he could understand everything he said.

'No my friend but I think we can both learn from the paths that we have followed.'

'I did not… follow a path.'

The two sat in silence for a moment.

'Perhaps not. Except we have both been survivors at the mercy of God.'

'I… I do not… seek his mercy Cardinal.'

The Cardinal coughed and turned red.

'I would like to offer you a new life Cieba. You could live here safe from Rodriguez Taveres. Agustin could teach you how to read and write, a man of your intellect could easily learn English and Latin. In time you will understand the peace and power of the Holy Spirit and the way of the civilised world. In return… you my friend could teach me about your fine art.'

'Fine art?' asked Cieba unmoved.

'Your ability.'

'My ability?'

'Your ability…' Alessandro shifted uncomfortably in his chair. 'Your ability to create such wondrous apparitions.'

Cieba held out the silence that followed at length, allowing the heat of the day to wade in. The Cardinal shifted uncomfortably in his chair and as he reached out to his Bible the light from the window caught the beads of sweat that collected at the edge of his receding hairline, they gathered to find a course down the side of his face, betraying his plummeting confidence.

'I would like to meet Rodriguez Tavares again,' Cieba said at the breaking point of patience.

'Yes of course. I can arrange that… if we have an agreement Cieba.'

'Yes Cardinal Rodiani we have.'

As Alessandro had predicted, it only took seven more days for him to complete his collation, though he decided after several attempts, to put aside his summary end note. In it he would conclude that his work in South America was done and having lived in complete abstinence from all his vices, he could now serve the church as a repentant man, a virtuous man, someone who had learned so much in his exile that he was now closer to God than he had ever been.

Agustin was allowed to regain order in the master's bedroom and was impressed to see the work compiled and ready for dispatch. He never caught sight of the two letters again and not for the first time he asked himself 'How long will this calm last I wonder?'

In accordance with Cardinal Rodiani's instruction, on top of his other chores, Agustin began to tutor Cieba, and his lessons steadily began to bear fruit. Cieba learned with remarkable ability for one whom had never held a pen. 'You learn with the speed of a gifted child!' Agustin noted as Cieba moved from Italian to English and to Portuguese with ease.

'Do I not have my whole new life in front of me like a child, Agustin?'

Relieved that his work was finally done, Alessandro rewarded himself by calling on Cieba's talents. Indulging himself with experiences that he brought closer together. He felt himself grow in stature. Rome would have to take him back, and if he had the art that the Indian did, he could remain pure. He could look once more down the length of the Arno and forget about this place. It was just the final summary which remained, a frustration that niggled and poked at him, until it finally spilled over.

'Agustin, I think your men should show me more respect. I have decided changes are needed.'

'How Cardinal?'

'Firstly how are the Latin lessons going with our maestro?'

'Basic, and not as well practiced as his other subjects Your Eminence,' Agustin replied as he poured the tea. 'My only fear is that in his thirst for knowledge I am neglecting my other duties.'

'The other two will have to pick up the slack.'

'With respect there is no slack,' Agustin's words fell silent, to a slight raise in the Cardinal's head.

'If Cieba is competent in the other subjects concentrate on the Latin for a while,' Alessandro's tone was tainted with his old self 'and I'm sick to death of seeing his lesson papers everywhere, use my coffee room. It can be your tutorial room.'

'As you wish Your Eminence, and which subjects would you like me to drop from his lessons?' Agustin asked with a slight sigh of resignation.

'Agustin I want you to concentrate on the Latin, I don't give a fuck about the rest, understood?' There it was, the storm brewing behind Alessandro's words.

'Yes Cardinal I understand,' Agustin replied, the cruel eye that looked at him burnt all the more for a break in its fire. Mustering some presence of mind whilst Alessandro slurped at his tea he remembered his duties.

'Forgive me Cardinal but a note arrived yesterday from Sao Louis. As you were so busy with Cieba I did not think it appropriate to disturb you. It has the port seal and arrived with some funds which I have placed in the safe as usual. While you slept I put the letter on your writing desk by the window.'

'Very well, leave me,' Alessandro ended their conversation with a dismissive wave of his hand.

Alessandro returned to his room and opened the letter. Excited that maybe Rome had written without him even having to finish his report. Surely in all that was holy he would be spared any more pressure from the Portuguese Marquis. But his shoulders dropped and the sight of his homeland disappeared when he unfolded the page to read in an elegant Spanish hand;

Cardinal Alessandro Porta Rodiani

Dear Cardinal,

How surprised I was to run into your aide Agustin in Praia da Viera. I was shocked to hear you are residing so very deeply in this endless forest and given your situation I was greatly relieved to learn that you are in good health.

Agustin may have informed you that I now have business interests in the borders and will pass by your home regularly.

Given the most honourable and influential position in which you reside, my interests may or may not bear impact on your records.

Cardinal, as it has been such a long time since we met, I think you will be pleased to hear that, on a recent visit to Rome, I was lucky enough to speak with Cardinal Andre Debois. He reassured me that the Vatican does recognise your excellent work and fortitude. The Cardinal Debois asked that, if ever I should have the good fortune to meet you again, I should pass on his respects. Rome, it seems, wishes you to remain until Spain and Portugal decide who will take over the Jesuit colonies. As a friend I thought I should let you know.

Lastly, having witnessed the solitude in which you have been placed, I can understand the difficulties and the huge expense you must be facing to obtain the finer things which might make your stay more bearable. I have, therefore, taken the liberty of enclosing a small gift.

I anticipate that once I have finished my business here at the Port, I will follow this letter toward Praia da Viera and so may have opportunity to bring similar gifts. Therefore, should you ever have need to contact me do not hesitate. I'm sure your men will know where to leave a message for me in the town.

Yours most sincerely,

Rodriguez Taveres

Alessandro moved to his favourite chair and looked back into the room. He held the letter in his lap and re-read it twice more. 'Fucking "honourable and influential",' he muttered to himself desperately. He had not been honourable, if he had, he would not be here in the first place. With tears of frustration welling in his eyes he realised he had sat on something. Shifting forward he found his black Bible beneath him and while his tears dried to leave reddened eyes of quiet rage he looked at it, turning it over several times and flicked through its pages. Finally he held it to his lips and kissed its old cover.

'Il diavolo non è mai lontano,' he said to himself. 'The Devil is never far away.'

TWENTY

Alassio

'Come on you two, let's go,' Philippe called up the stairs with a smile on his face. He could hear his boys giggling in their rooms above.

'I can't find my shirt Papa.'

'It's at the end of your bed Piero, where it was when you woke.'

'I can't find my shoes Papa.'

'They're down here by the door Agustin, where you left them last night.' He laughed shaking his head. 'Come on my boys. If we don't go soon, there'll be no fish left for our supper.' Philippe lifted a small satchel of food across his shoulder and waited at the threshold of his door. 'I'm going now boys. I'll have to leave you here, and fish on my own. See you tonight,' he called, stepping out and leaving the door open, but he didn't get far before he heard the boys clattering down the stairs after him.

'Papa wait for me,' Piero shouted. Two weeks ago he had received a necklace for his eighth birthday, it had a shark's tooth neatly threaded on to it and he wore it with pride and gusto. Behind him his younger brother Agustin tried to get past, but Piero was faster, and blocked the way as he pulled his shirt over his head.

'Hey, hey there you are Piero,' said Philippe laughing. 'All we need now is your little brother.'

'Wait for me, wait for me!' Agustin shouted, rushing out after them struggling to lace up one of his shoes.

'Ah there you are!' his father exclaimed. 'Come here little man, let me do that for you.'

'Then we can go and catch our supper!' Agustin shouted with a big grin on his face. He was six and believed wholeheartedly that he was the best fisherman in the world.

'Okay fine fishermen,' said Philippe, putting a guiding hand on each of their shoulders. 'Let's go!' They headed out of their gated garden and down the lane towards their village and the turquoise waters of the Mediterranean. The nearest town, Alassio, could be seen through breaking trees but was quickly lost as their lane curved west past their neighbours, whose house was covered with Abutilon and the finest figs.

'Papa?' Piero said, 'Did you know Mamma is still asleep.'

'Ah now Piero, it is still early in the day. I think we should let her rest don't you?'

'Is that because fishing is just for us men Papa?' asked Agustin.

Their father only laughed in reply, he ruffled their hair and gave them a gentle shove. 'Go on both of you. First one to the boat gets to be captain.'

Down they ran, with arms aloft and feet lifted high to stop them tripping. It was a ten minute walk or a five minute run and the boys loved to race. Above them, a cloudless sky offered a settled sea and Philippe soon lost sight of his sons, but he knew they were safe. Traders and other fishermen called to him as the houses became fronted with market stalls and the path opened up onto the sea. The community was close and its ties to the monastery provided trade and respect. Though Philippe left religion to others, he was happy for his wife to educate their boys as she thought best, just so long as once a week they could help him fish. They joined him when the sea was calm and breathless, and watched from the shore when the winds fought against the tide and unleashed its white horses across the breaking waves.

'Papa, as I'm captain, can I throw the net this time?' Agustin asked, still panting after he'd won the race. He and Piero were sitting on the jetty, their feet hanging over the edge.'

'No Papa let me,' shouted Piero.

'You know maybe today you can take it in turns to help me, then we will see how the water rocks the boat.'

'Ah papa you always say that,' Agustin looked disappointedly down at his feet.

'Then today Agustin, you can cast the net first, and catch us the biggest fish in the bay.'

'Really Papa?'

'Really my boy.'

'Agustin,' Francesco said, gently nudging his friend awake. After a search through the house, he'd finally found him dozing in the sun outside the archway.

'Ah Francesco, I must just have nodded off for a moment,' Agustin replied

'Just for a little while I'm sure. It's time we made the trip into town. We need supplies, and Mateus was wondering if we should take some of the Cardinal's bundle of papers. Get them dispatched to Rome.'

'If only I could look once more upon that sea,' Agustin said ignoring the question.

'What sea? I thought you hated the sea?' Francesco frowned.

'I was dreaming of my childhood home, and my father when you woke me Francesco.'

'Was it a nice dream?'

'Very much so, my father was a great man, and the sea near my home was clear and beautiful not dull and treacherous like the Atlantic.'

'Was your father a priest or a Cardinal?'

'No no,' Agustin laughed. 'He was a great fisherman.'

Francesco smiled and folded his arms. 'The forest has always been home for Mateus and I. Our fathers had little time for affection. They were too fierce; killers in the cloud forests until the Jesuits found us, and we moved to their mission.'

'Ad majorem Dei gloriam!' said Agustin.

'Mateus and I have always wanted to go back to the mountains. You know, I think we'd almost persuaded Father Matthew to go there on our return from Sao Luis. Then he fell ill. We should go back there Agustin, the three of us? Or even four, if Cieba is ever released from his lessons.'

'Maybe Francesco, I cannot tell…there is of course the small question of the Cardinal,' Agustin said. He closed his eyes, trying to remember his dream, but it was no use, and instead got up and continued. 'At the moment my friend, our Cardinal has requested that Cieba start…' He hesitated. 'He wants Cieba's secrets written down for his own. What have I started Francesco? I was just trying to give Cieba a little time.'

'Agustin I'm sure that you did what you thought best. Whatever Cieba is doing for the Cardinal, it has pleased him. Most of all he has saved us the sight and weight of his body.'

'I just don't like it,' Agustin said holding his head in his hands.

'You did what you thought was best. Agustin look at the funny side of it. The Vatican is hardly likely to encourage this new sexual magic. I'm not sure it was their intention for the Cardinal to develop his habits when he came out here.'

'No I doubt he'll want to share those secrets with the Pope.' Agustin laughed. 'I also have the feeling he won't want his work sending just yet. So Francesco, let's get a list together. If you are going to the town I need a few extra things myself.'

'Excellent, Mateus is most insistent that we go soon, he keeps saying the rains are coming, so with your permission we'll head off tomorrow.'

'Of course, but Francesco, I'm an old fool so don't listen to my complaints.' He tutted and got to his feet to find some paper for their list. When it was finished they parted company in the courtyard. 'Ah Francesco before I forget, please tell Cieba to bring only his Latin books this afternoon.'

Francesco and Mateus made their way into Praia da Viera the following day. Mateus was up first and had hooked up Luca to the cart before his cousin had appeared. The journey out passed in silence. Any attempt by Francesco to chat was met by distracted nods from Mateus. Once they reached the town the two split the shopping list in half and went their separate ways.

'Mateus, you are unsettled?' Francesco finally suggested as they made their way back. 'I thought you would be happier now that we are returning to our home, and it looks like we'll make it back before it rains.'

'It will rain soon enough!' Mateus replied flatly.

'Oh for the love of God, what is the matter with you?' Francesco shouted.

'It's Cieba… Having that shaman amongst us is,' Mateus exasperated, like they'd been discussing it for hours. 'Francesco why do you ignore it? Our fathers brought us up to believe in Pachamama and the other spirits of the forest. Then we are moved to the mission where we are taught that the love of Jesus is everything… he laid down his life for us. Do you not remember Father Matthew?'

'Of course I remember Father Matthew.'

'I heard Agustin say that, that Shaman has done a deal with the Cardinal. So I ask you cousin, what insanity is this? Surely this is not God's work!'

'Mateus, please.'

'And for Agustin and you, to allow this man to shadow the light of Christ. It makes me feel unsafe Francesco.'

'I see…'

'Whatever Cardinal Rodiani is, he provides us with security. If he loses his faith in Christ, I question that security. We should think of ourselves… Make plans. I do not want to end up in the sugar plantations because of a shaman's ability to satisfy that man's loins.' Mateus stopped, sighed deeply and shook his head. 'It was better when we brought down the girls from the town.'

'Mateus I don't know what to say.'

'Spirits should not be wielded Francesco. Even if we do trust in Agustin.'

'Ha my friend, you were right,' Francesco said suddenly brighter.

'Good then we will talk to him tonight…'

'No he has enough to trouble him.'

'But Francesco you just said that I was right,' Mateus held the reins up in disbelief.

'Not about that,' Francesco laughed, lifting up a hand. 'It's starting to rain.'

'Yes, even Cieba can't stop the rain from falling,' Mateus replied.

'No but I would bet that he could convince the Cardinal that he was still dry.' The two men laughed out loud, lifting the mood, as the rain quickly turned into a downpour.

It was dark and they were soaked to the skin by the time they pulled into the courtyard. Candle light flickered up in the Cardinal's room and in the windows of the chapel. Lit by the lanterns that they carried, Agustin and Cieba stepped out into the rain to help off load the cart and get Luca into his refurbished stable.

Days passed in the tutorial room. Cieba read and questioned, then listened and copied. His understanding grew apace, often studying into the night, whilst Agustin nodded off only waking up to end the session.

'Agustin,' Cieba said late one night. 'I think the time has come to give the Cardinal what he wants. I fear his patience is running out.'

'What can I do?' Agustin asked wearily.

'Nothing other than to trust me. I must go back into the darkness.'

'Cieba if there is any way I could go for you, or I could share your burden, you only have to say.'

'Agustin, you of all people I wish no harm to. All I ask is that you trust me. I will return.'

Agustin managed at first to lie about Cieba's whereabouts, except as one day became two, he felt the wrath of Alessandro without even telling him. On the third day he confessed to his friends and they prayed in the chapel fearing above all things that Cieba had gone for good. Together they decided Agustin should give Cieba two more days. Then they would face Rodiani together.

That night Agustin did not sleep. If Cieba did not return Alessandro would be in a murderous mood. Sometime after midnight he left his bed, pushed his rosary beads deep inside his pocket in fear that he might break them and went downstairs to polish everything that he could by candle light. The following day he emptied the chapel to sweep the floor and clean the windows. After he'd given Alessandro his supper, he returned, to polish the pews. Finally in the small hours of the night exhaustion overtook his old bones before he'd finished, a cloth still clutched in his hand, his knees tucked beneath him and his head rested on the shiny surface of the last bench.

Before dawn Mateus found Cieba slumped over the small table in the tutorial room, with a stack of papers clamped tight in both hands.

'He looks lighter than the Cardinal to carry. What do you say cousin?' Francesco asked quietly from the doorway. 'And a little less pink!'

'He looks half dead again, like a skeleton,' Mateus added. 'Lets get him back to his bed. I tell you what, you get the legs this time.'

Once they had delivered Cieba to the stable, they woke Agustin. Rubbing his eyes, and wiping his mouth the old man focused on the papers Francesco was proffering to him, and explaining their provenance.

'Well gentlemen,' Agustin said separating the pages and counting them, 'I have no idea what this all means, apart from, it is quite exquisite.'

'Do you think the Cardinal will be pleased?' asked Mateus.

'Ah' Agustin said suddenly remembering his duties, 'Francesco would you be kind enough to take the Cardinal his breakfast tea.'

'You slept in longer than you think Agustin! It is mid morning, but rest assured, the Cardinal has been fed and watered.'

'Then I shall go up to him. Let's get these under his nose as quickly as possible.'

'There is no need to trouble yourself Agustin,' the Cardinal's deep voice made them all turn with a start. He was standing just inside the chapel doorway, only God knew for how long. 'You can leave us,' he said waving the cousins out of the door.

'So this is it Agustin?' Alessandro's face was fixed on the scrawled paper. His eyes wide as he took them from Agustin. 'Lines and patterns Agustin! Pages and pages of circles and squares!'

'Twenty two pages in all I think. Cieba left them laid out ready to be bound. Which is what I was just going to do. Ready to be placed in your hands Cardinal.'

'It's very pretty, but what am I supposed to do with it?' Alessandro's eyes narrowed 'I recognise some of these lines but there are no words, what about the Latin you were supposed to be teaching him.'

'I'm sure Cieba will explain.'

Alessandro took a step back as if to leave, but instead he closed the door and leaned against it. He cleared his throat. 'Agustin, how many years have we lived in this dammed country. Surely you of all people can see that we can't go on like this.' He ran both hands through his hair. 'Get the shaman back to work. I want to know the rest of it!'

230

'I am here Cardinal,' Cieba said, appearing outside the door as Alessandro opened it to leave.

'I can see that you have been busy,' Alessandro said drawing a deep breath.

'Those pages are what you seek Cardinal.'

'Yes as we agreed, in return for the understanding of our languages, which you now speak so well,' said Alessandro.

'Agustin has taught me well.'

'Do not take me for a fool. These patterns, this magic, needs words to direct and control it. I have heard you whisper them!' Alessandro moved back into the room until his face was highlighted in the tints of the stained glass window.

'Some thing's are best kept unwritten,' Agustin said.

'Cieba, I did ask Agustin here to ensure that you get everything on paper!'

'You did Your Eminence, but…'Agustin tried once more to be heard.

'Leave us Agustin.'

'Please I implore you, Your Eminence.'

'Leave us.'

Agustin barely made it out of the door before terror caught up with him. It sapped the last strength from his legs, forcing a migraine over his left eye that closed it. It was a feeling he could not escape, it paralysed him, forcing his exhausted mind to blackout.

From the door of the stable Francesco saw Agustin fall and ran quickly over to gather him up.

Francesco carried his friend into the house, up the stairs and into his bedroom, lying him gently onto his bed.

'I will go and get the cart ready Agustin, get us out of here.' Francesco whispered. He closed the door and crept back down the stair and out across the courtyard to the stable without being seen.

'Cieba, we had an agreement,' Rodiani's voice filled the chapel, he was trying desperately to stay calm and he was sweating heavily. 'I have the key to a new life for you. Or do you want to be wasted on the plantation fields?' Alessandro touched the top of his fist to his mouth before continuing. 'Write down the words that you whisper to make these patterns work. Then bring them to me. Do that and this tardiness will be forgotten.'

'These patterns are keys Cardinal. They unlock secrets that are held in darkness.'

'Out of the darkness and desecration, and into the light,' said Alessandro. Pleased that this new religion had started to sound just like his last, he could not help but give a half smile. 'This is not just about sex,' Alessandro heard himself saying, turning red, his embarrassment quickly turning into rage. 'Don't try and trick me with fucking patterns. You call women out of thin air, visions, the past and I think also, the future, which you see. That is what I want and that was our deal!'

'Cardinal...' Cieba's words were cut short.

'Who are you I wonder?' the Cardinal asked, his voice trembling. He stepped back from the light of the window to stand in the shadow. 'Tell me if it were not for Agustin, would it be you who murdered me?'

'You must listen...' Cieba tried again, moving away from the door and around the light shaft so that he stood on the opposite side of the chapel.

'Why do I fear you more than I fear footsteps in the dark or the devil at the window?' Alessandro's voice was weak and detached.

'Because I can teach you how to control your fears,' Cieba replied.

'I'm rotting in this forest. So teach me, that I might go back to the world. Free me of the hold that the devil has on me. Show me how I can relive my life' He waved the pages into the light.

'Cardinal, what you ask I cannot give you.'

'Do not lie to me, there is far more inside you than decadence. I have seen that paper from 1968.' The Cardinal's voice was gaining confidence. 'If you will not teach me, then write down the fucking words that you would have me whisper. Then I will release you.'

Outside came the sound of horses' hooves in the courtyard.

'We had an understanding Cieba. If you do not wish to fulfil that understanding, then why do you tempt me?'

'To humble you.'

'To humble me! You fool! When you came into my home you were a breath short of death,' Alessandro seethed. 'What gives you the authority to judge whether I am worthy of your skills? Fucking hell, I have feared enough now, and I have given enough!' With a sudden movement Alessandro rushed across the chapel to the door. 'Rodriguez!' he shouted. 'You can come in now!'

Into the shadows of the room, bringing with him the oppressive humidity of mid day, walked the bounty hunter. His entrance brought back the pain which had struck as the bullet wedged into Cieba's shoulder. Yet worse than the twist in his flesh was the sight of Mateus standing behind him.

'Did he offer you safety Mateus?' Cieba asked. There was no escape and he did not fight as Alessandro moved behind him and gripped both of his arms.

'I am so sorry,' Mateus was weeping. The rope he held, was yanked from his hands by the yelling Rodriguez. 'Give me the rope you idiot!'

'Enough is enough Cieba,' said Alessandro. 'You will know your place as a slave. If you won't teach me your precious words then nobody will hear them.' Rodriguez tied Cieba's hands together behind his back. Rodiani ran a hand over his hair, and wiped the sweat from his brow. Calmer he repeated. 'You will know your place.'

'I am so sorry,' Mateus repeated. 'He promised me that he'd spare us all from the plantations when the Cardinal returns to Italy.'

'I lied,' said Rodriguez, a cruel smile spreading across his face. He pulled a knife from the scabbard at his waist and plunged deep into Mateus stomach then again into his side. Mateus did not scream as the blood rose into his mouth, nor did he fight back. His fate was set, his dignity was undone. With a satisfied huff Rodriguez wiped his blade clean on Mateus who slumped back against the wall, his life departing before he lay still on the chapel floor.

'Now kneel, Cieba, man of Spirits,' whispered Alessandro from behind him. He kicked the back of Cieba's knees sending him to the floor and without his hands to counter the drop, he fell forward smacking his face into Mateus' blood.

'Look at him', sneered Rodriguez. 'What is his name again?'

'His name is Cieba, and when I've finished with him, he will be yours to sell.'

Cieba's eyes flickered shut, unconscious and lost even to the Pelecaras. When he woke he found himself tied to a chair in the small tutorial room. On the opposite side of the table Agustin had been bound to the other chair, his cheeks already bruised.

'He's awake,' Rodriguez said, he was standing behind Agustin and Alessandro was in the doorway.

'Good,' said Alessandro. 'Remind him we mean business.'

Rodriguez punched Agustin on the back of the head so that his face hit the table. Taveres then pulled him back by his white hair so Cieba could see the damage he had done.

'Now slave, listen to me, this is the last time I'm going to ask. Write down the words that control these patterns. Or I'll cut out Agustin's tongue.' Rodriguez said flatly. 'Such a shame don't you think?'

On the table between them lay Cieba's work. Copies of the scratched out patterns, first made by the Pelecaras, now here in black ink. Next to the paper were an ink well, a pen and a few blank pages. The top blank page had a bloodied finger print on it. In the doorway Alessandro was rocking gently, his shirt undone, his hair ruffled and messy, and his eyes fixed on the table.

Cieba cursed the Pelecaras. This was their work, and he had paid for it. In the five days it had taken to record their now detailed pathways, they had aged him rapidly by three and half years as punishment and price for these pages, even though he had shown them the gateways out. To make the wound worse he was unable to help the one man in his life he could truly call a friend.

'Calm down Alessandro,' Rodriguez said. 'This may take some time.'

'Calm, calm you say!' The Cardinal erupted, his face puce. 'You expect me to be fucking calm! This man has the secret to life Rodriguez, and all its pleasures and… you shot this slave dead and he's here alive in this room. He's learnt languages and…'

'I've shot a lot of slaves and I couldn't tell one from another,' Rodriguez said beginning to wonder if he should have stayed back in the town with his wine and the soft thighs of the woman he was bedding when Mateus had arrived.

'Well remember this one's face Rodriguez. If this witch doctor can do it why can't I, a man of God, wield the same power, think about it man! How many lives of men could I, could you and I live? With your taste for women and gold, wouldn't you like the chance never to grow old?'

'Alessandro, if you don't calm down, all will be lost,' Rodriguez said quietly.

'You are right Rodriguez, forgive me.' Alessandro flattened his hair back down and took a deep breath. 'Above all else Rodriguez I want to look into the future, be in charge of my life.' He sighed, 'For what is left of it.'

'Excellent Alessandro. Cieba,' Cieba's eyes rolled open and tried to focus. Rodriguez pulled the patterns in front of him. 'Take your time,' said Rodriguez gently, 'I'm going to turn these patterns over in front of you and I want you to point to the one that will give Alessandro here a glimpse into the future. Give him what he wants, then I will take you and Agustin away.'

Cattleya had begged him to kill men just like these and revenge grew deep within him. He would undo these murderers wholly and give them to Huayna. It would give him time to get away, and somehow repay Agustin for his friendship.

'That one,' Cieba managed to say when Rodriguez turned the fifth page.

'Good, good,' said Rodriguez. 'Well done. Now I will release one arm and you will write down the words Alessandro needs. Agreed?'

Cieba nodded, looking at Agustin through swollen eyes.

Onto the spare paper he wrote out in Latin the whispers he had heard in the dark and the words his grandfather Nasua had taught him. 'You will need at least a little extra light,' he said when he had finished. He took hold of the patterned page and marked dashes at intervals onto the lines. 'Place candles where these marks are. Do not step over these lines Cardinal, or your demons will kill you before you have the chance to enjoy yourself.'

Alessandro moved behind him to look over his shoulder and retie Cieba's free arm. The shaman's words were forcing his anger to surface. He would have control over this slave, he would know his place. With a fury he could not control he grabbed Cieba's jaw with both hands.

'Now cut out his tongue Rodriguez.'

'Huayna!' Cieba cried, but his jaw was seized so he could not move and they grabbed hold of his tongue to stop his words, his struggle was useless. Cieba felt the cold steel of Rodriguez's dirty blade slice through his tongue. His own blood nearly choking him before searing, unfathomable pain overwhelmed him and unconsciousness took hold.

Xapiripe spirits, that he had not seen for an age, poured out of the forests. Unseen, they threw open the gates to stand at the window and the open door. Seldom did one such as Cieba pass from the world. But Aratum started to whisper amongst them that he was not ready to give up his life.

Through the open window another horse could be heard, followed by a cough and the smell of tobacco.

'We're in here Tristao,' Rodriguez called. He pushed Cieba forward so he bled freely onto the table. He persuaded Alessandro to go and sit at the base of the stair outside the room. Once he was gone he whispered into Agustin's ear. 'This better work old man, or you're next.'

'What bloodied mess is this Rodriguez?' Maglanis said stepping passed the Cardinal. 'I thought we were supposed to be keeping the slaves alive.'

'Very funny Tristao. I am, for once, glad you could make it,' said Rodriguez. 'Now help me get Alessandro a bit of air. Then I need you to tidy up.'

Francesco had had Luca ready when Tristao arrived and he'd just managed to duck back into the stable to avoid being seen. He had no idea what had happened to Agustin. All he knew was that Rodriguez and Rodiani had taken Cieba inside and luckily none of them had noticed the cart made ready. All Francesco could do was watch Rodriguez reassure the ashen faced Cardinal outside the door, only leaving him to pat both his horses, who neighed when he turned away.

Francesco and Luca could just hear what he was saying to Alessandro.

'You should rest Alessandro, it's getting dark and the sky is full of rain.'

'I've told you. I don't want to rest. I just want to get on with it!' Rodiani replied.

Tristao walked out into the yard and showed his master a piece of paper.

'Good work Maglanis. Now shut those gates and help me draw out this pattern into the dust. Then we'll find some candles, if there are any in this ridiculous place.'

'They are still alive Luca,' Francesco dared to murmur in the stable. He could just see Rodriguez and the bemused Maglanis at work through a small gap beside the bottom hinge.

'Alessandro, we have copied out the pattern,' said Rodriguez giving the sheet of paper to the Cardinal. 'Now you should call out these words he has written. I just hope it's worth it.'

'It's no use,' shouted Maglanis, 'if the wind doesn't blow them out, the rain in those clouds will.'

Alessandro read out the words on the paper as the candle flames struggled at to stay alive. Rodriguez knelt at the flame closest to him trying to nurture it against the breeze from the courtyard gate. Having succeeded with the first he moved onto the next.

'Maglanis, help me,' Rodriguez yelled at his captain, who did as he was told.

'Excellent,' shouted Rodiani as more flames grew in strength around him. They twisted and licked the darkening sky, growing in confidence, defying the thunder rumbling above.

'Repeat those words again,' Rodriguez shouted over his shoulder. Helped by a sudden drop in the breeze the flames lit up the three men, who drifted toward each other into the middle of the pattern.

'Il cerchio diavoli,' the Cardinal said under his breath reaching the bottom of the page for the third time. He folded the paper in half and pushed it into his shirt.

'Well, what now?' asked Maglanis

The question was answered firstly by the flame in front of him, then followed by the rest. All grew twice their height and more, then, as suddenly as they had risen, each flame simultaneously blew out, taking with them what was left of the daylight and plunging the men into a darkness so deep they could not see each other.

'What a waste of time,' Maglanis said, kicking the ground beneath him.

'Ssh look,' Rodriguez said, 'it's actually working.' He was pointing to the candle furthest from them that had re-kindled. Others followed, illuminating the courtyard buildings, except that in this light the stones and plaster had started to disintegrate and crumble, revealing behind them the trunks of the forest trees. With the buildings completely gone the men now stood in a wide woodland clearing, the candles just lighting the lowest leaves of the canopy above. No sooner had the image clarified itself, than it started to blur. Displaced by an unseen force, it began to rotate slowly.

Rodriguez felt the hand of Tristao upon his shoulder, Alessandro stood alone. The steady rotation gathered apace, pulling with it the candle flame so that they were surrounded by a smooth wall of flame, silent at first, then as the vortex gained momentum it hummed quickly creating a deafening, debilitating sheet of sound.

Images pushed aside the flame in front of them, as the Pelecaras depicted what they saw most in the three men's hearts; violence, greed, women and exploitation. It was a future without love, or embrace, and behind it all Huayna stood, his hands strong with flesh, dictating the flow of the flame.

The three men were transfixed as the voiceless visions grew and dispersed in turn. Amongst them the bitter war of American independence, and the flare-lit skies of World War One, both unbiased in their rotting corpses and unrelenting death. Momentarily through the flame a deep black line flickered and seeping through it came the faceless Pelecaras. Translucent and cold. More terrifying and unyielding than any nightmare, they cackled with delight, walking between the men as the wall began to form images again.

Then the five spirits started to whisper.

It was Rodriguez who first began to see profit in the evil in front of him and the women who appeared. Oh the women, at least a thousand, yes there must be a thousand. Except suddenly his revelation was badly marred by the increasingly deafening noise. Even with his hands clasped tightly to his bleeding ears, he was unable to concentrate. He felt sick and unsteady, and couldn't stop himself kneeling down to vomit. With his hands pressed hard at his ears he passed out.

For Alessandro and Maglanis, after the trenches, and a vision of desperate poverty they watched a crushed nation of thousands raise their angry arms to follow one man in his bid to create a German Reich.

'Oh but for the glory of God,' Alessandro wept as he saw what looked like angels fall from the sky. Thousands and thousands of them, white against a dark sky, illuminated by what must be the bellowing flames of hell.

Helped by Huayna, Maglanis saw the napalm clouds of Vietnam and there in the heart of the burning tree line stood a figure. It was the native, the one Rodriguez had shot in the town, and somehow the same one who sat in the house. He beckoned to Maglanis, tempting him to follow, but as the bounty hunter touched the wall of the vortex, the Indian disappeared only to be replaced by a dying woman who held her bloodied hands at her ruptured stomach. Tristao closed his eyes but the image was still there, no matter what he did the woman would not disappear. This was too much, this had to stop and it abruptly did when Atoc could stand his screaming no more.

With Maglanis at his feet, Alessandro watched another figure approach. It was a man, his devil incarnate in the form of Father Marcus. He was throwing something up into the air and catching it, at first Alessandro saw it as his sandal, but as he got closer the object was rounder and white. When he reached the edge of the swirling mass, Father Marcus was transformed into another who stood for a moment, the ball still in hand. The man pushed a hand through the vortex causing the interrupted flow to break in black veins that stretched out like the lead in the windows of St Sebastian.

'It's really quite beautiful isn't it,' the man said.

'Who are you?' Alessandro shouted.

'My name is Joshua,' the man replied. Reaching out a hand to touch the Cardinal's forehead, he ran his clean fingers over Rodiani's thinning hair, then back across his cheek and up over his eyebrows, where he hesitated to increase his pressure and close the Cardinal's eyes to darkness.

On the opposite side of the disappearing vortex, Francesco had waited for this moment to rescue his friends. Using his strength he managed to bundle them, one by one, into the open cart, and get the gate fully open. He shooed Rodriguez's frightened horses away and set off down the track.

'Come on Luca, we'll get to the town and make for the river,' Francesco said to his pony. 'If we're really lucky my friend, this lot will be dead!'

In the courtyard Rodriguez was the first to recover and was stumbling about trying not to be sick again. 'No no, no,' Rodriguez said, shaking, the noise still screaming in his head. He stumbled over to the house to get some water, when he realised that his two victims had fled.

'Maglanis!' he called 'We need to get that slave back.'

Tristao rose with a groan, his eyes hurt and his vision was blurred. He stumbled to his feet making his way to Rodriguez. 'Christ I feel like we've just woken from one of your parties back in Portugal,' he laughed.

'So long as we get that slave back, it's a night we can relive, now that Alessandro has the keys.'

'He can't be allowed to give up those secrets to anybody else,' said Maglanis.

'Then go and catch him. We'll take him to the Richardson Plantation,' said Alessandro sternly, rising from the ground and rubbing his eyes. Stepping forward he stumbled over an object, bent down and picked it up. 'If he is planting sugar cane, at least we know where to get him when we need to. The whip will keep him out of trouble.'

'And the other two?' Rodriguez asked. 'Agustin has been with you a long time?'

'Do as you please Rodriguez.'

'Right Maglanis,' said Rodriguez, 'it would appear that now we are both working for the Cardinal.' He called their horses, who had not gone far, and returned at his whistle. Maglanis loaded their muskets and they mounted their horses, swiftly riding out onto the track.

Francesco and Luca had made good headway under the starlit sky, but they were no match for the mounted steeds which pursued them. Hindered on the longest open part of the track where the rain had caused the ruts to deepen further, their journey was slowed to a crawl.

'I hope you get to gaze upon the sea again old man,' said Francesco. 'Just like in your dream.'

'Now that would be a fine thing,' Agustin replied groggily from behind him.

TWENTY-ONE

Catherine's last wish

A loud blast from the musket of Rodriguez Taveres sent birds into the night sky and silenced the monkeys of the forest. His shot just clipped the tail gate of Francesco's cart causing Luca to jerk forward. It was the second shot that thudded into the driver, who arched his back as it smashed into his vertebrae. All Agustin could do was try and reach out to Francesco, but it was too late, he was dead.

Frightened, Luca pulled as hard as he could, his lack of direction lifting the cart out of the ruts and tipping it over, spilling its load out into the road. Still semi-conscious, Cieba barely heard Rodriguez and Maglanis discuss how to dispose of the bodies of his friends.

'That, Maglanis, has to be one of the best shots I have ever seen!' Rodriguez said from his horse.

'Well, Rodriguez, it is good that you praise me. You just needed to be a little more patient and let that moonlight break through. You know when firing on horseback I always lean back a little more. If you are quick, the angle...'

'Yes Maglanis, I think I know how to shoot on horse back.'

'Of course Rodriguez but I always kill first time, and never try and kill more than one man with each shot.' Maglanis was going to enjoy his moment against his former employer.

244

'You know Maglanis, you should not let a bit of luck go to your head, now let's collect what we came for.'

Both men dismounted and inspected the bodies. They pulled Francesco into the trees and went back for Agustin who had hit his head badly and was barely breathing.

'Put a knife in him Maglanis, to finish him off. I've left my blade with Alessandro.'

'Rodriguez…'

'Just hurry up.'

'Rodriguez I cannot bring myself to kill him. He is a man of God.'

'So was that man,' Rodriguez pointed into the trees after Francesco.

'No Rodriguez, no this is completely different. This man is from Italy. A man who has stood inside the Vatican and kissed the hand of the Pope himself.'

'How do you know this?'

'Rodriguez, Let him die in peace, he has done us no harm.'

Rodriguez crouched down and thought. 'Very well. Let's drag him into the trees so Alessandro won't see him when we come this way later.'

When they had moved Agustin, Cieba felt himself pulled out of the mud and laid back onto the cart. He heard the thwack of the reins on Luca's back, followed by the turn of the wheels.

'We cannot turn Rodriguez, there is not enough room,' Maglanis said out of breath, after several attempts to get Luca to pull the cart in any direction but forward.

'Alright, alright. You take the cart into the town, and find a boat for us. I will follow with Alessandro. We will meet you by the well.'

'Please,' said Maglanis with a smirk.

'What?'

'I would like you to say please.'

'Tristao Maglanis I ask you to do this and you refuse, after the way I've always looked after you. Listen to me, we need to work together or that crazy bastard back there will ruin everything he has just stumbled upon. Unless, that is of course, you want to deal with him yourself.'

'No of course not.'

'So please,' Rodriguez said, pinching the bridge of his nose.

'Understood, I'll meet you in the town by the well,' Tristao pulled on the reins.

Even after all that had happened Rodriguez was disturbed to find the Cardinal walking down the moonlit track towards him. He wasn't carrying any bags and no longer wore any remnant of his fine clothes. Instead he had put on an old shirt, which he had left open, and he was toying with something, passing it between his hands and throwing into the air to catch it.

'Cardinal Rodiani are you quite well?' There was no response other than a half smile and a direct stare. 'Rodiani we have a long journey ahead. Would it not be wise to take a few financial provisions, rather than just that.'

Alessandro smiled again and pulled a ring from each index finger. 'These are set with precious stones and will fetch a small fortune at the docks.'

'What is that?' Rodriguez asked, pointing at Alessandro's hand.

'A ball. It's from in there... I think the man I saw, was trying to give it to me.'

'Again, Cardinal, I really think it would be best if we went back to your safe. Or dare I ask, have you spent all of the church's money?'

'No, I will not go back, and at least for now call me Alessandro. It's time for a change of faith I think. So, if you want to have any part of this magical future, we move only forward. Do you understand me?'

'Yes Alessandro, I hope that I do.'

Two hours after he had been left to die, Agustin heard his master's voice from the road and kept his body flat amongst the trees until they had gone. In the end is was an ant's bite which got him to his feet and where there was one, it rapidly felt like there were a thousand crawling down his shirt and across his back. Agustin swiped at his shoulders and grabbed at his shirt to try and remove them, he knew however that there was only one course of action. So, pushing his way back between the trees, he stumbled out onto the track and removed his shirt and trousers to be sure. It took him the whole length of the rosary prayer he was reciting to ensure he was clean. It was then he realised he was naked, his aging pale skin exposed to the night's wilderness.

'This would be funny if you were not lying there Francesco!' Agustin said catching his breath and looking into the trees. He picked up his clothes from the side of the track and contemplated his next move. His head ached from the blow to it, in fact his whole exhausted body hurt. Taking in a deep breath he straightened himself up and looked back down the track.

'I think I will put my trust in you Fernandez, drink a little wine and sleep. Maybe in the morning I will decide what to do,'

Agustin said. Trying not to fall over as he stepped down into the nearest rut, he spotted at the edge of the puddle, his beads. Still feeling nauseous he bent over to pick them up managing to drop his trousers into the water as he did so.

'You know even in death Francesco, I expect you're laughing.'

Straightening himself up once more, Agustin made his way slowly back to Alessandro's old fortress. He found clean clothes, ate, and was surprised to find Rodiani's room much the same as when he'd last cleaned it. He looked at the papers all ready to go and chanced to see if the safe had been emptied, it had not, so he emptied it himself, placing the money in a satchel of his own, and took it down to the kitchen.

It was only as he sat down to eat that he sensed he was not alone. 'Mateus,' he said to himself making his way out into the courtyard. He knew where his companion was without taking another step. He knew too that he was dead and that he himself should leave quickly. Gathering what food he could carry Agustin headed back towards the gate. With a bit of luck the others would have left by the time he arrived in the town.

'Forgive me Mateus but I have not the strength to bury you nor bring your cousin back here. I will, however, put an end to your ill fated house Fernandez. God willing, the trees will grow quickly over the track and leave my friends in more peace than he did.'

With everything he could carry at the gate ready, Agustin placed some straw and firewood as far into the chapel door as he dared. Signing the cross, he went back up to the Cardinal's room one last time. He lit the papers his master had toiled over and took the flame around the house and into the chapel doorway. Lastly he placed a lighted candle into the stable and watched it quickly ignite the straw.

'Time to leave you old fool' he said as he gathered his belongings and headed for Praia da Viera saying a short prayer for Francesco as he passed him, but he did not slow his pace, for fear his heart may break. Instead he walked on, more resolute in his faith with every step that he took. Not for the first time he surmised God had failed. Yet with the rosary in his hand, he was restored. How many had failed God? How many had been distracted away from the purity of his creation by their own greed? If God was guilty, it was in that alone, he would not be drawn by the demands of the individual, which, however wrong, would leave the Cardinal's indiscretions unnoticed and unpunished.

'Life should be simple,' Agustin said to himself, then laughed. 'You old fool,' he repeated.

Amongst the trees nothing mattered, especially when the open stretches lit by the moon ended, and the track turned to avoid some unforgiving obstacle. Here the canopy above touched, plunging his path into darkness and Agustin could do no more than place one foot in front of the other until the branches opened up again.

Having spent most of his journeys to Praia da Viera nodding off, Agustin had never marked their progress by feature, tree or turn in the track, only by the escape of sleep. However he noticed a hoof print in the mud, and then another marking out Luca's steady gait. Life, it would seem, had gone on, that thought was enough to bring bittersweet tears to his eyes.

Their pony had come with the property, so the story went. Chosen and named by Consuela at the port of St Paolo.

Originally from Argentina, Luca was a Criollo horse, who showed all the sturdy characteristics of his breed, except that he had never reached the same stature as his parents and his roan coat had been passed over in favour of the thirty or so chestnut mares which had been for sale at the market that day. All but Consuela had missed Luca's charm and so Fernandez had dutifully bought and transported him inland to their new home. Luca loved the cool of the stable and the care Consuela took to make sure her groom washed him everyday after her ride up the track. She had even insisted the men clear a loop around the house so she could gallop him through the trees.

Along with her affection Luca also felt her pain when he had to pull Fernandez from the chapel back into town to be buried. After the funeral, he carted what belongings Consuela had left up to the boat and felt her kiss as she departed. Then for five and a half years he was used to herd cattle or cart the town's people, until a rumour spread that a Cardinal would soon be residing amongst them. The town gave him the only gift they thought appropriate. Luca could cart him down to the Fernandez house and Luca, they assumed, would soon be carting such a dignitary back.

Older and wiser the pony remembered it all as he waited by the well in Praia da Viera. Maglanis had carried Cieba away as soon as Rodriguez had turned up with the Cardinal. All four had left without a word, leaving him strapped to the cart and exhausted. Hours passed, until just before the sun rose, two children ran over to him, stroked his nose and ran off. It was then that Agustin arrived, his arms aloft with a big smile on his face.

'Luca I have never been more glad to see you.'

With the rising sun came locals who found Luca and Agustin a stable to sleep in. They told of the theft of a canoe and the abandonment of two fine horses. They were willing to take Luca back too, but bowed to Agustin's wishes and sold him and the pony a place on a boat heading down river. If they got as far as Itaituba without incident, the crew would help secure the pair transport to St Santarem, from where he could travel to Sao Luis.

From the sea port of Sao Luis Agustin hoped to buy a place for them both on a ship heading home to Italy. For now, his oarsman reminded him, they had to make the first step and get Luca into a canoe which he would not tip over. After much discussion and a few more coins from Agustin's satchel the locals strapped three canoes together and gently persuaded the pony over some planks and on board. To everyone's relief Luca remembered his journey here and soon stood in the centre canoe. His weight counterbalanced by an oarsman in each corner of the outside canoes. Agustin took up position in front of Luca holding his reins and seated himself on a bundle of hay.

A bright morning welcomed their departure, and for the first week the weather stayed settled, allowing the group comfortable progress. Each night they camped on the shoreline and let Luca stretch his patient legs and after a few days the exercise seemed to stimulate his bowel movements which in turn made the journey more comfortable. Onward the river took them, meandering ever north and east, regularly picking up smaller streams that dissected the forest on either side, always pushing back the tree lined banks. The daily repetition took three and a half weeks before a village opened up on the left bank. Its occupants rushing down to the water's edge to see the travelling companions with Luca standing proud at the centre. Waving and laughing, the boys were quick to swim out to meet the boat.

They offered food and shelter in exchange for Luca's help to move a fallen tree. It gave a well earned rest and their two day stay set a precedent for the rest of their journey. A further four weeks passed before the town of Itaituba marked the end of the journey for the men from Praia da Viera. Except they would not be parted, such was the bond that had grown between them. They sent a letter back to the town with Agustin's word that he would turn them around at St Santarem, persuading the men that he feared further contact with the growing European population there, would expose them to diseases they had no protection from.

Their journey took fully eight more weeks to arrive at St Santarem. They'd been hampered by rain, humidity and the joining of rivers which pushed and fought for control of their makeshift boat. However, no matter how glad to be on dry land Agustin was, true to his word he insisted that as soon as they had unloaded on a sandy beach not far from the town's outskirts, the crew should turn round and return home. Dutifully they agreed and accepted the extra coins to spend on their families. The gold that they received from Agustin would at least pay for each to build a new family house in Praia da Viera.

Other than his crew, nobody had seen Agustin land that afternoon, so, as he walked into St Santarem, word of his arrival spread quickly before him. A man of God with nothing but a satchel and a pony walking out of nowhere was miraculous and worth attention. Of the many who came to bow their heads in respect, a few approached to seek his touch. Overwhelmed, and at first humoured Agustin could do little more than play along and hope to get transport to St Luis as quickly as possible.

After a mile or two, a monk moved forward from the back of the transitory crowd. He bowed and offered shelter, which was gratefully accepted. As they walked together, still with the crowd behind, Agustin felt suddenly resistant to discuss his history and, as the protection of a large church loomed in front, he felt anxiety rise from within. Claustrophobia crept across his back and he inadvertently pulled on Luca's rein.

'Forgive me but I must take care of Luca,' Agustin said.

'Of course but we have much to discuss, allow us to feed and bed your pony. All will be well Agustin.'

'No. No, with respect our journey has been long and I must see to him myself.'

'You are a devout and selfless friend indeed,' the monk replied showing Agustin the way and then dispersing the crowd.

Outside the stables, Agustin asked for water to wash down Luca and then requested solitude, he was tired he told them and needed to meditate before he could eat. Humbled by his intention, the monks agreed and thankfully left him in peace. Once they had gone Agustin sighed wearily and sat down on the hay beside Luca, who did not stir from his own recumbent position.

It did not take long for them to fall asleep, only to be woken by an English accent, something Agustin had not heard since two London dock hands had been unloading at the Lisbon quay.

'I tell you Peters, we could search from here to Rome itself, and we ain't never gonna find a priest to see him.'

'Well Mr Smith. He'll just have to die without a blessing. Some might say that's what he deserves anyhow.' This second voice was much younger than the first.

'You mind your tongue. We're doing what his missus would have wanted and that's a fact. You think of all the times she helped us out on that stinking plantation.' The first voice was deep and gritty, the second lighter but nonetheless coarse.

'Yeah sure, but who have we got to thank for bringing us here in the first place. Catherine didn't take us back with her did she Mr Smith, I mean if we meant that much to her she would have, wouldn't she?' Peters said.

'That's Mrs Richardson to you, and she left us here to look after him. She didn't know he was going to get sick, did she? So stop blaming her. All the time Mr Richardson is alive we have to honour her last wish and look after him till he's dead.' Smith was almost growling. 'So show some bloody respect boy or keep your mouth shut.'

'Sorry Mr Smith but… but we've been here for two days. What's the next town, Manaus? He'll be dead by the time we get back from there.'

'If we have to, that's where we'll go.'

'But…'

'But nothing… now that's enough. Get your head down I don't want to hear anymore from you till the morning.'

Despite the quiet that followed, Agustin could not get back to sleep. He waited many patient hours late into the night until he could no longer cope with his active mind. 'This is no good,' Agustin whispered to Luca, and stood up as quietly as possible to creep out of the stable into the empty, silent streets of the town. Thankful for the peace, he walked on, settling on a route which took him to the water's edge. It didn't take long for the river to come into view, the sound of its movement calming his mind. There was nothing for it but to remove his sandals and walk out onto the sand and into the water. Behind him a few house lights flickered to mark the town and in front the stars were mirrored by the water. Agustin took a deep breath and let his tight shoulders relax. He was at last peaceful enough to think properly of his brother.

'I miss you Piero. I am sorry my friend that you ever set foot on that ship, and I wish you were here with me now. My journey home brother... seems to only get harder.'

He stood in the water for so long that the stars began to fade and the first chink of dawn appeared on the eastern horizon. Agustin walked back, barefoot, to the stable passing the entrance to a church, its door was closed and he left it so, choosing instead to wake Mr Smith with his own broken English.

They would ride south east to their sugar plantation where Agustin would tend the last breaths of its master, Samuel Richardson. With a well cushioned saddle and a great deal of help to get onto Luca's forgiving back, Agustin rode for the first time in forty years and quickly remembered why it had been so long. He would endure the lack of dignity, provided the cushions protected his piles. Outside of the town the landscape changed dramatically, forest gave way to scattered trees and fields. Cattle grazed on either side of the road and ranchers acknowledged their passing by tilting their wide brimmed hats, whilst they smoked the potent cigars which, he remembered, Maglanis coveted so much.

During their journey Smith and Peters told of their employer, of his diligence to perfect efficiency and of his disregard of the slaves who died to achieve it.

'Course he's only gotten worse since his Mrs went home. She couldn't stand it anymore. Don't reckon she ever wanted to come here in the first place,' said Peters.

'It's her father's place you see,' Smith explained. 'Forced them to come here after they found out they couldn't give him a grandchild. She told me once that her father was ashamed.'

'Mr Smith, this sounds like your confession. Should I not be hearing this from Mr Richardson himself?' Agustin said. This silenced his companion's indiscretions for the rest of the journey and kept their chatter to the hot meals of their home countries and the praise they had for the ponies they rode.

They made as much progress as Agustin would let them, often slowing or even stopping Luca to adjust his seating position. They bedded down overnight in an empty building at the side of the road and made an early start the following morning. Within a few hours the open countryside reverted back to woodland that funnelled the road until they arrived at a set of huge metal gates crossing their path. On either side stood two uniformed guards armed with rifles and swords. Once greeted, one of them ran ahead, leaving the other to swing open and close one side of the gateway. Following the runner's lead, the company rode through an avenue of trees which curved away in a wide arch opening up to finally reveal a magnificent plantation house which rose three storeys high in front of them. The ground floor was fronted by a series of arches, dissected by a set of stone steps zigzagging up to meet a balustrade which ran the whole width of the first floor and concealed a balcony. Upwards, large blocks of grey stone assembled the first floor; the second was rendered and painted white. With five sash windows on the centre block and two on each of the wings, the building was finished with a greyish slate roof much the same colour as Luca's coat.

Just to the right of the centre stone steps a man appeared and lent against the balustrade. Tall, even by Maglanis' standards, Samuel Richardson was dressed in the finest of clothes, his hair was greyed and his face drawn.

'How deep is that planting on the far eastern bloc Mr Smith?' asked Richardson, disregarding any form of greeting. He was well spoken, his English diction perfect, given its volume.

'Six inches deep sir, as you prescribed,' replied Smith.

Samuel screwed his eyes up at Agustin before continuing his welcome.

'Don't just sit there both of you, get the priest off that cart horse before it collapses beneath him.' This time he just suppressed a cough at the end of his instruction. Waving his hand in the air he shouted as best he could. 'Now gentlemen. Now!' With that he disappeared inside the house.

'We'd best go after him Father Agustin,' Smith said dismounting his own horse and passing his reins to Peters, before helping the older man get off Luca.

'Don't worry; we'll take good care of your pony. If it's one thing we've got here, it's fine stables,' Peters said turning to gesture over two tall African men who kept their heads bent low as they approached. Dressed in white cotton shirts and blue waistcoats, they lead the horses away.

'Go with them Peters,' Richardson said unseen from above, unable to prevent a dry cough this time. 'Well don't just stand there, come up,' he called, his voice getting fainter as he walked away.

'This way Father,' Mr Smith gestured up the stone steps in front of them.

'Please Mr Smith. Just call me Agustin.'

On the first floor balcony they were met by the round smiling face of a buxom, middle aged woman. She held open her arms to greet them, and quickly became overwhelmed, wiping tears from her eyes with her apron.

'Oh thank God you could come Father!' she said, not knowing whether to curtsey, bow or cross herself, but her attempts to do all three at once made Agustin smile warmly.

'Please, my name is Agustin and you have Mr Smith to thank, not God this time.'

'Oh,' the woman replied, again not sure of what to do.

'This, Agustin, is my wife. Mrs Elsie Smith,' Mr Smith said proudly.

'And you must call me Elsie,' Elsie said settling on her own big smile this time.

'Very good,' Agustin nodded in acknowledgement, then looked towards the open door.

Just visible inside the shadows of the entrance hall stood a steely faced guard. He did not move as they passed, or utter a word. Agustin would have thought him cadaverous, but for a blink of the sentry's eye.

'When will that block be finished Mr Smith?' Richardson said out of sight, and above the stairs which curved up against the left hand wall of the room that was at least fifteen yards across.

'The block should be finished today,' replied Smith as he followed Agustin into the house. 'After that we'll be ready to start planting over on the western block tomorrow.'

'How many dead?' their employer asked his voice growing weary.

'None as of three days ago, but thirty-two over on the east side last week and I believe, sir, that they had to shoot three due to dysentery…'

There was no reply this time and they waited for some further indication as to how far they should go into the house.

'So all is well sir!' Smith said mustering a positive air.

'Yes I see Mr Smith. Elsie! Have the priest cleaned up. I'll be in my room,' This last sentence was finished with a tortuous cough from Richardson that was so agonisingly long it left even the guard looking painfully at Agustin.

'Follow me Agustin,' Elsie said reaching out to tug on his habit. She led him away from her husband and through a large ornately decorated room to their left. The ceilings were high and the large windows made the space light and airy. At the other end of the room Elsie turned and gave a half smile before she spoke. Nervously playing with her apron, her east end accent was as difficult for Agustin to follow as her husband's. 'I don't think he's got long left now. Hasn't left the house in two weeks. Just wanders up and down the stairs from his room to the balcony.'

'At least he is getting some air,' Agustin replied.

Elsie turned her back to him and headed off through a door to an adjoining room much the same as the one they were in, and then on through another door into a stairwell which led down to the washroom and kitchen. She kept talking, occasionally turning round to catch Agustin's eye. 'She left two years ago. Broke his heart it did. Ever since then, he ain't never been right. We reckon, course, that it was that what brought him down.'

'Has he been seen by a doctor?'

'Twice. Once to tell him he had cancer of the lungs. Then he came two weeks ago to tell us he…' Elsie had to stop and wipe away her gathering tears. 'That's when I insisted that Mr Smith went and found a priest. Catherine, that's his wife, well she said that he needs to make his peace with God before she would talk to him again. The saddest thing is he won't write, won't even tell her he's dying' Elsie had to stop to wipe her face again. When she had finished, Agustin took her hand in comfort.

'Hush my child,' he said plucking words out of the air. 'I will hear his confession and ease his passing.'

Left alone in the washroom at the bottom of the stairs, Agustin ran cold water over his face and through his white hair. He leant over to let the water fall from his head into the sink, watching the light from the window above catch the last droplets as they petered out. It had been a long time since he had heard confession from anyone other than Cardinal Rodiani, and those had always been steered by his mixture of sexual guilt and substance abuse. Often, those sessions had ended with a turning of the tables and a lecture about Agustin's own inadequacies; they always left the Cardinal free from absolution.

Agustin shook his head to dislodge more water from his hair. Since they had arrived here in Brazil the name of Samuel Richardson had been synonymous with the brutality of the sugar plantations. Richardson was, after all, supplied by Rodriguez, and if he and the Cardinal had been, or were still, here, his own life would surely be forfeit to this gamble.

Reaching for a towel to dry himself Agustin tried to clear his mind. The house was so silent he could hear the clock in the room above strike three then another followed suit in the kitchen outside. He heard Elsie's feet approach across the stone floor and her hand hesitating at the door before she knocked.

'Would you like a drink Agustin?' she asked quietly. 'Or... shall we just go up?'

'I would be grateful, I think Elsie, for a small glass of water.'

The water she gave him was warm, but still refreshing. Placing the empty glass back in Elsie's hand, Agustin waited for her to place it down then fill another and collect some handkerchiefs from her washroom. She led him back up the stairs and through the two ornate rooms into the entrance hall. The sentry acknowledged their presence with a raise of his head.

'Follow me,' Elsie said leading him up the wide stair. They ascended onto a landing that stretched the entire width of the building, at either end of which a window allowed light to spill in. The walls held no adornments and had been painted light blue to make the most of the natural light. On both sides closed white doors indicated the rooms beyond, and following Elsie to the left, Agustin waited as she knocked.

The door was opened by a negro slave dressed in the same uniform as the stable hands had been, white linen and blue waistcoat.

'Thank you William,' Elsie said. 'Is Mr Smith in here?'

'Yes Ma'am, he is with Mr Richardson.' William stood back from the door and bowed slightly to Agustin without ever taking his eyes off him.

'This is Father Agustin, William; don't look so fearful he is here to help Mr Richardson.'

'Yes Ma'am,' William replied still not taking his eyes off Agustin.

'I mean you no harm William…' Agustin tried to say.

'I think perhaps you may be excused William'

'Yes Ma'am,' William said backing out of the door and closing it as he left.

'He is more frightened of you than the slave traders, Agustin,' Elsie said leading him further into the first of two rooms which made up her employers quarters. The coughing from the other side of the adjoining door indicated where he was.

Mr Smith came through, looking worried, he seemed to have aged in the short time since they had last met. Smith silently exchanged the blooded handkerchiefs he held for the clean ones in Elsie's hand.

'Please, let me,' Agustin said taking the small cotton squares. 'Let me go to him.'

'As you wish Father,' Mr Smith said, conceding to the offer opening the door.

'So, priest. Have you come to crucify and damn my soul for the sins of my family?' Samuel asked, as soon as Agustin had closed the door behind him. He was seated facing towards a large window framed by long white linen drapes that brushed against the floor. Another step forward and Agustin could see out onto the estate beyond. The light that came in gave colour to the washed out face of a once tall and handsome man. His host coughed and continued 'Or have you come to give the absolution that Cardinal Rodiani would not?'

Stopped in his tracks by the Cardinal's name, Agustin watched Samuel spit into the last dry corner of his handkerchief. He had to dig deep to realise that their names had not been connected.

'How long has it been since your last confession child?'
Agustin asked as calmly as he could.

'How long, how long?' Samuel said pulling himself out of
his chair and crossing the room to the mantelpiece of an unlit
fire, the hearth stacked with wood in readiness. Samuel looked
above it to a painting of a woman. 'If you knew her, if only for
the briefest moments, you would understand why she left.' He
sighed. 'I doubt however you want to discuss the frailties of my
marriage.'

'God is listening,' Agustin said.

'Before we came to this place. Catherine and I travelled
through France, Italy, and Greece. Italy was by far our
favourite.' He laughed, almost beneath his breath. 'Catherine
fell pregnant, and we returned to England. But Father,
Catherine lost the baby. The physicians told us that the fever
which followed had rendered her infertile.' Samuel reached out
for the mantelpiece to steady himself.

'To us everything in society became staid and stuffy and
Catherine's mood darkened. Frustrated by her despair her
father decided that we were to move here, away from her
family. He gave us money to build this house on his plantation.'
Richardson laughed again. 'Catherine said we could make it into
a bit of Italy, a bit of that beauty, here in a place so raw. I even
used Palladio as my inspiration for the house.' There was a
moment's silence as he caught his breath, followed by an
attempt to laugh that turned into a disjointed snigger. 'You
know I even bought Vasari's books to inspire me to paint.'
Samuel moved back and sat in his chair. 'Her father of course
hated me for my love of art.'

'Here in our perfect home Father, a house so well
proportioned that you wouldn't want to leave its walls… that

was the idea… here I could paint and emulate great artists.' He pointed back to the canvas above the fire place. 'Her portrait is my best work I think.' Samuel sighed his mind drifting as he spoke. 'Catherine used to let her hand fall over the side of the gondola; she'd trail a finger in the water…'

Agustin followed Samuel and looked out of the window again.

'Disgusting isn't it Father?' Samuel said sitting back into his chair.

'The world changes under the influence of men Samuel. God it would seem is often powerless to stop that.'

'I had no choice, her father called in our debt. The man in charge here was moved on, and there isn't much time for painting when quotas need to be met.'

In the silence that followed a shot rang out from somewhere unseen, its resonance clawing into the room causing Samuel to draw his legs up as if he himself had been hit. He pulled his head down so he sat poised in the foetal position, a whimper underlining his broken resolve.

'Did Cardinal Rodiani have anybody with him?' Agustin asked without compassion.

'Tavares and two others.' Samuel slowly lifted his head and replied at length.

'One was a slave?'

'Yes, left here for safe keeping.' Samuel put his feet down and turned to face Agustin. 'They threatened me with my own daggers,' he pointed a shaking hand to a side board, where only one ceremonial dagger rested on a frame made for two. 'Why?' Samuel asked.

'There is a way, child, that you may be able to gain some redemption in my eyes, if not in the face of God.'

It took little over an hour for Cieba to arrive in Samuel's room. Dressed in the same muddied beige smocks that all the plantation workers wore, he looked as wasted as he had done when they had last met. His elation though was overwhelming, lighting up the depressed air that hung in the house and filling Agustin's heart with joy as they embraced.

'It's doubtful that Rodriguez will have time to inflict revenge on me for letting him go,' Samuel said. 'So take him Agustin, for what ever purpose you see fit. Be warned though, this man is a valuable asset that the Cardinal will seek out, wherever you may hide.'

'I think Samuel, from the little I understand, it's a risk I'm willing to take.'

'And my path is set,' Samuel replied, looking up to the painting of his wife.

'Your confession is done child,' Agustin said placing a hand upon Samuel's head.

'Without penitence?'

'Write to your wife Samuel. Tell her how much you love her and say goodbye.'

They left Samuel in front of his window with a small table to write on, and as the hot evening air was dispelled by a steady night breeze, he passed on from his life dreaming of Catherine's love, and the freedom they had once shared.

Agustin spoke quietly as they loaded Samuel's body into a cart at dawn the next day. Accompanied by Mr Smith and Peters they buried him not far from the derelict house they had slept in two days before. Better here than in a place he wholeheartedly despised.

'Take this,' Smith said, handing Agustin a dagger. 'It's the other dagger from his room. Sell it or use it to keep you safe.

Either way I think you should have it rather than the next governor!'

'Yeah, you never know when you'll need it. You might as well take this too,' Peters said producing a wallet of papers. 'This belonged to that Cardinal. Reckon it must be religious cos I ain't seen patterns like it for anything else.'

'Is that all of them?' Smith asked getting more agitated as he looked at the folder. 'You'll forgive me if it is religious Agustin, but I don't want that anywhere near me. God may strike me down if I burned it, so please take it.'

'It's alright Mr Smith, blimey. As far as I am aware yes that's all of it. There must be twenty all in all.'

'You are, I'm afraid two pages short,' Agustin said, realising what he was being proffered.

'I am so sorry Father,' Smith said, 'Peters here will return to the house and collect them for you.' Cieba raised a hand to decline the invitation. 'Then Peters, you can deal with them when we get back. I just hope that Rodiani don't come back for them.'

'Very well. Then these are yours I think,' Agustin passed the wallet of patterns to Cieba.

'Thank you Agustin for all that you have done for us,' Peters was unsure of how to conclude their time together. 'You are indeed a man of God,' he said as he patted Lucas' flank.

'Then God be with you both,' Agustin said flicking the reins to stir Luca and head toward St Luis.

'So we let time unfold my friend,' Agustin turned to Cieba at his side on the seat of the cart. 'I think, if you have no objections we'll change our names and wet our feet in the Alassio sea.'

PART THREE

TWENTY-TWO

Lilly Tastes Sweet Revenge

'I wish to God the spring would at least make an effort to break through,' Molly sighed, her breath clouding against the cold window pane. She was slight enough to fit into its recess without her silhouette obscuring the common beyond. Molly touched a finger against the new patch of condensation, clearing just enough to see the white frost on the trees outside. She shivered and pulled up the dark blue shawl around her shoulders. 'I'm so sick of the winter, so sick of the cold and...'

'Well, come and sit closer to the fire Molly, staring at the snow isn't going to make you feel any better!' interrupted Lilly, sitting in her dressing gown by the fire, brushing her hair. She'd been staring into the flames thinking back fondly to last summer when she'd sat on the beach, watching the sun melt into the cool waters of the English Channel. The summer seemed a long way away, she hoped they'd be lucky enough to escape London again this year; the war would surely be over soon.

Lilly closed her eyes in the warmth of the fire and remembered how the summer sun would light up the church at the entrance to the harbour. She loved how the setting rays would change with the tides, rolling with the waves or laying flat across many rock pools at low tide. Together with her daughter Emily, they stayed in the beachfront guest house every August for one week so far without fail. Under the gentle guidance of the housekeeper, Miss Madeline, they enjoyed many summers playing in the huge house and on its quiet beach. Emily stayed up a little later each year, often till she had fallen asleep wrapped in a blanket. Lilly sat up in front of the fire, rolled her shoulders to stretch her back, if they did get to return to the Island this year, Emily was going to be too big to be carry back from the beach.

The fire began to crackle and spit focusing Lilly's mind on the present. Little did she know this was the same March day of 1915 that Joshua was celebrating his fifteenth birthday in the halls of the Winchester school that would provide what his parents thought, would be the right start in life. However, she did know that the British Empire was realising that the war they had predicted would be over before Christmas 1914 was not going to go away. Across the hall in the drawing room Constance started to play the grand piano which had arrived in the house as a present from their employer, Rodriguez, two years ago. Her nimble touch on the keys pushed sound out into the room, except that today the sonata she played fell heavily on the ears of women in the room opposite.

'Can't she play something with a little more tempo?' asked Mollie. She left the deep window seat to sit opposite Lilly by the fire. Molly huffed, and pulled her knees up under her chin.

'Why don't you ask her to play your favourite "Appassionata",' Lilly said, looking across admiring Molly's illuminated face, so beautiful, so sultry. Self-consciously, Molly slowly guided her long black hair back behind each ear, and smiled at her thoughts.

'I'm not in the mood,' Molly said with a sly smile. 'Constance will only give me another lecture on adagios and allegrettos.'

'You're right,' laughed Lilly.

'Is the clock right today?' Molly asked in a lighter voice, looking towards the mantelpiece.

'Yes, I wound it before my bath,' Lilly said. 'And now it's about time I got dressed, and you love should be getting ready' Standing up, she offered a hand to Molly, who reached up with a touch that really was something else. Her touch matched her body, and could draw a breathless desire from her clients with the subtle decadent momentum they paid so handsomely for.

'Do you think the Admiral will bring his wife this time Lilly?' asked Molly, biting her soft lower lip and looking back into the fire.

In the eight years Lilly had lived here, she had given Rodriguez a daughter, and had looked after his house. In return, from the first night that they had slept together, he had pledged that he would never sleep with another. Emily, their daughter, had been born on the fourth of October 1907 but no further children were conceived. In 1911 Rodriguez had brought back Molly, a refugee from France. She was filthy and malnourished but her beauty was, even then, undeniable. Lilly refused to let her work. The girl was too young, she argued, but despite her fierce defence Rodriguez had got his way. Once Molly was well enough she was to be become part of the household or be thrown out onto the streets. His only concession to her fight was that Molly would be the last girl he would bring back to work here.

Lilly smiled to herself, now at thirty eight she was twice Molly's age. Why Rodriguez had promised himself to her she did not know, he could have any of the girls in the house. Yet he had courted Lilly with great affection, no matter how slow she had been to return his feelings. He was the owner of this house of prostitution, his reputation preceded him as a deliverer of violent reprisal to those who brought trouble to his door. Once a girl was in this house she was safe from back street blowjobs and concussed depravity. Why then, when they had met by accident, had he chosen her to lavish his wealth upon?

In his efforts to persuade Lilly of his love, Rodriguez had even closed his doors to all clientele for a month to concentrate all his girls' efforts to her pampering. Never again would she be bruised by the forceful exchange of flesh for cash. He worshipped her as if she held the stars in her hands. "One of a thousand equal parts of beauty," he'd said, "and you Lilly, are the hub of them all."

On the last night of that month he emptied the house and they had lain together. She shook with anticipation as she waited on his bed, and at his touch her pulse had raced, electrified by his caress. For all his brutalities they had made love with such gentle endeavour that it eased her contempt for men and she wished never to be parted from him.

'I think I'll go up then Lilly,' Molly said gliding out of the room focusing Lilly's mind back to the present.

'Yes,' agreed Lilly, 'and I shall dress to greet our guests,' but her mind wandered again as she dressed, to her absent lover.

'Why me Rodriguez, why pull me from the street over all the other women that you have at your disposal?' Lilly had asked him.

'Why put yourself down? Are you no better than them?' he had replied.

'Rodriguez, all those beautiful women…?'

'No more Lilly, you are the last, a thousand women are enough for any man, I dare not sleep with another.' He put a finger to her lips. 'Accept our fate, I shall love you like no other, and all I ask is that you run this house for me.'

'But I don't know how.'

Rodriguez gently took hold of her chin to affirm his response 'Lilly believe me, the women here will listen, and the drunken men will do as you bid.' Happy that she had understood, he left their bed and dressed.

Rodriguez came and went on business, away for a day or two, sometimes a week, sometimes a month. When Emily was born he bought the house three doors down for Eliza, Lilly's mother, she could look after his Emily away from the creaking bed springs, and Lilly could concentrate on the running of his brothel. With the solidarity of the other women there were few hang ups.

One morning in their fourth year together, as he dressed Rodriguez announced he had business in the Balkans, 'I'll have to leave at four to catch the overnight train, I may be gone some time.'

'Why go to such a troubled place?' she had asked.

'I simply have business with those who wish to make war,' Rodriguez said shrugging his shoulders.

Her daydream over, Lilly looked into the mirror which hung in the hallway. She checked her dress and make up. Clients for the other three girls had already arrived by appointment, and the door bell now rang for Molly's rendezvous. The Admiral and his wife greeted her with the same wide eyes of anticipation that they always did. Once inside Lilly took their winter coats and left the couple in the drawing room to warm themselves by the fire.

'Here we are,' said Lilly holding a silver tray with two full glasses of a sherry which Rodriguez insisted was the best in Europe. 'This should warm you through a little,' she said. 'What a pleasure it is to see you both again during such troubled times.'

'Ah yes,' replied the Admiral remembering his duty for a moment. 'But I think we will get the better of the Hun before too long.'

Anna looked up to her husband; he stood at least a foot taller than her in his fine uniform and slick hair. The doubt in her eyes gave away her fear that he might be deployed abroad to direct his men, instead of from his comfortable office in London. Lilly placed a gentle hand on the Admiral's sleeve and smiled at them both, 'Well here in this house, our little oasis of pleasure, we can forget the world around us. At least for an hour or two.'

'Erm…' said Anna blushing. 'I wonder if we might meet with Molly again?'

Lilly smiled warmly. 'Yes, I believe she's doing a little bit of reading upstairs. Shall we go on up?'

'Ah yes,' said the Admiral following Lilly's lead up the stairs to the closed door of the library. There, they waited a well choreographed second. Anna looked down at her shoes and the Admiral straightened his tie.

'Ready?' Lilly asked them. But she could see from Anna's flushed neck that they were. Lilly knocked and called out, 'Molly?'

The Admiral swallowed hard and his wife reached out for his hand seeking his assurance.

'Yes, come in,' Molly called back.

'Enjoy,' Lilly said to them both, opening the door to let them in. Rodriguez was right; he'd never have to bring back another girl.

As the months passed by into years, the war continued, bludgeoning its horrific mark on history.

Rodriguez continued to stay away for longer periods and when he did return it was in the dead of night, only staying long enough to deposit cash in the cellar and without fail, make love to Lilly.

Then one night in July 1918 he arrived on foot rather than in his car. The last client had left two hours ago, Constance had gently closed the lid on her piano keys and the calm of sleep had spread across the house. It was instinct that woke Lilly from her dreams and desire that roused her from her bed. She could hear the unmistakable confident footsteps of Rodriguez mounting the stairs towards her. Quickly Lilly flattened her hair and let her night dress fall. Anticipation closed her eyes, she wanted to feel him before she saw him. 'Ah Lilly,' her lover said, his breath against her neck, his kiss soft, his touch subtle. 'Keep your eyes closed my love,' his accent divine. Lilly felt the weighted chill of gold, like gilded rain, against her chest and around her neck. 'Come,' Rodriguez said guiding Lilly to her dressing table.

'Now open your eyes.'

In the dull light of the room her new diamond necklace shimmered, backed by a golden hue. Rodriguez placed a solitary kiss onto her neck and whispered.

'I must go my love, but the war will not last much longer. If I can survive Rodiani one more year I shall return a wealthier man.' With that he was gone.

Beyond anything she had ever imagined his gift moved her, not because of its content but because of the manner in which it had been given. It would sustain her through the months to come and the men that dwindled at their door. On a Saturday morning in March, 1919, Rodriguez returned in a 1910 Delage motor car which caused great excitement. Strapped to the back of the car was a bicycle brought back for Emily. Rodriguez even played with her on that cold day, wobbling along on the bike giggling like a child himself. Lilly looked on, laughing for her daughter who had found a new friend and that night at the supper table he produced with a cheer, a large picnic hamper. It was packed full with oranges, Clementine's, bananas and other exotic fruits. Some were a little battered after the journey but on the whole they tasted delicious.

'Fresh from the south of France by virtue of my trusted car,' Rodriguez announced. Beneath the fruit, spread out in two layers, were chocolate bars 'The finest chocolate in Italy for you both.'

Drunk from the wine he had brought back they asked Eliza to take Emily home and then made love on the stairs and again in Lilly's bed. In the morning she woke him with tea and asked, 'Where have you been, I wonder. That so many have died, and yet the war has not aged you by a day.'

'Never ask my Lilly. Never ask what I cannot tell!'

A week went by, then months flew past, pushing spring into summer. Though they expected Rodriguez to interfere with the books or the order of the house, he did little but read the daily paper and sip coffee, or wine depending on his mood. In July he gave the whole house a month off, he gave each of the girls one hundred pounds and told them to rest, and stay out of sight. It was a generous side that the girls had not seen before. Perhaps the war had changed him after all.

He spent much of that month with Emily, leaving Lilly at the window with her finger tips touching the warming panes of summer. A warmth spread through the house as father and daughter became wrapped up in each other like long lost friends never to be parted again. For Lilly trips to the theatre were accompanied by fine dining and laughter.

'We should go to the Island?' Lilly asked.

'Of course.'

Sitting in the garden of their holiday home on the Isle of Wight, Rodriguez sipped the coffee Madeline had brought him, and pondered over a letter he had received that morning. The long garden faced east and was sheltered on both sides by sporadic trees which marked the boundaries with other, similar properties. The lawn ran out from the house to the beach, separated from the shore by a six foot stone wall, only breached by the high spring and winter tides which crashed up and over it. Rodriguez had moved a table around the garden until he was happy that he would get maximum morning sun and minimum wind. Content that he had achieved the perfect spot, he was now so engrossed that he hadn't noticed Lilly climb up from the beach and walk over to him.

'Rodriguez, what troubles you?' she asked.

'I have been called and so I must go.' His voice was flat with resignation.

'Rodriguez surely not now…' Lilly pointed back down to the beach to where Emily was playing. 'Won't you come and join us?'

'You don't understand Lilly.' He stood up and reached out to touch her cheek. 'Spend some money on the house; Molly knows where I keep it. I will try and return before Christmas.'

'Now that the war is over, can't Emily and I travel with you, my love?' Lilly asked

'No Lilly don't ask me that,' Rodriguez lowered his voice.

'We'll miss you,' Lilly pouted.

Rodriguez half laughed. 'It would be for the best if you stay here until the end of the week. Madeline will look after you. Make your way back to London, Molly will meet you at the station.'

'Then you must go,' Lilly replied, wiping away the only tear she had ever seen from Rodriguez's face.

'Say goodbye for me.' Then without a kiss he pushed the letter into his pocket and was gone.

At the end of that week Madeline drove them to Ryde to catch the ferry that would take them to Portsmouth and the train home. With the memory of sand and chilled lemonade still at the forefront of Emily's mind, she held her mother's hand as they opened the front door. Inside, their friends were there to greet them with open arms.

That night, with Constance at the piano, the women closed the door to custom, and sent Molly to find something expensive to drink from the cellar. Emily joined them for a while, Lilly wanted her daughter close, and it was late when she finally drifted off to sleep in her mother's arms to the sound of chatter. Together the ladies laid Emily on the drawing room sofa in front of the fire.

With Emily out of the room, the stories concentrated on their clients, laughing at their special requests, and taunting each other for the prices they charged to satisfy them. They sang a few songs as the wine flowed and more bottles were called for. It was two in the morning when the candles flickered low, and the temperature dropped. Too tired to talk anymore only half of them made it to their beds that night, and as Lilly finally closed her eyes to the fading embers of the fire, it was to the gentle breathing of Emily on the sofa beside her that she fell asleep.

The following morning the ladies of the house made toast and drank sweet tea together in the large kitchen. They nursed their sore heads and Lilly sat back in a chair with a great sense of camaraderie.

'Molly,' Lilly said nursing her sore throat. 'As beautiful and sumptuous as you are I think you should rest your tired fanny again today!' Everyone burst into laughter.

'And you Lottie, Constance and Anna. You can all keep your legs closed too. We'll stay closed a day or two longer I think.'

'But what if…?' asked Anna.

'Ladies I think we can afford to stay closed for a while.'

The other women looked at each other, the good humour seemed to have left the room.

'I'm not sure that it's such a good idea without Rodriguez's say so,' Molly said.

'Ladies,' Lilly continued, 'I think there is enough money in the cellar of this house…'

'Lilly!' Anna said trying to interrupt.

'Anna, much as I love him, I know about his bank books. Not only English, but he also has accounts in the United States of America and Switzerland. I think we can safely take a little while off to plan some redecoration. Rodriguez was most insistent that the job be done for Christmas.'

'Those things that you found in the cellar Lilly...' Lottie said standing up.

'What else is there to find other than that old grubby dagger?' Lilly said somewhat confused.

'Lilly,' Anna finally spoke up to confess 'We all know about the money and the dagger it's just that... we were told to keep quiet.'

'Lilly, unless Rodriguez gives us time off, we must open our doors and our legs,' added Lottie moving towards the door. 'And that's all I'm going to say.'

'So it seems, even after all these years, you still know more about him than I do.'

'Do you not remember Alessandro Rodiani, Lilly?' asked Lottie now agitated at everyone.

'Only that Rodriguez has mentioned his name in passing.'

'Lottie be quiet,' Molly said.

'Don't you think it's about time Lilly knew the truth?' said Lottie resting against the door frame.

'What do you mean, what's going on?' asked Emily.

'It wasn't Rodriguez's idea to drag you out of the gutter Lilly,' said Anna. 'It was a taunt from Alessandro, a bet if you like?'

'Lottie no,' said Constance. 'I'm imploring you to stop.'

'Emily,' said Lilly nervously. 'I think it's time Grandma took you home to get changed. Please could you do that Eliza. Maybe take Emily up to the shops, bring us back some... some,' Lilly did not finish her thought pattern. Instead she got up to give her daughter a hug and a kiss on the cheek. 'Be good,' she said.

'Come on Emily, sounds like your mum's got some business to attend to,' Eliza lied putting her arm round Emily, she gave a half smile to Lilly.

'Tell me before I change my mind' Lilly said her hands shaking as she sat back down.

'Rodriguez had always had this brag that he was destined to sleep with a thousand of the best women in the world before he died,' continued Lottie. 'One day, it'll have been about six months after I started here, I heard Rodriguez come up from the cellar. Alessandro was laughing at him, shouting at him. "Times up Rodriguez. You need to choose your last lover". He kept on taunting him Lilly. "You know, seeing as it's my book, I think I shall pick for you". You were Alessandro's choice Lilly; it had nothing to do with Rodriguez.'

'They brought you here pissed out of your head,' said Constance. 'You and two other women, all of you were drugged. We waited on the stair, me and Lottie, didn't we?' Lottie nodded. 'But this time, fuck me they had a big fight. Alessandro left with Rodriguez's book held tight to his chest.'

'We left you down there,' said Lottie finally, 'thought you were all dead, we waited for Rodriguez to come up, but he didn't, we waited an hour or more. I can tell you it felt like an age.'

'When we couldn't bear it no more, we had to go down, and there you all were naked on the floor. You were alive but... the other two girls were... cut,' Constance's words faltered, holding back the memory by placing her hand to her mouth. 'They were both dead. There was a big drawing on the floor, weird like. We cleaned you up first. Rodriguez was so cold; we thought you had the best chance. You were out of it for days after. He'd fucked you till you bled, and then he'd beaten you black and blue, he had.'

'When Rodriguez woke he had a rage like I'd never seen. Took to his opium house, where you live now with Emily' Anna said. '"Fucking Alessandro," he yelled as he left, "you've left me with a whore!" We took him what he wanted while he yelled, "For all the women I've ever had." Never asked about you, not once, and for a month, just jabbered on, off his head he was, and never looked at us like he used to after that, never even reached out for any of us. Then one morning he walks out the door into the sun and says to me, "If she is my last, then I'll love her or be damned." We were told to pamper you. Lastly, he told us we were to do as you bid, and we have.'

'I don't remember it that way at all,' Lilly said. 'I thought he'd rescued me.'

'In a way Lilly, he did,' said Molly.

'I thought, you know, after all these years I just thought that he loved me in some small way. He swore that he'd be faithful,' Lilly was speaking very slowly now struggling with each word and stretching out her hands in front of her, they gave her something to focus on.

'If what Alessandro said was true then he will have been faithful,' Anna said trying to reassure her friend.

'So he has built everything we have on the direction and taunts of this Alessandro.' Lilly was crying as the realisation of his deception sank in.

'Alessandro is…' Anna started, but stopped, looking at Lottie for help.

'Don't cross him Lilly,' said Lottie. 'For all our sakes.'

'You know he's gone to meet Alessandro don't you Lilly?' Lilly nodded. 'Pray Lilly that their war-mongering is over, and

282

that Rodriguez does not bring him back here,' Molly said. 'I never want to meet Alessandro again. Lilly, he has people who watch this place, not least some of our clients, so that we do as he asks when he leaves each time.'

'He is bound to you by Alessandro's demons,' Anna said, crouching down in front of Lilly to take her hands in her own.

'Through all the uncertainty of war why did you never tell me this before?' asked Lilly.

'Rodriguez told us there was no uncertainty. He said he knew the outcome before it began,' Anna said.

Lilly felt the eyes of her peers upon her, and remembered the bruises they had tended, and the friendship they had offered. She lifted her head and saw the fear in their eyes and swallowing her pride she suggested, 'Well, we had best ready ourselves for the day ahead. I'm afraid Molly; the Admiralty may have need for your still perfect beauty, and your perfect fanny, for a while longer.'

The women laughed with Lilly's understanding, then kissed her wet cheeks and left for their rooms. All alone in the kitchen, Lilly sat back in her chair to re-evaluate her feelings for Rodriguez Taveres.

September passed, and Emily rode her bike each day until the afternoon light faded. Whatever had been said, Rodriguez was still her father. Whatever it meant for her mother she wanted him back even if he missed her twelfth birthday. Through October it was too dark to ride after school and she had to wait until the weekend, but as November began the cold wind brought the bike into the hallway and then up into her room, much to her mother's disapproval.

In the early cold hours of the third of December, the sound of a diesel truck woke Emily, and then her mother three doors down, as it clattered to a halt outside the brothel. In front of it, leading the way, was the Delage car. By the time the vehicles' doors slammed shut, all the girls including Lilly, saw Rodriguez pay off the truck driver, who walked off into the night. Rodriguez returned to his car and opened the passenger door. From inside, the slender hand of a woman took his, as she stepped out into the cold. With their breath escaping into the dark night, they whispered to each other and waited to be let in to the house.

It took about half an hour for Rodriguez to walk through Lilly's bedroom door. Without speaking he laid on top of the bed in his thick overcoat and within seconds began snoring.

Molly found the new woman asleep on the sofa in the drawing room. Apart from the feeble embers' light out of the grate, the woman lay in the dark, allowing Molly to sit opposite her, and wait. Anger tensed Molly's shoulders and kept her awake until the late cold dawn brought a grey light to the freezing wind that rattled the trees outside. Molly could see the sleeping face now. It wasn't a woman at all, but a girl of maybe fourteen at most, innocent, like Emily still was. Molly sighed to herself. Taking pity on the girl, she flattened out the ashes and built the fire to give a little more heat to the room.

When Lilly appeared an hour later she found Molly in her favourite window seat. She crouched beside the sofa and looked, shaking her head as she did so. 'So young,' she whispered, 'what was he thinking of?'

'His pocket, no doubt,' replied Molly. 'Just like it was with me.'

'His cock more like,' said Lilly keeping her voice low, and standing up to face Molly.

'It was not so long ago that I was laid there,' Molly said drawing her knees up tighter under her chin.

'It was not so long ago Molly that you were to be the last girl he ever brought back. He said your beauty was incomparable.'

'And you were his last love, without question.' They sat for awhile listening to the fire and the clock above it. At last Lilly stood up. Her face set, her mind made up. 'Can you get a bath ready for her Molly? And I will wake Mr Taveres. Oh, and Molly get Constance to play a little 'Appassionata' will you?'

Rodriguez was still on the bed fully clothed when Lilly tenderly woke him.

'Did you have a good trip?' she asked. Rodriguez sat up grinning at the sight of the breakfast tray Lilly had brought to him.

'You know,' he replied, 'Alessandro is so often right. He was so right about you'

'Oh, will he be right about the girl who sleeps down stairs?' she replied pouring his coffee.

'She is the most beautiful creature I have ever seen.' He took the cup from her with both hands, sipped the hot fluid, then smiled with smug satisfaction. 'I shall never have to bring back another woman.'

'How do you do it Rodriguez?' she asked leaning forward and caressing his brow. 'The lines on your face have not grown like they have on mine. Where men have returned broken or not at all, Rodriguez only flourishes.'

'Never ask Lilly. I told you never ask,' he replied draining his cup, and changing the subject. 'Have you thought of me often Lilly?'

'More this time than any other Rodriguez, more than any other,' Lilly replied, filling his cup and catching his eye with a seductive smile.

'Oh I see,' said Rodriguez taking a bite of his toast. She was beginning to stir him.

He put the toast down and moved to take off his overcoat. Lilly helped him, and whispered into his ear. 'She really is quite the most gorgeous girl you have ever brought here,' she breathed seductively. 'So innocent and ripe Rodriguez.'

'Yes, oh yes, Alessandro was so right,' Rodriguez shifted forward and started to unbutton his shirt.

'And you are such a handsome man. Seeing the girl makes me realise I cannot possibly keep you satisfied, why don't you have her for yourself.'

'Lilly I brought her here for the business, for you, to keep the heart of this house beating.'

'She's unspoilt, just as Molly was,' Lilly said seductively. 'What is her name Rodriguez?'

'Isabella.'

'You gave Molly away, why miss the chance with Isabella?'

'I'm bound to you Lilly, don't tempt me with my own desires.'

'I would share her with you Rodriguez. Then surely my love, you wouldn't be breaking that bond you have with me,' Lilly opened his shirt a little more, kissing his cheek, and then his neck.

'No, no, Lilly don't tease me please. The girl, she must be starving.' Rodriguez's voice hesitated for the first time in the fourteen years that she had known him. 'Please... make sure...'

'Sshh my love,' Lilly reached inside his shirt and felt his thudding heart. 'Isabella is being looked after. Come it's about time we got you out of these dirty clothes.' Rodriguez reached up and stayed her hand, stopping her before she fully undid the next button.

'What about the girl?' he asked again.

'Maybe if we went down to the bathroom we might find her,' Lilly kept her voice low and he relinquished his button to her touch. She moved round, kneeling between his legs and continued with her gentle fingers until his shirt lay completely undone and his trousers were unhooked. She ran her hand beneath his crotch then stood to take hold of his hand. 'Come let me lead you.'

'What is that noise?' Rodriguez asked resisting her pull.

'It's Constance; she likes to practice each morning. The clients like her playing so much she's worth more with her fingers on those keys than she is on her back.'

Downstairs, Constance directed the soft felted hammers and started to play a polished sonata. The sound gliding up through the house, softening with each step and each door until it caressed the nerves like the most subtle liqueur.

Of the thousand women whom he had slept with he could count on his fingers those who had not been paid to speak to him the way that Lilly spoke to him now. He took her hand and felt her touch, she smelt so, so good. He sighed, feeling like his long journey through life was worth it for this moment. This woman who had faithfully remained here in London for him, bringing up his only child. He was helpless to her desire as she led him out of the room, turning as they reached the door.

'Close your eyes Rodriguez,' Lilly said.

This woman, this mother, this beautiful gem filled his mind with an enticing simplicity that cut loose his memories and concentrated his ego. Gone was his doubt. Alessandro was right, he repeated in his own mind, she was better than the rest and he had not been unfaithful. His reward was that she now offered the girl freely. No Alessandro. No demons would stalk him.

Maybe, just maybe, he thought as he closed his eyes to her instruction he should close this place, take his family high up into the mountains of Spain and try for another child. Lilly was gently tying a scarf around his head. 'Don't you trust me?' he questioned.

'A little darkness will heighten your senses my love,' she replied, pulling the shirt from his breeches. He had lost weight, she thought, as she led him along the hall. Downstairs the piano recital gathered pace and Rodriguez felt the heat on his body as they stepped into the bathroom and heard the door shut behind them.

'Ah Rodriguez. I wondered if you'd come and join me' said Isabella in Italian.

'Isabella,' he reached up to remove the scarf.

'No, no, Rodriguez leave that on a little longer,' Lilly said, pulling his hand down to touch the soft skin of her neck and her silk dressing gown gave way under the momentum of his hand.

He heard the movement of water, as someone got out of the bath and wet feet crossed the floor.

'Isabella?' he asked.

'Yes,' said Lilly, guiding his hand to the warm damp flesh of the girl's slender frame. She sighed under his touch, her wet hand loosened his trouser belt and reached inside to his swollen groin.

'Rodriguez, let's get you out of these clothes.' Lilly's voice sent another shudder down his spine.

Fuck Alessandro and his demons, fuck the predictions he had seen in the forest so many years ago. He was sick of living in fear. Alessandro had the book anyway. Rodriguez could bear it no longer and pulled off his blindfold. There, in front of him, in the thick white steam of the room, stood Molly, not Isabella.

'I am not going to let you ruin that girl as your last conquest Rodriguez' said Lilly from somewhere out of sight.

'What are you doing, you silly bitches?' Rodriguez shouted angrily.

'Trying to raise your demons Rodriguez!' Lilly yelled at him.

'But I haven't touched this stupid whore.'

'That's not fair Rodriguez. I wanted to be your last,' said Molly, backing away into the thickening steam leaving him in the white out.

'What are you doing Lilly?' his voice suddenly vulnerable. 'Who amongst you fine ladies can conjure up my demise?' He grew angry again as he reached for his trousers. 'You know I think I'll fuck another thousand and another if it suits me. I've been a fool to waste so much time.'

'I think a thousand is enough,' said Lilly, passing behind him in the mist, slicing across his back with a blade. He span to hit his attacker but she side stepped him and plunged the long sharp blade effortlessly between his ribs.

'Lilly,' he growled desperately holding his side.

'Enough of your lies Rodriguez,' Lilly said firmly, pulling the dagger from between his fingers. 'How many have felt this blade like you do now, I wonder?'

'None, none since… what does it matter,' Rodriguez dropped to his knees, with blood bubbling from the wound and filling his lung, he tasted it in his mouth. Fury overcame pain and he tried to get to his feet, but Molly took the dagger and scored another cut so deep into his back that he could do little more than close his eyes to the pain.

'Look up Rodriguez,' Isabella said softly. Her hands were around the handle of Samuel's dagger that waited beneath his chin. 'Look at us Rodriguez,' she whispered.

Lilly stood beside the girl. A girl, he realised now as he looked up, she was only a girl.

'Did you know, Rodriguez,' Isabella said, her soft voice gaining aggression, 'that Alessandro killed my mother and father the night before he dressed me up and handed me over to you?'

'All the years… we have spent together… Lilly, don't you see, that I love you,' Rodriguez pleaded.

Lilly said nothing as she drove the blade deep into his throat. She held onto to the handle while the other women left. His eyes still fixed on hers, his pain agonising.

'Now that I think about it Rodriguez,' she said into his ear. 'I never loved you. I just accepted your fears.'

It took a day to discreetly gather anything of value from the two houses and a further day for Lilly and Emily to walk into three banks across London removing as much money as they could from Rodriguez's accounts, without raising suspicion. They used Emily's forgery of her father's signature, so good that it did not raise any eyebrows.

Added to the cash from the house they had forty six thousand and seventy pounds, they left Lilly's mother with two thousand, and one bank book in the name of a Mrs J Canterbury. This and the other accounts would need forged papers, eagerly created by an old client in exchange for a night in Molly's bed. It was the last man Molly ever slept with.

A week after Rodriguez had met his end, four women and a young girl left their street at midnight in the old Delage car. They had access to sufficient means, if they were careful, to sustain travel for many years. Their last act was to set a fire ablaze which quickly consumed the house, Rodriguez, and the last of his cruelty.

The women who remained safely behind, three doors down, watched the following day as two men they'd not seen for a long time, poked through what was left at the Taveres brothel.

'I think we should stay in England for a while, don't you Maglanis?'

'I would agree. As long as we find a decent place, it'll be safer than Europe to ride out the coming storm. You know however, that we need to tidy up our business in Bellagio,' replied Maglanis.

'Yes of course. Very well, that's settled. Send a telegram to Madeline; we'll stay there until we can find a new place in town. In fact, Maglanis, go to the Island, take Madeline the Pipp ball, it will be safer there than with us. I'll join you later, when I've finished our business on the lake.'

TWENTY-THREE

Mary

In response to the car bomb which exploded outside the U.S. Embassy in Saigon on March 30th 1965, Jerry Swartz had done what his mother had asked him not to do, and signed up to join his brother John, as a Marine in Vietnam. It wasn't just the two Americans and the twenty Vietnamese who had been killed, but also the 200 people who were wounded, that had made his mind up. He had stood on the veranda of his parents' homestead and checked the reflection of himself in the window before opening the door. From the look on his face, Evelyn knew what her son was about to tell her.

'Your father will be proud,' Evelyn said, wiping a tear away with her small handkerchief before pushing it back inside her sleeve. She smiled at her son, flattened the collar of his shirt and returned her attention to the bread she was kneading .

Inside their house there was little sign of the changing ideals of the 1960s. The family's American mid-west farm had stayed with its deep religious culture, their lifestyle left little room for profit and free thought. All the men in the surrounding community served their country when called for, and the women did the best they could to build homes and feed their families. Dreams and aspirations were placed behind duty.

On the 22nd of August that year it was Mary, the eldest child of Evelyn and Joseph Swartz, who opened the door to two men in military uniform. The news they carried with them brought Evelyn to her knees, Jerry had been killed during Operation Starlite against the Viet Cong in the Van Tuong peninsula. It was the largest marine operation of the war so far and he had fought bravely.

The following week Joseph took the advice of his neighbour, James Johnston "JJ", and hired a mute labourer.

"He's a good man Joseph," JJ said. "Nathaniel is strong, he likes to read, he don't eat much and don't hardly drink, just likes to work.'

'Well I don't know JJ, he's an Indian after all,' Joseph had replied. 'Does he worship the good Lord, or is he just full of Indian dances and those blasphemous chants?'

'No Joseph, he doesn't go to church,' JJ frowned. 'But you need help, at least until John comes back.' Joseph had turned away at the mention of his son. 'Listen, John will be home before you know it, and you can send Nathaniel on his way. Mary is strong but she ain't no man.'

Six months after JJ dropped Nathaniel in the Swartz yard, the military men were back to tell Joseph that his beloved eldest son, John was missing in action. Joseph knew that his son could still be alive. He felt it had to be true, and under the grace of God he would live to see John again. In his deep belief, his temper grew shorter and his waist narrower. He would need Nathaniel's help for a little longer yet.

With everything under control at the farm, Joseph and Evelyn were encouraged by their daughter and JJ's wife, to allow themselves time to dance once a fortnight at the local school house. The dances were well attended by church goers and others alike, sometimes the moonshine would flow and the dancing would go on well into the night. However, as all the eligible men in the area either spoke only of Vietnam or their disgust at it, Mary had decided some time ago to stay at home, it gave her time to breath and relax in her own way.

'You know,' Mary said, as she turned to her lover. 'Apart from your name, there's little about you that I know.' The drying sweat on her back tingled down to the base of her spine, and a gentle shiver ran through her. Mary ran a finger down her lover's chest to his navel, then leant forward to kiss his cheek.

Nathaniel turned his head towards Mary, and looked into her blue eyes. Tenderly he lifted away the wisps of hair that fell against her cheek so that all her beauty could be seen. Her skin glowed in the gentle light of the room, it softened her sculptured body, lean from a life time of hard work and little money.

'We risk so much to be together. I just wish sometimes I knew more about you,' Mary hesitated looking Nathaniel's body up and down. His dark skin inviting her caress. Was there any point in her questions she wondered. Was it not better to be satisfied having sex with this man who had taken her virginity, this lover who had jump-started an emotion that church only sought to suppress? Why challenge the thrill of illicit sex with a man who would, nor could ever bring their affair to anyone's attention? She smiled, remembering how she had flirted with him, trying to catch his eye. Jeez she was twenty eight, yet right now she felt ten years younger, she remembered when they had first made love together here in this bed. How patient he had been then, and how she had come under his caress. The guilt that had followed, Mary managed to quickly squash. The death of her brother changed her, his faith had not saved his life, and the girl in Wood River he had been dating would, without doubt, move on. What would be better? She asked herself; to enjoy this man until he moved on, or leave. The latter was not an option, her parents were not getting any younger and if John did not return to run the farm her father would surely sell all he had worked for. Mary had put any thought of John's survival to one side. Nathaniel would only stay until John came home. Until then, as long as she was careful, she would enjoy his touch and indulge her passion. Her plan was straightforward except for the last month or more, the embraces that had once been fleeting exchanges now lasted longer, and the way that his hand held onto her's meant so much more.

'Jeez Nathaniel,' she said in her bed. 'I wish I could hear the thoughts in your head. Do you think me as sexy as that grin of yours says, or am I just another lay, on a different farm?'

Nathaniel returned her smile, and his brown eyes flashed with desire. Lifting a hand to his heart, he blew her a kiss. Mary airily rejecting his foolery with a gentle nudge to his shoulder.

'Listen,' she said, gently prodding him. 'The whole goddamn world is intent upon its own destruction, and I only know your name cos you wrote it down over a year ago.' she sighed and lay back staring up at the ceiling. 'Each day that passes, I see my mother pray that God will keep John safe, and my Pa, he barely says a word to anyone and… and you, the only man I can speak to… and you can't say a word to me!' Mary rolled over and sat on the edge of the bed. She was growing angry, her knuckles whitening as she pulled at the bed cover beneath her. 'Jeez you know how much trouble we'd be in if we got caught here?'

Nathaniel saw the likeness now as he'd seen it before throughout her life. Fuelled by a scrap of paper, an article that had not yet been written. Yet the likeness had always been there. Even when he had first traced Mary's family here when she was twelve, unmistakably he'd seen in her, Cattleya's strength and fight.

When Mary was fifteen, he'd caught sight of her playing with her brothers outside the stores in Wood River. From behind the wheel of his car he'd seen Evelyn lifting up the groceries into the flat bed of their truck. Evelyn had accidentally snagged one of the bags on the tail gate, leaving its contents to roll out into the road. The teenage Mary had scurried to help, while the two boys laughed, blaming each other when their mother scolded them. Nathaniel had found himself unable to move, transfixed until the last lost apple had been collected from the road. Only when Mary looked up and caught his eye had he looked the other way.

On that day disbelief had overtaken him, the one absolute of his long life had stared back at him. The girl he had rescued from a car crash as a woman so many times before, had stared back at him in real, unadulterated time. Shaking nervously he'd driven non stop to Kearney, where he sat for a while in a parking lot. The incident had unnerved him so much, he walked into the nearest bar. At eleven thirty, four hours after he had entered, he left. Drunk and to the amusement of everyone else inside, he unsteadily got back into his car and weaved his way out of town.

Nathaniel drove until tears overtook him and he had to pull over. Having pulled the key from the ignition and thrown it out into the field, his frustration boiled over. Kicking the door open, he had punched at the car until his fists bled. It took an hour of caressing his sore knuckles and searching, before he managed to find the discarded key and calm down.

Settling back inside the car, Nathaniel had slept an unconscious sleep. He woke when the sun pushed through the dust of the windscreen, bringing with it a headache of epic proportion. Half blinded by the pain, Nathaniel just managed to open the door quick enough to vomit onto the dirt. His stomach churned repeatedly reminding him that he should not drink and as the last of the bourbon turned into bile, he swore, for as long as possible, he wouldn't drink again.

It had been thirteen years since that day to this moment. Mary was talking on the bed, but her words were not reaching his ears, his mind was too focused on the last year that had brought his long trail to this bed. A bed he had never even given thought to getting into until he gave into her kiss.

Of the lovers Nathaniel had had as time passed by, some lasted at most a month or two but none ever lasted longer. The rich ones had loved his silence, the poor ones had asked too many questions. Mary took him for what he was, only ever enjoying their time together for what it was, and the more they began to fall for each other, the more he became resolute that this woman he thought he was to save, had no connection with New York at all.

Maybe he should listen to his cold heart, maybe he had saved her and should love her for who she was.

'I don't even know how old you are,' Mary's voice was audible again. 'What are you thirty five at the most? I mean what brought you to our farm miles from fucking anywhere. It's not even as if your choice of country is great. Who sends its sons to die in Vietnam. You know my brother Jerry was twenty, Jesus Christ, and John is twenty four.'

Nathaniel sat up beside her and placed a hand over hers. Mary let go of the blanket and turned her hand over to let their fingers intertwine.

'Nathaniel we've been hiding for months, sneaking about to be together.' Mary threw caution to the wind, 'Could it be that you have grown to love me as much as I have come to love you?'

Nathaniel lifted his hand from hers and started to rise from the bed.

'Nathaniel,' Mary said, reaching out to try and regain his touch. 'I'm sorry, don't go,' but he pulled on his clothes and walked towards the door. 'Please, there's no need, Ma and Pa won't be back till tomorrow morning.' But he was gone.

Mary flopped back on her bed. 'Ah shit,' she scolded herself. 'You had to go and ask, you had to go and fucking ask.'

She waited for the sound of the back door to shut behind him as he left. But instead there was a moment of quiet as if her lover was deciding his next move. When Nathaniel did, footsteps returned up the stairs. He was holding a piece of paper, a book to lean on, and a pencil. Mary sat up and flattened the blankets for him to sit down.

Holding the pencil awkwardly he sketched what Mary recognised as the outlines of North, then South America. He marked cities with large dots. New York, then across to Seattle, then Denver, Louisiana down into Mexico then Brazil. He marked Salvador de Bahia, and with unsteady line, the Andes stretching down the continent picking out Lima and Concepcion (a city he had spent several years in). He pushed the lead back over the Andes northward until he hesitated where the cloud forests of his birth had been. He smiled to himself. Where his life had begun.

'I'm nearly thirty and I've only been as far as the falls, and only to Omaha twice,' Mary said studying the drawing. 'Jerry did show me on our map where France and Germany were, where Pa fought. Over here right?' Mary pointed into an undrawn Atlantic, 'Why did you travel so far away from your home?'

Nathaniel didn't give an answer, he had never thought this far ahead.

'Nathaniel, are you married or something? Oh shit man I never thought.' It was Mary's turn to get up and put on her clothes, and Nathaniel's to try and stop her leave.

'If you've got a wife you should... you should just go get...' Mary stopped herself. Nathaniel's waves of protest barely calming her. 'So if you're not married, what is it? Write something down for God's sake.'

Nathaniel looked at her with his hands aloft and nodded his head.

'Come downstairs, I'll get you some more paper.'

'Nathaniel write something. Help me to understand even just a little bit about you,' she said when they'd sat down in the comfy chairs by the fire place. The clock across the room showed eleven thirty, its second hand pushing on around its white face. The weight of each day, over so many untold years, started to fall heavily on him. Agustin had warned him to stay away from Mary and to use his life more wisely, let love come to him.

'Besides, how can you be sure?' Agustin had said as they walked along the shores of Alassio. 'How can you be sure that the newspaper clipping is not just another trick by the Pelecaras?' The thought had been enough to stay his mind while Agustin had lived. 'Do not give me extra life Cieba,'

299

Agustin had said as he reached his nineties. 'You have brought me home and that is more than an old fool like me deserves.'

Mary was no spirit's trick, of that Nathaniel had made sure.

'Nathaniel,' Mary said softly, trying to stir him and realising it didn't matter one bit where he had come from, or where he was going. If they only had this last moment, then so be it, she loved him and told him once more, her words slow and affectionate.

Mary didn't even stop him as Nathaniel went to fetch his bag, but couldn't hold back the tears when he returned and sat beside her.

From inside his battered duffel bag he pulled an old book, its cover cracking with age. It was held together by just enough dirty brown string to stop the pages inside falling out and Nathaniel placed it onto her lap.

'I don't understand Nathaniel,' Mary said confused. Exhausted and unsure of her earlier resolve she tried to give the book back. 'Stay and we'll face my father together.' Though she did not know how. Pa would shoot them both rather than let their affair come out in church. 'Better still, take me with you Nathaniel'

Nathaniel shook his head, he would not put her at risk. He would face Rodiani, and stop waiting for him to die.

"Pitiful creature," Agustin had called Rodiani. A pitiful creature whom Nathaniel had kept at the fingertips of his own life. No matter how secretive Rodiani became, his success had always left a trace, whether it was one or twenty years apart.

The last time Nathaniel had located Rodiani was in 1958 from a tip-off that a report in an Italian newspaper, All'interno di stampa, had dared to question whether there were players behind the mafia bosses in Rome. He'd collected the paper from a friend who lived on a side street to the Piazza Cesare Beccaria in Florence and read it in front of the Porta alla Croce. The paper not only questioned the power of the most influential families, but linked several businessmen in their front cover photo to America and Manhattan families who had strong links to the old prohibition days. It was fortunate that the copy was saved for him, the All'interno di stampa had been raised to the ground a month later.

"How can you bare to let time slip?" Cattleya had once asked.

"Patience," he had replied. Now, he realised, he had been patient enough.

Nathaniel grabbed a piece of paper from Mary's table, his hand wavered above the page and determination grew. Followed instantly by fear that all this time he'd been putting Mary in danger. The ink blotted onto the page but he managed to pull a few words through with the nib.

Forgive me Mary, wait for me I will return and explain this life.

His heart grated as he gave her the page. He pointed at the word "this", then at the journal. She smiled at him through her tears and nodded. He then scribbled, "Hide this". He pointed again at the journal, then finally wrote, "I Love You".

Enough now of hurt and pain. Nathaniel kissed Mary on the cheek, stood up and stepped away grabbing his bag as he walked out of the door.

TWENTY-FOUR

New Print

Driven by a bitter wind, an unseasonable dust rose up from the back roads in Nebraska. It was clouding not only the cold, clear blue sky, but the view ahead and had halted Nathaniel's progress. Having unintentionally bought the slowest truck he could have out of the McGraw's yard in Gibbon, there was no chance of outrunning the dust ball it was creating. Frustrated, Nathaniel pulled over as much as he could and took a swig of cold water from his canteen. He'd have to wait a while and let the wind that followed him drop or change direction. He closed his eyes and leant back in his seat, fighting the thought that he'd have made better progress hitching. He huddled up and closed his eyes.

'Cold huh?' said a voice, stirring Nathaniel from his short sleep.

Nathaniel wiped his mouth, sat up and smiled at the stranger outside the truck. He was young, perhaps early twenties and chubby. His dark hair matched his black slacks, black shoes and a coat that was too small for him. Judging by the dust in his hair and the way he held tightly onto the collar of his overcoat, he'd been walking for a long time.

Nathaniel smiled, wondering what had brought this young man to this back road. The stranger felt his gaze and dusted off his trousers and his coat.

'Sure is a long road. Bad enough in that old Ford, worse when you're on your feet!. Say are you headed into Grand Island by any chance?' he asked Nathaniel, his voice raised unsure whether he could be heard through the window. Nathaniel's response was to remove the cap of his canteen and take another sip.

'Have you driven out of Kearney?' The man said waiting as Nathaniel studied him a moment longer then wound down his window.

'Gibbon or Shelton maybe?' he asked lowering his voice. 'Say do you understand me buddy, can you speak American?' Now the man looked past the driver and around the vehicle, he spied on the passenger seat Nathaniel's bag laying slightly open, beside it lay an old battered paper which he made out as the New York Times. 'You're a long way from home, huh,' he suggested.

Nathaniel laughed; nodding his head then proffered his canteen toward the stranger.

'Are you headed all the way to the Big Apple?' he asked almost before he'd finished drinking so that some of the water escaped his mouth falling onto his coat. He wiped his face with his sleeve, then conscious of his action, he tried to wipe away the moisture with the other arm.

'Can't you speak man? Jeez,' he said redirecting attention from himself. Nathaniel shook his head and opened his mouth to reveal the short stump of a tongue that Rodriguez had left him with.

'Shit Mr, I'm sorry. Shit that must have hurt man.' The stranger held his hand to his mouth and winced as if experiencing the pain. Then held out his hand in a greeting. 'I'm Charles Hirsch, recently of Kearney, now of this road, looking for a lift to anywhere near Grand Island, or Lincoln, or shit, right now I'd even go as far as New York. That is if you're going all that way?'

Nathaniel accepted his hand shake and laughed gently, causing a look of doubt to cross Charles's face as he handed back the canteen. 'Ah shit man I'm sorry I bothered you. I guess you must be a farm worker from round these parts, and I guess from how you're parked up, you're heading east. Would you be kind enough to give me a lift as far as Wood River maybe?' he hesitated putting his hands in his pockets, as if looking for something to show Nathaniel, then changed his mind. Then less confidently than he had begun, he said, 'I would kinda like to stay off Highway 30.'

Nathaniel lifted a hand to halt Charles from any further explanation and waved him to get in.

'Thanks man I really appreciate it,' sighed Charles. Nathaniel took the bag out of his passenger's hands, reached into it to find a pencil, and wrote his name at the top of the newspaper.

'Nice to meet you Nathaniel,' said Charles Hirsch

Nathaniel started the old Ford flatbed and continued to follow the straight road ahead. It became the Wood River Road leading to the junction with the Nebraska Highway. As they pulled up at the crossroads Charles looked uneasily south toward Wood River Town.

'Do you have business in Wood River Mr Nathaniel?' Nathaniel shook his head. Charles looked exhausted and about as uncomfortable as a man could be, but more than anything else he looked frightened.

Charles closed his eyes, bit his lip and opened his hands, looking desperately at Nathaniel. 'Okay your choice Nathaniel, I can't think about it any more. I'm running from the Vietnam draft,' Charles swallowed hard. 'Leave me here and I'll go jump the train, once I'm past Grand Island I should be safe for a while. Or if you're going on past Grand Island to wherever you're going, take me with you. I know someone in Omaha who can feed us and I can pay you gas money for your journey on, or back.'

Charles had felt the Indian looking at him while he'd considered his next move from Wood River. He knew he was being sized up. But strangely Nathaniel's silence was comforting, that, and the turn of the old engine distancing him from the conscription letter he'd left in his sideboard draw.

He didn't have to wait long for a reply. Nathaniel shifted the gear stick and pulled left across the road junction, heading north towards Cairo. Less than a mile up the road he turned right, heading east again down another of the long straight roads that crisscross the endless agricultural land. Nathaniel pulled over where the road temporarily widened and wrote onto a space of his paper again.

I CAN TAKE YOU TO YOUR FRIEND. I MAY HAVE BUSINESS IN OMAHA.

'WOO!' shouted Charles suddenly exploding into life. 'Business is what I'm all about Nathaniel, I don't want to die in fucking Nam. Jeez I've got so much more to offer the world than just my fat ass as cannon fodder.'

Nathaniel stopped Charles from any further talk with a straight face and a short wave of the paper. It was only 20 miles to the outskirts of Grand Island where they would have to fill up with gas and get some food. Nathaniel knew the back roads nearly all the way to Omaha, he'd worked on many farms across the state, always moving far enough away to let memories fade. By the time they pulled up at the gas station Charles was asleep and Nathaniel left him that way. They crossed the Platte River in darkness just north of Central City on the 92 and headed east again for thirty or forty miles until Nathaniel finally turned south and switched off the engine. It was time he slept, if only for an hour or two.

Stirred by the sound of food being unwrapped, Nathaniel did not open his eyes until a sense of unease overcame him. From the rear view mirror he could see Charles looking through his bag. He'd lowered the tailgate and was handling the dollar bills that Nathaniel had saved over the last four years. Charles counted the tight rolls, inspecting them with widening eyes. All in all, he reckoned with the loose change there must be nearly seven grand. He'd also found Samuel's dagger which he'd laid on the tailgate. Preoccupied by mentally spending the money, he didn't hear the driver's door open, but he did feel Nathaniel's hands suddenly grip his throat from behind.

Charles knew no more until he woke up to find he had been propped up against the back wheel. Nathaniel was sitting a few yards away on a rise, silhouetted by the rising sun. He was playing with the dagger, twisting and spinning it in his hands.

'Hey man,' Charles croaked holding a hand to his neck 'I was just trying to find some ID.'

Nathaniel did not look up.

'I guess I'm not the only one trying to change the direction of his life, huh?'

Still there was no response.

'I was not trying to rob you Nathaniel! Jeez you've saved me from the certain death of Nam. I'm not going to tempt fate any time soon.' He pulled his knees up and started to sob. Charles was only a kid, Nathaniel saw it now, why had he not before. Just overfed by a college education that bred arrogance with no depth, and this break for freedom had drained what was left of his confidence. Charles was clearly desperate for life not to be sucked out of him by duty.

Nathaniel stood up and offered out his hand in pity, and Charles took the act of kindness with both hands. 'I was just trying to find out a little about you man. No ID? No drivers licence?' Nathaniel shrugged his shoulders in response. He'd bought his last passport in Chicago in 1933, but lost it on his return journey from Florence twenty five years later. Since then Nathaniel had had no need to travel. He'd wanted to stay in Nebraska. Charles reached into his coat and produced his own identification papers. 'It's the one thing that I have got over you. Now that we're close to Omaha, you should let me drive into town. If the cops pull us for anything at all, and you're at the wheel... well you'll get us in the shit Nathaniel. I don't suppose they'll be looking for me out here just yet.'

It had been over fifty years since Nathaniel had been detained by the law over a brawl in Manhattan, it had been a bloody incident and as a result, he'd spent three days in detention, until his employer at the time had paid his bail. Nathaniel had had to work for free for two months to repay him. He recognised the sense in Charles' gesture and waved the dagger in the direction of the driving seat.

They crossed back over the Grand Platte River heading into Omaha on the West Central Road. Charles shifted down a gear just before they entered the city. They headed north, meandering their way into the suburbs. Somewhere off North 72nd street they turned left for the last time, and a couple of hundred yards down, pulled up in front of a single storey house, little different from the hundred or more in the many neighbourhoods they had passed by so far.

With the engine turned off they sat in silence looking at the white timbers of the house. Charles turned to Nathaniel. The Indian needed a haircut, a shave, and most of all a bath, he watched him reach for his bag and write on his paper.

YOU STINK!

'Ha, you and that fucking smile man. You don't smell so good yourself,' Charles replied, climbing out of the truck. He crossed a short patch of grass and knocked on the porch door. After a second wrap of knuckles, a scruffy looking bearded man opened the door. Genuinely surprised to see Charles, he embraced him with great affection. Charles waved and Nathaniel left the safety of the truck.

'William H Jefferson, I'd like you to meet my saviour, Nathaniel.'

TWENTY-FIVE

A Club for Discerning Gentlemen

As Alessandro had neglected to give him an address, it took Joshua most of his first day in New York to find the 'Il Circolo' Club. The first, then second cab driver on the Airport ranks hadn't had any idea of the club's location, the third said he'd find out for an extra fifty, "seeing as how the place sounds kinda kinky", Joshua had declined his kind offer. Instead, he got dropped off where 84th Street met 5th Avenue beside Central Park; the cab driver had spent the entire journey giving his insight into the Air France robbery that had taken place that April. Leaving the streets, Joshua walked along a pathway to the park reservoir and looked across the water towards Upper East Harlem. It was then, as the last effects of the gin and tonic he'd consumed on the flight over left him, that he realised he was probably looking for the club in the wrong way.

Half an hour later with cold air in his lungs and a clear head, he walked into one of the city's finest hotels. Above the reception desk, which dripped with Christmas decorations, the clock ticked just past five fifteen pm. To the hotel staff Joshua looked and sounded quite the English aristocrat as he checked in. With a hundred dollar tip to accompany a discrete tone, he asked the concierge to arrange some tea from the restaurant, and contact with the most exclusive escort service in the city.

The concierge politely nodded his head, he loved the English, they always said please.

The statuesque brunette who arrived at six pm sharp, would, Joshua thought, have made Tristao grin like a Cheshire Cat. Gliding across the foyer, turning heads with her beauty. With consummate ease she met the concierge, who indicated Joshua's position, now patiently reading a paper in a high backed leather chair at one end of the bar. The concierge obligingly accepted a second hundred for his efforts and assured Joshua that he would take care of the rest of his luggage when it arrived from the airport.

Joshua enjoyed playing the part, his mentor would have been proud. With the escort on his arm he headed out to the waiting limousine, lying to the concierge that he would settle on a room upon his return.

Another hundred dollars, placed into the driver's hand, saw him on the steps of Il Circolo on the Upper East Side. Joshua turned and thanked them both explaining that he felt unwell but gave them another hundred each for their trouble. Tristao would have cursed the woman's departure.

After using his most confident knock, the large black front door of the club opened. The doorman listened to the name of Daniel Weaver in connection with Alessandro Rodiani, and asked Joshua to wait just inside the door for one moment. It didn't take long for a second man to arrive. Albert introduced himself with the same efficient and emotionless style that Stevens had mastered. He was the manager of the club and would be pleased to show Joshua to the drawing room where he could await Mr Weaver.

Joshua accepted a pot of tea, and the use of the facilities. The interior of the club shone with polish and when he glanced back Joshua could see that his footsteps had marked the brushed red carpet that lined all the hallways. Even the lavatories were elegant, with marble walls and gold taps. Joshua laughed wryly as he checked his eyes in the mirror; it was good to appreciate a posh loo in full Technicolor, without the need of smell to direct him.

Back in the drawing room he found his teapot was waiting. Once he was settled, it was poured by a polite young man, who moved so efficiently around the room he barely made a sound. Albert returned before Joshua could request a second cup, and informed him that Mr Weaver was stuck in a meeting and would pick him up for a late supper around nine thirty. Mr Rodiani requested that Joshua was to make himself comfortable in Daniel's own personal suite on the fourth floor.

For all those years on the street, Joshua had never been more grateful to change his clothes. His suit was taken away to be freshened and he allowed himself a bath, his first decent emersion into warm water since leaving the Notting Hill house. Relaxed and strangely comfortable in the chic surroundings of the club he felt the confidence of his twenties return. He ignored the choice of new underwear and shirt that had been lain out on the bed, and stayed in his dressing gown. He ignored too the television, he didn't know what to do with it. Instead Joshua turned the armchair in the corner of the room so he could look out through the window and watch the lives of others play out in the illuminated windows of the buildings opposite.

Ready and dressed Joshua was collected at nine twenty five precisely by Albert who escorted him and his suitcase down through the building and into the waiting black limousine outside.

'Would you prefer to leave your suitcase at the club, or should I place it in the trunk Sir?' Albert inquired.

'I think close by, thank you,' Joshua replied, not relinquishing it at all.

Albert nodded for the chauffeur to open the car door in order for Joshua to step inside. Once seated he took in a deep breath and exhaled slowly.

The man beside him was sipping from a glass of water which had been half wrapped in a white paper napkin. He was suited in pinstripe and looked to be mid to late fifties. Joshua thought him up to sixteen stone and six three possibly six foot four tall. The man's polished exterior was finished with blond hair, neatly and precisely parted to the left. At first he gave an air of calm, wealth and power, but as he introduced himself, Joshua noted the slight shake in his cold and clammy hand.

'Hello Joshua, my name is Daniel Weaver, his New York accent strong.

'I see you have also visited Savile Row,' Joshua said, ignoring the need to introduce himself or get into character.

'Well. Yes I have,' Daniel replied slightly bemused by the question but he followed the lead. 'And we are fortunate to have their craftsman visit us here in New York on occasion.' He shifted in his seat touched his collar and checked the position of his tie. Joshua settled back into the beige leather seat and sighed, he was tired.

'So Joshua, Alessandro wanted us to meet?' Daniel said trying to raise the tempo of his persona. He moved forward to tap gently on the glass panel that separated them from the driver, in response the car started to roll forward. Daniel coughed as if to highlight his question.

'Yes,' replied Joshua. 'He did.'

'I know you have no reason to agree...'Daniel said hesitantly, 'but if you are here as a professional, then can I just sign a few things over... to my wife... downtown. I won't run. After all there's no point,' he waited, while Joshua's laughter filled the car. 'Don't taunt me' Daniel said. 'Just let me sign some papers then you should carry out your instruction.'

'Relax Daniel; I'm not here to kill you. Not yet.'

'It's just that Alessandro never sends anyone unless...'

'Yes. I can see the reason for your concern,' Joshua replied. 'Mr Rodiani merely thought you could be of some assistance, to get me started on a little errand.'

'In that case Joshua, I would of course be pleased to help in any way possible,' Daniel said relaxing. He put down his glass of water onto the shelf which was moulded onto the door, then lifted a section of the seat next to him and pulled out a bottle of whiskey. Adding a large measure to the water he replaced the bottle and sat back.

'Forgive me Joshua would you like a drink?'

'No thank you. I only really drink when I'm flying. Helps the nerves you know.'

With the reflections of Manhattan sliding over the black polished surface of their car, Joshua gave Daniel the rundown of his mission, and Daniel responded with suggestions of how he could help, including his own financial input. With business out of the way they stopped to eat downtown. In the restaurant they found common ground on the subject of jazz and talked on for what seemed hours. In the end it was Joshua who suggested a return to the club where maybe they could both get some rest.

The following morning Joshua broke from his usual breakfast of steaming tea and ate a good meal. He hadn't had

313

scrambled eggs that tasted as good since his days at Winchester and he enjoyed a read of the New York Times. Having stayed in other rooms Daniel joined him, declining eggs for his favourite bagels and coffee.

'Just one thing that nearly slipped my mind,' Joshua said placing his cup back in its saucer. He reached into his blazer pocket and pulled out the baseball Rodiani had entrusted to him in London.

'Ah the Pipp ball, I wondered when that would come back for safe keeping.'

'It is obviously something of great value. Forgive me, I should have given it to you before.'

'It is valuable Joshua,' Daniel said running his fingers over the red lacing. 'And extremely valuable to Alessandro.'

'Is it part of a collection?'

'Not in a collection, I'm sure there would be too many other balls that Wally Pipp touched... Besides, his signature has almost completely gone. See here that's all that remains of it,' Daniel lifted the ball up for Joshua to see.

'So why the significance?'

'That, Joshua, is something that Alessandro would have to explain, all I know is that he has had it a long time, and he only entrusts it to a few.'

'It probably seems like an obvious question, but why doesn't it go into a safe?'

'The one thing Alessandro has always been adamant about, is that it never leaves the direct contact of the person who is looking after it.'

'Surely he would never know and if it's so personal, it seems a little odd that he does not keep it himself.'

314

'He told me once, Joshua, that he had learned from his mistakes, said that he had a few different items which he liked to keep transient. The guy was steaming at the time Joshua, but deadly serious. As for the safe, I would not dare risk it. I know if I were to lose this ball, well, I doubt death would be a release from Alessandro's anger. He's a lunatic when he gets mad. There are only two people in the States whom he would trust with it, that's myself and my friend Robert Faulkner.' Daniel took a last sip of his coffee and placed his cup back down. He pushed his chair back from the table a little and folded his arms. 'Alessandro must really trust you. He only ever lets that crazy Maglanis bring it over.'

'Then, that perhaps is the second thing I should have relayed earlier.' Joshua chose, rather than reveal the truth, to blame Tristao's death on his failed drugs deal. Weaver accepted the news with sadness, but commented that though Maglanis had always been reckless he had not expected him to die by anyone's hand other than Alessandro's. At 11 am, the limo returned outside to take them both to the JFK airport. Their journey through the streets of Manhattan passed with ease, their mutual love of jazz filling the car with shared stories. When this business was complete, Daniel offered to fly Joshua to the Lighthouse, where he could hear the best of the east coast jazz bands. At the airport they shook hands in the limo.

'So Joshua, I'll contact our man Lieutenant Hathaway. I think I'll put the feelers out to Philip Wilson too; he's what I call a bit of a wild card. Alessandro likes and trusts him, though many others would not. I will wait for your call at the club. Good luck Joshua and let me know your destination from Omaha, that way I can keep Alessandro informed.'

'Thank you Daniel, you have been most accommodating,' Joshua said closing the door.

Around the same time as Nathaniel arrived outside the inconspicuous house of William H Jefferson, the tyres of flight 873 left a stream of smoke on the Omaha runway. Joshua had always hated flying and despite his usual disregard for alcohol, he had drunk two double gin and tonics in the New York terminal while he waited for his flight. It had worked on the flight over from London, so surely it would work again 48 hrs later. Whilst in the air he got the taste for more and had a measure for each state which passed below. Unfortunately, when they landed, he was so unsteady he had had to use his age for sympathetic guidance into the Omaha terminal. With only his battered suitcase to think about, he retreated into the nearest toilets to relieve his bowels. Relieved that within the confines of the cubicle there were less spinning objects he promptly fell asleep.

Two hours later the sounds of a man whistling woke him.

'Fuck,' Joshua said out loud, his backside felt as if the rim of the seat had been burnt into his cheeks. 'Fuck,' he said again as he realised his left leg had gone completely numb. He stumbled against the door almost tripping over his case as he tried to dress himself, a migraine rapidly spreading across his face.

'Are you okay in there?' the man called from outside the cubicle.

Joshua didn't reply, instantly embarrassed, he was very aware that if he left the cubicle now, disorientated, limping and clutching his backside, his ability to explain himself would be limited.

'Hey are you okay,' the caller now knocked on the door. 'Do you want me to call someone'

'No, no thank you. I just had a bit of an upset stomach. I, I think it's passed now, thank you.'

'Are you sure buddy?' the man asked again, it sounded like he had his hand on the door. Joshua realised from the gentle concern in the voice that the man couldn't be airport security.

'Yes, sorry to have bothered you.'

'English, huh!'

'Yes.'

'So polite even when you're holed up blowing chunks.' With that, the man's footsteps shuffled off out of the toilets, and Joshua took this opportunity to leave before he drew any more unwanted attention.

Once outside the airport amongst the sounds of Christmas songs, he found a cab, and asked the driver to take him downtown, somewhere central, where he could get a sandwich and a cup of tea. The unshaven driver had long greasy hair and kept staring at Joshua, who was in no fit state to defend himself. He just hoped the Christmas hit parade that blared out of the radio would stop the driver asking him questions, or require the use of violence. Bodies were always harder to hide in a strange town, especially when hung over. Finally as he pulled over to drop Joshua off, the driver handed over a small card which read, FINNEGAN'S OPTICIANS. 'My father uses them, they might be able to help you, you know, with your eyes.' The driver said gruffly yet sincerely.

'Thank you, you are very kind,' said Joshua reaching up to feel the wet of blood under his eyes.

He sighed, he had not even felt the blood, and couldn't hide his desperate disappointment as he found some money for the fare. 'Keep the change,' he said.

Joshua found a handkerchief and cleaned himself up the best he could using the window of a parked car. His eyesight was now irritating him, often blurring into the negative when he blinked, so he walked into the first bar he found. He desperately needed to sit down and gather his thoughts, but he had to walk straight out again. The lights were so low he couldn't see the bar, and the migraine he'd developed in the airport was now threatening to paralyse all his senses, not least his eyesight. Back outside Joshua walked a little way then took a moment to lean against a car and steady himself.

The stillness calmed him and oddly so did the concern of an elderly gentleman who pointed him across the road to the yellow sign of Ben's Bar and Tea House. Realising that his vision was settled Joshua crossed the road and stepped inside. There was a large window looking back out onto the sidewalk, so he sat at the end of the long bar closest to it and ordered a pot of tea. While he waited Joshua watched what was now a steady stream of human traffic outside, their motion further relaxing his mind, better than television he said to himself. Reaching inside his jacket pocket Joshua touched his passport and return tickets to New York. They reminded him of Tristao and he smiled at his memory. Tristao's company, no matter how crass, had been as sincere and welcome as Daniel's had been.

Joshua's daydream was interrupted by the tap of a spoon on a metal pot. 'I said here's your tea Mr.' It was the bartender. If he could have seen the colour of the tea, Joshua would never have put it to his lips. The underground café in London had dished up some bad brews, but none compared with this mixture of coffee, sugar, and stale tea. Al would never have been happy here.

'I think I'd better stick with coffee, if you don't have any tea,' Joshua said after spitting the fluid back into his cup.

'One coffee coming up,' said the bartender taking the offensive tea away. He wasn't sure whether he should apologise. In the three years since he'd had the place, nobody had ever asked for tea, so the bags he'd just used, had been inherited from the last owner.

'This place has the best coffee in town, though I usually stick to the bourbon,' said the man three stools down, raising his glass in confirmation. He looked about the same age as Joshua and sat with a straight back, with a paper laid out on the bar in front of him. The stranger wore a well ironed shirt, its collar starched, his greyed regulation hair style, was neatly parted on the left. One hand held the crease of his trouser leg, in the other a glass, empty but for a lonely ice cube which he was spinning round and round.

The two of them were the only customers sitting on the bar stools. Behind them and towards the back of the bar, at a wall table, two other men sat opposite each other. Joshua could make out that one was skinny and bearded, bit of a hippy, the other shorter, chubby, and looked like he'd been in the same clothes far too long. The two looked like reunited friends, and were talking happily over a pitcher of beer.

'Forgive me for saying mister, but you look like you're new in town,' said the other man on the stool.

'Yes,' replied Joshua, 'I arrived today.'

'Are you here for business or leisure?' At this question, Joshua turned his head from the stranger and looked out of the window.

'Louis give the guy a break,' the bartender said. 'I'm sorry mister, Louis can be a real pain in the ass.'

'No, it's okay,' said Joshua turning back to Louis, it was obvious he was a retired cop. 'I'm just passing through, Louis.'

'You're British, right?' asked the barman.

'No shit, Sherlock,' said Louis.

'Who?' asked the barman.

'Sherlock Holmes,' put in Joshua. 'And yes, I am British, Louis.'

'What brings you to Omaha mister?' Louis persisted, sipping his refilled drink, the ice clinking in his glass.

'My name is Joshua, and I'm just passing through. I'm intending to do some demographic research in the farmlands around the Kearney area.' He found himself saying. It sounded convincing, no matter how unprepared he was for any questions it might raise.

'Oh,' replied Louis, draining his glass again and raising it for a refill. 'Thought maybe you'd come here to visit that fancy eye doc, what's his name Ben? Is it Finnegan or something?' He'd been a cop thirty two years. Twenty two here in Omaha, ten before that in Lincoln, and a soldier before that. Louis thought he knew all about the criminal life of the city, and had even been out to Grand Island once or twice a year, he knew nothing nor wanted to know anything about farming. Joshua's coffee arrived. The barman had taken his time over its preparation, hoping to show off, thinking maybe this Joshua could recommend the bar to others.

Louis went back to his paper, leaving the silence to be filled by the two strangers talking about old times. Though Joshua wasn't listening, he could tell that Louis was.

'You know Ben, it's no wonder that your generation is going off the rails,' Louis said loudly, doing his best to emphasize his patronising tone, to which Ben responded with raised eyebrows, and a shake of the head. 'I mean Jimi Hendrix, and The Rolling Stones. Hippies and bums the lot of them.' He looked back, clearly trying to provoke the other two customers. The bearded guy looked up, but said nothing his expression said it all.

'Listen Louis, you've been in here all day, maybe it's time you took a break, get some air. Come back later for a night cap,' Ben suggested. Joshua guessed he'd been through this before.

'I bet a well dressed guy like you would agree huh?' Louis said, turning to Joshua. 'I mean Jeez a man who wears a suit like that must appreciate what I'm saying. I mean, with rock star bums as role models, how in the hell are kids supposed to have any morals themselves?'

'You'll have to forgive him Joshua; I expect you were looking for a club for more discerning gentlemen. Listen I can give you the name of a real nice place, about ten minutes from here,' Ben said leaning against the bar, with a note pad, his back towards Louis.

'Please, no need to apologise at all,' replied Joshua, raising a hand to stop Ben writing down the address. 'I'm sure I've heard far worse.'

'I lived near Gibbon, Buffalo County,' Ben said, trying to be of help in another way. He felt sorry for Joshua now. 'I can tell you that life is hard out there. I was raised on the farm and worked the cornfields with my family.'

'May I ask what brought you here?' Asked Joshua.

'My elder brother was killed in Okinawa leaving me and my father to run the place. When he died three years ago, I had to sell up, and move here with my mother. You see, Ricky wanted to settle down when he left the navy, I wanted an education.

But hey, here I am, forty one, and the owner of this fine establishment.' Ben stood up and gestured around the room to the pictures of baseball stars past and present. Joshua could just about make out that one or two of them were signed. In pride of place behind the bar, a smiling Smoky Burgess.

'That guy should be in the baseball hall of fame,' Louis said, following Joshua's eyes.

'You're a big fan?' Joshua asked Ben.

'It's the only time I get to travel, I try to get to a game two or three times a year. Mostly though I listen to it on the radio, or the T.V. That was until Louis here pushed it off the bar last week. Which was pretty dumb because he's the real White Sox fan.'

'Hell Ben, and you say I go on,' said Louis proffering his empty glass again.

'I'm actually doing some research on the migration of workers through the mid west' said Joshua, following on from his earlier lies.

'Jesus, at this time of year, you must be nuts. Haven't you got no family to be with during the holidays?' Louis asked.

'Unfortunately not Louis.'

'See Ben. I'm not the only lonely old bastard in the world!'

'Louis, for God's sake give the guy a break. Tell us a bit more about your research Joshua, if you've got time that is. Be nice to talk about something other than baseball, just for a change you know,' said Ben, throwing Louis a disgusted look.

'Well Joshua my man, there are enough fucking Spics, Ities and Greeks round here, oh don't forget the Jews, starting their own farms. Jeez somebody ought to have bought up all that land years ago for the Yanks to keep,' said Louis with increasing volume. 'You see, all it would take is enough cash...'

Louis realised nobody was listening, and stopped talking to cup his glass with both hands, staring down at the ice.

'I'm also interested in the integration of the native Americans into the farmlands,' Joshua continued spurred on by Ben.

'Jeez fella you do talk fancy and clever,' said Louis still staring into his glass, his tone now becoming bitter. 'You some sort of professor?'

'I'm really sorry Joshua about Louis. He helps me out from time to time. So I'm sorta stuck with him. All those years on the force have messed with his head and it's not the sort of welcome to Omaha that's good for trade. Listen if it'll help you, I'll give you the name of my buddy back home,' said Ben reaching for his note book and writing down an address. 'He'll know most of the farms up to and around Kearney.'

'I know some officers in Grand Island who'd like to give you a hand with those fucking immigrants,' said Louis, his voice slurring badly. 'If they want to stay here, they should be sent to Nam, prove themselves worthy. I bet the cops would help you with that too. They'd add them to the list of fucking hippy draft dodgers they're chasing.' Louis looked round the room making sure everybody heard him. 'A bullet up the ass would sort their heads out Ben, get them off the dope they smoke too.'

'Come on now Louis, take off will you,' Ben said taking the glass out of Louis' hands. 'It's not just your bar. Jeez, how many more times. Go home, eat something. Be an asshole somewhere else.'

From the corner of the room the two men stood up, leaving their pitcher of beer empty. As they walked past Joshua and Louis, the bearded man shook his head at the cop.

'Thanks buddy,' the chubby man said, thanking Ben for the beer as he settled the tab. 'But you know, I don't think we'll be back, the air is far too heavy.'

'Jesus Christ Louis!' Ben said under his breath.

'Just another twisted fucked up cop,' said the bearded man. Louis stood up ready for a fight, only to find he was too unsteady, and a good foot shorter than his intended opponent so quickly sat back on his stool and resumed his attack with a snarl.

'Leave it Will, will you,' the chubby man said, grabbing hold of his friend's arm.

Through the window Joshua could see the two men talk briefly, then walk off. Following their lead Joshua drained his cup and thanked Ben and Louis for their company. The coffee hadn't been much better than the tea, but the caffeine and sugar would sustain him until he could find a bed for the night, hopefully with a good breakfast the next morning.

'Whatever happened to admiring the great stars?' said Louis, once again the lone customer of Ben's Bar. 'James Stuart, Cary Grant, Doris Day. They not only make great icons but star in great films. Hitchcock thrillers! Now that's good entertainment, not all this fucking hippy love.'

'Ah shut up Louis,' said Ben.

TWENTY-SIX

The Media Room

After Nathaniel left, Mary sat alone until the sun started to shine in through the windows of her home. Drained, she looked around the room which had once been so familiar and comforting, but now felt stifled and binding. She had not, nor could not, move since he had left. She felt sick and empty.

The crude map and the notes Nathaniel had made lay on top of the old journal he'd given her. His last note stared up at her:

I will return and explain this life.

What the hell it meant, she had no idea.

'Who are you Nathaniel?' Mary said out loud, only one of a thousand thoughts which had rattled around in her head, as one morning hour had merged into another. Now this thought had been vocalised, anger rapidly spread through her, replacing despair with disgust. She threw his journal to the floor and ran from the house. Out through the yard, until the bitter winds of December cut hard through her shirt and old jeans, checking her pace until she had to stop. She stood shaking, looking down the road, wiping the tears from her eyes and running her cold hands through her hair. She looked back at the farm buildings and felt the dirt between her bare feet. It all fought to smart her emotions and bring her back to reality. Except her lover's kiss and the unravelling night that they had just spent together would not be chilled. Mary closed her eyes into the wind and raised her arms to the God she had prayed to for so long. Neither were forgiving or forthcoming, only unrelenting, the only change was in her.

Returning to the house, Mary ignored the journal, made herself some coffee but always kept the pages within her view. With a mug cupped between her hands, she returned to her chair and stared at its cover in front of her. His life was in that battered journal, held tightly closed by leather laces that ached to be undone. In the shortening shadows of the house, Mary drained her mug and reached forward to pick up the book and lay it on the table, her hands trembling as she untied its bindings. She counted twenty pages which had been bound to form a spine against the leather cover, the thread was fraying and Mary had to be careful not to pull the pages away completely. The pages were of thick, faded parchment onto which were drawn circles and squares that made up patterns, some complex some simple. Lain flat in between many of these pages were four or more clippings, either cut or torn from newspapers, some so thin and faded that they were transparent.

She debated for a moment if this were stolen, was this man she loved a thief? Was that the secret of his silence? So it was a mixture of anger and curiosity that forced her hand to turn the pages.

The patterned leaves held no writing, if they were religious it was not obvious, a knot in her stomach considered the devil's foul hand in her lover's tale. Though this thought quickly passed when she began to study the varied newspaper off-cuts.

On many there were dates, a few stretching back into the 19th Century. Not all were American or English, she recognised others as French, then guessed at some being German, and had to look over onto Pa's bookshelves to confirm it. He'd collected books from Europe as mementos of his time there as a soldier during the second world war. Others in his company had collected knives, money or bits of uniform, but not Joseph, he wanted to bring something back that reminded him of the journey and not of his friends who had fallen. Mary could only guess at the origin of other clippings, they could be Chinese, Russian or Italian, yes she was sure some were in Italian. She grinned, father had often joked about the Italians he had met. Joseph had even learnt to write a bit of their language and Ma had always teased him with her own poor impressions.

On some of the newspapers were pictures of varied quality, which changed as the print houses had changed their methods over time, starting with drawings and etchings and transcending into photos. The earliest was March 5th 1861 declaring Abraham Lincoln as president. In the same fragile pile, an article, dated Wednesday 15th July 1863, reported from New York, on the third day of the Civil War draft riots that were bloodying the streets. Mesmerised, Mary read on tracking history through different languages. Between the last two pieces of parchment only one of the five were written in English, it was dated 8th May 1945, and celebrated VE Day.

'Explain this life,' Mary said shaking her head again. 'All I wanted was to grow old with you.'

She was numb and had to move, turn her eyes away and get a drink. Ma and Pa would be home soon and what in God's name was she going to say to them. She'd have to explain some part of Nathaniel's departure. After pouring a glass of water in the kitchen, Mary sat back down for one last look.

It was on an Italian paper that she first saw him, in a photo of a group of men. They were all dressed in suits and appeared to be celebrating. Of the five men, the one second from the left looked familiar. Mary turned a few pages, and a few years back, and there he was again, this time on page twenty five of the English Times. The man was, say, fifty five, and of stocky build. He had receding hair, but there was no record of his name. Intrigued, Mary looked through the pages again, again separated by another ten years his picture appeared, this time only as part of a much larger group and only his head was visible. Her stomach cramped as she looked on. The same man 1875, 1898, 1912 in France, 1917 in Germany, 1929 in New York. Surely this could not be the same person. The last clipping had his clearest photo, from a 1958 copy of the All'interno di stampa a once popular but short lived paper from Florence.

'Well Nathaniel, whoever this man is or whatever this book is, it's got you scared,' Mary sighed, and looked back out of the window to the cold morning outside.

'Ah Shit,' she said her stomach wrenching. 'Why did I have to go and fall in love with you.'

TWENTY-SEVEN

Back to the City

Even though William had cleared the spare bed of old clothes and opened the window, the room was still stuffy. Nathaniel was so tired he didn't mind, it was no worse than many of the houses and stables he had stayed in. So, on the soft mattress he was more than comfortable, and it was to the muffled sound of friendship from the next room that he fell into a long sleep.

When he finally woke the following morning, Nathaniel found Charles sipping coffee with Will in his ramshackle kitchen. They were still reminiscing, and rather than disturb them Nathaniel chose to get some cold December air and stepped outside. The neighbourhood was quiet, save a passing car whose driver barely fit behind the wheel, and a little old lady who walked with a determined gait dragging her small yappy dog behind her. Once he reached the brow of the hill ten houses up from William's own, he turned back. Outside the Jefferson house he saw the two men still chatting through the window. He wanted solitude, so opened up the truck, pulled out the blanket from behind the seat and settled into the passenger side.

It didn't take long for Charles to knock on the window as he had done before. This time offering a mug of coffee which was so full it was spilling over the edge. Charles explained he and

William had a plan to drive into town, visit some of their old haunts, grab something to eat and plan their next move. Nathaniel declined the offer to join them; he needed time to think but was glad to give them the use of the truck.

Watching them drive away Nathaniel made his way back into the spare room. He lay down on the bed and watched the dust play in the late morning sunshine, until he closed his eyes and nodded off. When he woke the sun was setting and he was still alone. He managed to make coffee in the cluttered kitchen and resigned himself to heading off as soon as the others returned. Moving through into the lounge he sat back on an old couch that faced towards the kitchen, and not toward the T.V, which was the only other piece of furniture in the room. Nathaniel finished his coffee stretched his arms out in front of himself and thought about taking off regardless of the truck. He could buy another one and head across state, this time without any freeloaders. It was then that the two men returned muttering about some old cop they'd just met in a bar.

'So Nathaniel,' Charles said loudly, 'William and I have been thinking of a way forward. I mean to say, how we could work together.' He waited for a reaction, but Nathaniel looked unimpressed. 'Well we've thought of a way to increase your savings and make us all some real money.'

Nathaniel looked the two men up and down to weigh up his options. He reached for the newspaper-come-notepad and started to write his departure note, enough was enough.

'A business proposition you could say,' Will added, the alcohol bringing a smile to his face as he reached out for his friend's shoulder. 'Chuck here says you want to get to New York and well, seeing as you are a bit restricted without I.D to fly. You could come with us... we'd work together to get you there. We'll explain on the way but with the right roll of the dice, we could take down a few business men on the way,' the grin left his face before he concluded, 'Redistribute their wealth a little. What do you say?'

Nathaniel sat back on the couch. The bitterness in William's voice smacked of a vengeance he easily identified with. It was risky to mix another man's revenge with his own. The saving grace here though, was that it was low key, and he could always get out if it got too messy. With his decision made Nathaniel wrote on the paper:

AS LONG AS WE'RE HEADING IN THE RIGHT DIRECTION.

'Fucking A, man!' Charles exploded punching the air.

'The plan needs a little work, but basically we heard this guy in a bar downtown talking about buying up land... we'll use that as the basis of a hustle.'

They loaded up the old ford and headed out the following day. After a fuel stop at Big Len's diner they headed for Des Moines, taking it in turns to drive and sleep, always pushing on until they crossed the state line into Illinois where they spent a night and a day in Davenport.

After leaving Ben's bar, Joshua walked through downtown Omaha. Like New York, it felt good to be in a town where he knew nobody and with his vision thankfully clearing he remembered his promise to Daniel Weaver. He found a bar with a phone in, and dialled out to the Il Circolo. Albert picked up the phone, and was quick to get Daniel.

'Hi Joshua,' said Daniel, clearly relieved to speak to him again.

'Hello Daniel,' Joshua replied.

'Your timing is great. I've just had a call from Alessandro, making sure we met, checking up on your progress.'

'Oh I see,' replied Joshua annoyed at Rodiani's pressure. 'Yes well, my progress is satisfactory thank you.'

'Great,' Daniel said, unsure of how to continue.

'I would be grateful perhaps, if you could tell Mr Rodiani I've remembered all the things I love about this great country of yours. I'm going to drive to Grand Island, Daniel, and I'll ring when I get there. Goodbye.' Joshua didn't wait for a reply and hung up.

Waiting in the parking lot of a Davenport motel, Nathaniel and Charles watched their companion walk back to pay for their rooms from the previous night. After spending several days cramped in the truck they'd all benefited from a decent bed to stretch out on, and some solitude.

'You made the right choice man,' Charles said excitedly. 'William's a real talent, you'll see what I mean when we hit Chicago.'

Nathaniel grabbed the local paper he had been reading and a pencil from his bag, to write:

CHICAGO IS NOT NEW YORK!

'Like he said Nathaniel, he wants to get into some business deals, redistribute some wealth, maybe play some cards; from there we head straight to New York. What do you say?'

IT SOUNDS LIKE A DANGEROUS DISTRACTION.

'Relax Nathaniel, we've come this far. Before you know it we'll have you in New York wealthier than you could have dreamed of!' Charles was nodding his head rhythmically and rubbing his hands together.

Nathaniel opened his door, this was a bad plan.

'Just hang on, let William explain when he's ready,' Charles leaned forward to stop Nathaniel leaving. 'Here he comes now.'

Joshua arrived in Grand Island after a long uncomfortable drive. He'd not driven alone since 1952, and five years before that in the States. Although Tristao had tried to help him with some time behind the wheel in London, it hadn't taken long for Joshua to hit a couple of parked cars and his mentor to run out of patience. The lessons had ended with an argument, Tristao throwing his arms in the air and walking off down the street, leaving Joshua to reverse away from a post box and slowly crawl back in first gear toward Ealing. Now, with colour back to his vision he drove without incident. He found, however, the concentration needed was extremely tiring, especially after having so little sleep since arriving in Omaha.

Joshua drove for as long as he could into the night until his eyes started to close. He decided it was time to stop when he saw the vacancy sign flash at the entrance to Kimball's Motel. Fortunately, Kimball's only had a few seasonal decorations on the outside, and when he walked in through the open door he was pleased to find a tiny representation of a Christmas tree, placed in one corner.

Behind the counter at reception a woman, whom Joshua thought was in her early twenties, flicked over the pages of a book. She barely acknowledged his arrival leaving him to wait patiently.

'Hey,' the girl said not looking up.

'Hello,' Joshua replied

'I guess you're looking for a room?'

'Yes,' Joshua looked over at the Christmas tree again. 'For a few days I think.'

'Sure, we're pretty empty so take your pick,' the girl was finally looking at him and gesturing behind herself at three rows of keys that hung from neatly lined hooks.

'Please, you choose. However I would be grateful for a room with a kettle.'

'You're British right? You visiting family here in Grand Island?'

They stood in silence for a moment, in an oddly comfortable silence between two strangers. Joshua liked the way her blonde hair fell around her turtleneck sweater and she had a nice face, unaffected by her position or the season.

'I'm actually on my own. and not visiting anyone' Joshua replied.

'Oh,' the girl said 'that's kinda sad?'

Joshua again took a moment to reply. 'You are so very right young lady, I miss my family.'

'Well, you seem like a kind man, so take this key. 57 is a nice big room, it's just up the stairs and about fourth on the right. I'll do you the same rate for the smaller rooms, you know, as you're here for a few days. You got any more bags apart from that old case?'

'No, this is all I've come with.'

'Well I'm here all through Christmas too, so anything that you need just give me a call.'

'Thank you,' Joshua replied taking the keys from her outstretched hand. Her touch was so soft against his tired tight skin. Both sensuous and soothing, the contact brought an appreciative lightness to his weary body and in response the girl stood up as the keys left her fingers.

'I hope you like your room,' she said, as the moment was broken and Joshua headed toward the stairs, except after a few steps he turned back to catch her eye.

'Forgive me but...' he started but his words faltered, as he rationalised his thoughts.

'Yes?'

'May I just ask why you're not playing Carols or Sinatra classics?'

She returned his smile and said. 'The manager's away now, and including you there are three people staying here Mr ...' She looked down at the register to remind herself, but Joshua hadn't signed in. 'Mr?' she asked.

'My name is Joshua, and why are you not out dancing?'

'Well Joshua. I just don't get Christmas or men no matter how much I try, so well, I work instead.'

Joshua nodded his understanding, and turned back towards the stairs. While he stayed at the hotel he never asked the girl's name, nor did she offer it, but he gladly accepted her company and the fresh pot of tea she brought him on Christmas morning. Why? He didn't know, but he listened to the stories about her family and her father, who hated the fact his little girl was growing up. In return he told her about his son and how he'd taught him to swim in the sea. With the mention of the sea the girl told him how much she wanted to travel. Another month here, two at the most and she was heading for L.A. where she could be free.

Four days after he entered Kimball's yard Joshua left the hotel with a gentle kiss from the girl and his old battered suitcase. An hour later he found breakfast in a diner and looked up the contact Ben had given him. He did make some further inquiries in the morning but decided by the time he was eating lunch Ben's lead was still the strongest, it had a good feel about it.

Joshua tutted to himself as he got behind the wheel, there was something about those two men that had left the bar in Omaha. It was something he couldn't quite put his finger on as he drove onto the long straight roads that crisscrossed toward and beyond Wood River town. The endless, crop-less, cold landscape surrounding him was dusted with snow and soon tired him out. Deciding that he needed a break, Joshua chose to knock on a couple of doors, it would help warm up his persona. It was a doorstep manner that he'd come up with on the road from Omaha. He would say he was following a research line backed by the University in Kearney.

When questioned on his timing he would apologise and say the research was actually government funded and he had a limited time scale to deliver results. So conservatively dressed, armed with pencil and notepad, most who opened their doors to him were friendly and sympathetic to his cause.

William brought the old Ford to a stop outside the Johnston's Guest house on the outskirts of Aurora and turned to his fellow companions. 'Time to level with our friend, Charles. I've been in the speculations business for twelve years Nathaniel. I've played the best and most simplest scams. I've always kept safe by aiming low and getting out quick.' He hesitated and took a deep breath, slowly exhaling. Suddenly, struggling to explain anymore, he got out, stretched and looked back at them. 'It has always gone to plan. That is, up until last year when I over stepped the mark a little. I didn't have enough cash to back up my mouth. I lost and I got my legs broke you see.'

Nathaniel rested his head back on the car seat and sighed.

'Listen to me. At least I'm being honest with you and I can see I'll have to prove myself. Now I'm not no queer here but there's something about you Nathaniel. It was you brought us together, it's something that makes me think we can really do this.'

Charles was nodding enthusiastically in agreement looking for Nathaniel's approval.

But Nathaniel closed his eyes.

'Listen I've been counting decks since I was twelve man. So you lend me a hundred dollars and if I don't at least double your money tonight you can dump us here and move on to the Big Apple.'

'Come on man, one more night's not going to hurt is it?' Charles said, his voice shaky as he looked down at his trembling hands. 'Nathaniel without you, we're screwed.'

ONE NIGHT! Nathaniel wrote, then handed over the money.

The following morning after a sleepless night in a cheap bed, Nathaniel let himself into his companion's shared room. There was no sign of William and the clock read ten past five. Frustrated, Nathaniel closed the door and returned to his room. He washed, dressed and in an effort to clear his head he stepped outside. He found William asleep in the truck, four hundred and twenty three dollars up.

On his second day of knocking on doors, Joshua was pointed in the direction of the Schwartz farm by a delivery truck driver who had stopped to make sure he was alright. The driver had seen Joshua lain across the back seat of his rented Chevrolet. Tiredness had again caught up with him and he had needed forty winks on the side of this empty road. By the time Joshua had been woken a tractor had approached from the other direction. Neither driver understood Joshua's joke about three London buses, but were interested in what an Englishman was doing out here, dressed the way he was at this time of year.

The Schwartz family farm was about a half hour north west of Wood River. 'They have a Brazilian guy working for them. Quiet guy never talks to me, but might be able to help.'

After another hour's drive, Joshua saw the white painted wood of the Schwartz farm house reflecting grey in the dark sky. The exact same house he had seen in Rodiani's basement. He parked the Chevrolet in front and with pen and paper in hand, he knocked on the fly screen door.

'It's all in the wrist' said William to the other men as they sat in the Jackson's basic diner. Charles and he were slurping coffee to wash down a breakfast of pancakes and bacon that Nathaniel had abstained from. Having accidentally stumbled into the kitchen in the early hours, he had opted for toast and orange juice instead, he felt safer as both items either needed their surfaces burning or had been stored in a sealed container. Unaware of Nathaniel's concern for the discoloured drying meats he had found in the rudimentary kitchen, both William and Charles had eaten well. If fate was driving this road trip, Nathaniel decided, he would give into its whim.

William pushed his plate away and mimicked his winning throwing action. 'Craps was always a favourite of mine as a kid. Did us well again last night huh gentlemen, what do you say?' He high five'd Charles, who whooped with delight. 'Dice are one thing, but cards, now that's where the big bucks start to fall.' He sat back making sure his audience was as ready as they could be for his romantic recollection. 'Poker Nathaniel, that's what I like to play. I love the way those two cards, laid flat in front of you, just ache to be turned. There's nothing like that feeling when you just know enough about the others at the table, to see the fading look in their eyes. That's when you know the hand you've got is the one to bring them down.'

'What did I tell you Nathaniel, is this guy good or what?' Charles said, high fiving William again.

Nathaniel was struggling to match the image of this thirty something bum with the clean cut poker players he had watched during the twenties and thirties. Class was gone he assumed, the last war had done its damned best to reset the levels. 'Money will always flow with the repetition of war,' Agustin had often said during their time together. He was right of course, the money just got dirtier with the passing of time.

'The anticipation in the room,' William was still talking. 'Man it drips from their foreheads. The air is electric. It's all about holding your nerve. The queen of spades, now that's a card, last time she fell on the sweet green cloth I took home fifty thousand dollars…' Nathaniel totally tuned out this time and looked out of the window at the gathering snow clouds.

'He's got that look again,' Charles said, nudging his friend to stop talking.

'I'm telling you, it's a better drug than the coke they snort up their noses,' said William agitated that he had been stopped in mid flow. Fortunately for the other two the waitress came over to clear the table, her actions stalling William long enough for Nathaniel to pull a clean napkin from the next table and write on it.

WHAT'S NEXT?

'Chicago!' said Charles, taking on the actions of a jazz singer. 'It's Christmas time, and we reckon the big players will be out with their bonuses, handing over what's left anyway, after the turkey and the tree, and little Jimmy's train set.'

SO? Nathaniel wrote, tired of their bullshit and speculation.

'The money men love Chicago,' said William. 'It may take a game or two to get us into the right circles, but I've done it before. We need to be slick, and quick. No faltering. Don't worry Nathaniel I have a plan.'

YOU'LL NEED TO SHAVE AND HAIR CUT Nathaniel
wrote, laughing as he did.

'Yeah and we all need to be dressed for the job. I can't do this alone. That's where your money comes in Nathaniel.'

Nathaniel bought them the best suits he could afford. William was changing, the kid had guts and a spark. There was also a slim chance that Alessandro had left some trail to follow. But the more Nathaniel found confidence in his move the more he felt the pull of the Pelecaras, gnawing at him, desperate to show him the frailty of his pursuit. Just like they had always done when he spoke about Mary. 'What's the point' they had cackled. 'She's already dead?'

Nathaniel shook the memory and scribbled down:

WHAT ABOUT THE FARM DEALS?

'Good question,' agreed Charles 'Once William here has opened the door I'll introduce us as a company speculatively buying up struggling agricultural land to form an alternative alliance, we can convince prospective employers that you have all the experience to advise us.'

WRONG TIME OF YEAR?

'It's never the wrong time for these guys Nathaniel. They are businessmen through and through.' Nathaniel nodded his head in agreement. It was another long shot that might just work.

Alive with the beats and vivid with the colours of the season, Chicago was full of opportunities for William to indulge his passion. With the calculating head of a pro he quickly generated enough cash in three different establishments to raise capital and move up a level, always mindful that his left leg had never properly healed.

Nathaniel was more impressed though by Charles, who had picked up on a conversation with two men at a bar in the early hours of the morning. His awkwardness smoothed by martini, he had blagged a seat for William at a poker game with Philip Wilson, a business tycoon out of the Big Apple. Charles was given a number to call the next morning to confirm their inclusion in the game. The buy in was twenty five thousand and it would take nearly all of William's winnings to get them in. If he got into trouble they'd have just enough to feed themselves for a day or two, at which point Nathaniel would leave them once and for all.

The next day was spent in preparation and sleep, this might be the only chance they would get for a day or so. Charles called the number he had been given, and set about locating the venue. They were to arrive no later than nine, so William was left as long as possible before they woke him.

With the temperature dropping quickly on the Chicago streets which were already covered in snow, the company set off. They got a cab to cross the five blocks from their hotel, and with only five minutes to spare they walked down the narrow flight of steps that marked the entrance to Louisiana House. On the other side of the door they were frisked for guns and knives, the doormen didn't question the cash. William was nervous and Charles was running on caffeine having not slept at all. Nathaniel just hoped his nerve would hold out. They were shown through to a large bar area where twenty or so people were sipping drinks and a girl in the corner sang soul music in a dress that shimmered in the low lights every time she moved.

Philip Wilson didn't arrive until just after eleven, accompanied by a body guard and a young woman at least twenty years his junior. His entrance was well received by handshakes and kisses from those who knew him, which made it obvious who did not. Those left out, Charles assumed correctly, were here to play.

Evelyn Schwartz opened her farmhouse door to a man she reckoned to be about the same age as her husband, she squinted, but accepted Joshua's explanation and invited him inside for a warm drink. Irritated with herself that she had left her annoying glasses on her bedside table, it was obvious to Joshua that she couldn't quite focus as well as she once had.

'Sit down, sit down,' Evelyn said, 'I'll put the kettle on the stove, help yourself to cookies. You look like you could do with a bit more than that though. Man of your age should have a bit more weight on him.'

'Thank you Mrs Schwartz that is very kind of you. But alas as I have grown older, my appetite has dwindled. However, no man could resist just the smell of those cookies, they look delicious,' said Joshua. He sat down placing his suitcase on the floor beside him and took a cookie. 'These are very good Mrs Schwartz. Forgive my prying, but is there anybody else in?'

'Well yes my daughter is upstairs. She's not very well, and… She's taken to her bed. I'm sure I can help you with your questions, seeing as you have come such a long way.'

'Thank you. I would be extremely grateful if you could help,' Joshua was enjoying this. 'Again forgive the question but shouldn't we be sharing these with somebody else?'

'Apart from my husband, he's out on the farm, fussing over some tiny oil leak.' Evelyn suddenly felt weak and just caught hold of the couch's arm in time to prevent her legs giving way beneath her. Joshua found himself reaching out, but Evelyn found the seat without him. Overcome, Evelyn sat back and took a deep breath before she spoke. 'Jerry was my youngest, I'm afraid he… Just had to go to the war,' her eyes swelled with tears. 'My eldest boy John is now missing out there.'

'Oh Mrs Schwartz I'm so sorry, here I am disturbing you,' Joshua made a move to stand up. 'I'll come back another day?'

'No no it's alright, my husband Joseph will be back soon, he's just twice as busy since Nathaniel left.'

'Oh,' said Joshua.

'Joseph was posted to England during the last war, just before he headed off to France. He'll be interested to meet you. It'll be a nice distraction. Now, no more of my troubles, I can hear the pot bubbling. Speak up while I make us some coffee.'

343

'Did Nathaniel leave recently?' Joshua asked, repeating the question twice for Evelyn to register it.

'Yes, he was such a good helper, never spoke, had no tongue. Worked from dawn to dusk and stayed with us through all the hard times we've had. Now God save us, I don't know what we're going to do.'

The back door into the kitchen opened and Evelyn collected up a mug for her husband who greeted her with a nod and frowned at their guest. Joseph Schwartz was a farmer through and through, tanned by the wind and wizened with bitterness for his years of toil, 'Hello,' he said, his tone hard. His stare questioning.

'Joseph, this is Joshua. He is doing some research, he's come all the way from England.'

'Oh has he. Funny time of year to be doing research?'

'I was telling him about Nathaniel...'

'I told you not to mention that God damn Indian's name again Evelyn!' Joseph interrupted sternly.

'But I just don't understand why he left dear.'

'If you want to turn out our dirty washing carry on woman. Why not call down Mary, see what she has to say!'

'Please, I must take my leave, did this Nathaniel say where he was going to?' Joshua said.

'No, he left in the dead of night whilst we were out dancing. Who are you, the police'? Joseph asked eyeing up Joshua's suit.

'As a matter of fact yes,' lied Joshua 'I must apologise Mrs Schwartz you understand this is a delicate matter.'

Joseph didn't reply, he just walked over to the stairwell and yelled up for his daughter. 'Mary!! The cops are here looking for your lover. I hope they shoot the little Indian bastard.'

'Lover? What ever has he done? He was such a nice man,' asked Evelyn, the shock raising a hand to her mouth.

'Murder. Mrs Schwartz,' Joshua lied again.

Evelyn fainted, collapsing onto the floor.

'Mary get down here now,' Joseph shouted, crouching beside his wife and holding her head in his hands.

'Ma!' shouted the woman above quickly running down to her father. Except Joshua stepped forward, stopping Mary at the bottom step, grabbing her by the arms and pushing her against the wall, only to have Joseph attack him from behind.

'Let me go, you idiot!' yelled Mary.

'No, I won't Mary,' replied Joshua 'No, I won't.'

For Mary, the speed at which the stranger knocked her father to the floor totally threw her off guard and she could do little but watch Joshua's hand return to a fist before it connected with the side of her head.

In the back room of Louisiana House the clock staggered past four am. Most of the original onlookers were either too drunk to stand or had gone home. Philip Wilson shook his head. 'That's it,' he said 'You play hard William and I'm guessing you've more than broken even. A good time to quit. I can't focus on the cards anymore, let alone talk business.'

'That's a shame,' said Charles 'I was hoping we could interest you in our project. It's a real gem.'

'Yes, so it would seem,' Wilson replied. 'You said you're off to New York, right?'

'Well that was the plan,' said William, he was going to say more but Nathaniel's look stopped him.

'You know I shouldn't do this and I cannot promise anything,' Wilson sighed and sat back in his chair. He eyed

William up for a moment then rubbed his head with his hand. 'I might regret not seeing this through myself,' he stood up, removed the tie that hung loosely round his neck and tucked it into his pocket. 'Like I say I shouldn't do this, but look up my friend Robert Faulkner, you'll find him at the address on this,' he pulled a card from inside his jacket as he stood up, flicking it onto the table. 'Keep it to yourself, it's an exclusive place. Give Robert a call, tell him you've spoken to me and tell him you've got a deal the Yankees would be proud of.'

After only a few hours sleep, the three men climbed back into the old Ford. Momentum was with them, the plan was working and they should not let the snow gather to any depth or they might just falter. Nathaniel was first to drive. Proud of their achievements and pleased that his judgement had been right, he let the other two sleep. It was a long drive to the Big Apple.

A drip of fluid woke Mary. Her eyes flickered open to focus on a second drop falling from the end of needle, menacingly blurring too close to her face for her to move.

'You'll have to forgive this torture Mary. I'm too old to bare knuckle fight and too wise to carry a gun.'

'Who are you? What have you done with my Ma?' Mary seethed in anger. She began to kick but Joshua placed a foot on her chest and leant forward, the needle ever closer to her eye.

'They'll be alright, I think young lady. Now where has Nathaniel gone?'

'I don't know, away from you and…' Suddenly she had a gut feeling that the man in the newspaper clippings and this man were connected, 'and that other man…'

'Who would that be Mary?'

'The grey haired guy in the newspapers, the one… in that book. You work for him don't you?'

'You'll have to forgive me but I'd rather not answer that. However, it may help you if you told me which book you are referring to.'

'The one on the bed upstairs. It's his, it's Nathaniel's.'

'Oh now, if you have the Journal,' Joshua gave a chuckle. 'If it's the one I'm looking for, it would certainly ease your suffering considerably. I am afraid however, whilst I look, I will need to give you Tristao's medicine, it'll stop you running away.' Joshua stuck the needle into the side of Mary's neck and made his way up to her room.

Instantly Mary's fight was gone, disappearing with the needle's nick. The heroin flowed through to her blood stream like a disoriented orgasm, uncontrollable, blissful and deadly. It left no allowance for rebellion, and transformed the room into a sickening claustrophobic state, through which Joshua drifted in and out in a blur. All she could hear before she blacked out was the snap of a suitcase lock and Joshua's phone call out to the Il Circolo.

TWENTY-EIGHT

Plans and Misdemeanours

'My father used to say that there are few things in life better than an Havana cigar, a fine cognac and good company,' said Robert Faulkner, draining his second glass.

'He was right,' replied Charles, exhaling a plume of cigar smoke that gently rose into the low lit room. The touch of the leather chair all the more luxurious after the cramped conditions of the truck. As soon as they'd walked through the door of the Il Circolo, Charles felt like the deal in front of them was already done. 'Just stay confident,' he said to himself, 'I'm a successful business man.'

He looked around again at the framed photos which adorned the walls. Though mostly of retired gentlemen who must have been long serving members, there were one or two that captured other moments in time. A proud soldier distracted Charles for a moment with the memory of the draft, so he refocused on a photo of two cops shaking hands, beneath them a plaque that he could not read. Charles shuffled forward in his chair; the new suit he had bought on the way over had started to cut into him during the dessert. All he had to do was stay calm.

'I can only agree with you Charles,' said William, choosing his words carefully.

'What is your view Nathaniel?' asked Robert.

Nathaniel lifted his glass to signal his approval at the mingling flavours which lingered around the stump of his tongue.

It had been quite a journey from the Wood River road junction, where he had first met Charles to this room. So much so, that he'd had to pull the truck to a halt on the west side of the George Washington Bridge. Much to the dislike of his new friends, he needed to walk across the bridge alone, smell the sea and run his hands over the peeling paint. No matter how tense his shoulders stiffened, he just needed to remember that inside him lay the deep sense of relief that he had saved Mary. Despite what the Pelecaras had taunted, she was not already dead, and with the journal safe in her hands he would be able to explain everything to her when he returned.

Beside the bridge, Nathaniel had pulled out a fresh paper and scribbled:

I'M GOING TO WALK, IT'S BEEN A LONG TIME SINCE I WAS LAST HERE

'Are you fucking nuts it's freezing?' William had shouted in frustration.

I WANT TO TAKE IT ALL IN
CLEAR MY HEAD

'Let him go Will,' Charles had said. He could have used a walk himself but not in this weather. 'Nathaniel it's nine forty seven am. We're meeting at eight tonight, here, write down the address and don't be late. Oh and don't go messing up those fine clothes we just bought.' What harm could it do? Charles thought, as he moved into the driving seat and shifted the Ford into gear. The three of them were on the roll of a lifetime.

With a briefcase in his hand rather than a bag over his back, Nathaniel's new suit didn't stop the bitter wind cutting through to his skin, nor stop his determination to visit the junction of 142nd Street and 7th Avenue. He managed to avoid the worst of the snowy slush on the road, until he stood still at the crossing, where it washed over onto the sidewalk to wet his shoes and dampen the edges of his trouser legs. As the cars rolled by, Nathaniel took a moment to take in the street signs he had seen so many years before. He found himself staring at the tarmac and sighed, so relieved that he was here alone. It took the crashing siren of an NYPD squad car to distract him from his thoughts, its swirling lights turning right in front of him and heading toward Il Circolo.

Nathaniel walked on pulling his overcoat closer, each footstep clearing his mind further; he told himself he was doing the right thing. Nearly two hundred years of waiting had to come to an end, so if he had the chance to love again he had to find Rodiani. Whether he was in this city or not, Nathaniel suddenly felt closer to him than he had done for many years.

Robert Faulkner raised his hand to signal Albert, who nodded in recognition and brought over a crystal decanter to top up their empty glasses. The very same brand of Cognac that had been favoured by the Club for the last century. 'This is an amazing place,' said Charles, the alcohol releasing his thoughts as he sipped it.

Robert took a taste from his own glass. 'You know, I think you gentlemen were very lucky to meet up,' he said.

'You could look at it that way,' replied Charles before the others could speak, 'but I think it...'

William coughed an interruption. 'Charles and I had been looking for business opportunities within the farming communities separately for some time. It was lucky we were brought together by Nathaniel. So Charles, I hate to stop you, but I would have to agree with Mr Faulkner here.'

'Please as I said before, call me Robert.'

'Thank you Robert, you have made us feel most welcome,' William was doing his best not to become nervous. Charles was starting to look the worse for wear; too much booze would always spoil a deal. Just enough for everyone and you're home free. The last thing they needed was for the kid to mess up. 'Mr Wilson was very impressed by our presentation in Chicago. In fact, like we said earlier, he appeared very interested himself. For us it's a once in a lifetime opportunity.' William lied convincingly, they had all practiced the routine exhaustively along the open road until they'd stood on the steps outside.

'Yes and his good word has got you through the door and a seat at my table,' said Robert.

With four other New Yorkers, Robert's grandfather, James, had founded the 'Il Circolo,' to find solace from the world around them. With their acquired wealth and connections they had plotted politically and socially until they sat on the inner circles of business, subtly influencing administrations during the heyday of the stock markets and many years of war. They had stood strong during the boom times and stronger still during the stock market crash. Whatever happened, they always came away with a margin.

Since the day the club had opened in 1832 there had been few additions to the members list. After their controlled success and survival, they had had to be extremely select, a multimillion dollar bank balance, or a position of high power soon did not guarantee a place amongst these chairs. Even guests were only allowed in with the agreement of a family member. Under no circumstances would the club be compromised, business was business after all.

Albert moved between them again to fill their glasses. After thirty years at the club he had perfected a presence likened to a shadow, always at hand to refill, collect or guide, he was as much a part of the club as Robert. Placing the tray back beside the drinks cabinet, he left the room momentarily, returning to hand a small note to their host.

'Thank you Albert. Please tell Mr Weaver he can join us when he arrives,' Robert said passing the note back for Albert to dispose of.

Robert took a puff of his cigar aware that the others were watching, he exhaled releasing an expensive plume up into the hazy room.

'So,' he said, 'where were we gentlemen?'

'The deal is a sound proposition,' Charles said. William thought his voice irritatingly nervous.

'Yes, so you say Charles. Maybe it's the wine but I'd like you to re-cap. Whilst we ate you broadly went through the figures which in theory sound great... I think now... I need Charles for you to firm up the profit projection for my two million input?' Robert was looking straight at an increasingly sweaty Charles.

'Well Robert, from what Nathaniel has shown us you can expect a 200% return after five years... Er...' Charles coughed to clear his throat. 'Obviously, we are hoping that as wheat prices continue to rise... erm as we expect them to... to rise,' his confidence was going. Shit two million dollars. Stay calm, stay calm. 'Nathaniel has lined up three farms for you to view and he has given extensive advice on the equipment we need to invest in.'

'It's prime for development,' said William trying to ease the pressure on his friend. 'We know agricultural markets are still moving slow but it's a huge untamed market, with farmers who would sell for the right price, to a co-operative.'

'Tell me Charles about the families, the cost of re-housing, what percentage of my investment does that require' Robert wasn't letting go of Charles.

Albert had seen and heard this all before. There was an art to listening to the conversations which were held within these walls, and it took experience to forget what you had heard when you left the room, as he did now. Daniel would be here soon and he'd asked for some coffee to be made ready.

Albert had been at work since three this afternoon, his pocket watch now read twelve thirty. He shrugged his shoulders and stretched his neck trying to shake off his tiredness. This meeting could be over in five minutes or five hours, he could never predict which. Tucking the watch back into his waist coat, he left the coffee to brew, and discreetly returned to refill their drinks again. This time however, as Albert opened the door, Robert indicated that he should stay outside. He closed the door and listened, beginning to wonder why Daniel Weaver would want to be involved in an investment out of Chicago. Anyway, he thought to himself, it was a first to have a man from Brazil in the house. They'd had all creeds and colours here especially the Italians, but no Brazilians.

No matter what colour they were, the deal had to be big to be invited here to the club. Albert could just here Robert's voice.

'Okay gentlemen I'm still finding it hard to place all of the figures of my investment, a quick mental tot up and you've only spent one and three quarter million,' Robert said re-lighting his cigar.

'Well as we said there are … There are a few loose ends to tie up,' said Charles, looking at William for help now. 'It's very late, maybe we should meet again tomorrow afternoon. Get everything sewn up?'

'Charles you're not going anywhere until the rest of the figures are accounted for.' Robert slowly exhaled allowing the cigar smoke to roll out and up from his lips. 'Before you arrived I'd heard interesting things are happening in the Mid West. So time is short. Even as we speak, I'm awaiting on news from a colleague who has his own interests in the farming communities.' He took a moment to sip from his glass, swilling the liquid round his mouth and swallowed, looking William in the eye. 'Therefore, gentlemen, you should play your cards now.'

Charles shuffled forward, and placed his glass on the table. Its placement was deliberate, as if letting go would sober and steady his mind. Each of them must have consumed a bottle of wine at the table followed by a glass or two of dessert wine before starting on this cognac.

Why the fuck couldn't this billionaire go with the principal of the deal and why the fuck had they all drunk so much? Charles felt as if he was going to pass out.

Nathaniel watched the wisps of cigar smoke rise slowly and confidently into the room, lifting to roll along the ceiling. They were close, he could feel them.

A knock at the door disturbed them all from their thoughts. Robert called to allow the entry standing up as he did so, happy to greet his dear friend Daniel Weaver. They were as tall as each other, equally well suited and though Daniel was the younger, he was so tired he could have been ten years older. He whispered into Robert's ear, passing him an object as he did so.

Whilst his employers shook hands, Albert was distracted by Nathaniel who appeared to be listening to an unheard voice. To his right, the chubby kid, Charles, suddenly looked to be struggling to breathe. He shifted unsteadily to the edge of his chair and loosened his collar, turning pale as he did so. It was then that the Indian moved, with an action so subtle it went unseen by the others, and afterwards Albert had questioned himself. Except that he had definitely seen the silent stranger move forward, to embrace and comfort his companion without actually leaving his own seat. The whole calming and sobering action had taken less than a second but had unravelled like the slow motion shots at his beloved cinema. Albert tutted to himself, he was too tired and closed his eyes, pinched the bridge of his nose and sighed.

When he opened his eyes again he saw Charles calmly sitting upright, straightening his tie and producing a handkerchief to mop his brow. The kid reacquainted his hand with his glass, which reminded Albert of the coffee on the stove. Then he heard the phone ringing.

'Forgive me gentlemen, but you'll have to excuse me,' Albert said and Robert acknowledged his departure as Daniel sat down beside him.

'I think our intentions are obvious here Mr Faulkner,' Charles said, his tone now calm and steady. 'I fear we have all drunk too much, and to shake on a deal you are uncertain about, would be a mistake for all of us.'

Robert laughed, rolling the object he'd been given between his hands as he spoke. 'A man has his cards dealt to him, and he must play them the best he can. What do you say William?'

'That's an old ball huh?' William said.

'Yes William, once signed by the 1920 Yankees team. You used to be able to make out the signatures but they're all faded now. It's been held in the hand too long you see.'

'That will make it less valuable,' William said, his voice losing its confidence.

'Except this ball is far too valuable to us for it ever to become worthless.'

'Was it a home run ball?' William asked, getting to his feet and standing behind his chair. 'You know if it is, I'll bet it would be worth a fortune.'

Nathaniel felt the cold that darkness brings and he reached down to feel the briefcase beside his chair. Underneath the facts and bullshit figures, lay Samuel's dagger, still as sharp as the day he had first held it.

'It was Joshua on the phone Mr Peterson,' Albert said re-entering.

'Thank you I'll come straight away.'

'Unfortunately he hung up Sir. He did however leave a message.'

'What was it Albert?' Robert said firmly. 'Don't worry we're all friends here.'

'We gave it our best shot. I think we should leave you gentlemen,' William interrupted indicating that Charles and

Nathaniel follow his lead and stand up, it was time to make a retreat. Nathaniel rested his briefcase on the back of his chair, his thumbs on the two clasps.

'I make no apologies, gentlemen,' said Robert. 'This news, I think will be of interest, so tell us Albert, what did Joshua say?'

'That he has the patterned journal sir, and that he is bringing a woman with him, who he described as negotiable material.'

'I wonder, Albert, would you give Captain Hathaway a call, ask him to come down. If you could explain the situation here, I'm sure he won't mind being disturbed,' Robert said. He got to his feet and crossed the room as he spoke, closing the door as Albert departed.

'Stocks and shares, speculations and accumulations are one of the foundations of this place gentlemen,' Robert said firmly 'Forty years ago, Charles, your scam would have worked very well, and who knows maybe in the future you will be able to repeat the past, but not on this occasion. What do you say Daniel?'

'I believe Charles, that your business career will have to wait, while you catch up with you're old pals from Kearney in Vietnam,' Daniel said, his hands pushed into his trouser pockets.

'What the fuck is going on here?' Charles said.

'We've been set up. Played by that guy in Chicago,' William said desperately.

'Mr Jefferson you really should stick to rolling your weighted dice and counting cards,' Daniel continued.

'Listen Mr, whoever you are, just let us go!' Charles said. 'We don't want any trouble…'

'Be quiet now Charles, this has got nothing to do with you. In fact, given the company you're in, both of you are extremely lucky to be alive. It's Nathaniel we all have the honour of meeting.'

William stood back from his chair; with the door closed they were trapped. The only weapon they had was in front of Nathaniel. All he could do was try and blag his way out. 'I think Mr Faulkner; you mistake me for someone else. We've come out of the mid west to set up a new company. Nathaniel here wouldn't hurt a fly. Look at him, hardly a murderer!'

'William we've heard enough of your bullshit. It's Nathaniel I'm interested in. Mr Rodiani has waited a long time to catch up with him.'

Nathaniel drew the dagger letting the case fall into the chair.

'Relax Nathaniel,' Robert said holding up his hands. 'Alessandro doesn't know you're here yet.'

Nathaniel's knuckles whitened on the dagger handle, his heart racing. How could have been so stupid as to get trapped in this house? He cursed his voiceless mouth and his ignorance. He wanted to kill Rodiani without looking at him again, and yet more now than the sight of his nemesis was the fear of torture. He had been trapped like this before and lost his tongue, what Rodiani would do to Mary was unthinkable. He took a step past his chair towards Faulkner.

'You might want to wait Nathaniel,' Robert said, stepping back to block the exit. Nathaniel strode forward, grabbed him with ease and held the blade up under his throat.

'What the fuck is going on Nathaniel?' Charles shouted.

Albert entered the room, his eyes full of fear. 'Please don't hurt Robert. Please Sir, don't hurt him. Robert, I think you've got this wrong. Please let these men go, before Hathaway's men arrive.'

'Listen, we've got nothing to do with this man. Whatever trouble he is in, it has nothing to do with us,' William said as calmly as he could, his hands splayed out in denial.

'What else did Joshua say Albert?' Robert spoke as best he could.

'Daniel?' Albert said, looking for his approval to continue.

'What was it?' Daniel said, he didn't know what else to say.

'Joshua told me the woman is with child sir. She is pregnant and her name is Mary.'

Nathaniel lifted the dagger, drawing blood from Robert's neck.

'Alessandro is staying two blocks from here in an apartment on 78th Street,' Albert said quietly.

'She's pregnant Nathaniel, think about what you're doing,' Robert said, as aggressively as he could, almost gagging on his own words as the blade was pulled harder against his windpipe. Nathaniel didn't let him talk anymore, he eased Napoleon's fine dagger away then pushed it into Robert's throat, killing him in seconds. Once the body slumped down out of his grasp he plucked the ball out of his dead hand.

'The cops will be here any minute,' Albert said slowly and shakily. He looked down at the bloodied body, a man he had loved like a part of his family 'You all need to leave now.'

'Albert what are you doing?' Daniel shouted. He moved to the far side of the room away from the knife, his friend was dead and unless he could get to the armoury in the next room there was nothing he could do to avenge him.

'Oh Shit,' Charles was shouting. 'Hide us.'

'No,' Albert shook his head. 'Get out of this house.'

'I just hope it's that easy,' said Charles. He and William pushed the butler to the front door by his collar insisting that

359

he look out and make sure the route was clear. They were followed by Nathaniel, who still held the knife in one hand, the bloodied ball in the other. But they were too late, the scuffles of organised feet on the other side of the door proved Hathaway's efficiency. Nathaniel placed a sticky hand on Albert's cheek, somehow Albert understood him.

'The girl will be here soon, maybe as soon as tomorrow morning. I'll do what I can but Alessandro will not stop until he gets what he wants,' Albert said, turning from Nathaniel's hand. 'Let me talk to them,' he said, opening the door and stepping out into the darkness.

There was no alternative route because Daniel now stood behind them blocking their way, feverishly pushing shells into a shot gun and snapping it shut. Then, out front, before they could react, a heavy shoulder pushed open the front door with such force that the handle was smashed into the plasterwork. Stunned and frightened each of the three men were pulled from the house and thrown down across the steps. They barely had time to stand before the first batons of the NYPD struck.

'Hurt them boys, so they don't know who they are. Then dump them. Fucking vermin!' Oz Patterson growled. 'Hathaway says he wants to start the new year with a clean slate.'

With the cops work done Albert watched the four bodies shoved into the back of separate cars, and sat ashen faced on the club's steps. Daniel finally appeared in the doorway just as Oz Patterson loomed up the steps towards him proffering the dagger. 'I've put the ball in the Indian's pants, but you'd better take this, it's far too pretty to be on my shelf,' he said.

Applauded in the shadows by the Pelecaras the violence of Oz continued. Carrying out his Captain's orders to the letter,

Falkner was not to be found, the two hicks could fit into a case somewhere, Hathaway insisted the Indian should receive maximum pain and be left with his last breaths deep up an alley to rot. 'Make absolutely sure he will die,' Hathaway said.

It was only as the cars departed and Daniel returned to his rooms that Albert was left alone to clear the blood from the floor before the day shift started. Finally, as he washed the last blood from the mop bucket in the cellar, a cold hard hand found his shoulder and he met a creature that almost stopped his heart.

The news crews briefly recorded the bodies of Charles Hirsch and William H Jefferson as they were tagged, covered and wheeled out of a side street in the Bronx. It took two more days for Albert to find Nathaniel, on the lower east side, stinking of the piss of others, he was barely alive. Albert placed the newspaper clipping which the Pelecaras had given him into his hand, and what was left of the whiskey he had been drinking in the other. There was little point calling 911, so he stayed, not that he had been instructed to, but as his father had always said, no man should die alone.

TWENTY-NINE

Nathaniel Explains to Mary

Mary felt the car lolling from side to side again, and again she tried to lift her head up, but her neck hurt like hell, and she couldn't work out why. She felt cold, hung-over, but much worse than Joseph's whiskey ever punished her. Mary tried to flicker an eye open but it was too much, she'd have to settle on having her head up straight. The car hit a hole in the road, jerking her sideways, forcing her head against the window. She wanted to scream but could not even mumble a curse.

Trying to sit upright Mary could hear the radio was being tuned between barely audible tracks of New Year cheer. Then several long horn blasts from the oncoming traffic heralded a swerve that caused her face to judder against the glass. Again Mary tried to shout out in pain, this time succeeding with a muffled sound, that came out with dribble, blown out over her dress. The radio crackled and was switched off allowing the drone of the engine to take over.

'Hello Mary,' said a man's voice. It took a moment to register the accent and then she remembered and tried to cry out her disgust, with only the same bubbled affect as before.

'I must apologise for the bumpy ride,' Joshua said, 'I'm afraid my driving isn't as good as it once was. I'll put the radio back on, we'll chat later. Oh and don't worry I picked up the book.'

Mary passed out, lost in Tristao's toxic injection. Her disoriented mind wandered to her Mother, who would need a hand with her bath, and she'd have to get Pa, who must still be working. She'd have to go and get him now that Nathaniel was gone. Nathaniel, her lover was gone and she was trapped, confined, her retaliation reduced to phlegm. Mary tried to lift her arms to fight her way free, but they only landed in her lap. Claustrophobia clawed at her, weighing down her arms with fear.

'Do you know Mary,' Joshua said with a gentle laugh. 'Tristao did teach me something after all, that medication I gave you is very effective.'

Whether it was ten minutes or an hour later Mary had no idea, but when she opened her eyes again, her focus was better and the music a little clearer.

'Ah hello,' Joshua said, reaching over to pat Mary's hands. 'I think we've got about two or three hours before we hit the Big Apple, so you've got plenty of time to wake up. You'll be glad when you do Mary, your friend Nathaniel is waiting for us. And I hope you'll be pleased to hear, I've passed on your good news. You'll make a great mother I'm sure. It's just a shame we have had to drive. Unfortunately there was no way of getting you onto a plane… Nonetheless we've made good time.'

In the concentration of the miles that had passed since leaving the mid west, Joshua had not had much time to think about what torture lay ahead for Mary. He had done enough he thought, and would happily hand her, and this book, over to Rodiani. This he hoped would conclude their business, and with one hunt over, the search for his son's forgiveness might, perhaps, begin.

'I think we'll go over the George Washington Bridge if that's alright with you,' he said trying to distract himself from the memories of his contracted life. He began to think of Ruiz and their first meeting in Italy. Just as he had done on the streets of Milan, Joshua wondered if he should have escorted those women home, or walked away when he'd first seen the glimmer on the edge of Ruiz's blade. Would it have changed the course of his life? Would he have done things differently, if he had known what was to come?

Joshua relaxed his grip on the wheel and sighed. He wasn't the sort of man who taught his son to play cricket on a Sunday afternoon, no matter how much he longed to do so. He wiped a bloodied tear away from his cheek; his eyesight was beginning to fail, not only in colour, but in light.

The engine rolled on and the wheels clawed at the road. Mary kept her face towards the side window and finally managed to open both eyes. How long had she been like this? She smelt like death and she was wet.

The radio crackled as Joshua turned the dial once more.

'Maybe that cop Louis was right about modern music Mary,' Joshua said, sighing again. 'Ah there we are, signs for the bridge. What a way for you to see Manhattan for the first time. And on New Years Day!'

As Joshua's eyesight darkened, Mary started to see buildings blur past with the city traffic. Gradually the colours started to solidify, and as the sun made its way up into the sky it breathed life into her, Nathaniel had always said that it would. With a massive effort her hand began to respond to her thought, he would not have wanted this. That's why he left her.

Above them, shadows from the bridge's framework made the sun's rays flicker across their faces and over their hands.

Joshua's voice grated on her. 'He chose well, that man of yours. Not long now Mary.' She wanted to scream at him, what the hell had he done with her parents.

'You know, I think Mr Rodiani will be extremely grateful that you have brought his journal back. Maybe with you up for negotiation, Nathaniel might just give up some of the secrets that it holds.'

Mary couldn't take it any more. She was trapped and incontinent inside this bastard's car, her guts churned into such a knot of disgust that she began to vomit. Sure, she should have warned Nathaniel that she might be pregnant. Her fears churned out her stomach again. How could she bring a child into the hands of this abandoned nightmare? With all the dignity she could muster, Mary got a hand up to her face and wiped her mouth with such a basic motion that she only made the mess worse and caused Joshua to open his window letting in the chill.

Outside, as the morning shadows were being interrupted by the red lights of the city junctions ahead, Mary felt a strength that she had never had before. It wrenched her from within, seething and screaming to be released, until almost uncontrollably her hands responded and she grabbed the steering wheel.

The heroin took the pain of the impact when they collided with the other car. But Mary could see that her captor had felt everything. She closed her eyes to him, happy at the pain he was in, hoping that he would not escape and that they would not be rescued. Mary smelt gasoline and smiled, it wouldn't be long now, death is what she wanted more than the life she had dreamed of.

From somewhere the smell of a cigarette drifted into the car, its sweet deathly allure making her seek one last look at the outside world. Except there in the space once filled by the windscreen was Nathaniel. Like a final dream, his beautiful almost adolescent face, looked down. She could only smile, as she felt his touch. 'Thank you,' she wanted to say. 'You've come back to me.'

'Help me free her Joshua,' Nathaniel said as her eyes started to close. 'She doesn't have to die.' Then something more solid pulled her up and out through the windscreen, free.

At his death in the alley, Nathaniel had felt Albert's soft hands close his eyelids and his muscles let go of the cold that had bound them. Albert had done all that he had been bid, his face resigned to his own small part of guilt, just as Agustin had once looked. Albert left, deciding after this brush with the spirit world and the death of Robert he would not return to 'Il Circolo.' Instead he would leave this city for good.

Free from his body Nathaniel had looked back at his frail muted shell, huddled and pale. It would not be long before it was found. Any sadness though, was quickly replaced by the feeling of freedom, he could no longer be hurt by hunger or the biting wind. He grabbed the newspaper clipping from his dead hand and read it through. Every single thing that he had felt sure to have avoided, was wrapped up in the accident about to happen this very morning and undoubtedly the Pelecaras were already waiting. Nathaniel turned away and out into a side street on Manhattan's lower east side. Up through the city he moved, quickly crossing 14th and 21st Street, then left, down 34th Street to 7th Avenue. The lights of the city were so defined and free from the blurred edges of alcohol. Nathaniel had missed the crowd of thousands who had met last night in Times Square to welcome in 1968. The celebrations now replaced by its bleary eyed citizens and, prompted by the coca cola clock, taxis rolled by. Not bound by the tick of any clock his spirit moved effortlessly, first walking, then running without exhaustion through the streets at ease, unhindered by the living.

He crossed Central Park, where the tips of bare tree skeletons were touched by the sun that had started to rise above the horizon of towers. At the north end of the park, 7th Avenue beckoned as his fastest route, and so up into Harlem he went, passing the library where he had once spent many hours in research.

For the mortal lives around him, the only trace of his passing was the newspaper clipping as it danced through the streets, unabated, clutched in an invisible hand, until finally at the cross-roads of 7th Avenue and 142nd Street, it hovered momentarily then dropped into the road side sludge. Unbiased by emotion, moisture spread from letter to word, telling its story one last time.

From a cloudless sky, snow began to fall, and with desperate slow motion two cars collided in front of him. There were few pedestrians to witness the crash, but one quickly rushed to call 911. Those who stood back in terror or tentatively approached would never know how Captain Hathaway could have arrived so quickly, or how he could seem so relaxed as he smoked his last cigarette. In front of the captain, Oz Patterson directed five new police officers into the gasoline that was flowing out onto the road.

Within minutes, the sirens of the emergency services announced the arrival of Fire Chief Bill Maguire, who shouted at the men to retreat. His cries distracting them long enough for Nathaniel to climb up onto the bonnet of Joshua's car and pull Mary into the hands of the determined fire crew.

Once she was safe on the gurney, Maguire had no choice but to call off the rescue. Unaware of the creatures he was forcing back he yelled. 'Get out of the gasoline gentlemen, even you will burn!' Maguire could not see the nod from Hathaway that consented their withdrawal, he was just happy they had moved, those who were left in the vehicles were dead anyhow. 'Nobody else goes in,' Maguire shouted managing to push the men away just in time before the cars ignited.

In the second it took for the air to bloom with flame, Nathaniel pulled Joshua's spirit onto the sidewalk.

'So you got to me first,' Joshua's spirit said brushing himself down.

'Yes but it doesn't matter.'

'Death is then the final release,' Joshua laughed, as the cars in front of them lifted from the ground, encased in flame.

'It's just another journey Joshua, and I think I can help you.'

'What about your child, surely the child… I see it now; you must keep the child out of Rodiani's hands.' Joshua's words were stopped by Nathaniel's.

'Mary will be safe. Alessandro might pray that our child does not survive but look, she is in the best possible hands,' Nathaniel nodded toward the disappearing ambulance. 'Agustin used to say there is always hope, even in the darkest of places, you just need to be patient. You know Joshua, Rodiani played you from the moment you met Ruiz. He's your devil, Joshua.'

'I think it is time then, to repay him for his troubles,' Joshua said.

'They will guide you,' Nathaniel said pointing through the settling flame to the five new officers who had now donned their long winter coats, their faces lacking solidity even from where they stood. 'Ask them to take you to my body first; they'll know what they're looking for. Give what they find to the Cardinal for safe keeping. He'll need that now, more than he ever has.'

For Mary, the blue lights and sirens faded into a clear silent bright light that left her mind blank and calm. If this was the transition into death, she was glad. Occasionally a muffled voice pierced its brilliance, or a face tried to break into her vision, but neither lasted long before the white out returned. She smelt a hospital's disinfectant, and the motion of the surface she was on. A lift, a voice, then nothing until she felt what must be Nathaniel's touch, it was definitely him.

'Mary,' Nathaniel called, but her mouth would not reply and her eyes would not open to see.

'She's badly traumatised,' the nurse was saying from the foot of her bed. 'High on heroin and pregnant. Not the best example of a new mum!'

'She's messed up pretty good,' said another. 'Just keep her here in ICU and Keep Me Informed!'

'Mary', Nathaniel called, his touch to her hand real. 'I need to explain this life.'

Mary managed the slightest pull of her fingers to approve the same voice from the crash.

'I was named Cieba by my father, the last Shaman of our village.'

Mary pulled her fingers again, she wanted to hear, before she died, she wanted an explanation from a voice she had barely heard, yet knew, above all else, was his.

'Eubucco, my father, left me at the side of the Apurimac river, his love for me gone. I was the last. I was to be the shaman of my grandfather's dreams. But Mary, I betrayed them. Even then I betrayed them. As they left me in the cold, my father asked for a forgiveness that I could not give. "'Forgive me my son. I call to Pachamama to guide you, and pray that the Pelecaras leave you to grow old".'

'Mary, the Pelecaras had infected my pregnant mother when the fierce people raped her, and discarded her battered body. When my father found her he felt nothing but pity. He took me for his own son. A son that would bring them nothing but death. It was not Pachamama or the Xapiripe who kept me safe, it was Huayna. He protected me when Iquitos wanted to kill me and when Alessandro cut out my tongue. You must understand Mary, the Pelecaras offered me love, the one thing they could never have, and kept me alive to watch this desperate world grow older. You see they wanted their son to truly understand what it is to be them.'

Mary was squirming trying to fight him away, the vomit churning inside her stomach again.

'Doctor!' the nurse was shouting. 'The Schwartz woman is fitting. She needs sedation or we're going to lose the baby.'

'Alright,' the doctor called over 'Increase the dose and hold her down.'

'My grandfather used to say that no man was beyond redemption, but after so many years of trying, I disagree. There are seven of us now Mary. We will withdraw into the darkness and await my son's atonement. For we are the Pelecaras and we shall protect our child and let him grow old.'

In his luxurious bed Alessandro Porta Rodiani lay asleep, until a cold breeze from the window woke him from his stupor.

'Argh,' he grumbled and reached out to find his light switch. Despite the click, the light did not come on. 'Oh Fuck It!' he shouted annoyed, then winced at the sound of his own voice. His head was pounding and his eyes were stinging badly. Too much cheap wine, he thought to himself, it had been a hell of a night, but he swore that it would be the last time he'd get drunk in the Bronx. There was nothing for it, he'd have to get up in the darkness and shut the window or he would get no peace.

'Cardinal Rodiani,' said a voice he recognised.

'Joshua, is that you?'

'Yes Alessandro it is. I found you in New York just like we agreed.'

'Joshua, I thought,' the Cardinal faltered, 'Joshua, I can't see you. Please… put the light on for me.'

'The light is on Cardinal. I just thought a little dark reflection might do you some good.'

Alessandro's hands shook even before they reached the blood on his cheeks and he screamed as he found his empty eye sockets.

'Now Your Eminence, in the dark it's just you and I.'